"SOMEON̶   ̶"

"Why wou̶   ̶g like that in ̶

Sweat had formed on ̶   ̶er lip.

"How come none of this makes sense? How come you had trouble during the polygraph when you were asked about the initials M-T-R . . . about Exodus-Five?"

He didn't say anything.

"Let me be real generous with you. Let's say you do sensitive work for military intelligence, and you're afraid to talk about it. Maybe you've encountered some intelligence about a terrorist operation that the FBI doesn't know about."

Kathryn got up, walked around the table and put her hand on his shoulder. "I want to help you, but you have to cooperate. Do you know anything about the initials M-T-R?"

"No comment."

The response caught her off guard. No comment? His shoulder felt cold. Had she heard him correctly? "What? Do you know anything about Exodus-Five, anything at all?"

He knows what happened to his daughter, she thought. *He knows.*

DUST TO DUST

DUST TO DUST

C. N. Bean

AN ONYX BOOK

ONYX
Published by the Penguin Group
Penguin Putnam Inc., 375 Hudson Street,
New York, New York 10014, U.S.A.
Penguin Books Ltd, 27 Wrights Lane,
London W8 5TZ, England
Penguin Books Australia Ltd, Ringwood,
Victoria, Australia
Penguin Books Canada Ltd, 10 Alcorn Avenue,
Toronto, Ontario, Canada M4V 3B2
Penguin Books (N.Z.) Ltd, 182–190 Wairau Road,
Auckland 10, New Zealand

Penguin Books Ltd, Registered Offices:
Harmondsworth, Middlesex, England

First published by Onyx, an imprint of Dutton Signet,
a member of Penguin Putnam Inc.

First Printing, May, 1998
10 9 8 7 6 5 4 3 2 1

 REGISTERED TRADEMARK—MARCA REGISTRADA

Printed in the United States of America

PUBLISHER'S NOTE
This is a work of fiction. Names, characters, places, and incidents either are
the product of the author's imagination or are used fictitiously, and any resemblance to actual persons, living or dead, events, or locales is entirely
coincidental.

BOOKS ARE AVAILABLE AT QUANTITY DISCOUNTS WHEN USED TO PROMOTE
PRODUCTS OR SERVICES. FOR INFORMATION PLEASE WRITE TO PREMIUM MAR-
KETING DIVISION, PENGUIN PUTNAM INC., 375 HUDSON STREET, NEW YORK, NEW
YORK 10014.

Dedicated to fsh,

three angels—
M.J.
Jessica Marie
Sarah Elizabeth

and those who stand up to corruption
and the abuse of power,
regardless of the consequences.

As always, I thank those who have supported me, especially Audrey LaFehr.

Valerie Miner, I'm glad you never break a leg. Your fine example encourages my own balance. Love.

I thank the Sewanee Writers' Conference, 1996, for a generous fellowship. I especially thank Tim O'Brien. Tim, I appreciate the insightful comments on the overall idea and your scrutiny of the early pages. Oh, by the way, Tim, fill in the blanks: "Don't try it . . . Street."

Ann Hood, I hate to mention it, but I believe you still owe me two dollars for making time travel backward.

You are dust,
and to dust you shall return . . .

the curse of Genesis
the Hebrew Bible

Ashes to ashes,
Dust to dust . . .

"Burial of the Dead"
Book of Common Prayer

1

In the wooded marsh where she hid, she heard footsteps. "Angela," he said, "come back." Scared, she tried to run through the thick fog. Mud sucked off a shoe. She left it. She flung her schoolbag and the flute she played in the seventh-grade band. She only wanted to escape, but everything went against her. The dog tags around her neck clattered as she ran through the thick muck. "Angela," he said, and caught her. "I told you to stop!" He slapped her. She cried out. He hit her again. "Shut up!" He spoke through clenched teeth.

The hunchback with the cottony hair held her tightly. "Shut up," he repeated. There was fire in his eyes, magnified by glasses that looked almost as large as his hot face, a face whose pink color was intensified by a white mustache and beard, like a goat's beard. "That's better," he told her, breathing heavily. His breath smelled like cigarettes. There was a bumpy rash across his cheeks. The heat in his face intensified it.

Through the tears that blurred her vision, she tried to think of what to do. Fog hid Wainwright Heights. Somewhere there was a rickety bridge made of boards thrown in muck, the "swamp." People said that's where the boogeyman lived. At least that's where he had been waiting for her, at the bridge, smoking a cigarette. If only she could get back to the boards, she would know how to get home. But she couldn't remember where the boards were.

Why me? was all she could think. Was it because she hadn't done what she was supposed to do—that is, she had cut through the swamp to the bus stop, which was the way her parents had told her never to go?

"You shouldn't have run," he told her, more composed. His breathing had evened out. That scared her because he seemed more in control.

Her foot was numb from the cold of the November morning. She wondered if she would ever find the black gym shoe that had been sucked off by the mud. She hoped so. She liked those shoes. They were her favorites. "Please, don't hurt me," she said.

"That's right," he told her. "Beg." In a sudden move he slapped her mouth. "Beg! I like it when people beg!" He so caught her off guard that she couldn't move, couldn't even breathe, then she fought as wildly as she had ever fought. His slaps turned into slugs. Next thing she knew she was in the mud. He was holding her down with a knee, still slugging her. Then he clasped her hands in one of his hands. His other hand squeezed her windpipe. Through clenched teeth he whispered, "Beg, or I'll kill you."

She could hear the bus and the distant voices of children. Then the voices were closed up in the bus. The sound of the bus moved on. "Please," she said, and gasped for air. He released her windpipe. Oxygen returned to her.

"That's right, I like it when people beg."

He hoisted her by the bulky field jacket she wore, lifted her right out of the mud, off her feet, though he was short. Fingers digging into the back of her neck while his other hand covered her mouth, he carried her by her head, as if she were a bowl or dish. She could smell cigarettes on his fingers. She hated the smell of cigarettes.

Once out of the swamp, he walked faster. She tried to get her feet to the ground, but he walked so quickly her feet dropped out from under her when he did lower her enough that they would touch the ground.

At a battered blue sedan, out jumped a wiry, old man, his dark hair slicked back. He was in his fifties, maybe sixties—had a dried-up face—and wore combat boots. "Is it her, Michael?" he asked. He tightened the leather belt that held up his polyester slacks. The belt was already so tight it bunched up the pants.

"Never call me by my first name, Lieutenant. Do you understand?"

Fidgety as he was, the lieutenant tried to stand at attention. "Sorry, sir."

Michael jerked back her hair. She tried not to cry, but couldn't help herself. "Tell me, Lieutenant McCabe, does it look like I got the right one?—no thanks to you."

Lieutenant McCabe nodded. "That's her all right." He smiled, showing yellow teeth. Old, but straight. Big. "Very good, sir."

"Then, get her in the car before something else goes wrong." His voice was impatient.

The lieutenant opened the back door, pulled down the seat, which opened to the trunk, and crawled across the lowered seat as Michael swung Angela in feetfirst. It was everything the lieutenant could do to keep up with the short, strong boogeyman. The lieutenant wound rope around her feet while Michael tore a piece of gray tape from a roll and slapped it on her mouth. She wept openly. She didn't want to go with them, didn't want to die. They were going to murder her, she was sure of it.

Michael said, "Shut up," and raised a hand. While his other hand pinned her hands behind her, he said, "Get her hands." He flipped her on her belly.

The lieutenant bound them. Together the men heaved her facedown into the trunk.

Michael said, "Make a sound, and I'll slit your throat." His fiery eyes glowed. He popped open a shiny knife that had a dark red handle. "I mean it." He barely touched the blade with his thumb, as if to show how sharp the blade was. She could hear the blade scraping skin. She tried to keep silent, though she felt her body jerking with sobs.

He threw up the seat, leaving her in darkness.

The car started. She could feel movement, not abrupt movement, as if the car were racing away, but a casual pulling forward. The men who had grabbed her so quickly now seemed to be in no great hurry. All she could think about was her father and mother. How would they know where she was? How would they find her? How could they help? She tried to get her lips free so she could breathe better, but the tape was strong. She cried silently as she listened to the men talk:

"Captain McCanles—"

"What?"

"I didn't mean to question your authority back there, sir. I apologize. I guess I was worried what the major would do if we screwed up."

Major? She thought. Her father was a major. Had he arranged this—arranged it to teach her a lesson for crossing the swamp?

"Johnny, I know all about you," McCanles continued. "You're a coward, and that explains everything to me."

"Begging the captain's pardon, but if I'm a coward, what am I doing here?"

The captain laughed. "Oh, I'm trembling all over. I should stop the car this minute and slap the shit out of you."

The lieutenant didn't respond to that.

"Let me tell you why you're here, and don't you forget it. You're here because you've never amounted to a damn thing in life, and you know I'm going to be someone. That's why you're here. You're hoping I'll take care of you just because you have an Irish name like I do. But when it comes to courage, you're not Irish, you're a coward. Is that clear?"

"Yes, sir."

They became silent.

The ride turned bumpy. Angela could smell dust in the trunk. The day was heating up. It was that time of year when the nights and mornings were cold, but the days were still warm. Despite the warmth, though, she shivered from the grime and mud covering her. She sneezed. A couple of times, her head struck the floor of the trunk. She cried. She wished she hadn't lost her shoe.

The car stopped. Car doors slammed. The trunk opened, throwing in sunlight. Captain McCanles yanked her into the bright air. Lieutenant McCabe tried to pull the tape off her mouth. McCanles shoved him aside, saying, "You're useless." He jerked the tape. She screamed. He slapped her. "Shut up!" Her face stung from where he slapped her.

"Please, let me go," she mumbled.

He slapped her again. "I said, shut up, retard!"

She began to cry. "I'm not retarded."

He slapped her harder. Again she cried out. "Shut up!" he screamed. His face was the color of his knife's handle—dark red. She tried not to make a sound.

Lieutenant McCabe said, "I don't think you should push me around like that in front of the prisoner."

In an instant McCabe fired off a volley of fists at the lieutenant's face. Blood spattered Angela. She screamed. He slapped her so hard she spun to the ground. The next thing she knew, she was watching the lieutenant get to his knees, his face a bloody mess. He had a dazed expression about him.

Breathing heavily, the rash standing out on his face, the captain told him, "Now, call the major and tell him we have his girl. Do you understand?"

"Yes, sir." The lieutenant, a dazed look on his bloody face, went inside the run-down house where the car had stopped. The porch swing was broken, hanging only by a chain on one end. There were no curtains in the front windows. Through one of them, she could see the lieutenant talking on a portable telephone.

Was he talking to her father? she wondered. Was he asking her father whether she had learned her lesson?

While Captain McCanles cut loose her hands and feet with his sharp knife, she looked around. The yard had several large trees—brown and almost naked from the changing season—and tall grass, also turning brown. There was a lot of sticks and trash in the yard. Nearby was a barn, which was as old as the house, and an autumn forest. Taking her by the arm, the captain led her inside the house, the downstairs of which had been swept, though not well. She could see broom marks in the dust as he led her to the second floor. The lieutenant was still on the telephone. She could hear him talking, but couldn't tell what he was saying. She wanted to say that she would never do anything wrong again, but she kept silent, afraid to make any sound.

The captain stopped at an upstairs door with a shiny brass lock on it. Shavings from where the lock had been installed littered the floor. Holding her with one hand, he shook a ring of keys until he found the right key, unlocked the door, and opened it to a dirty room whose only furnishing was a military blanket. It was heaped in the corner.

Before she realized what had happened, he shoved her. She hit the wall, and she remembered the automobile accident she had been in. The door slammed. She heard the key in the lock. The captain's footsteps left.

Dazed, she began to cry again. What was happening? Why were they being mean to her? What had she done to deserve this? Was it because of how she treated her parents? Or her teachers—they often lost patience with her. Sometimes they got so angry they squeezed her arm, hand, or neck. But was any of that so bad they had taken her away from home? Crying, she tried the door. The doorknob was loose, but the door wouldn't budge.

She went to the dirty window. Two stories down was a dump of broken glass and rusty cans. She opened a second door. In the closet ceiling was a panel. She wiped her eyes and nose on the sleeve of the field jacket her father had given her. In her closet at home was a panel to the attic. She hid things up there, notes and valuables. She closed the door, went to the blanket, and sat down. The blanket smelled musty, but she didn't care. She was too busy thinking about the panel in the closet. Fingering the dog tags her father had had made for her—in case she ever got lost—she tried to concentrate on the attic panel.

She returned to the window, where she looked out at the road. It didn't look like it had been used much. Probably not much chance anyone would pass along it. She wondered how far it was to the next house. She glanced at the closet door. Was there a way to escape through the attic?

Footsteps approached. She returned to the blanket, where she sat down. The lieutenant appeared, holding a paper plate of food. "The captain said eat," he told her. His nose was pink and puffy. The skin near his eyes was purplish black. There were bloodstains on his shirt. "Take it," he said, a hum in his nose, like he had a cold.

The food didn't look appetizing. A cup of water, a piece of ham, potato salad, and a slice of bread. No fork or spoon.

He said, "Take it now or I'll get the captain."

She took the plate.

"And you better eat every drop. The captain doesn't like it when his orders aren't followed."

"What do I eat with?" She said it to let him know she was willing to cooperate so long as they didn't hurt her.

"With your damned fingers for all I care," he told her, a sour look on his face. "Just make sure there's nothing left when I get back, or I'll tell the captain."

"When do I get to go home?"

The lieutenant left without answering her question.

She looked at the food. She wasn't hungry, but knew if she didn't eat, the lieutenant would do what he had said—he would tell the captain—and she didn't want that, didn't want more trouble. At the same time she wondered why they wanted her to eat so soon. Had the food been poisoned? That must be why they wanted her to eat. She went inside the closet and scraped the food off on the floor. She poured out the water. She closed the door.

Then she returned to the blanket and sat down, placing the empty plate and cup near her. She had to pee. Her face was sore from where she had been beaten. She went to the window and looked at her reflection. Her face had shadows on it. From the mud, she guessed. Also it was puffy, like the lieutenant's nose. Her stringy hair looked like it didn't belong to her. She pushed back some of the hair above her left ear. She could see the scar in her scalp, the scar from the automobile accident she had been in. She remembered being in the hospital.

The longer she waited for the lieutenant to return, the more she had to pee. She paced the room. She knew she couldn't say anything, because the lieutenant would want to take her to the bathroom. He would watch her go too; or, worse still, the captain would watch her go. She found herself crying silently as she pranced about the room, trying not to pee her pants.

The lieutenant returned for the plate and cup. "Quit your sniveling," he told her, watching her as she immediately crouched in a corner near the window.

She was sure he would look in the closet, at which point he would discover the food and water, but he didn't. He didn't say or do anything except take the plate, pull the door shut, and relock it. His footsteps retreated. She leaned back and closed her eyes. Her feet slid out from under her, and she sat down heavily. She tried not to think about what was happening.

The next thing she knew, she awakened. The room

was orange. She had to pee so badly, she thought she would explode. She jumped up, thinking it was morning and she had slept through the night. They would be coming to murder her, she knew. She opened the closet and tried to pull herself up by the bar for hanging clothes. In her physical therapy after the automobile accident, she had worked with exercise bars. Those, along with the wheelchair and walker that had once been a part of her daily life, had made her arms strong. But now she was having trouble coordinating her feet. She thought it was because she had to pee so badly. Again and again she tried to get a foot on the shelf while holding the bar. Each time her foot dropped, it made her more angry because she had been able to do the same thing at home. It's how she had gotten into the attic at home. She told herself what others had told her, that she was stupid. She could go to the bathroom as soon as she escaped, she told herself. She heard sounds downstairs. She was sure the captain was on his way up to murder her. In her panic she got a foot on the shelf. Then, with a struggle, she was up.

The panel was easy to shift aside. Straining under her weight, she pulled herself through the opening.

It was lukewarm in the near darkness. Once she put the panel back in place, she experienced a sense of relief, knowing the captain and lieutenant would never find her. There was a window. She got it partially open, but in the outside corner of the window frame was a wasps' nest. A wasp that had settled in for the night stirred to life. It seemed angry and flew in the opening. She swatted at the air, knocking the wasp to the floor. She stomped the insect with her bare foot before she realized she had done it. Her heart pounding, she looked out the window.

There was a short stretch of roof, from which hung a gutter. All she had to do was crawl out on the roof and climb down the drain. Then she would hide in the forest.

Panting, she tried to get the window up enough to squeeze through. It was stuck. She pushed and tugged on it until she thought the glass would break, but the window wouldn't budge. She shook it. She found herself gasping for breath. She struck the window. Its frame broke loose, and the window slid up all at once, which brought down the nest. It broke like a dirt clod on the sill. Two dazed wasps flew up from the broken nest. She jerked down the window. One of the wasps left. The other remained, apparently searching for a way in. The second wasp returned, flew close to the window, then left again. The first wasp left. No sooner did Angela get the window up than one of the wasps returned, flying in before she could jerk the window down.

The wasp headed straight for her. She swatted at it, which disturbed the air enough to throw the wasp off course. It returned. She heard her voice making sounds of panic. She swatted at the elusive wasp again and again until she knocked it down. She stomped it with her bare foot. The foot stung.

She squeezed out the window and was crawling down the slope of the roof when she heard activity in the room below. The lieutenant yelled, "Captain McCanles!"

She knew there wasn't time to climb down the gutter. They would catch her before she got down; or, in her panic, she would fall. She crawled back in the window and looked around. Most of the attic had a crude floor, but there was a floorless area where the rafters met the structure of the walls. She crawled into that dark space, careful to keep her weight on the rafters. It was the same in her house. Her father had once taken her across the rafters and told her never to put her weight on anything else.

It didn't take long for the attic panel to burst open and the captain's head to appear. "Hold still," he said, his head jerking this way and that. "She's out. She got out the window. Get me down!" His head disappeared. She could hear footsteps running down the stairs. Then the voices were outside. The captain said, "She couldn't have gotten far. It hasn't been that long since you brought down the plate." She knew then it wasn't morning, but was the same day. "Head for the woods. I'll check the barn. Holler if you see her. I'll kill her!" Footsteps ran away.

The house was quiet. The attic smelled like old lumber and was stuffy. She found herself sweating. It was hard to breathe. She wondered whether she should climb down through the attic panel and hide in the house, then she remembered what had happened earlier that morning when she had tried to run. The captain had caught her. She didn't want that to happen again. Crouched, she trembled, which caused her dog tags to rattle, so she held them.

The captain's head reappeared in the attic panel. She hadn't heard him return to the house. He pulled himself up into the attic. "She must be here somewhere," he said. He walked right past her as he went to the window to look out. She noticed that despite his shortness, he was still too tall to stand upright, so he had to walk bent forward, which increased the prominence of his hunchback.

He knelt at the window and looked out. For several moments he remained in that position. Then for some reason he looked behind him. "I know you're here," he said. She didn't think he could see her, but the way he said it, it was like he could feel her presence. He said, "Come out, and we'll take you downstairs and give you a warm room. Right now you don't care, but tonight it'll get cold, and then you'll care."

She didn't move.

He said, "Don't make me find you."

She felt herself begin to tremble. The awkward position she was in made the trembling more pronounced. Her dog tags rattled as she let go of them to steady herself. She grabbed them, making them clatter.

The lieutenant said, "There she is, Captain!" The

lieutenant's head was in the attic opening. He had pulled himself up. "There." He was looking straight at her.

"Where?"

The lieutenant pointed at her.

"No," she said, the word slipping out before she could stop it. "Please, no!" She couldn't withdraw any farther, though she tried to pull back. She screamed as the captain dragged her out and slapped her face and arms with his hot hands. His slaps turned to punches and kicks. "I'll teach you to run away from me!" he yelled. "Beg me to stop!"

She peed and peed as he beat her.

2

⬥

After her shower, Kathryn Stanton untangled her blond hair with a hair pick. The hair looked good. After her last hairdresser had moved to Kentucky, she had finally found a new one she liked. The right amount of curl was there, and so was the right amount of color. Not that she was vain. It wasn't that. It was just that when she got her hair fixed in the morning, she didn't want to mess with it anymore that day, no matter how long the day lasted, and she was used to long days. In fact, after months of long days she had finally managed to have a weekend off. She needed it. She didn't want anything to ruin it, and the hair, at least, was cooperating. She needed the hair to cooperate.

At the mirror she applied makeup. She wiped out the crow's-feet at the corners of her sea-green eyes. The eyes had tiny flecks of yellow in them. The eyes watched everything her hands were doing, missing nothing. She wiped away most of the scar from her left cheek.

On November 21, she would be forty-five. She could look at herself and see she was getting older. What did Randy Lewis see in her? she wondered. He was eight, almost nine years younger than she was. She had a teenage daughter. Though Kathryn kept in shape, delivering a child thirteen years before had done something to her. Maybe it had made her more mature, more worldly—she couldn't be sure. But de-

livering a child did something to a woman. She knew
that. She looked in the mirror and could tell she was
a mother. Did Randy care?

Appearing behind her, he began to massage her
shoulders. "You ready?" he asked.

She looked at him. His wet hair, dark like his eyes
and scanty beard, had been given a good roughing up
with a towel. He smelled like Polo aftershave. He always wore Polo. She liked the smell of it.

She closed her eyes as he massaged her neck and
shoulders. "That feels good," she told him, smiling.

"You haven't seen anything yet. The weekend's
only beginning."

"What about room service and a quiet evening together?" she asked, her eyes still closed.

"First things first. Let's hit the slots." She looked
at him. He had said it in a joking manner, but she
could tell he was serious. He wanted to get out, to
have fun. He popped the top of a Coors Light and
took a long drink.

Wrapping a towel around her, she headed for the
kitchenette, where she opened a diet Coke from the
refrigerator and took a couple swallows. The Coke
was cold.

The telephone rang. She sat on the sofa, put her
bare feet on the coffee table, and answered the phone
on the lamp table. It was her mother.

"What are you doing calling so soon, Mom?" Kathryn looked at the gray light that engulfed the wall-to-
wall windows. She wanted to remind her mother she
was with Randy, but she didn't. From the angle where
she sat, there was not much to see twenty-two stories
up, not even the ocean. Only her reflection, staring
back at her between bare knees. She thought her expression looked perturbed, as if to say, "Can't I even
get away for two days? Don't you realize how important this weekend is?"

"I just wanted to make sure you got there okay."

Kathryn immediately sensed the "something's wrong" tone in her mother's voice. "Mom, what's wrong? Did something happen to Wendy?"

Her mother gave one of those long, deep exhales through her nose. "Nothing we can't take care of."

"What happened?" Why are you calling, then?

"I'll tell you when you get back. I don't want to ruin your trip."

Randy sat on the arm of the sofa. "Is everything all right?" he asked.

She held up a finger as a signal that he needed to give her a chance to figure things out for herself. At the same time she was instantly irritated with her mother. Why had she called if she didn't want to ruin the trip? Wasn't that the whole purpose of calling? "Mom, tell me what happened."

"Chester and I have handled it. We've been up since five this morning, but we've handled it."

"Five this morning? Mom, don't ruin my trip by playing these games with me. Don't make me sit here all weekend trying to figure out what's going on."

With that, her mother poured out everything, which was obviously what she had wanted to do from the beginning. Wendy had stayed overnight at Holly's house, her mother explained. Ashley had been there, too. "You remember that boy Eric, whose father you called?"

Eric Mullins was a seventeen-year-old who spent a lot of time hanging out at the middle school that Wendy attended. He and a couple other teenagers his age or older attended all the sports events such as basketball games and track meets. There the older boys tried to pick up the thirteen-year-old girls, to "break them in" before high school. Yes, Kathryn said, she knew Eric. He was a mother's worst nightmare.

"It all began at five o'clock this morning, when Holly's mother called Chester and me to tell us that Ashley had been picked up by the police."

"What!" Kathryn dropped her feet off the coffee table and sat forward.

"Wendy wasn't in the car, but according to Holly's mother, Wendy and Holly had snuck out with Ashley and had gone with these big boys. Wendy says she got scared and started crying, so the boys took her and Holly home, but Ashley stayed. The boys got stopped for having a headlight out on their car, the police saw Ashley in the car, and took them all to the police station."

Holding the phone between her shoulder and her tilted head, Kathryn buried her face in her hands. "Oh, God," she said. She hated Eric. She wished she was back in Dallas. She'd probably have him arrested herself.

"What's wrong?" Randy repeated.

She held up a finger again.

"Believe me, Chester and I have taken care of everything. We've kept her home today, she's not allowed to have any calls or anything, and Chester's been trying to get in touch with the father of this Eric boy. Wendy's even been studying all afternoon."

I bet she has, Kathryn thought. She said, "Let me talk to her."

Wendy got on the phone. Her voice was weak and nervous. "Hi, Mom."

Kathryn tried to remain calm. "I understand you had some problems last night and today?"

Wendy didn't say anything.

Kathryn broke. "Wendy, how could you do this to me? It wasn't two weeks ago you promised me you wouldn't have anything to do with this Eric boy. I told you how I felt, told you he was too old for you, and that he only wanted one thing, and you promised me." She wished Randy wasn't listening.

"I didn't go with him," her weak voice said.

"You did go with them, and then you got scared."

"And I made him take us back home."

That was true. It made Kathryn realize how thankful she was that Wendy hadn't been in the car when the police had stopped it. "Put your grandmother back on," Kathryn told her, then added, "Wendy?"

"Yes."

"I still love you. I don't agree with what you did, but I love you."

"I love you too, Mom."

"Aren't you going to say something else?"

"What?"

"You know what."

"I'm sorry."

Kathryn's mother assured her that Wendy was on complete restriction for that weekend. "Don't you worry about another thing," she said at the close of the conversation.

Afterward, Kathryn told Randy what had happened. She didn't hold anything back. If he was really interested in her, she thought, he needed to know the truth about what he was getting into. She had a thirteen-year-old daughter, and he needed to understand what all that entailed.

To her surprise, he was understanding. While she was horrified by the news she had received—that is, thought she was losing her daughter and there was nothing she could do—he told her that at least Wendy had had enough of a conscience and a sense of right and wrong to know that she needed to get out of the car. What Randy said made sense, and she started feeling better about Wendy. She felt better about Randy, too.

He guzzled his beer. "She's going to survive," he told her. "Sure, it's a rough time in life, but you made it through, I made it through, and she'll make it through. Come on, let's get out and do something."

He belched under his breath. "It'll take your mind off of things." He slapped his hands together. "Besides, we need to celebrate. It isn't every day that a woman is promoted to assistant special-agent-in-charge of an important FBI region like Dallas."

"It's not that big a deal." It really was, though, and she knew it. The Bureau was still a man's world.

"And to head up an elite terrorism unit." He whistled. He shook a hand as if it were on fire. "This is hot." He smiled at her with his even white teeth.

Sometimes he was hard to resist. She studied his ragged clothes, a tattered undershirt too small—his muscular arms bulged in it—and jeans whose knees were ripped out. Treasury's Alcohol, Tobacco, and Firearms always attracted the jocks. "When are you going to grow up?" she asked.

He was still smiling. "It's what you like about me. I bring out the best in you. Are you ready?"

"Let's do it."

He stood. "That's more like it. I'll dry my hair, and we'll be out of here."

While he returned to the bathroom, she threw on a blouse, windbreaker, jeans, tennis shoes, and socks, and went out on the balcony, where she looked down at the ocean. On the twenty-second floor, the wind was gusty. People looked like toys on the Atlantic City boardwalk. Not many people, she thought. The sounds of the ocean made her feel better. Randy was right. Those early teen years were rough, but countless generations had faced the same age and had survived. Wendy would survive. What was important now was the weekend.

As soon as Randy came out of the bathroom, she and he left the hotel.

They went down to the beach. The air was cold, gusty, and filled with the cries of gulls. She and Randy took off their shoes and socks, and carried them as they walked. The water was cold, too, but the open air felt good. For the first time, she felt free of Dallas. Everything was behind her.

The salt air made her skin tighten as the wind braced her. She stopped to pick up a shell. Like a cup, it still held a small amount of water and sand in it. Glancing at Randy, she asked, "It doesn't drive you crazy about my daughter?"

"Like I said, she's going to survive. Come on, let's go put a few quarters in the slot machines."

She liked Randy. At the same time she realized she had invested a lot of hope and faith in her getaway for the weekend, and that worried her. She wanted the relationship to work, somehow wanted to prove that it wasn't her that made all the relationships she had been in turn sour.

They walked through the thick sand that led to the boardwalk. It wasn't that she thought she needed a husband. Even when she had discovered she was pregnant with Wendy, she hadn't gone out in desperation and tried to scare the father into marrying her. Yet Randy was different from any other man she had ever known. Would he marry her? Was that why he had invited her on a weekend getaway? Was their relationship leading to something serious? It frightened her that she so badly wanted a marriage proposal that weekend.

At the boardwalk she sat on a bench and tried to clean her feet of sand. Randy didn't worry about the sand. He put on his socks and shoes. No matter how hard she brushed, the sand clung to her. She was freezing, so she eventually put on her shoes, sand and all, and moved on. She shoved her socks into her coat pocket. She felt good.

She and he headed for Ocean One, a shopping mall on the ocean front, shaped like a riverboat about to set out to sea. But before they got there, she had to empty her shoes of sand. It was driving her crazy. She wished she had brought a heavier coat, too. She told Randy she was cold. He pointed out Caesars casino.

They took an escalator up to a warehouse filled with slot machines, card tables, and roulette wheels. There was no music or entertainment, only the incessant sounds of bells ringing and electronic wheels turning. Despite the sparsity of people on the boardwalk, there was no shortage of people in the casino. They were everywhere.

Kathryn didn't play, but she did watch Randy feed a roll of quarters into a slot machine. She ordered him a Coors Light to drink while he played. She nursed a diet Coke. Within minutes Randy had used up his quarters. He gulped down his beer.

They walked to Ocean One, where they took an elevator up to the Italian Bistro. It didn't take long for them to get a table. The restaurant wasn't crowded. The maître d' led them to a table overlooking the ocean. "How's this?" he asked.

Both she and Randy said the table was fine. It was strange to see the ocean below, but not hear it.

"Russ will be your waiter this evening," said the maître d'. "He'll be right with you."

Sure enough, no sooner had the maître d' withdrawn than Russ appeared. He was a tall, handsome youth with tanned skin and straight blond hair, oiled down. He looked like he needed a haircut.

Randy asked him where all the tourists were.

Russ said the regular season was over. "Until spring, the gamblers eat and sleep right in the hotels— to be near the casinos." He asked them if they wanted anything from the bar.

She ordered a diet Coke. Randy teased her. He said she had to order something with alcohol in it so they could have a legitimate toast. She ordered a glass of Chianti.

He ordered Chivas Regal and water, a double.

While they waited for the drinks, Randy asked her

if she would miss the streets now that she was in the administrative end of the Bureau.

She shrugged. The new assignment would involve administrative work, she agreed, but she would still see the streets. That was the luxury of being an assistant SAC. Besides, the assignment would give her more time for Wendy. She made sure he understood how important her family was to her.

When the drinks arrived, Randy raised his glass to hers. "Congratulations on a miracle promotion," he said. Their glasses touched. They looked at each other without saying anything, only smiled simultaneously, then drank.

As if embarrassed to mention anything, he asked her if she had any idea how long the Bureau would take to act on his application. He played with his drink's red stir stick. He twisted the plastic stick this way and that.

He had asked the same question several times during the previous month. He had applied to transfer from Treasury to the Bureau. She had offered to give a recommendation for his application, and he had been excited. She thought he'd make a good agent. She and he had been assigned to the same violent crime task force in the past—before she had moved to the terrorism unit. That's how they had met—while working violent crime together. She told him, "I think you'll hear something in the next few weeks."

He took a big drink of his scotch. The ice cubes rattled in the empty glass, which he set on the table before him. He told her, "That's what I really want, you know. I've wanted it from the beginning. But they wouldn't consider me before now." With open hands, he rubbed his scraggly beard. "I guess I was too wild for them. But now I've settled down and proven myself, thanks to your help. I appreciate all your support, and with it I may even stand a chance." He winked.

They kissed across the table. "It may get you in trouble, too."

Russ returned to take their order.

Randy picked up the menu. As he opened it, he said, "Tell me, Russ, what are your specials this evening?" Randy seemed in a better mood.

Russ said he recommended the fresh crabmeat over the linguine. "It's in a tasty white sauce," he said.

Both of them ordered it.

Russ opened a package of crackers and buttered one. "Isn't it great getting away like this?" He consumed the buttered cracker.

They exchanged small talk until their meals arrived. Randy ordered another Chivas, another double.

They ate in silence for a few minutes. The crab was very good, though occasionally she came across a piece of shell. She didn't mind. She could tell by the taste the meat was fresh.

Randy asked, "You think they'll let me in?"

Why was he back to that again? "I'd say you have as good a chance of getting in as anyone else does." Was he paying her back for talking so much about Wendy?

"Has anyone said anything about my paperwork?"

No, she told him, no one had said anything. She went on to say she had reservations about making any inquiries because every time someone pulled his file, it slowed the process. It could have a negative effect. "You know, someone might get pissed."

"No, don't do that. I don't want to do anything to screw things up."

She noticed he was drinking more than he was eating. Was he nervous? He ate mainly buttered crackers. What was he planning? she suddenly wondered. Why had he asked her away for the weekend? She became excited. It was to propose. She was sure it was. Nothing could be more perfect

Outside it was getting dark. She and he headed toward the hotel. He put his arm around her and pulled her close. "Come here, it's cold," he told her.

It felt good to have his arm around her. She listened to the ocean. She mentioned that he hadn't eaten very well at supper. "Is something on your mind?"

He was evasive. He told her he didn't care for the sauce over the crabmeat.

"Why didn't you say something?" she asked. "You could have ordered something different."

"I didn't want to keep you sitting around," he said.

That was nice, she thought.

In the distant night a trumpet played. It was an eerie sound for being as cold as it was, with its backdrop the sounds of the ocean. Even stranger was the song the horn played, "Amazing Grace." The closer they got, the louder the sound became. Kathryn mentioned how strange it was that someone would be playing a funeral song on the boardwalk.

They passed the alcove of an abandoned building, where the trumpet player stood in the dark, still playing "Amazing Grace." As the song receded in the background, Randy asked, "If I run up and get you a heavier coat, you want to walk awhile?"

She said a coat would be nice.

He didn't take long to go up to the hotel room for the coat and return.

They stopped at an arcade. He bought a corn dog and lemonade. They passed through the arcade that was noisy with game machines and went out on the pier, where there was a small carnival still set up, though the rides were shut down. It was too cold for rides. Only a few stands were open for the last of the autumn crowd. She and he sat on a bench.

He took a big bite of his corn dog and, speaking through the steaming food, he asked, "You want a bite?"

She shook her head.

He sucked lemonade through a straw. "It feels good to be out like this, doesn't it?" He handed her the lemonade. "To be free, completely free."

She took a sip and handed the cup back. "I think I like the weather better back in Texas."

He finished the corn dog. "Maybe."

She asked, "You ever think about us?" Why not break the ice?

"What do you mean?" He was chewing the food.

She thought he knew what she meant and was teasing her. "I mean, you ever wonder where our relationship is going—what you want out of it?"

He smiled with his big white teeth. "Sure, I think about us."

Good, we're getting somewhere. Getting such a concession from him was like pulling teeth, but she was satisfied by what he had said. Okay, let's do it the hard way. Be coy. "You think what we have going will ever turn into anything more serious?"

He shrugged. "Sure. You know, it has been nice. But, I think right now the big thing is to get this business of my application settled, so I have some stability in my life; and, then, once I'm in the Bureau and have been through the academy, it'll be time to start thinking about the two of us." He looked at her. "I can tell you right now, I'd be a damned good agent."

She stood. Wrong answer. She felt numb. "I'm cold," she said. "Let's go back." Even with her coat, she was freezing cold.

At the hotel she heard the signal of her pager. She had left it in the room while she and Randy had gone to supper. Using a portable phone from her luggage, a secure phone she always carried, she dialed the number displayed on the pager. It was the private number of the special-agent-in-charge of the Dallas region,

Grant Smythers. He was at the office. Not a good sign. Not on a Saturday night.

He asked her if she was on a secure line. She told him she was. He told her a twelve-year-old girl had disappeared from Fort Hood, Texas, and the base's commander had received a note about her. Kathryn thought of Wendy. Almost the same age.

"Have you heard of any terrorist group or militia with the initials MTR?"

No, the initials didn't ring a bell.

He told her no one else had heard of the group either—he had run the initials through the computer. "That's who's claiming responsibility," he said. "As far as we can tell, there is no such group, but whoever sent the note is also claiming to have a biological weapon. They want three U.S. Army Lance missiles with thermonuclear warheads, and they want the missile launchers also. Otherwise, they threaten to use the biological weapon."

Kathryn was trying to concentrate on what he was saying, but it was confusing. "What would all of that have to do with kidnapping a girl? Is the father or mother someone important?"

"No. Like I said, it sounds like a hoax. To tell you the truth, probably one of the parents murdered her and is trying to make it seem like she was kidnapped. Overcompensation. Typical. It would explain this sensational claim about a terrorist group and the weapons in question."

"Okay, so why do you need me on this? Sounds open and shut."

That brought silence.

"What?"

"This is the strange part," he said, "the part that makes me a little nervous. As a matter of fact, there are exactly three Lances already at Fort Hood."

"I didn't know they stored nuclear weapons at Hood."

"I didn't either. Until now this has been highly classified information. You see the dilemma, don't you? We can't move the ones that are there because someone obviously knows they're there—or made a damned good guess. If this is legitimate, someone's trying to flush the missiles out into the open. Let me put it this way, it's been over twenty-four hours, the girl is still missing, and someone seems to know about the nuclear missiles down there. Sure, they're small field missiles, but each one is the equivalent of the Hiroshima bomb."

She took a deep breath and muttered, "Damn."

"I was hoping you'd go down to Hood—just to be on the safe side. I've already sent down that new agent, David Gonzalez, with an advance team."

She barely knew Gonzalez. He was new to the division she had inherited.

"I told him to take over from the resident agent."

"And?"

"And, if it turns out to be nothing, you come back home. Leave Gonzalez to wrap things up."

She didn't say anything.

"I just think it'd be better if you were there—someone with some authority. That way if the media gets a hold of the story, we'll have someone there who knows what she's doing."

"Okay, I'll go down and check it out." The weekend had been ruined anyway.

While she put away the phone, Randy asked her what was wrong. He looked excited, the way she had seen him look on raids when he got to use a battering ram to break down a door.

Nothing, she told him. A routine kidnapping case that would probably turn out to be a homicide on the part of one of the parents. All she could think about was Wendy, a little older than the victim. How many times had she herself lost her temper with Wendy? It was a frightening thought. Had one of the parents so lost his or her temper as to be unable to control the rage?

She dreaded what she was about to discover.

3

Agents from the FBI's Evidence Response Team were still at the Robleses' Fort Hood house when Kathryn arrived early Sunday morning. She arrived around five-thirty, having flown from Dallas to Fort Hood by army helicopter, and found agents finishing up a meticulous search. The ERT had been there all night. It was standard procedure—start at the family home in a kidnapping case and move outward. Assume one of the parents murdered the victim. Assume the kidnapping was a hoax. Assume the worst. Search the house from top to bottom for clues to support those assumptions. Of course, no one said that was what the agents were doing, but everyone understood.

As Kathryn walked through the living room of the impoverished home, she listened vaguely to a flurry of radio transmissions about a gunshot victim who was being transported by helicopter to Darnall Army Hospital. Apparently, the soldier had been shot with his M-16 while out on field maneuvers. It wasn't clear whether the shooting was accidental, intentional, or a suicide. The radio transmissions reminded her of routine radio traffic in the Fort Worth/Dallas area—the sort of thing one heard night and day—but it seemed high profile for Fort Hood, a military installation that stretched across more than 340 miles of central Texas. Agents from the Army's Criminal Investigation Command (CID) had been dispatched to investigate the shooting.

FBI Agent David Gonzalez, talking on a portable phone, nodded when he saw her, but continued talking. His dark, curly hair going this way and that, a shadow of stubble on his face, and his clothes wrinkled, he looked like he had just crawled out of bed. His eyes were bloodshot. He wore a navy windbreaker that had the large gold letters FBI on its left breast, dirty jeans, and scuffed loafers. No socks. He handed her an evidence bag that contained the note about Angela.

Still talking on the telephone, he asked the person on the other end, "How extensive has the search been?" Group laughter came from one of the back rooms of the house. David turned his back to Kathryn and covered the ear that wasn't pressed against the telephone receiver. "Say again? As you can hear, people are getting a bit slaphappy by this time of the morning."

It was the first time she and he had worked together on an investigation. He had transferred to the Dallas terrorism unit from the Los Angeles region, but she hadn't been the one to bring him on board, so she didn't know much about him—other than what was in his personnel file. Her predecessor had approved the transfer. It had been one of his final acts before being shipped to the resident office in Fairbanks, Alaska. Not a promotion either. He had supervised a case that had resulted in bad publicity. The Bureau was cutthroat that way. Bad publicity could destroy a career. Everyone understood that.

She moved close to a lighted lamp in the living room and read the note in the evidence bag:

We have the Robles girl. "We have enough of the biological agent Exodus-V to destroy a major city. Unless you respond to our demands, you will have a disaster on your hands. We want the 3 U.S. Army Lance missiles that are at Fort Hood, the ones with thermonuclear warheads. We also want the mobile launchers for them. Move them to the Fort Hood airfield within

72 hours from the time you receive this. More instructions will follow.
    MTR.

Next to the note was an envelope. Its address, that of the commanding general of Fort Hood, was printed in the same crude hand. There was no return address, but the envelope had a local postmark on it. The postmark was from three days before, Thursday, October 30.

When she looked around for David, she couldn't find him. She asked Cindy Kurtz, an evidence specialist, if she knew where he had gone. Cindy said she thought he had gone outside. Cindy was a pretty woman, blond, in her twenties, and with an expressive face, especially a pleasant smile.

Sure enough, Kathryn found David at the side of the garage, smoking a cigarette. Nodding, his eyes almost closed, he said, "I needed a wake-me-up." He extended a hand. She took it. "Good to see you again," he said. "As you can tell, I've been at this all night." He pinched the wrinkled shirt he wore, lifting it away from his chest, as if to call attention to his appearance.

She asked him what he knew about Exodus-V. She waved smoke away from her face.

He held the cigarette behind his back so smoke wouldn't get near her, and said as far as anyone could tell, there wasn't such a germ. "That's what I've been on the phone about," he told her. "They're still running the name through the computers, but right now there's nothing." He took a puff of his cigarette. "If you ask me, I say there's no kidnapping at all. I mean, the information about three Lance warheads could be discovered by anyone from the military police to base commanders; but other than that, nothing else adds up. No biological weapon, no group called MTR. One of the Robleses is hiding something. That's what's happening."

She stepped away from the smoke. "And what makes you think one of the Robleses is hiding something?" Since he had been at it all night, he was obviously a lot better informed than she.

"A hunch." He smiled smugly, not enough to show his teeth.

Where were the Robleses? she wanted to know.

He told her that the parents were in their bedroom. "They returned about five minutes before you arrived," he said. "I asked them to wait in the bedroom until we finished."

"Where'd they spend the night?"

"Friends of theirs. After my initial interview with them, they said they wanted to cooperate in any way they could and asked what they could do to help. I told them it would be better if they and the children were out of the house while we searched. The children are still gone." Turning his head, he took a puff of his cigarette and blew the smoke over his shoulder.

She asked him how long he had smoked. She didn't know why she asked it, perhaps to tell him she didn't like him smoking around her.

"I'm going through a divorce," he told her. He forced a smile, again without showing any teeth. "My wife of fifteen years suddenly said she doesn't love me anymore. She and my two sons stayed behind in Los Angeles."

She said she hadn't heard about the divorce.

Rolling the burning end of the cigarette between his fingers, he sprinkled tobacco on the ground in front of him. He put the butt in his coat pocket. He told her he hadn't heard about it either until very recently. "I kept thinking things were going to work out, but then she dropped the bombshell on me. I wanted to talk to you about it—maybe take off a few days and see if Libby and I could patch things up—but she said there was nothing to patch up, so this is where I'm at." He removed the butt from his pocket and held it out. "Trying to handle things the best I know how given the fact that I've never been through a divorce before."

She studied the ground where he had sprinkled tobacco from his cigarette. "Let me know if there's anything I can do to help," she told him.

"We've finished the search out here."

She pondered him.

He pointed at the tobacco droppings. "In case you were looking at the mess I made."

Turning the evidence bag in her hands, she asked the obvious: Had the letter and envelope been checked for prints?

He took off his coat and slung it across his shoulder, leaving it hooked on a raised finger. The bulge along his waistline was noticeable, despite the loose-fitting, faded navy shirt he wore. Shoved inside the waist of his jeans, in a holster that was held in place by a clip that attached to his pants, was his 9mm service weapon. He told her the letter and envelope had passed through multiple hands before getting to the desk of the commanding general. "It wasn't until the commanding general's office that someone had the common sense to notify the Army's Criminal Investigation Command," he said. "CID called us." He told her there were many prints. He explained everything with an unhurried thoroughness. "I'm running them all of course," he said. "Anyone who's touched it, I'm checking his or her background. So far only obvious people have touched it."

What about the search of the house? she wanted to know. Had it turned up anything?

ERT had inventoried everything in the house, he replied. The only thing they couldn't account for was a small key that had been found in Angela's room. "The key was hidden in a cup with a small stuffed animal shoved down on it. You know, an animal like one of those stocking stuffers you give at Christmas."

He stretched out the thumb and index finger of his left hand, as if to illustrate the size of the stuffed animal.

"And what did the parents say the key belongs to?"

"They don't know. All they could think of is that it's probably something she picked up somewhere. They say that ever since the automobile accident, she's been a pack rat." He told her about the hit-and-run accident the previous May. A car had turned onto a highway, not seeing Mrs. Robles. Angela had been the only one not wearing a seat belt. She had been thrown from the van. "Apparently, she was in a coma for six weeks or so," he explained, "then she went through a couple of months of intense rehab. They let her go back to school this past September, but I guess she's in special education classes, tends to be a discipline problem, and needs a lot of extra care and attention. The perfect motivation to cause a parent to lose control and do away with her."

Odd he should tack that thought on. She thought about Wendy. Wendy was a handful too, but even at the worst moments, Kathryn had never thought about killing her. "When was the last time Angela was seen?"

"Friday morning. She didn't get on the bus for school."

She handed him the evidence bag and shoved her hands into the pockets of the FBI windbreaker she wore. Her hands were cold. She commented about the postmark on the letter's envelope. "Whoever mailed that letter appears to have known exactly how long it would take for the letter to get to its destination, and knew exactly when Angela was going to disappear. Either that or it's all pure coincidence, though I can't help but think someone realized that if he or she wasn't careful, the letter would actually get to its destination before Angela disappeared."

"I guess you lost me."

"The postmark is Thursday. Someone seemed to know precisely how long it would take once a letter was dropped in a box for it to arrive at its destination. A slight miscalculation and the letter would have arrived even before the kidnapper could get away with Angela." A precise operation that was designed to look slipshod? Hands still in her pockets, she said, "Let's go in and look around."

On their way back to the house, she asked him to refresh her memory about how it had been discovered that Angela was missing.

David told her that parents were required to call the school if a student was going to be absent. He opened the door for her. Since there was no call from the Robleses, he said, the school secretary called and left a message on the Robleses' answering machine. "Of course, Mrs. Robles was at work, as was her husband, so no one got the message; but, at lunch, the older Robles girl, Susana, noticed that her sister was not in the cafeteria like she was supposed to be, so Susana mentioned it to her teacher. The teacher talked to the school secretary, who then called Mrs. Robles at work."

They walked through the house.

"And the computer turned up nothing about the initials MTR?" she asked.

"Nothing obvious," he told her. "Naturally, there are a number of things in the files, but none of them match this location or modus operandi." Again he stopped. If there was any possibility the note was legitimate, he said, he had a theory about the letters.

She asked him about his theory.

He told her that at one time the ancient Hebrews had left out the vowels in their written language. "Of course you can see the inherent strategy. If you leave out the vowels, it's harder for the enemy to figure out what you've written. Even a cache of secret documents is of little value to an enemy that encounters such a system."

"Do you see some message in the letters MTR?" she asked.

He smiled smugly. "Given my Mexican-American heritage," he said, "I may be reading too much into this, but I see the consonants for the Spanish word *matar,* which could literally mean killer. Or it could be something to do with the verb that means kill. The word matador comes from it. It refers to the one who kills the bull."

She nodded. "And do you think the letter is from an individual or a group?"

Again he smiled smugly. This time he lowered his voice. "What do I really think? Given the Robleses' Mexican-American heritage, I would say one of them signed the note with something a little too predictable and obvious."

"Well, let's see what they have to say," she told him. "Why don't you bring them out and introduce me."

The first thing Kathryn thought when the Robleses appeared was how unlike each other they looked, Mary Belle and her husband, Tony. He was short and overweight, she was skinny. He had short black hair that looked like it had hair oil on it. She had extremely long, shiny, dark hair. Tony looked rough, distinctly Mexican-American. She was petite and delicate-looking. If she was Mexican-American, the blood was more of a mix. He had a couple of hairline scars on his face, one right above his upper lip. Mary Belle was flawlessly attractive, despite her age. She looked to be in her forties. The age was in her eyes and in her teeth that showed when she said hello and right away asked what the FBI was doing to find her daughter. She sounded like a worried mother. Her nose was red, and her eyes were glazed with tears.

Kathryn couldn't tell if Major Robles had been crying, though his nose was red also. He wore sunglasses. He wasn't in uniform.

Kathryn told Mary Belle that agents were actively

searching for Angela. Then she asked them, "Have you
two seen the note we've received about your daughter?"

They both said, no, they hadn't.

Kathryn took the note from David, and gave it to
Mary Belle to read. The major read with her. The
note caused Mary Belle to bring a tissue out of the
front pocket of the new jeans she was wearing. "Then
this is real," she said.

Kathryn was surprised by the statement. "Did you
think Angela hadn't been kidnapped? Is there something we should know about?"

Mary Belle shook her head. "It seems like everything bad is happening to that poor girl." She began
to cry silently, tears streaming down her face. Tony
put his arm around her. "If this is real, why are you
hanging around here? Why don't you get out and find
her?" There was anger in her voice. She shook the
evidence package that held the note.

Kathryn assured her that the FBI was taking aggressive measures to find Angela. Then she asked, "Did
you notice anything unusual about the letter?"

"No," Mary Belle said, using a tissue to wipe her eyes.

"The initials MTR don't strike you as being unusual?"

Tony turned pale.

"The letter says 'we,' " Mary Belle said, "like there's
more than one. A group has kidnaped our daughter."
Her husband rubbed her back. When Kathryn's silence
made it obvious she was waiting for something more,
Mary Belle said, "MTR could be my husband's initials,
Major Tony Robles, if that's what you're getting at, but
I resent such an insinuation on your part. Why don't you
go out and find our baby rather than stand around here
and ask rude questions like that?" For being such a
small and delicate woman, her tone was quite imposing.
No sooner had she said that, however, than she began
to weep, and her husband held her. "I'm scared," she
said. "Oh, Mother of Jesus, I'm scared."

Kathryn was satisfied by Mary Belle's response. It

was cruel to have to push her, but Kathryn had noticed the coincidence in the initials immediately and wanted to hear what Mary Belle and Tony would say. It often happened that people who committed crimes committed careless mistakes in the process. She wouldn't put it past someone to draft an elaborate note in which he or she used plural pronouns to make it appear as if there were more than one person involved, and also concoct a fictitious acronym to imply that a terrorist group was responsible for the crime, only to use his or her own initials or some other personally identifiable marker. That Mary Belle had volunteered her observation about the coincidence in initials tended to support her innocence of any corroboration in the letter, though it did nothing to eliminate her husband as a suspect. Kathryn had noticed a change in his color when she had called attention to the initials. She wondered whether David had noticed the change. She asked the major, "Have you heard of any group that goes by MTR?"

No, he said in a dignified tone.

What about Exodus-V, she wanted to know, had he heard of it?

He said, no, but again she thought she noticed an almost imperceptible change in him. She looked at her surroundings. Major Robles was definitely a suspect, she told herself. He was hiding something.

For a moment, she walked away from the Robleses and David. What about a motive? The daughter's mental and physical condition? Or did the Robleses resent the way they lived? The walls of the furniture-laden house were a dull yellow. There were smudges and stains on them. Given her experience with the bureaucracy of the federal government, she assumed that only government painters could make improvements in military quarters. That would explain the poor condition of the walls, she thought, but why was the place so cluttered? It looked as if the Robleses had been forced to

live in housing that was less than adequate for their
needs. Could it be they couldn't afford to live in a larger
place? Were they in financial trouble? Tony was a major
in the United States Army. She was sure he wasn't
wealthy, but he and his family should be living better
than they were. Where was their money going to? Medical bills? The army would cover all that. Where else
could the money go to?

The furnishings of the house consisted of odds and
ends, the kinds of furnishings one might pick up at a
used furniture store, or at an auction. Green shag carpet
covered the floors. It too was worn, stained, and needed
to be replaced. There were a lot of hanging plants and
cheap paintings. The house smelled musty, perhaps from
the baseboard heaters, perhaps from months of summer
heat, or perhaps from age. Maybe all three.

As she stood removed from the Robleses and
David, Kathryn wondered if Major Robles had murdered his daughter in order to collect the insurance
on her. Because of the military's cheap insurance system, she knew that members of the armed forces routinely insured all their family members. Was that it?
The signs were all there. Angela was apparently a
physical and psychological burden to the family. The
family obviously could use money. They needed a bigger house, and many of their furnishings looked
threadbare, even worn out. What kind of insurance
did they have on their daughter?

She moved back to the Robleses and David. She
asked about the physical and mental status of Angela.

Mary Belle repeated most of what David had already reported. Without going into detail about the
circumstances of the accident, Mary Belle said that
Angela had received serious head injuries during an
automobile accident. She had been in a coma for several weeks. For a month or so, she had been confined
to a wheelchair. Then with continuous physical therapy she had eventually learned to walk again, first

with a walker, then with a cane, and then on her own, though she still wasn't completely coordinated. Her mental status? Mary Belle admitted that Angela had become a discipline problem in school.

What was she doing at the bus stop by herself? Kathryn wanted to know.

It was a part of her rehabilitation, Mary Belle explained. Doctors wanted Angela to assume more responsibility for herself. The special bus for handicapped children no longer picked her up at the house, but she walked two blocks to another house, where there was a child in a wheelchair. Angela got on the bus there.

Where were her other children on Friday morning? Kathryn asked Mary Belle.

They got on the regular school bus and thought Angela had made it to her bus all right. "Angela's in special classes in a separate part of the school, so the children seldom see each other during the day. My oldest daughter and her are in the cafeteria at the same time, but that's about it."

The telephone rang. Kathryn followed Mary Belle into the living room, where a special recorder had already been attached to the telephone. Kathryn nodded for Mary Belle to answer. It was Mary Belle's mother. Mary Belle began to cry.

Kathryn and David went to Angela's bedroom. Major Robles stayed with his wife.

The bedroom was neat. That bothered Kathryn. While it was true that Angela was a year younger than Wendy, twelve- and thirteen-year-olds didn't keep their rooms so neat. The bed was made. Wendy never made her bed. On Angela's bed was a stuffed green frog made from what seemed to be a tube sock. There was a shelf above the head of the bed, upon which stood photographs and knickknacks. Everything was too organized. The shelf shined with polish. On a lamp table was a collection of more stuffed animals—a black and white panda, a pink bear with a large red heart, and a small pink bear stuffed into a white mug.

David pointed out that the white mug was where the key had been discovered.

There was a shelf with some books on it. The floor seemed to have been recently vacuumed.

Kathryn put on a pair of plastic gloves. She pulled open the top dresser drawer. It was crammed with junk—fingernail polish, polish remover, pens, pencils, papers, and loose change. Now this is a twelve-year-old, she told herself. As she moved things around in the drawer, she asked David, "What do you think?"

He said, "The person who bothers me is the major."

She looked at him.

He asked, "Did you notice how he looked when he read the note?"

She went back to digging through the dresser. She said, "He was bothered about something, wasn't he?"

"That was good about the initials. I didn't even catch it until you mentioned something. That's probably what got to him."

She glanced his way. "Let's get them scheduled for polygraphs. What's his work anyway?"

"He works for the 504th Military Intelligence Brigade."

She stopped searching and looked at him, struck by the title of the major's unit. Then likely he would know that the army kept nuclear Lance missiles at Fort Hood. He would know how many, too.

"I doubt it has much to do with anything," he told her, seeming to sense what she was thinking. "I understand he's only a translator of some sort."

"What do you mean, translator?"

"I work with encoded messages," Major Robles said. He was standing in the doorway. Though he seemed to try to stand with the dignity of a military officer, his belly protruded over his thick brown belt. The belt buckle was slightly off center. She saw a tear slide down onto the left side of his chin. The tear didn't seem to want to drop, and might have been mistaken for sweat or something else had the circumstances been different. He entered the bedroom and sat on the edge of his daughter's bed.

She stared at him, wanting to ask him to take off his glasses. "What kind of insurance do you have on Angela?" Normally, she wasn't so blunt, but she wanted to see what kind of a reaction she would get.

"I know what you're getting at," he said soberly. "Unlike my wife, I understand. My wife and I will have to be eliminated as suspects. You already think I'm one. It's a shame things have to work that way, but I understand. We have a standard government policy on each of the children. Actually, I'm not sure of the amount. I think ten, maybe fifteen thousand. It's standard. Nothing more. It's what the military gives us. It's what they give all the families of soldiers. I'd be happy to dig out the papers."

She wondered what his eyes were doing. She thought she was a good judge of character based upon what she saw in a person's eyes. "It's not necessary at this time," she said. "But we would like to ask if you and your wife would take polygraph examinations. Do you have any problems with that?"

"You'll have to ask Mary Belle about herself, but I have no problem."

"You're welcome to consult with an attorney," she told him.

"I don't need one." His voice sounded sure of itself. "All I want is our daughter back."

David said, "I notice from the ring on your hand that you're a West Point graduate."

She glanced at his hand.

"How did you know that?" the major asked.

"My older brother went to West Point. He was killed in 'Nam."

"Sorry."

David nodded. "I received a nomination to go to the academy, but that's all the farther it went. I didn't have the grades. Not like my brother. He had a lot of gifts."

She went back to looking through Angela's dresser. Her back to Robles, she asked, "So why do you suppose anyone would kidnap Angela?" Unless she could see his eyes, it didn't matter whether she looked directly at him. She wondered how extensive his military intelligence training had been. Was he in counterintelligence? She would want to review his military records thoroughly.

"The truth?"

She turned to him. "Of course," she told him. "The truth."

"It's ugly what I think," he replied. "I think this whole letter business is a hoax."

Interesting, Kathryn thought.

The major sighed. "We've always noticed how well developed Angela is for her age. She looks like a woman. She looks older than she is." He took off his sunglasses. His eyes looked bloody. "Please, don't say anything to Mary Belle about this"—he put back on his sunglasses—"but I'm afraid someone has taken my baby to have his way with her." Another tear ran down his face. This one broke from his chin.

Kathryn had considered such a possibility. Maybe one of Tony's colleagues had raped and murdered her. Any of his colleagues could know about nuclear weapons at Hood.

"Ever since the accident, she's been different. I admit, it's been difficult. Everything in our day-to-day lives has changed. We can't even go to church anymore. There was a time when we did, back when she was in a wheelchair, but we had to stop because she was always hanging onto the men there. She even went up to the minister and asked him to kiss her. He had to have a talk with her, to tell her it wasn't right, but she didn't care. I'm afraid someone's taken her to have his way with her." He inhaled quickly through his nose. It was runny.

"Then, why pretend it's a kidnapping?" she asked, studying him. "And why this business about Exodus-Five—you're sure you've never heard of Exodus-five?"

"Everything is so confusing right now," he said. "I don't know what I've heard and what I haven't heard. You ever get that way—when you feel like your life's been turned upside down, and you can't think, you can't remember, you can't do much of anything? I guess I'm like my wife. I'm so terrified by what's happened that I can't think straight."

Kathryn couldn't help but notice that the major's response was evasive. He was lying. He knew something. She was sure of it.

After moving items around in different drawers, she went to the closet. She opened the door and turned on the light. The closet was as neatly organized as the room. All of Angela's clothes hung neatly on hangers. Her shoes were lined up.

Major Robles must have noticed her pondering the closet because he said, "Mary Belle babies her now. I guess she feels so guilty about what happened that she wants to do everything for the girl. She doesn't want to let her out of her sight, not even for a moment. I was the one who talked to the doctors and asked them to make sure Angela had to walk to the bus stop. If it was up to Mary Belle, the bus would still be coming to the front door."

At the closet Kathryn knew she wasn't looking for anything in particular. ERT would have been through everything, but she wanted to get a feel for the place. She especially wanted to know what Major Robles was hiding. She didn't trust him. She felt the pockets of the clothes—for notes. Wendy wrote a lot of notes in school. Kathryn was always finding them when she washed laundry. Note writing was characteristic for that age group.

Mary Belle entered the room, sat on the bed, and took her husband's hand. She told him the entire family was on their way up from San Antonio. "Everyone's coming. They want to help."

Kathryn asked her, "Once again, how did you discover Angela was missing from school?"

Mary Belle told her she had been at work at the hospital in Killeen—she was a registered nurse there—when the school had called her at around noon. She explained everything just as David had.

The major spoke up: "Mary Belle called me, and we contacted the military police, who contacted Army CID. Agents there weren't too concerned. They said she had probably run away. I don't know if you knew, but she did it once before—didn't really run away, but we couldn't find her, so we called the military police, who found her at a friend's house. Apparently, she had gone home with another girl without telling us. She told the girl's parents we were mistreating her."

Kathryn was about to pull the string to turn off the closet light when she noticed the attic panel. It seemed to have been moved. It didn't quite line up with the attic opening. "Did ERT check up in the attic?" she asked David.

He told her he was certain they had—he had seen them with a ladder.

She asked the major if he'd ever been up in the attic.

"I took Angela up there this past summer," Major Robles said. "One thing about it, after the accident she's been curious about everything. She wanted to see what was up there, so I took her up."

Kathryn asked him if he had something she could stand on—a chair or ladder—and a flashlight. He left the room. She used the opportunity to mention to Mary Belle that they would need to talk to the children, and to ask her if she'd be willing to take a polygraph examination.

Mary Belle, unlike her husband, seemed resentful. She said she would take a polygraph, but she was going to make sure people knew how the FBI was treating her and the case. "If we were white and you didn't look upon me as a mixed-breed, you wouldn't be standing here right now. You'd have the whole United States searching for my daughter."

Kathryn didn't say anything. She felt sorry for the mother. If the tables had been turned, and it was her facing the disappearance of Wendy, Kathryn realized she would have been the same way, probably worse. She would have been angry and frantic at the same time.

The major returned with a stepladder and flashlight. Kathryn pushed side the attic panel and stuck her head up in the warm attic. She flashed a light onto an ocean of insulation. She began to move the insulation. Wendy hid things in the attic. Kathryn lifted a thick piece of yellow insulation, under which were some folded notes, some money, a transistor radio, and a diary. Yes, this was a twelve-year-old. She brought the items down.

Everyone seemed stunned, even Cindy Kurtz of the ERT, who had stopped in to see what was going on. Cindy looked embarrassed.

The major said he hadn't ever seen the diary. Right away he was defensive.

Mary Belle contradicted him. She said, "Tony, you've seen that. We bought it for her."

Major Robles' sunglasses looked in the direction of his wife. He was clearly caught off guard. He said, "We did? I don't remember it."

Mary Belle told how they had given Angela the diary at Christmas the year before.

The sunglasses moved in the direction of Kathryn.

"My wife does the Christmas shopping," he explained. He looked uncomfortable.

Kathryn told David, "Get me the key that you found."

David left the room, which became very quiet. Momentarily, he returned with a small key. It fit the diary's lock.

Kathryn began flipping pages of the diary, scanning the entries that had been made in a crude hand. She looked up at Tony and Mary Belle and said, "I think there are some things we need to talk about."

4

The handwriting in the diary was neater than Kathryn had expected, given what she had heard about Angela's injuries from the accident. In fact, the writing was quite neat, though the entries were brief. One entry was as simple as "Everyone hates me." Another, "The kids hit me and run away. They call me stupid." A couple were troubling: "Mom slapped me in the face." "Dad hit me with a belt. I promised to be good." Kathryn turned to the last entry in the diary: "A man who looks like the devil and his helper have been watching me from their car. I told Dad, but he didn't care. I'm scared."

In one of the upstairs interrogation rooms at the Army's CID unit, Kathryn held out the diary, which was turned to the last entry. The major took it. "Take a look at this," she told him. David watched without saying anything.

The wood interrogation room was in an old barracks: a two-story yellow building with green trim that had been painted so many times, the paint seemed to hold the building together. Inside, the walls were shiny yellow enamel.

She said, "Would you please read it aloud?"

The major read aloud the entry.

Kathryn took a drink of her diet Coke. The air in the room was warm and stale—smelled like old lumber—from the steam heat. The heat register was clanking. There was no insulation in the walls, no wall-

board. Kathryn could tell the government spent a fortune heating the building in the winter. It was like the
government, she thought. Always wasting money—
throwing away taxpayer dollars. She could tell David
wanted a cigarette, so she told him, "David, why don't
you give us a few moments alone together."

Even when David had stepped out of the room,
she didn't say anything right away. She listened to his
footsteps go down the hall. She could hear him in the
stairwell. At the window she looked out. Why would
Major Robles hit his daughter with a belt? she wondered. He didn't seem like the type. The thought of
physical contact made her sick to her stomach. At the
same time it frightened her. There had been moments,
especially in recent days, when Kathryn had come very
close to slapping Wendy, especially when Wendy
talked back to her or used curse words. It was almost
as if Wendy were trying to push her to the limit. Still,
Kathryn didn't think it was possible that she could
beat Wendy. Slap her yes, beat her with a belt, no. In
fact, other than a rare smack on the hand when
Wendy had been a baby, Kathryn had never used
physical punishment on her daughter. It was frightening to think some people did use physical punishment
without restraint.

Leaning near the dirty glass, she could see David at
the side of the building, where he lit a cigarette.
Watching him, her back to the major, she said, "Major
Robles, do you know who these men are that Angela
is making reference to?"

"No, I don't. This is all new to me."

"Major, we have a problem here, you know." She
returned to the table.

He didn't say anything, only watched her.

"Angela even wrote that she told you about someone watching her. You say you don't remember her
telling you that?"

He shrugged. "You know how kids are—they tell

you all kinds of things. As difficult as it might be to believe, I can't remember her saying anything about someone watching her. It seems like if she would have said something, I would have at least gone out and taken a look." He shook his head. "I can't remember, though."

"Why would she make something like that up in her diary?"

He forced a smile. Sweat had formed on his upper lip. "She has a vivid imagination. If some strangers had been hanging around the house, I'm sure someone else would have noticed them."

"Who said someone was watching her at the house? I can't remember." Yes, she could remember. She had mentioned nothing about the house. "Did I say that?"

His color had turned an almost sickly yellow. "I guess I assumed that was what Angela was talking about in her diary."

Odd, she thought. He was lying so much she didn't know what to believe. She finished her diet Coke and put the can on the table. She shoved her hands in her pants pockets and told him, "You had some slips in your polygraph exam, you know."

He didn't say anything.

"I think you know that. Some troubling responses to important questions." As a matter of fact, she was very bothered by the number of inconsistencies there had been. "No one's trying to harm you or cause you trouble—if anything, I want to give you a chance to get out of a mess if you're in one. This is the chance to get out—a chance to put your cards on the table."

Silence.

"Would you please take off those sunglasses?"

He took them off, exposing his red eyes, but he told her he couldn't see without them. "They're prescription," he said. "My regular glasses are broken. I sat on them. I know these seem rude, but I can't see a thing without glasses."

"Go ahead, put them back on."

He did.

She picked up a manila folder on the table, opened it, and said, "When you were asked if the initials MTR meant anything to you, you answered, no, they didn't. Didn't mean a thing. You emphasized your response because the examiner questioned you about it. What you told us, and what your body told us are two different stories, though. Major, you're not stupid, you know what a polygraph is. You know all about it. This can't be new to you."

"I guess I was a bit nervous about the whole thing," he admitted.

Don't give me that, she wanted to say, but instead said, "When you were asked if Exodus-Five meant anything to you, you answered, no, it didn't. Didn't mean a thing. You emphasized your response because the examiner questioned you about it. Again, what you told us, and what your body told us are two different stories. Can you explain that?"

"No," he answered, he couldn't explain.

"Did you write the note that was sent to the commanding general of Fort Hood?"

"No."

"Did your wife write the note?"

"Of course not!"

"How do you know?"

"I know my wife."

"If you didn't write the note, and your wife didn't write it, you know who did, then, don't you?"

"No."

"Are you sure?"

"Positive."

She got up and walked around the table. "How come none of this makes sense, then?" She stopped near his chair. "How come you had trouble during the polygraph when you were asked about the initials MTR, and you had trouble when you were asked about Exodus-Five, and you had trouble when you were asked about who wrote the note?" She stared at him. From where she stood she could see his eyes. They were fixed straight forward behind the glasses, as if they were intentionally avoiding her. "Don't you care about your daughter?" His eyes jumped slightly, the way eyes jump when a door slams unexpectedly.

"Of course, I care," he told her. "What kind of a father do you think I am?"

She returned to her chair. "A father who's not being very truthful."

His glasses fixed on her. "What are you implying?" His voice had turned cold. "You don't know who or what you're dealing with."

She shrugged. "Maybe I do, maybe I don't. Why don't you clear things up for me by telling me who or what I'm dealing with."

He didn't say anything.

"Let me be real generous with you. Let's say you didn't kill her, but you do sensitive work for military intelligence, and you're afraid to talk about it. Maybe you've encountered some intelligence about a terrorist operation that the FBI doesn't know about. I don't know. All I do know is you're not telling everything, and if this kidnapping is legitimate, you're putting your daughter's life in jeopardy." She opened her hands to him. "This is your opportunity. The reason I asked Agent Gonzalez to step out for a few moments is so that we could talk off the record. Talk. It's off the record." She waited. She didn't believe any of the scenario she had just conveyed to him. What she really believed was that he had killed his daughter, and that someone had helped him. He had fifteen thousand dollars' worth of life insurance through the military. Even if he had taken five thousand of that to pay a helper, he would still walk away with ten thousand dollars, minus any future medical bills—as it turned out Mary Belle had been carting Angela around to private physicians and specialists.

"I know how it is," Kathryn conceded. "I've seen it before. I know how you can get caught up in something and can't get out. Off the record, is there a way I can help you out of a mess you're in? Is there something you haven't told us that you think might help in our investigation?"

He didn't say anything. In fact, he seemed to be glaring at her, though it was difficult to tell because of the sunglasses.

"Is someone blackmailing you?"

No response.

She got up, walked around the table and put a hand on his shoulder. To touch him made her feel dirty. "I want to help you, but you have to help me. Do you know who wrote the letter?"

"No."

"Do you know anything about the initials MTR?"

"No comment."

The response caught her off guard. No comment? His shoulder felt cold. She removed her hand from it. Had she heard him correctly? "What?"

"I'm sorry, but I don't want to comment."

"Do you know anything about Exodus-Five, anything at all?"

"I think I want to talk to a lawyer."

He knew—knew what had happened to his daughter. He had arranged it all. "Do you ever neglect or abuse Angela?"

"I want a lawyer."

David returned. He reeked of cigarette smoke and had a smirk on his face.

In a cold voice Kathryn told him, "Agent Gonzalez, can I see you for a moment?"

She and David went down the hall to the men's bathroom. Inside, she told him what had happened while he had been outside smoking.

Still smirking, he said, "See, I told you something was rotten in Denmark. I told you I had a hunch about him. He killed her, didn't he?"

Instead of responding to his question, she said, "While I get started with Mary Belle, you get someone to give the major a ride home, and then set up a surveillance team so we can keep our eyes on him. I want him watched around the clock. I want to know if he consults an attorney. I want to know every single thing he does."

She went downstairs to get Mary Belle, who had been waiting in the reception area. "Sorry to keep you waiting," Kathryn told her. Kathryn's whole attitude had changed, almost to the point that she wanted to hug Mary Belle and tell her how sorry she was that Mary Belle was tied to someone who was lying and who knew something about what had happened to Angela. She resisted that temptation, though.

Mary Belle put down an old magazine with no covers. All of the magazines on the table in the reception area looked old. "That's okay," she said, watching Kathryn. There wasn't much enthusiasm in her voice. She sounded empty, lost.

Kathryn could hear David and Major Robles in the hallway and then going out the door. She said, "They're going to run your husband home—that way he doesn't have to sit around waiting for you. Don't worry, we'll make sure you get a ride back once we're done." She held an open hand toward the door. "Let's go upstairs and talk."

On their way up the stairs, Kathryn mentioned, "It looks like we may be in for a cold winter this year."

Mary Belle didn't say anything.

Kathryn could tell she wasn't in the mood for small talk.

Inside the interrogation room, Kathryn apologized for sounding so insensitive. She said, "The fact of the matter is that in most cases like this, it turns out to be someone who knows the victim. Often it turns out to be a family member." She wanted to prepare Mary Belle for the worst.

"And you think it's me?" Her dark eyes seemed to say, How could you believe that?

"No, I don't." Kathryn touched Mary Belle's thin arm. "I don't think it's you, but the kinds of judgments I have to make doesn't allow me ten or fifteen years to get to know you and all there is about you, so I end up saying and doing things that seem insensitive, but get me where I need to be. Bear with me, please."

Mary Belle gave an almost imperceptible nod.

Kathryn asked if she wanted anything to drink.

Mary Belle's expression softened. "To tell you the truth, I feel a little shaky. Are there any potato chips or something I could get to eat. I mean, if there's a snack machine downstairs." She touched her stomach. "I'm pregnant, you know."

The news came as a shock. It was the last thing Kathryn had suspected or expected to hear. As it was, Mary Belle looked unhealthily thin. Kathryn replied, "No, I didn't know that."

Mary Belle nodded. "Actually, it's quite embarrassing. We didn't expect it at all. I didn't even know I could still get pregnant." She blushed. "Imagine that—me a nurse, and not knowing any better." Her cheeks stayed a rosy color for a long time.

They still had color in them when Kathryn returned with a bag of pretzels. She put down a Sprite too. "Sorry about the pretzels," she said. "It's the closest thing they had to chips." She nodded at the Sprite. "I thought you might want something to wash them down with. Sprite doesn't have caffeine, so I figured it'd be all right for the baby. When's it due?"

"The end of May."

"How are you holding up?"

"Not very good."

Kathryn felt sorry for her. She looked like someone

who had just gotten out of the hospital. All of the trauma with Angela had to be taking its toll. "We're working as hard as we can to find Angela," Kathryn said.

"I know you are, and I'm sorry if I don't sound grateful."

Kathryn allowed a few moments of silence to pass before she said, "Tell me about Angela."

Mary Belle looked very pale. She opened the bag of pretzels, took out a pretzel, and began nibbling it. "What do you want to know?" Her hand was trembling.

Kathryn sat down. "Tell me about her health. Her physical status, mental status—"

Mary Belle popped the top on the Sprite. "Looking at her, you wouldn't know anything was wrong," she said. She took a drink of Sprite. "She's actually quite pretty, and quite a young lady." She chewed on another pretzel. "Her left eye droops a little." She touched right below her own left eye. "That's only since the accident—well, since she woke up. She was in a coma for six weeks, you know."

"That's a long time. It must have been extremely difficult for you."

Her eyes became glassy. "We thought we were going to lose her. And now this."

"Does she still have a lot of problems?"

Mary Belle looked through glassy eyes as if she were trying to think the tears away, then she barely blinked, and the tears rolled down her cheeks. They got in the blush that didn't look like it was there. "Her feet are still uncoordinated—she's getting better, but they still give her trouble. Kids that age tend to be clumsy anyway, but with Angela I think it's more than clumsiness." She shook her head. "I don't know—are you a mother? You look like a mother."

Kathryn nodded.

"Then you'll know how it is when I tell you that

even when they say everything's all right, you worry about your children. Maybe I worry too much. Maybe I blame myself for the accident and what's happened to her. Maybe I do everything for her because I feel guilty. I don't know. I don't care. The doctors say she's fine. Tony says she's fine. The teachers say she's fine—they want to move her to regular classes, but I don't want to rush." She wiped her cheeks with a small hand. It made the tears blend with her blush. "Now all I can think of is that if I had insisted on having my way, the kidnappers wouldn't have gotten her because she wouldn't have been walking to the bus stop. That was Tony's idea."

"I thought it was the doctor's idea." Kathryn knew it was Tony's idea, but she wanted to know how much Mary Belle knew.

"Tony put the doctor up to it. Later I learned that Tony persuaded the doctor to insist with me." Her voice didn't sound bitter. It was as if she blamed herself for everything.

Why would Major Robles murder his daughter if she was getting better? Kathryn wondered. Why would he go through so much trouble? What was his motivation? Had he been sexually abusing her while she was so incapacitated from the accident? Was that it? Had she gotten better, then threatened to tell on him, which made him desperate to silence her?

From her pocket, Mary Belle removed a tissue. "Some things have definitely changed about her. For example, she used to be a very talented musician. Now it seems like she can't play at all. I mean she blows on her flute, but that's about it, and she only does that when I make her." She began to cry. "She doesn't realize it was my fault—can't even remember the accident." The tissue became saturated. She pushed the pretzels and Sprite away from her.

Staring at her, Kathryn said, "It must be terribly difficult for." Mary Belle didn't say anything. "I mean what with Angela and the accident, three other children in the home, both you and your husband working, and now another child on the way."

Mary Belle nodded. "It is hard," she admitted. "Hard to make ends meet."

"Financially?"

"It seems like it's one thing after another." She was trying to wipe her eyes, but the tissue was falling apart.

Kathryn got up. "Let me see if I can find some more tissue." She left the room. All she could find were paper towels from the men's rest room. They were the brown, rough towels. Kathryn apologized, but Mary Belle didn't seem to mind. She blew her nose in one of the towels. Kathryn asked, "Are you going to be all right?"

"Something's got to give," Mary Belle replied, wiping her face with a new towel. "I can't take much more. We can't even pay our bills right now, and we live from check to check. I don't know how long it can go on this way."

If things were that bad, Kathryn thought, even a standard life insurance policy would promise relief. "What all's going on?"

Mary Belle folded the brown paper towel again and again. "There's the extra medical bills with Angela. You know, you always wonder about the military doctors, so you go out searching for second and third opinions, but they cost money. Then, there are the moves. I wish we'd have never moved here. We just got here, and I had the accident with Angela. I never wanted to move in the first place. They never give you enough money to move. It never covers everything. Then we send money home to our families. Tony supports his family. I support mine. We're like the only people in our family who have gone to college or who have gotten good jobs." She shook her head. "And Tony, I don't even understand him. If he would go to the civilian side of his work, he'd make three times what he is making as a major in the army." She said it again as if to emphasize it. "If he went to the civilian status, he could have the same job, and make three times as much money. This whole business about loyalty to his country and to West Point is absurd."

"Do you ever talk to him about all this?"

She let out a deep breath. "He goes one way, I go another. That's what I've discovered marriage is all about."

"How much do you know about Tony's work?"

"Nothing."

"Nothing?"

"Not a thing."

"You're his wife. He never talks to you about his work?"

"He's not allowed to. He's not allowed to talk to anyone. In fact, if anyone starts asking him questions, he's supposed to report that person to his superiors."

"He's never mentioned MTR, or Exodus-Five?"

"No, but he wouldn't tell me even if he did know something. He'd just tell me he could go to jail for talking."

Kathryn opened the diary and turned to the last entry. She let Mary Belle read it, and was satisfied when she saw an appropriate shocked expression on her face. She asked, "Did you know Angela was keeping a diary?"

David returned. He looked cold. His cheeks were red, and he was rubbing his hands together. The smell of fresh cigarette smoke came with him. "Hi." He sat down in a chair and leaned back so that the chair was balanced on its rear legs near the radiator.

Watching David, Mary Belle said she had forgotten that Angela had even had a diary. "When I saw you bring it down from the attic, I remembered, but I hadn't the slightest idea she was keeping one."

Before Kathryn could say anything, David asked

Mary Belle if she had seen any strangers hanging around the house or the neighborhood.

No, Mary Belle said, shaking her head. "But I wouldn't be surprised if Angela saw someone. She sees a lot more than people give her credit for. Sometimes she shows us all up by noticing someone we all miss, or by remembering something we've all forgotten about. Someone can call on the telephone, and Angela will recognize immediately who it is. She'll call that person by name. A lot of times, with me, I have to talk for a few moments before I figure out who it is. It'll even be someone we haven't talked to for a long time, and she'll recognize that person's voice immediately."

Kathryn asked, "Had Angela mentioned anything about someone watching her?"

"No." The shake of her head was emphatic. "And I'm surprised Tony never mentioned anything to me as soon as Angela had said what she saw. That's not like him." There was a fresh look of concern on her face, as if she just realized Tony had kept a secret from her.

"Had you noticed any changes in her personality, habits, anything?"

Mary Belle gave a subtle smile. She had a delicate face. "I think she's like all children at that age. They're prone to mood swings. One moment they can be laughing, and the next moment they'll be screaming or crying for no apparent reason."

Kathryn had noticed the same thing with Wendy. She shoved her hands into her pants pockets and asked, "Mary Belle, have you told us everything you can think of?"

"I guess so." Then she added, "I hope so at least."

Hands still in her pockets, Kathryn said, "Sometimes, especially in criminal investigations, witnesses tell what they think they know, only to remember later that they've forgotten some important detail. Then they get scared that someone's going to accuse them of lying, or of withholding evidence, or with trying to hide something, and they don't know what to do."

Mary Belle got a concerned look on her face. "I'm not sure what you mean."

"You've talked to a number of people since all of this started. Have you remembered anything you think we ought to know?"

The confused look lingered. "Is there something I should remember?"

"There's a little inconsistency we need to iron out," Kathryn told her, ever so gently.

"Inconsistency?" She put the folded brown paper towel on the table. "What do you mean, inconsistency?"

"Mary Belle, there was a problem with your polygraph examination."

Mary Belle's face reddened with embarrassment. She picked up the folded paper towel.

"You know what I'm talking about, don't you?" Kathryn said. "The examiner asked if you were hiding anything about Angela, and you said, no. What bothered you when you said that?"

Before Mary Belle could answer, David asked, "Were you worried about something Angela might have written in her diary?"

"What?" Mary Belle seemed to have trouble concentrating.

"Were you worried she might have written some things about the way you treated her, things you wouldn't want others to know about?"

What was he doing? Kathryn wondered, panic filling her.

"What?" Mary Belle repeated, looking at him.

David said, "Were you worried she might have written about the times you and your husband mistreated her, or the kinds of punishments you gave her?"

Mary Belle's confusion turned to anger. She said, "How dare you."

Kathryn glared at David. Shut up, she wanted to say. Look at me, and shut up. To Mary Belle, she said, "Let's go back to this inconsistency in your polygraph examination."

Mary Belle looked back and forth between them, as if she didn't know whom to trust.

"You know what that little problem was all about, don't you?"

Mary Belle took a breath through her nose, obviously still ruffled by what David had said, exhaled forcefully, and nodded. "Yes, I know." Her voice was no longer kind.

In a gentle tone Kathryn asked, "Can you explain what troubled you when you were taking the polygraph?"

"When Tony and I were first married, we wanted children very badly," Mary Belle said. "We tried and tried, but couldn't conceive. We even went to the doctors, who said they couldn't find anything wrong. They told us some people couldn't have children for one reason or another. These days that's not the case. Today almost anyone can have a child, what with all the modern technology and things." She shook her head. "Right when we decided to adopt, I got pregnant." She smiled slightly. "I know this sounds strange because you hear this kind of story all the time, but it's the truth." The slightest smile of amusement lingered on her face. "Tony and I were worried at first. We were afraid we might not be able to love Angela as much as we loved our own child. It was a foolish thought. We loved her as much as we loved our own. It's funny love is that way. You learn to love, and you love each one differently."

Kathryn said, "Angela is adopted?"

"Yes. We adopted her because we had given up on ever having children on our own, then we had three"—she snapped her fingers three times—"one after another." She touched her stomach. "Now there's another one." Her eyes filled with tears. She tried to keep the tears wiped from her eyes. The roughness of the paper towels was abrading her face.

Kathryn folded her hands on the table in front of her. Again, she had been surprised to discover that key information had been withheld from her. "Why didn't you tell us about this before?"

"It's not like when we introduce our children, we introduce Angela as our adopted daughter. I guess we were scared."

"Scared?"

"Angela doesn't know she's adopted. No one does. It's not the kind of thing you want your child to find out before you're ready to tell her yourself, and then you want to be the one to do it and not have someone else do it." She shook her head. She blotted a tear from her right eye. "Tony and I hadn't had a chance to talk things over—things have been happening so quickly. When everyone showed up, he didn't say anything about Angela being adopted, so I thought I better not say anything. I was worried that television or news reporters might show up, find out about her past, and make a big deal out of it. I thought that would devastate Angela." Mary Belle gave an angry glance at David. "Then, when we talked about it, we decided the FBI might not give as much attention to an adopted child who was also a Mexican-American— that you might not be as sensitive."

David looked at his lap. Kathryn was sure he had gotten the message.

"So that was what was bothering you when you took your polygraph?" Kathryn asked.

Mary Belle nodded. "We didn't want the news about the adoption to come out before we had had a chance to tell Angela ourselves, then before we had a chance to talk to our own children."

Kathryn asked, "Where did you adopt her?"

"She came from an adoption agency in Dallas," she said. "It was all legal—I promise."

"I'm sure it was. Do you remember the name of the adoption agency?"

"Intercountry Adoption Services, or something like that." She arched her back. "How much longer?"

"A few more questions. Do you know anything about the biological parents?"

Mary Belle shook her head. "No, as far as I know, there was only the mother, and she didn't want any part of the process. Do you really think it's important that she's adopted?" She looked tired.

"Not particularly," Kathryn replied, "but it is something we definitely should check out. It could provide a motive for a kidnapper." She didn't believe that, but she had to cover all the bases. "One or both of the biological parents might be trying to get her back. Has the adoption agency been in contact with you—such as to notify you that the biological parents were searching for their daughter?"

"No, why?"

"Sometimes biological parents try to find adopted children for medical reasons," she said. "Say one or both of the parents go on to have another child, and that child ends up with a medical problem such as a rare kidney disease. If the child is going to die without a new kidney, doctors might encourage the family to hunt for a relative who can provide a donor match." Kathryn didn't believe any of that was the case, but she had to let Mary Belle know that they needed all the information they could get—that is, nothing could be held back.

"No, we've never been contacted by anyone." Mary Belle drank some of her Sprite.

Kathryn asked about the adoption papers.

Mary Belle explained there weren't any. "We kept them for a while," she said, "but Tony and I worried about them constantly. We thought that as the kids got older, no matter where we hid the papers, someone would end up finding them. We knew that would be a disaster."

"What about a recent photograph of Angela? I assume you have one. I haven't even seen what she looks like."

David produced a photograph. He said he had taken it to make copies.

The photograph was one of the entire family standing in front of their Fort Hood house. Mary Belle said a friend had taken it. While the others were smiling at the camera, there was Angela standing with a blank expression on her face. She looked like a young woman—funny how girls grew up so quickly—even wore lipstick that matched Mary Belle's lipstick in the photograph. At the same time the twelve-year-old with the adult's body seemed detached from the world of the photograph. Her left eye was drooping. It stared at the ground. Her right eye stared into space. A girl in a world of her own.

5

When Angela closed her eyes, everything moved in slow motion and had a black outline around it, as had happened after the accident, only now the blackness closed in on her and wouldn't go away. Even with her eyes closed, the images she saw were outlined in black. It wasn't like on the day she had left the hospital. Then the sun had been shining following a morning rain, and her father had pushed her wheelchair into the wet sunshine. The blackness had begun to fade then, as if the sun had burned it away.

Now, bound in the cold darkness of the car's trunk, she knew McCanles and McCabe were taking her someplace to kill her. She could feel death, could feel herself locked in the slow motion of her own end, cold blackness all around, no way out. No help. All she could think of was her father saying, "You've made your bed, now lie in it." It was his favorite saying. Her doctor had told her something like that after the accident, too. He had told her if she didn't start taking care of herself—she had broken her arm the year before—she was going to end up with a problem no one could fix.

The road changed. She bounced around in the trunk. After a while, she could hear popping and crackling, like fireworks, first distant, then nearby, then distant, then nearby. The pops and crackles grew very loud. With her hands tied behind her, she couldn't cover her ears or protect her head. Her head hit the trunk floor several times. In her frustration, she tried to cry out, but the tape over her mouth muffled the sound. The car stopped. The trunk opened; in rushed intense popping, crackling, cold gray, and moisture. She withdrew in reflex, terrified someone would hit her. Hands grabbed her. The army of hands lifted her from the trunk, untied her, and dropped her into a wheelchair, where she was restrained with hand straps, feet straps, and a lap belt. She struggled. She didn't want to return to a wheelchair, but it was impossible to overpower the soldiers who tied her into the chair. McCanles ripped the tape off her mouth. Her mouth stung, as her shoeless foot stung from where she had stomped the wasp, but she didn't cry out.

Only then did she realize the popping and crackling had stopped. Soldiers gathered around her in the drizzling rain. Thirty or more. Their faces were camouflaged with green, black, and brown paint, and they wore rain-soaked jungle fatigues and full field gear—bulging packs and belts with canteens—like she had occasionally seen on soldiers at Fort Hood. These soldiers also carried weapons. One soldier in particular caught her attention, a colonel who towered over everyone else. The men seemed to sense his approach and moved back. He had the black insignia of an eagle sewn into his left collar and on his cap. His face wasn't painted.

"Attention!" someone yelled. The soldiers straightened and froze.

Captain McCanles saluted. "Captain McCanles and Lieutenant McCabe reporting, sir," he said. McCanles and McCabe were still in civilian clothes.

"As you were," the colonel said, returning the salute. He wasn't wearing field gear. Only a sidearm. All the soldiers relaxed. The colonel was so unnaturally tall that he had to bend to see her face. His face was pockmarked. He had thick gray hair that was wavy. On his hand he wore a ring like her father wore and was so proud of, the ring of West Point.

He straightened. In a loud voice of authority, he said, "Operation Exodus-Five has begun." His eyes made a sweeping study of the camouflaged men. "You are to treat everything we do from this moment on as a part of a real Military Situation. We are as of this moment on the highest state of alert. No communications with the outside world, no unauthorized travel, and no discussions among yourselves. You get caught doing any of those things, and it's grounds for a general court-martial with serious consequences." He pointed at Angela. "I want everyone here to take a good look at our hostage. From this moment until the end of this operation, you'll eat, sleep, and train with her, around-the-clock. Not a moment will pass in which she will be out of our presence. She is more important even than your M-16. If you lose her, or anything happens to her, you will be held strictly accountable. She is the daughter of a very influential political leader. Is that clear?"

In unison the soldiers replied, "Yes, sir!"

Despite their loudness, the colonel insisted: "Is that clear!"

"Yes, sir!" The words filled the air.

"There will be a full briefing in the mess hall at eleven hundred hours." He glanced at his watch. "Until that time, Corporal Klock, you take charge of the prisoner."

A burly, crewcut soldier saluted and said, "Yes, sir." He was wearing a thick black band on his left arm with the white letters "MP" on it.

The colonel returned Klock's salute. "Captain McCanles and Lieutenant McCabe, you two are to report to the major."

McCanles and McCabe saluted. McCabe's salute was not very precise.

"The rest of you, carry on."

A fat black sergeant who wore a camouflaged bush hat yelled, "Attention!" and the soldiers snapped to attention. Once the colonel, McCanles, and McCabe had departed, the sergeant commanded them, "Fall in!" The soldiers, including Klock, gathered in a formation. "Corporal Klock, you and your prisoner take up the rear!" Klock hastily moved Angela to the end of the formation. "Right face!" In unison, the soldiers spun to the right. "Forward," called the sergeant, dragging out the word, "march!"

The soldiers marched in unison as the sergeant walked alongside calling a cadence: "Your left, your left, your left, right, left . . ."

They followed a dirt road, whose dust had become a paste in the drizzle.

After a while the sergeant called out the words to a song, which the soldiers sang:

"A little bird—"
"A little bird!"
"On the windowsill—"
"On the windowsill!"
"I opened up—"
"I opened up!"
"And let her in—"
"And let her in!"
"I made her warm—"
"I made her warm!"
"And kept her fed—"
"And kept her fed!"
"And then I smashed her ugly head—"
"And then I smashed her ugly head!"

"Ya left, ya left, ya left, right, left," the sergeant continued. "Ya left, ya left, ya left, right, left. Double time, march!"

The soldiers jogged, the fat sergeant running alongside them.

Klock and Angela followed. Despite the pasty road, Klock didn't fall behind. With ease he kept up with the others, running as Angela bounced roughly in her wheelchair. A couple of times she thought she was going to tip over, but he didn't let her. His firm grip kept the wheelchair balanced. The wheels of the wheelchair spun off a reddish paste like an electric beater spinning off cookie dough.

The soldiers ran in formation for a long time, a mile or so, before being called to a stop at a clearing in the wooded, hilly landscape. There was a wood observation tower, some wood bleachers, and a row of muddy patches that overlooked a gully. The sergeant said, "Light 'em up if you got 'em!" He took off his bush hat and wiped his shiny bald head with a dirty handkerchief. He was having trouble catching his breath.

A number of soldiers lit cigarettes. The men stood in groups and talked until the sergeant called them to the muddy patches that overlooked the gully. He assigned individual soldiers to individual patches while another soldier came along and passed out ammunition.

From a loudspeaker came the words: "Ready on the firing line!"

Soldiers positioned themselves on the muddy patches.

"Lock and load."

The soldiers inserted magazines of ammunition in their M-16s. A number of men were still putting in earplugs. Corporal Klock twisted earplugs into Angela's ears, then took his place at the firing line.

"Fire!"

The air filled with loud pops and crackles.

In the gully, in the field, and on the horizon, drab green silhouettes randomly rose and lowered in the rain. As quickly as the silhouettes rose, the soldiers fired off rounds from their M-16s. Even with the earplugs, Angela found the popping and crackling painfully loud.

The soldiers fired from different positions: lying, kneeling, and standing. They didn't care about the mud.

While Klock was standing, firing off rounds at a silhouette on the distant horizon, the colonel appeared again. McCanles and McCabe were nowhere in sight, but soon the training sergeant joined the colonel. Each time the silhouette rose, Klock squeezed off a round and the silhouette dropped. Angela could hear the sergeant yelling at the colonel, "He's knocking them down one after another at three hundred yards, sir! That's damned good!"

The colonel patted Klock's shoulder.

Klock looked back, but was careful to keep his M-16 pointed downrange.

"That's good shooting, soldier!" the colonel said, his voice competing with the other sounds of the firing range.

"Thank you, sir!" Klock yelled back, but kept his weapon pointed downrange.

"This is the moment we've all been chosen for, soldier!"

"Yes, sir!" Klock's voice was enthusiastic.

Later, the soldiers jogged in formation from the firing range to an obstacle course, where they made timed runs through the course. Angela was positioned along the sidelines to watch. The soldiers jumped over long configurations, ran across them, crawled under them, climbed ropes, and dropped over walls. Everyone was in excellent shape.

Then the soldiers double-timed to a shack that looked like a sauna. Soon thick smoke was rolling from under the door of the shack. Groups of soldiers would go inside and come out coughing. Though their eyes would be filled with tears, the soldiers laughed about it. They bragged about how a little tear gas couldn't stop them. Nothing could stop them, they bragged.

The sergeant told them they would be whistling a different tune during the night maneuvers. He said he had something that would throw a wrench in the works. The soldiers argued with him. One man said he had been training for two months for the present moment, and nothing short of death would stop him. The sergeant made the soldiers double-time back to the main camp, but they didn't complain. If anything, they seemed determined to meet any challenge the sergeant sent their way.

At the camp, outside on the ground, their ponchos spread as work areas, the soldiers disassembled their M-16s, cleaned them, and reassembled them. The rain had stopped. While the sergeant watched, he rubbed his bald head with his dirty handkerchief. His lips were pursed in such a way as to suggest he was trying to keep from smiling. The soldiers disassembled and reassembled their weapons with ease.

Then Corporal Klock wheeled Angela through the center of camp. She looked around at the yellow buildings she passed, buildings that were in bad need of paint and repairs. Klock took her to a long yellow building. Inside were many tables and chairs at which the soldiers were gathering. The building was loud with talk and laughter. Klock wheeled her to the front of the hall and put her near the podium, where the colonel was standing. With a pen, he was making notes on paper.

To her surprise, the colonel was pleasant, even polite. Corporal Klock saluted him.

As Klock took his position near the stage, standing with his feet spread to shoulder width and his hands locked in the small of his back, the training sergeant approached the podium.

"Attention!" he bellowed as soon as he had received a nod from the colonel. Everyone jumped up and stood stiffly. After that there wasn't another movement or sound in the mess hall.

The colonel leaned toward a microphone at the podium. In a doubly loud voice he said, "Thank you, Sergeant Copeland. Be seated." Everyone sat down. Klock found a seat near McCanles and McCabe, who were in uniform. There was silence. A long silence. The colonel contemplated the soldiers. He contemplated them for at least two minutes, perhaps as many as three. The soldiers didn't take their eyes off him.

Finally he spoke: "Good afternoon." He had a voice that would have carried even without the microphone.

"Good afternoon!" the men yelled in unison.

He allowed for another silence before he said, "As all of you know, we are officially engaged in a top-secret training exercise that has been approved at the highest level, Operation Exodus-Five." He smiled. "We have been assigned the task of playing the bad guys, a group of terrorists who are carrying out an attack against Fort Hood." He collected his notes and stepped away from the podium. "There are many different people involved in this major training exercise." His voice was loud, as loud as it had been at the microphone. He opened a large, ringed hand toward Angela. "This is our hostage, an actress"—he smiled—"she hardly looks eighteen, does she?" Angela noticed how surprised everyone looked. What was the colonel talking about? she wondered. She wasn't eighteen.

"She has volunteered to participate in this training exercise with us, understanding we are trying to re-create as accurately as possible the kind of environment and circumstances a real hostage would be faced with. She is pretending to be the daughter of a very powerful figure in our government." He glanced at the notes in his hands, then continued. "In a little over a week, on November the eleventh, Fort Hood will host a Veteran's Day ceremony. That is the day we are scheduled to strike. We will use our hostage until that time to gain leverage in this operation. The opposing forces will be trying everything between now and then to stop us. We will not let them stop us, will we?"

"No, sir!"

"We want our military and our United States government to be as prepared as possible for this kind of thing, and we're going to give them a run for their money, aren't we?"

"Yes, sir!"

"From this moment on, then, we will treat everything as real, as a matter of the highest national interest. In fact, beginning tonight, for your night maneuvers, and from then on, you will be issued special ammunition for your weapons. This ammunition looks real and sounds real, but it is not real. Do not point your weapons at anyone except the enemy. Do not fire off any rounds except during an attack, or if you encounter an infiltrator while you are on guard duty. Do not play. If you fire off a round in horseplay, it will sound just like a regular round. You will be identified immediately, taken into custody, dismissed from your special duty, and sent back to your original unit, where you will face severe disciplinary action." At that particular moment his face took on a mean, even brutal look. "Is that clear?"

"Yes, sir!"

"By severe disciplinary action, I mean the punishment will ruin your military record. In that respect, I repeat, this is not a game. You'll hear it a hundred times before this is over, but everyone is taking this seriously. This is not a game. A lot of important people are watching, including the President of the United States. Do not assume it is a game. Do not assume what we've been doing is unimportant." He put the top page of his notes on the bottom and looked at the next page.

"Each of you has been handpicked to participate in this exercise because you are the best, the best our country has to offer. That you are here is a very high honor for you. Do not disappoint me or your country. Is that clear?"

"Yes, sir!"

"Up until now, you have been kept in the dark about the particulars of our exercise. One more time, so you understand completely, our unit has been designated as a terrorist group that is planning a domestic attack against Fort Hood. It is like we are playing the role of one of those modern militias that we hear so much about these days. You must understand that everyone, I repeat, everyone, will be attempting to stop us. In that respect, we really are the most elite unit of them all. We are the center of attention." He smiled.

"Our weapon will be a biological weapon, to be delivered in a few days. It will be a down-sized version of the real thing. Each of you has already been immunized on a number of occasions during the past two months. This is to protect you from any effects of the weapon that we will use if our counterparts do not stop us first. And they will not stop us first, will they?"

"No, sir!"

"No one can stop us, can they?"

"No, sir!"

"If anyone attempts to infiltrate our defenses here, we will treat it as a real situation. Treat any stranger as the enemy, and take the most aggressive measures against any infiltration. The enemy will try with all they have to rescue the hostage we have taken, but we are not going to let them get her, are we?"

"No, sir!"

The colonel turned another page of his notes. "One last thing," he said. "In the next few days, there will be many briefings as we get closer to the moment in which we make our attack. The last point is this, the biological weapon we will be using has been designed to imitate what really happens in biological warfare. It actually contains a stun agent, so you can expect to encounter victims, many victims, people who look like they have been killed by a biological weapon. Remember, this is a training exercise, and those victims have only been stunned with an agent that will cause them to be incapacitated for approximately thirty minutes. You are not to be alarmed by what you see, no matter what you see—there will be a lot of theatrics involved—but you are expected to treat this exercise as real." He collected his notes. "We are going to be successful with this exercise, aren't we?"

"Yes, sir!"

"They're not going to stop us, are they?"

"No, sir!"

"We are the best of the best, aren't we?"

"Yes, sir!"

The soldiers were filled with enthusiasm.

"Right. Now, all but the officers will train and have a late lunch in the field. The officers will remain for an additional briefing."

Sergeant Copeland yelled, "Attention!"

The men in the room snapped to their feet.

The colonel commanded, "Dismissed!" Before Klock could get Angela out of the mess hall, the colonel stopped him. "Corporal Klock, you can leave the hostage with us. You'll train with the others until the night exercises are over. You'll resume custody tomorrow morning at oh-six-hundred hours."

Corporal Klock saluted, and did as he was commanded. He wheeled Angela to the table where the officers were meeting, then he followed the other soldiers out the door.

Within seconds all that remained in the mess hall was a group of officers. The colonel looked at Captain McCanles and asked, "Captain, were you careful to do everything as we planned with the girl?"

"Yes, Colonel Lazarus," McCanles answered.

Colonel Lazarus glanced at McCabe. "What happened to your nose, Lieutenant?" he asked.

Lieutenant McCabe looked nervous. He even

seemed a little pale, and his lips were bluish. That turned his dried-out face a steel-gray color. He said, "I fell, sir."

Colonel Lazarus didn't say anything at first, then he asked, "What happened to the hostage's shoe?"

McCabe shifted in his chair. "We took it so she wouldn't run off on us."

Colonel Lazarus studied McCabe.

Somewhere beyond the mess hall there rose popping and crackling sounds.

To another officer, a lieutenant with a fat nose that had no bruises or swelling, the colonel said, "Lieutenant Rivero, you are supposed to be my pencil pusher."

Lieutenant Rivero had almost a tanned complexion. Angela wondered if he were Mexican-American. "Yes, sir, I am." Rivero was soft-spoken. His voice reminded her of a woman's voice.

"That's not a very complicated job."

"No, sir, it isn't." Again Rivero didn't raise his voice at all. Not like the others.

"I trust you now realize the seriousness of the error you made."

Rivero said, "I admit I made an error, sir. There's no sense trying to gloss over an error. I apologize."

"Lieutenant, you act like errors are something that mean nothing to you. You act like if you make an error someone should just trust your judgment afterward."

Rivero looked like he wanted to cry.

"You assured me that a personnel officer, or even a personnel clerk, could manipulate paperwork to make anything happen he wanted to make happen in the army. It's a good thing we had a few checks and balances built into that system because you had Klock's commander at the Eighty-ninth Military Police Unit calling about Klock's status at the same time we were listing him in our unit."

Rivero didn't say anything.

"You could have compromised this entire operation, Lieutenant," the colonel told him. "And it would have happened all because you made a mistake. The kind of questions his company commander was asking were questions of a nature that should never have come up in the first place. As far as I'm concerned, you're grossly incompetent. You jeopardized all we're trying to do because you think it's a big game that doesn't deserve to be taken seriously. Is that how you feel?"

"It was a mistake, sir, and I promise you it won't happen again."

"Begging the colonel's pardon, sir," said a short, flabby second lieutenant, "but I don't see why we should have to get bent out of shape about some paperwork when what we're really trying to give our attention to is an important exercise." He had curly, reddish hair and a bumpy face whose pine-green eyes looked like they had been glued onto his head.

"You'd just as soon we didn't have any paperwork at all, wouldn't you, Lieutenant Duffy?"

Lieutenant Duffy gave a smile that made his face look stupid. He drank some of the bottled water in front of him. "Sir, if you ask me, it seems a bit like holding a hearing every time a soldier fires a weapon on the battlefield. I say we make decisions, and we don't worry about what other people say. We say the hell with them and do what we want to do. We're on an important mission."

That brought smiles to every face at the table, except the colonel's. Colonel Lazarus responded, "You don't believe in any kind of standards but your own, do you Duffy?"

Duffy's face reddened.

"You believe in going into the back room and a few of you talking over what you want to do, and then that's what you do, isn't that right? You think that since a few of you decided to stick together, that's good enough."

Duffy's face seemed to withdraw from the bumps and marks on it, making his eyes stand out.

The colonel finally gave a slight smile. "I have to admit that I'm usually a bit put off by paperwork myself. But just remember that we can basically do what you want—go into the back room and make a decision—as long as we file the proper paperwork afterward. That way no one comes back to question our decision. It's all about pencil pushing. You understand?"

Lieutenant Duffy had withdrawn to the point that he wasn't doing anything, only sitting there, his hands on his bottled water.

Colonel Lazarus said, "In a week, all hell's going to break loose. People are going to run to their paperwork to try to figure out what's going on. Now more than ever it's important that we stick together and do everything by the book. That includes paperwork. We can't afford to make even the slightest mistake, especially on paper. Is that clear?"

There were nods at the table.

"Once again, I want to emphasize, no mistakes. Make sure the men understand that too, because I'll hold each of you personally accountable for any mistakes your men make. Is that clear?"

The officers said, "Yes, sir," though it wasn't in unison, and it wasn't enthusiastic.

"Captain McCanles—"

"Yes, sir." McCanles straightened in his chair, though he was still shorter than everyone else at the table.

"I'm placing the hostage in your hands while the men are out on night maneuvers. You and Lieutenant McCabe make sure you take good care of her."

"Yes, sir.'

The colonel leaned back and smiled serenely. He

said, "I hope to have a high-level guest visit within the next couple of days, someone who's been instrumental in helping get all of this set up." He looked at McCanles and McCabe. "You two are dismissed," he told them.

McCanles and McCabe stood and saluted.

They wheeled Angela out into the sounds of a nearby firing range. The sky looked bruised, like more rain.

Down a narrow sidewalk between the mess hall and a barracks, McCabe wheeled her. McCanles walked in the grass. McCabe said, "Don't you think we should have told the colonel we had to change the major's plans slightly?"

What major was he talking about? Angela kept wondering. Was it her father? She hadn't seen any major.

McCanles told him, "I didn't change his plans that much. I met the objective."

"But you changed the schedule he set up. You should have told the colonel that."

"Lieutenant, I don't appreciate you continually questioning my authority," McCanles snapped. "I wasn't required to report to the colonel. The colonel doesn't care about the details. The major is the one responsible for the details. Besides, it made no difference whatsoever that I got her in the field instead of on the street. I got her. That's the only thing that's important. Is that clear?"

"Yes, sir."

They came to a small wood building with a padlock on the door. McCanles unlocked the lock with one of the keys on his key ring. He pushed open the door for McCabe, who turned the wheelchair around and pulled it up the steps and into the small room that smelled like wood. There was sawdust on the floor. It looked like a converted wood shop. Gray light leaned against two dusty windows. Angela could see the shadows of bars on the outside of the windows.

As soon as McCabe got her unstrapped, McCanles shoved her out on the floor. They took the wheelchair and closed the door, leaving her inside. She could hear the lock being fastened. She got up. She was so sore she could barely walk. She felt sick to her stomach and dizzy. She went to the door. It was locked. She went to one of the windows to look out, but it was dirty. She wiped off some of the dirt, only to discover the windowpanes were of frosted glass. She looked around at the room. There were a couple of barrels of wood scraps.

She sat down in the sawdust, brought her knees to her chest, and, placing one silver dog tag on each knee, she studied her name and address engraved on each tag. She pulled her father's field jacket around her knees to keep them warm.

The next thing she knew she heard the door rattling. It opened, letting in the smell of rain.

McCanles appeared with a plate of steaming spaghetti that included a slice of bread and a cup of milk. Angela could tell by looking at it that the spaghetti wasn't homemade. It was like the kind one bought in a can, the bright orange kind without meat.

"Lunch," he told her, putting the plate and cup on the floor near her. "Better late than never."

He raised his hand.

She scooted back.

"Eat."

She took a bite of the spaghetti, which was hot.

He squatted near her, removed a package of cigarettes from his fatigue shirt, and gave the package a shake. Up popped a cigarette.

She had never seen anyone do that with a cigarette.

"You like that trick, don't you?" he asked, smiling. "My brother taught it to me. You should see him do it."

She took another bite of her spaghetti. She was hungry.

Cigarette between his lips, he removed a book of matches that had been stuffed down in the cellophane of the cigarette package, and lit the cigarette. He replaced the matches in the cellophane. He studied the package of cigarettes at the same time he talked to her. "If you're nice to me, I'll be nice to you."

She didn't know what he was talking about.

"I can give you things. Maybe a Coke, or some candy. The colonel says you need a shower tonight."

She glanced at him in horror. She hadn't heard the colonel say that.

"He said you stink. I told him you pissed in your pants." He laughed.

She started to cry.

He raised an open hand. "Don't start with me!" he told her. "You know what I'll do if you start with me."

She wiped away her tears.

"Finish your food."

She looked at the food.

"Eat!" He smacked the side of her head with his open hand. "I'm getting tired of always having to repeat myself with you."

She took another bite.

"That's more like it." He watched her eat. "Eat your bread."

She took a bite of the bread.

He took a long pull on the cigarette. "Hurry," he said, smoke coming out of his mouth. "That's right, do everything I tell you."

She wished he would leave.

"Drink your milk."

She drank some of the milk.

"You're learning now." He ground out his cigarette on the floor, took what was left of the bread, wiped up the remaining spaghetti sauce, and shoved the bread in his mouth. He chased it down with the remaining milk in her cup. "Later, when it's time for your shower, you're not going to give me any trouble, are you?"

She didn't answer.

He smiled. "The colonel is right, you really do look like a young woman. You almost look eighteen." He touched her hair. Then, dishes in hand, he left. The door closed. She could hear the lock snap in place.

The smell of cigarette smoke lingered in the air. It nauseated her. She coughed. She took her dog tags in her hand and studied them. She remembered the last time she and her family had visited the military academy at West Point. Her father usually liked to visit the academy every year. She had gotten her dog tags made at the bookstore during the most recent visit, a year before. They usually went there every summer, but last summer she had been in the automobile accident. Last summer she had been in the hospital. It seemed like her life was full of problems like that.

As she studied the tags, she remembered something else about their trip to New York the summer before. She felt the large pockets of the field jacket. From an oversize pocket, she removed a navy baseball cap with the gold letters "NIAGARA FALLS" printed on it. The cap had been folded down in the pocket. She had seen her father fold his military cap the same way. When he wore jungle fatigues, he folded his cap and shoved it in one of his large pants' pockets. Her father loved the army. It was his entire life. She thought her father loved the army more than he loved his family.

She opened the cap and put it on. That's when she noticed the pack of cigarettes on the floor. McCanles had forgotten it. She picked up the package. Inside the cellophane was the book of matches. She removed the matches and opened its cover. There were several matches left.

She went to the barrels of wood scraps. In one, she found some old rags. She smelled them. They smelled like varnish, the liquid her mother used when she refinished furniture. At one time, before she had become so busy, she had liked to refinish things.

With much effort Angela dragged one of the barrels to the door. The other barrel she dragged to the opposite corner of the room, near the wall. She positioned some rags in both barrels, under the wood. She tried to light a match. Again and again she struck it against the cover, but the match head broke. Her hands were shaking. She knew if she could build a fire, someone would see the smoke and help her.

She pulled off another match. This one she held closer to the head, so it wouldn't break. It lit right away, but she dropped it because it burned her fingers. The match went out.

The third match lit, and she touched it to the rags in the barrel near the door. A flame grew. She moved back. The room began to fill with smoke. Fire climbed from the barrel. Wood snapped and popped. With the last match she lit a rag in the second barrel. The second barrel, which contained the other rags, was more flammable. There was a "whoosh!" and flames licked the walls of the room. The wood was old. It burned easily, popping and crackling, almost like the weapons the soldiers fired. Flames spread in all directions, consuming everything they encountered. She found herself coughing from the smoke. What had she done? she wondered. The flames and heat overpowered her, forcing her to the floor in a fit of coughing. In that moment she knew she had made a huge mistake, knew there was no escaping the fire. She tried crawling to safety, but didn't know where it was. The flames were everywhere. Thick, brown-black smoke billowed downward, making everything dark as night. She crawled headfirst into a wall, striking her head so hard that she was certain she split it open. Disoriented, she sat clasping her head, coughing and crying for help at the same time.

At that moment a wave of heat hit her as a wall collapsed onto another wall, breaking as an ocean wave breaks on the sand. It brought with it the light and cool of early afternoon. She escaped from the back of the building and ran for a patch of trees. She didn't know what she was doing or where she was going. Her skin was hot, as if it had been badly sunburned. Her hair was singed, her cap gone.

Beneath the trees, she collapsed. Only then did she look down and notice that her hands and coat had been burned. So was her foot that didn't have a shoe. The pain was intense. But at the same time, she knew she was alive and free. For some reason she looked at her bright red hand, which was clenched shut. She could see that the hair on the backs of her fingers, hair she hadn't really noticed before, was singed, calling attention to itself. She thought maybe her hand had been burned shut. By staring at it, she was able to open the hand slowly. There she saw the matchbook Michael had left behind.

From back in the camp came the sound of a clanging bell. She could see the flames jumping into the sky. She better get away, she thought. She got up and ran, cursing herself that she was so clumsy. Her feet wouldn't work right. The dog tags clattered as she ran. Rain cut loose. The sound of the rain reminded her of the rushing water at Niagara Falls.

6

The Robles house was alive with laughter, conversation, and activity. Tony Robles could hear his young cousin Felipe trying to get everyone's attention. He was speaking in Spanish. "Quiet!" he said. "Quiet!" The house fell silent. "Tony and Mary Belle's little girl has been kidnapped, and we're here to help to find her."

There were mumblings.

"Quiet!"

He was a wild one, Tony knew, someone who could stir up a group, someone people listened to—because if they didn't listen, he had hard-hitting fists, and he wasn't shy about physically slapping someone around. People said there was no one who could beat him in a fight. In fact, they often placed bets on him and let him win them money. The biggest brutes from local communities would come to fight Felipe and would lose, though it was always a friendly fight. Amid the cheers, Felipe would beat the hell out of his opponent, then he would help him up, hug him, and the two men would sit down to have a few beers together.

Felipe was talking again: "We need someone to make up some sheets that we can xerox—something with Angela's picture on it."

There were voices. Tony thought he recognized Azita's voice. She was his niece, a pretty young woman of twenty.

"Good, good. Yes, you Trina, and you Azita. Pete, you help the ladies."

There was laughter.

Pete must have been overly anxious about his assignment because there was more laughter.

Sitting in his bedroom, on the bed whose mattress and box spring were so old that there were permanent sags in them, Tony listened to the activity in the other room, and stared at the well-oiled .45 automatic pistol in his hand. He slid a round into the chamber and gently rubbed beneath his chin with the barrel. He told himself not to think about it. He tried his right temple. Gently, he lowered the weapon's hammer.

He heard Felipe yelling again. "Quiet!" Then his voice bellowed, "Quiet!" There wasn't a sound. "Listen, we're talking about a little girl's life. We're talking about many attacks on Mexican-Americans in this community in the last few months! And all of you are sitting around jabbering like this is some kind of a social event." The silence remained. "Okay, that's better"—he was still speaking in Spanish—"now, I need someone to coordinate publicity. Yes, Maria, you have a mother's face, they'll trust you."

More laughter.

"You go to all the television stations, all the radio stations, all the newspapers, and you get them to do stories. Take Angela's photograph with you . . ."

Tony looked around at his and his wife's bedroom. Every day his family moved dangerously closer to poverty. All of his dreams of success and prosperity were gone, somewhere in the past—in his youth, those days when life seemed to promise everything and when nothing was impossible. Now, he realized, any unbudgeted disaster would bring his family to an end. He and Mary Belle were even having trouble making their monthly bills. Only a few days before, he had had to send another late payment on a Visa bill. Late payments and charges on bounced checks were killing them. What else could he do? he asked himself. His life was a mess.

He examined his cordovan shoes. He had tried to keep them polished, but they were so worn that in a couple of places he could tell they weren't really leather shoes. Where the scuffs had worn through to the material beneath, there were patches of what looked like cardboard. Threads were giving way in the seams of the shoes. It had been the story of his life. Everything was falling apart.

He took off his sunglasses. His surroundings went out of focus. If he stopped sending money to his family, and Mary Belle stopped sending money to her family, then their own family would be more comfortable. But what about the cousins and nieces and nephews in San Antonio? They would have no milk, no books, no food. As it was, aside from the school lunches for the children, sometimes days would pass without a hot meal. Xavier was out of work. So was Thomas. Julia had leukemia. Roberta was pregnant. It wasn't just his own house and family that he had to think about. A lot of people depended upon him and Mary Belle. In fact, it had gotten so bad that in recent months, he had been cashing in savings bonds to buy basic necessities like food. Mary Belle didn't know that part. He hadn't had the courage to tell her.

He put sunglasses back on and looked at the bedroom: a bed, two stereo speakers, and a dresser that he and Mary Belle shared. The stereo was gone—it had broken and been discarded years before—though Mary Belle, practical, had insisted they keep the speakers and use them as side tables for the bed. At her speaker was an alarm clock and a lamp. On his speaker was an empty glass. He was embarrassed when he looked at the life he had given his family.

Yes, he had brought his family down, too, and he knew it.

The house fell silent. He could hear grocery bags.

Mary Belle was home. There was weeping as Mary Belle greeted the newly arrived family members.

Tony shoved the .45 into the back of his pants and made sure his coat covered it.

The door opened. Mary Belle stood in the doorway. "Where are you going?" she asked. She entered the bedroom, and closed the door behind her. The noise and activity resumed in the other room.

"To buy some beer and drinks."

"We can't afford that. Already we're over two hundred dollars in the hole. We can't write any more checks until my pay gets deposited on Thursday."

"We can't just let them not have any food or drink."

"They're here to help us. We've been helping them, now they're here to help us."

"I'll just get some beer and soft drinks."

She shook her head in exasperation and took off her coat. Hanging the coat in the closet, she said, "I told the FBI about Angela being adopted."

He told her that was all right.

"What did they ask you?"

Her voice sounded soft and pleasant to him, the way it always did. He hated the way he treated her. He shrugged. "The same thing they asked you, I guess."

"I told them about Angela because I didn't think we should hide it."

She never had been able to lie. She wasn't good at it, not like him. He said, "What else did you tell them?"

She sat on the bed beside him and arched her back. "You mean about you?"

He didn't say.

"Yes, they asked about you. They asked about your work. They seemed real curious."

"What did you tell them?"

"What could I tell them?"

He reached out a hand and massaged the small of her back. "Did they show you the diary?"

She looked at him with her large brown eyes. The eyes seemed to say that she had been waiting for him to bring up the topic. "Yes, they showed me the time Angela wrote about being scared because people were watching her. She wrote that she told you about the men."

"I don't remember her telling me anything like that. I read it, but I don't remember."

"Don't lie to me. I'm tired of that. All our married life you've been playing the same game, telling me how you're working on this top secret project and that top secret project, and you're not allowed to talk about any of it. I'm tired of that."

He stood, stepped away from the bed, and turned. "Mary Belle, you have to trust me, now more than ever."

She was shaking her head. "What do you mean?" she asked. Her hands were neatly folded in her lap, and her voice was as calm as he had ever heard it.

"Just what I said."

"I think you know something, and you're lying to me, and I don't trust you." She rose from the bed. "You know something about Angela."

"Don't do this, Mary Belle."

"I'm not playing," she said. "In fact, I've never been more serious in my life. I've never asked you where you've been all of those nights you weren't in bed, I've never pushed about what exactly you do, and I've created all my own little ways of talking to people who ask questions, but when it comes to our family"— she was shaking her head—"I'm not playing."

He took off his glasses. She was blurred, but he didn't want to see her the way she was.

"You wrote that ransom note, didn't you?" she said.

"No."

"Don't lie to me. I saw it the moment you looked

at that note. I saw it in your eyes. You're lying to me, you can't lie to me. I can tell when you're lying. You may have the others fooled, but I've lived with you long enough to know."

As he looked at her blurred image, he wondered how they had managed to stay together for so many years. There had been many times when he thought the marriage was coming to an end. Somehow it had always worked out. But this time, he had that feeling again—that things wouldn't work out. This time it seemed for real.

"You've ruined our lives," she said. "For some ungodly reason you insist on staying in the army when you could do the same work as a civilian and make so much money that we wouldn't even have to worry about the way we lived." She raised her hands. "You have us living in a dump like this. I could live better than this by taking the children and setting out on my own. And now you've done something to our daughter. What have you done to her?" She got her coat back out of the closet and put it on.

"Where are you going?" he asked her.

"I'm going back to the FBI. I'm going to tell them everything I know. I'm going to tell them what I know about your work. I'm going to tell them that you're lying."

He caught her arm. "Please, Mary Belle, whatever's happened to Angela is not my fault."

"If you're not directly at fault, you're somehow involved. I know you."

"That's like saying the accident last summer was your fault and me blaming you."

She turned instantly chalky.

The moment he had said it, he regretted what he had said. "I'm sorry," he told her.

"That's the worst thing you've ever said to me," she said coldly, her voice almost a whisper. "I can't believe you said that."

"Well, now you know how I feel," he told her, not knowing what else to say. "You're placing the blame on me for what's happened to Angela, and I don't think it's fair. I didn't kidnap her."

There was still a cold expression on her face. "So it's finally come to this, huh?"

"What?"

"You're blaming me for what's happened to Angela. A car pulled out, I swerved."

He was confused. He was having trouble figuring out what to say.

"You're blaming me for the accident."

"I said I was sorry." He was holding up his hands as if they were stop signals, and she shouldn't go beyond them. "I didn't mean any of that."

"Yes, you did. You wouldn't have said it unless you were thinking it, unless it was in the back of your mind. You blame me for the accident last summer."

"No, I don't! I said we can't be blaming each other for things that are beyond our control."

She stared at him.

He used that moment to move closer to her, to put his arms around her. She stood stiffly. He was gentle with her. "We're going to get Angela back," he told her.

Then she was crying on his shoulder. "How?"

There was a loud burst of noise in the other room. It sounded like an argument. Felipe yelled, "Stop! What are you fighting about?"

The reply was in the form of a mumble from both sides.

"And you think this is more important than the little girl we're trying to find?" Felipe spoke loud enough for everyone to hear. "Come on, everyone, come on. This isn't the time to be fighting with each other. I know all about fighting, and this isn't the time to be fighting."

"Why do these things keep happening to us?" Mary Belle asked Tony, laying her head on his chest.

"I don't know." It was true, he didn't know, didn't know why life kept beating him down. Didn't know why he kept getting back up when it beat him down. Didn't know much of anything. He thought how nice it would be if he could only get Angela back and move the family as far away as possible from the rest of the world. Perhaps buy a ranch down in the San Antonio area. Or maybe in New Mexico. That would be wonderful—to live off the land, to leave the mad world behind. He asked Mary Belle if she would like the same thing.

She said she would, said it would be nice to be near her family again.

Patting her back, he said, "I'm going to go get beer and drinks."

"Don't spend too much," she said. "Be careful. We're two hundred dollars in the hole, and we don't get paid again until Thursday."

Felipe met Tony in the kitchen and grabbed his shoulder. "Where do you think you're going?" he asked. Felipe was a giant. All but the top of his head, where there was a tuft of dark hair, had been shaved. He was still wearing a long overcoat, which he hadn't taken off since he had arrived.

"To get beer."

Felipe pulled out his wallet. A couple other wallets appeared.

"Keep your money. Mary Belle and I'll buy the beer," he told them. They insisted. He took the money, but felt cheap as he left the house. As he got in the car, he noticed the FBI surveillance team. They were watching his every move, he knew.

7

Kathryn and David signed out a government sedan from the Fort Hood motor pool and drove to Killeen, so she could pick up her raincoat at her motel room. The rain was persistent. She thought about calling Wendy while she was in the room, but she didn't want to keep David waiting. She wondered whether he had thought about his sons during the whole ordeal. Did he miss them? Had he called them yet? What was the real story behind his separation from his wife? He had made it sound as if his wife had simply gotten tired of him, but she wondered if there was more to it. She figured there was. There always was.

When she got back to the car, she asked him if he wanted to stop at McDonald's for a bite to eat. He said fine. She realized she was starved, having not eaten since the night before on the airplane. She had been running on adrenaline all day. She glanced at her watch as she put the car in gear. Two in the afternoon. They weren't scheduled to meet the Robles children until six. She had hoped to see them earlier, but Mrs. Reising had taken them and her own children to a movie. Major Russ Reising had said he expected everyone back at around five-thirty. He had assured her the children would be available when the agents arrived at six.

On their way to McDonald's, Kathryn talked about

Mary Belle's interview earlier that day. She told him about Mary Belle being pregnant.

"I know, I saw the note you made and was shocked, to tell you the truth."

"Yes, I was shocked myself."

He smiled smugly.

"What's wrong?"

"Our Robleses are full of surprises, aren't they?"

She had been thinking the same thing. "Yes, they are," she told him. "Take, for example, the news about Angela being adopted."

He let out a short breath from his nose as his head nodded. There was still the same smug smile on his face.

"If it takes this long to find out about something so straightforward, it makes you wonder what else we're going to discover before it's all over."

"I'd like to know more about how Tony and Mary Belle were treating Angela," David said. "A couple of those diary entries really bothered me."

She was glad he had mentioned that. She had been waiting for him to do so, still upset by what had happened earlier that day. Might as well get it out in the open. "I don't mean to be picky," she said, "but I wanted to say something about how you brought up those entries with Mary Belle. I didn't really want her to know what was in the diary, and I was trying to get a line of questioning going with her. Next thing I know, you took us on a tangent." She glanced at him. He had a smirk on his face. Odd, she thought. Does he find everything amusing?

"You have to admit, I caught her off guard," he said. He laughed. His eyes made him look like he was on some type of drug. They were glassy, almost as if there were a touch of fog in them.

"Yes, you did catch her off guard, all right," she admitted. "You also caught me off guard too, and threw the interview into a precarious position." She glanced again. The smirk was gone. "I think if we're going to be on the same team, we should work with each other and not try to catch each other off guard. Don't you feel the same way?" He was silent. "I mean, sometimes tactics like you attempted do more harm than good—they break up the coherence of a good interview. Sometimes they even backfire on you." She thought of Randy. He would have tried something like that. He was often reckless in his enthusiasm. Was that what had frightened her? Had she seen Randy in David? Was she being excessively critical because of that?

David apologized. He said he hadn't meant to cause a problem. He didn't look at her. He told her he guessed he was trying too hard to do a good job.

An apology wasn't what she had expected. Rude comment, yes. Defensiveness, yes. Apology, no. "Forget it," she told him. She knew he hadn't had any sleep in over twenty-four hours. That would explain a slip in good interview technique. They hadn't worked together either. They would have to get used to each other.

They rode in silence for a few moments before she said, "I don't mind trying things like that now and then—as long as we discuss them beforehand."

Again, they rode in silence, mostly taking in their surroundings.

Killeen was a typical military town. Kathryn had seen a number of such towns in her days with Naval Intelligence, and then in her fourteen years with the Bureau. They were all the same. Taverns, nightclubs, pawnshops, and businesses advertising "instant loans." Congested streets. Military uniforms everywhere. A lot of petty crime.

David finally spoke: "That was a stroke of genius to find that diary. How did you ever think to dig around up in the attic?"

She smiled. "Special training," she said. "I have a thirteen-year-old daughter."

He smiled too.

The atmosphere in the car warmed up again.

"She loves to hide things on me."

He said, "There was one thing that bothered me, though."

"What's that?"

"The neatness of the journal entries."

It frightened her how much they thought alike. She said, "Yes, my first thought was someone had composed the entries in the diary and planted it." She wouldn't put it past Major Robles to have done such a thing.

He agreed, saying he was convinced the major was involved in his daughter's disappearance. "I'm sure whatever he did, he did it with compassion," he told her, glancing in her direction. He looked back out his window. "Probably smothered her with a pillow or something." He shook his head. "But he's smart. You can tell. I wouldn't put it past him to put together the diary himself—to make it look like someone else was involved." Again she was frightened by their similar thoughts. "It's really too bad. He basically seems like a nice guy, like someone with a conscience. It never ceases to amaze me how good people can get caught up in bad situations."

For some reason she got the distinct impression he was talking from experience, or might even be suggesting that he could sympathize with someone who had snapped under pressure.

"You can tell he's bothered by whatever's happened," he continued.

She wasn't sure she had noticed that. Had he seen something she hadn't seen?

"His conscience is eating away at him. I'm sure of it. As soon as we can sit him down and work on him, he'll break. He'll decide the right thing to do is to bring everything out in the open and at least give his daughter a decent burial. She's probably buried out in a field somewhere . . .''

What if something were to happen to Wendy? Kathryn wondered. The thought kept haunting her. What would I do? She wished she had taken a few minutes to call her daughter while at the motel.

The portable phone buzzed. David answered it, talked for a few seconds, then told her she was needed back at the base.

They drove through McDonald's and ate in the car as they returned to Fort Hood, where, at the 89th Military Police Headquarters, Colonel George Hendrick was waiting. He introduced himself as the provost marshal, the chief law enforcement officer of Fort Hood.

An older black man with salt-and-pepper hair and a salt-and-pepper mustache, Colonel Hendrick wore starched fatigues and spit-shined boots. Everything about him was military. He mentioned, "I heard you found a diary at the Robleses' house." His voice was thick and rich.

How had he heard about that? Kathryn wondered. Who had told him?

"That was good work," the colonel continued. He held open a hand toward a corridor. "There's a visitor who'll be here to see you in a couple of minutes. We can meet in my office."

Hands in the pockets of her overcoat, she glanced at a wall clock as she passed it: 4:48. She hoped the visitor wouldn't take long. Probably a formality. She was anxious to talk to the Robles children.

Colonel Hendrick led her and David into his private office. He shut the door. The blinds on the windows were down but had been turned so that the louvers let in light. The afternoon was dismal. Rain hit the windows. "Please sit down." They sat in chairs in front of his desk. He sat on the edge of the desk, close to them. The office was as neat and orderly as the colonel was.

He said, "Lieutenant General Hale has asked that we give you as much cooperation as possible."

So that was it, she thought. The commanding general wanted to drop by and give them a pep talk.

"He's quite concerned about finding this girl, and he's naturally concerned about the physical security of the base. As you know, this is an open post. Visitors come and go all the time. In my command, I know we're extremely proud of our reputation for being able to maintain the security of the post without excessively restricting the public's access to our facilities." He studied her. "The one thing he mentioned that we won't tolerate, and we're launching a full-scale investigation to uncover the problem, is hate groups. I understand there are some around, and we're going to weed them out immediately. They're the kind of people who do things like this. Unfortunately, we've had a few such incidents during the past couple of months—not kidnapping or anything, but some disturbing incidents."

Did he know something about the initials MTR? she wondered. Was there a local group using those initials? She asked, "Can you be more specific about these hate groups?"

He explained how over the period of the past two months or so there had been a rash of hate crimes against Mexican-Americans in the area. "You know the sort of thing—windows broken out, garbage dumped in yards, spray paint on cars and houses." He had a look of disgust on his face. "One Mexican-American corporal was beaten out at a park, but that might have been something else. It seems the person in question is also a homosexual, so it may have been some people who knew him. In any case, the only common element seems to be that all the victims are Mexican-American."

David asked, "And how long did you say this has been going on?"

"The past couple of months."

Kathryn sat forward in her chair. "Have there been any notes or messages associated with these attacks?" she asked.

Before he could answer, there came a tap at the door. Colonel Hendrick went to the door and opened it.

The sixtyish man at the door looked vaguely familiar, though Kathryn couldn't quite place him. He had silver hair neatly trimmed at the sides of his bald head, was tanned, as if he spent a great deal of time outdoors, and wore casual, but expensive clothes—a navy sweater and tan slacks. He definitely wasn't a commanding general, whom she had expected. Didn't look the type. Colonel Hendrick said, "Agents Stanton and Gonzalez, this is Edward Brennan from out of Fort Meade, Maryland."

Kathryn knew immediately who he was—or at least she knew the agency he worked for. "The National Security Agency?" she said, puzzled, as she took the hand Brennan extended. It was cold and dry. "Now, what does NSA"—she pronounced it "naza," like the space agency, only with a "z"—"want to see us about?"

Sea-green eyes staring at her through wire-rimmed glasses, Brennan brought a hand to his chin, which he held between his thumb and forefinger. She noticed his wedding band and watch, both expensive. Without looking at Colonel Hendrick, Brennan said, "Colonel, would you mind excusing us for a few minutes?"

In a formal manner, as if he had been given an order he had to obey, Colonel Hendrick started for the door.

"Colonel," Kathryn said. He turned to her. "Would it be possible to get copies of any incident reports involving attacks on Mexican-Americans?"

He nodded and left.

As soon as the door closed, Brennan came right to the point. He said, "I'm here because we may have a situation that involves national security." He motioned to the chairs at Colonel Hendrick's desk. She and David sat down again. Still standing, Brennan said, "Major Robles works for us. He's a cryptographer on temporary duty from Fort Meade. I'm here to debrief him."

Which explained the crowded conditions of the Robleses' house, she thought. The furnishings didn't look like they fit because the house was only a temporary residence. It also explained the references Mary Belle had made to Tony's position. She had said that the same position as a civilian would have brought Tony three times more pay. Why would he stay in the army when he could be a civilian employee of NSA, a super-secret governmental agency. Kathryn asked, "Is this visit because you're worried about us exposing one of your people?"

Brennan pulled a chair close to them so they could talk quietly. He said, "Not many Americans even know about NSA. Naturally, we'd like to keep it that way, but my visit today is a bit more serious. I'm worried about a biological weapon known as Exodus-Five."

A chill shot through her, despite the overcoat she wore. She tried not to react too overtly, but she found herself shifting in her chair. "Do you know something we don't know?"

David mentioned, "We ran an extensive search, and it turned up nothing about the agent known as Exodus-Five."

"Exodus-Five is a highly toxic strain of *Bacillus anthracis*," Brennan explained, ignoring David's comment.

"Anthrax?" she said.

"Yes."

She had had training in chemical and biological weapons. She knew the dangers they could pose, especially anthrax. It was one of the more popular biological weapons—one that poor nations, modern militias, and terrorists were quite interested in. It was a cheap weapon that could inflict mass destruction.

"It was developed by the army's Medical Research Institute of Infectious Diseases, though it's been kept under tight lock and key. You can't find anything out about it because it's protected by a black box of secrecy."

"And why would NSA be able to penetrate that black box and we wouldn't?" Kathryn asked. "Tell me, what else do you know that we don't know?" She could hear anger in her voice.

Brennan told her, "Not much more than that. I know Exodus-Five is named after a story in the Bible. The story may or may not have a historical foundation." He went on to explain about the plagues that set the stage for Israel's exodus from Egypt. The fifth plague, he told her, was the one that killed the cattle. "Most experts think the fifth plague was anthrax, a very old bacterium. It's actually closely affiliated with dirt and dust itself."

Kathryn asked, "And what makes this particular strain of anthrax such a concern to you?"

"The mortality rate for normal anthrax is five to twenty percent, depending on how soon the patient is treated with a vaccine. Exodus-Five has been genetically engineered to make it far more toxic, and to make its life span much more conducive to warfare."

David interrupted, saying, "Can you translate that?" He had a smirk on his face, as if he didn't quite take seriously what he was hearing, or as if he didn't want to take seriously what he was hearing.

"Normal anthrax spores can stay infective for over a hundred years," Brennan said. "Off the coast of Scotland is an island known as Gruinard. During

World War II, the British and Americans conducted biological warfare experiments with anthrax there. Even today, more than fifty years later, the island's still contaminated. It's always been one of the drawbacks of anthrax. You can't go in and claim the spoils of war when you use anthrax because they end up being contaminated for years. Exodus-Five has a life span of twenty-four hours or less."

Kathryn asked, "And how toxic is it?"

"Please understand Exodus-Five has never been tested on humans as far as I know," Brennan said, looking at her. "But the army predicts it is as deadly as the Ebola virus—maybe an eighty percent mortality rate."

David mumbled, "My God, you are serious."

She glanced at him. His face had turned chalky. The smirk had vanished.

"I thought biological weapons had been outlawed in the United States," David said. "And you're telling us our own government has been involved in the development of Exodus-Five?"

Brennan said, "This is strictly a defensive weapon, please understand. Biological weapons are the weapons of the future. We know that. Yes, they have been outlawed, but military leaders still have an obligation to protect our nation. We're dealing with a new type of enemy, new weapons, and a new type of threat to national security. We have to keep up with the times. What we do and what we tell the American people have always been two different things. You know that as well as I do."

A cold expression on his face, David spoke before she had a chance. "If the military's done what you say they've done," he said, "it's strictly illegal, and the NSA doesn't have jurisdiction, as far as I know, in that particular type of threat to national security." He got a confused expression on his face. "Isn't the NSA concerned with electronic surveillance? Am I wrong?"

Kathryn finally managed to say, "Has someone stolen some of the army's stock of Exodus-Five? Is that what you're telling us?"

"We don't think so—at least none is missing from the inventory at Fort Detrick in Maryland. We think they only have the name, which is why Major Robles is here. About six months ago, we picked up transmissions by someone using the letters MTR."

That would have been approximately the same time as Angela's accident, Kathryn thought. She wondered if there was a relationship between the two.

"The transmissions made reference to Exodus-Five. At first we didn't know what it was either, but when we were able to confirm what it was, we immediately dispatched Robles to Texas. He's an expert cryptographer, you know. Unfortunately, MTR stopped transmitting a couple of weeks ago, or seems to have stopped. In fact, we hadn't heard anything at all until this whole matter of Tony's daughter took place. We had already arranged for Robles and his family to return to Meade, thinking it was all a hoax."

"Did you notify the Bureau about these transmissions you had been deciphering?" Kathryn asked. "I assume you did."

"We were waiting until we had something more substantive to go on."

She took that to mean no.

David leaned forward. "Mr. Brennan, you say Major Robles knew he was being transferred back to Fort Meade? You say you were in the process of transferring him back to Fort Meade."

Brennan studied him. "Yes, he knew. We had already notified him, and he asked to stay. Why?"

Kathryn looked at David. Why hadn't Major Robles told them about all of this? Was he involved? She asked, "Is there a vaccine for Exodus-Five?"

Brennan rubbed his chin between his index finger and thumb. "I believe the army has experimented with

C. N. Bean

one, but has given up on it." He brushed some lint off his sweater. "Obviously, you see there's really not much use for a vaccine. By the time you got the people inoculated, it would be too late. This probably signals a whole new line of biological weapons—weapons sure to kill and be medically stable at the same time." A slight smile came to his face. "Almost like a surgeon's scalpel."

"What would happen if that surgeon's scalpel was used here?" David asked.

Brennan looked at him. "If a terrorist group were to, say, explode an aerosol bomb of Exodus-Five in an area such as this? Is that what you're asking?" His eyebrows raised.

No one said anything.

"That's why I'm here. If that were by some off-the-wall chance to happen, a lot of people would die, plain and simple. That's what would happen."

Kathryn went to the window, whose blind she opened even more. Beyond the window was a peaceful world, soothed by rain. "How many is a lot?"

From behind her, she could hear Brennan talking. "Let's say some terrorist group targeted Fort Hood for an attack. I mean, it's not like there aren't obvious incentives for choosing Hood. For one, it's the largest armored post in the military. A center of power for the United States military. Imagine the message a successful terrorist attack would send to the world. Two, in weaponry, Fort Hood has it all. It could be that some group is looking for weapons. Three, there's a population of at least a hundred and fifty thousand people in this area alone. A small bomb of Exodus-Five would kill them all, almost instantly."

"I see you've done your homework," she told him. Done it too well, she thought, though he didn't seem to know about the Lance missiles.

There was a sobering silence in the room.

"There's still something that doesn't add up here,"

David said, breaking the silence. "How does the NSA know all this? With what we've heard in this room, it's obvious that our inquiries haven't even scratched the surface of what's going on here. That makes it seem like someone in your organization knew exactly what black box to look in in the first place. I'm back to my original question: Isn't your agency primarily concerned with electronic surveillance?"

Kathryn stared hard at David. Now, this was someone who knew how to interview.

"I told you," Brennan explained, "we picked up some transmissions and followed up on them. That's all."

Kathryn said, "We picked up a ransom note and followed up on it. Why is it we didn't have the same luck that you had?"

He shrugged. "What you have to remember here is that we've had more time to search than you've had. It isn't like we just found out about this overnight. We've done some digging in the past six months."

Kathryn approached where Brennan sat. She said, "That's what bothers me. You've been digging for six months and haven't notified the agency that has jurisdiction in these matters. Do you have some kind of an operation going on?"

He smiled. "That's absurd, something that doesn't even merit a response."

Kathryn experienced a dazed feeling. She massaged her temples with her fingertips. She could feel a headache coming on. "Even if none of the army's Exodus-Five has been stolen, and we can't be positive about that because NSA doesn't have the investigative authority to go in and force the issue, there are a number of reasons why the Bureau should have been informed about all of this. Six months you've been holding back information from us. Do you realize there may be an obstruction of justice here? That's criminal."

Brennan looked composed. "I assure you, no one's

intentionally tried to hide anything," he told her. "There is no obstruction, and I don't appreciate your insinuations. If we had thought for a moment this was anything more than a lot of empty talk, we would have contacted the Bureau immediately. In fact, we would have had a briefing with the national security adviser, because we would be talking about something with potentially devastating national security consequences. There is no Exodus-Five missing."

Pressing her fingertips into her temples, she said, "If this is a lot of empty talk, what are you doing here?"

He didn't answer, though he had a resentful look on his face.

She asked, "What do you suppose Angela Robles has to do with all of this?" She released the pressure. No sense running Brennan into the ground. He was probably only a mouthpiece.

"I suppose because Major Robles is the cryptologist who caught on to the transmissions in the first place," Brennan said. "That's why we dispatched him to Fort Hood. He was the one most familiar with the case. Apparently, someone felt the heat, identified him as being the one responsible, and decided to compromise his work." He took off his glasses, held them in his right hand, and looked at her. He told her, "Whoever this group is knows that now this case has gone public, we have to relieve Tony of his duties. To me the strategy is obvious—compromise the person who's causing the heat." Brennan crossed his arms across his chest. "It's worked. I'm here to relieve him of his duties. Standard operating procedure."

David said, "During this past six months, as the NSA has been putting all this together, I assume you sent Major Robles or someone over to Fort Detrick to do some digging."

Brennan responded, "I believe Major Robles did make a trip over there once we determined that Exodus-Five was a legitimate biological weapon. Of course, we wanted to make sure none had been stolen. Had we discovered there had been any missing, we would have immediately notified the FBI."

Kathryn said, "I want copies of all the transmissions associated with either MTR or Exodus-Five, and I want them immediately. I want a comprehensive log of all inquiries NSA has made, whether those inquiries were in person or by electronic means. I want the log immediately, and I want it to be certified by someone who understands he or she is going to jail if the log turns out to be incomplete or inaccurate. Last, I want you to talk to Major Robles and let him know he better be answering our questions as truthfully and straightforwardly as possible." She headed for the door, neither shaking Brennan's hand nor saying good-bye.

Outside the rain had turned to a fine mist.

David caught up with her.

"David—" she began.

"What did I do wrong this time?" he said, shaking his head.

She could tell he was tense.

"You're going to chew me out again because you didn't like how I handled things in there, right? What is it about me? I've worked with you a day, and you make me feel like some recruit right out of the academy. You don't have to train me—I'm a damned good agent." He lit a cigarette. She stepped back from him. "I know, you don't like my smoking either." He took a puff of the cigarette. It was a forced puff. Defiant. "I know all about you," he told her, blowing out the smoke. "I've heard the rumors. I know how you're a stickler for going by the book and doing everything a certain way. I know you're a hardass."

She smiled. "A little tense, aren't you?"

He took a puff of his cigarette. "The man just told us there may be a highly toxic weapon in the hands of a terrorist group. That means there probably is one.

The son of a bitch is lying out his ass. Yes, I guess I'm a little tense. I have two sons. I guess I don't exactly relish the thought of them or anyone else dying from a germ that our own military developed to kill people, especially a germ that's been developed illegally. So if I get on your nerves, I really don't give a damn, because right now I think there are a few more important things to focus on than whether our personalities are in sync."

She smiled. "My, when you get going, you're hard to shut down, aren't you? I was only about to say that you did a nice job in there."

"Oh." A slight laugh escaped his mouth. "Sorry."

"And what's this about my reputation?"

He laughed at himself, looked at the wet pavement, and scratched his right temple. "I can't remember. Did I say something that slightly offended you?"

She told him she needed the secure phone so she could call Grant.

He handed it to her, asking, "Aren't you the least bit rattled?"

"Yes, I'm terrified," she said as she pressed the buttons on the phone.

"I'll be in the car," he told her. He headed for the sedan.

She got through to Grant and began to brief him about the developments in the case, and their meeting with Brennan. As she talked, she watched David. He was sitting in the passenger side of the sedan, staring straight ahead.

Grant said he had already begun to receive information from FBI headquarters. "NSA is racing to cover its ass on this," he told her.

She figured as much.

"I'm sending down an additional twenty-five agents to give you some support." There was a moment of silence. Then, "Kathryn, the director wants us to set up a command center at Fort Hood—just in case."

Another moment of silence. "I guess you know what that means."

She did.

He told her anyway. "With something potentially big like this, the protocol is to put one of the special-agents-in-charge at the center, sometimes someone from headquarters, such as an assistant director."

She felt her stomach tighten. She turned her back to David, who was watching from the car. "Grant, I can handle this," she told him.

"Come on, Kathryn, I know that, and you know that. And you also know that if it were up to me, I'd let you run the show. That's why I sent you down there in the first place. But this thing may turn out to be something bigger than all of us, and if that's the case, important people are going to be asking tough questions. They'll want to know if the investigation was handled by the book—the way we always do things. We have to tell them, yes."

She gazed at the wet pavement.

"Kathryn, are you still there?"

The mist turned to rain again, not a heavy rain, but persistent nevertheless. "Yes, I'm here."

"You know I've put in a good word for you," he told her, "but again we both know how things work in cases like this. They assign the most senior agent. It's standard operating procedure."

Yes, she knew how things worked. It was still the old boys' school. If she had been a man, she would have already been a special-agent-in-charge at some major city such as Los Angeles, Houston, or Dallas, and the investigation would have automatically been hers. As it was, however, on high-profile cases, one never saw a woman as the chief investigator, not on any serious case that is. It had to be a man. He looked better.

"Come on, Kathryn, you know I'm behind you. Now, as soon as the new agents arrive, get a command

center established. We'll play it by ear from there."
There was a long pause, then a sigh. "Kathryn, there's
one other thing I need to drop on you, and I hate to,
but I know you'll appreciate me for coming right out
and being honest. I've always been straightforward
with you. Your friend Randy—his application was
turned down."

Her stomach tightened more. Her mouth was dry.
"Does he know?" Everything was going wrong.

"Yes."

Once she got off the phone with Grant, she tried
to call Randy, but all she got was his answering machine. She left a message that she was sorry to hear
the news about his application. She also left the telephone number for her motel room and asked him to
call.

She dialed her mother's number. "Hi, Mom, I only
have a couple minutes. Is Wendy there?"

"Yes—Wendy!"

While she was waiting for Wendy to get on the
phone, Kathryn asked, "How's she doing?"

"She's on her extra good behavior, that's how she's
doing. She knows if she isn't, she's going to be on
total restriction forever, or at least until you get back."

Wendy got on the telephone. "Hang up, Grandmother," she said. There was a click.

"Hi, sweetheart," Kathryn said. She glanced back
at David. He was standing outside the car, smoking
a cigarette.

"Mom, when are you coming home?"

"I should be home in a few days, hon. Are you
being good?"

She gave an exasperated sigh. "Yes, but can you
talk to Grandmother and tell her to let me off
grounding?"

"Let's not get into that right now. Have you been
studying and doing all of your homework?"

"Yes."

"Wendy, you know I didn't really emphasize this, but I was proud of you for getting out of that car the other night."

"A lot of good it did me."

"I love you."

"I love you too, Mom." She didn't sound enthusiastic.

As Kathryn headed toward the car, feeling good that she had called Wendy, she got another call. More bad news. Major Robles was gone.

"What do you mean, gone?"

"He drove to a grocery store in Killeen," the head of surveillance said. "We kept the store under surveillance. He didn't come back out."

"You searched thoroughly?"

"Yes, he had to have gone out the back."

"Have you talked to Mary Belle?"

"She was as surprised as we were."

"Get a warrant to pick him up as a material witness. Let me know the moment you have him."

She got in the car and slammed the door.

"What's wrong?" David wanted to know.

She told him. She also told him about a case that had been in the back of her mind. It involved two brothers in Massachusetts who had been caught manufacturing the deadly toxin ricin. At the time FBI agents had made their seizure, they had no idea how deadly the toxin was that they had in their possession. Only later did they learn that it was a thousand times more deadly than one of the military's most potent, known nerve agents.

David said, "You think Major Robles walked into Fort Detrick and stole the Exodus-Five formula right from under the army's noses, don't you?"

She didn't answer immediately. Don't panic, she told herself. Don't panic. "Yes."

8

Through the sudden downpour Kathryn and David made a dash for the porch of the Reisings' house. The brick ranch was in North Fort Hood, between Killeen and Copperas Cove, a small community on government property.

Standing under the porch and waiting for someone to answer the door, Kathryn noticed the disparity between where the Robleses lived and the Reisings' neighborhood. North Fort, she understood, primarily housed officers and their families. Wainwright Heights, where the Robleses lived, housed mainly enlisted families and temporary personnel. She made a comment about the disparity to David, who smiled smugly and nodded, as if to say he wasn't surprised.

Russ Reising, a tall, stocky man with oily brown hair, answered the door, letting out the sounds of playing children. Wearing a pale green shirt and olive slacks, he introduced himself as Major Reising of Military Intelligence. Kathryn was sure his hair was longer than what military regulations allowed.

She showed her credentials, as did David.

A young woman in jeans and a lime cashmere sweater appeared. She had long, reddish hair. Russ introduced her as his wife, "Suzonne," though he went on to say she spelled the name the traditional way: S-u-z-a-n-n-e. She had been born and raised in Louisiana, which is why her name was pronounced the way it was.

She had a distinct southern accent too and a voice forceful enough that it didn't take long for her to round up the Robles children. Two other children appeared, blond girls. One looked to be about twelve, the other nine.

Suzanne said, "Kids," and pointed at Kathryn and David, "these people work for the FBI, and they're here to ask some questions." Putting her hand on the oldest blonde, she said, "This is my daughter Heather."

Kathryn thought of Wendy. She said, "I have a daughter about your age. What are you, twelve, thirteen?"

"Twelve."

"Mine's thirteen."

Suzanne moved her hand to the next blond girl. "And here is Meredith. Can you say hello?" Meredith said hello. Suzanne touched the shoulder of the oldest Robles child, a chunky girl with stringy dark hair tied back by a white band. "This is someone who has almost the same name I have, Susana Robles, one 'n.' She's ten." Susana smiled nervously.

Suzanne moved her hand to the next girl, also chunky. Her dark hair was short, which made her face look fat. She wore a red dress, one that appeared to have been handed down, perhaps from Susana. "This is Carmela. She's nine." Without touching him, Suzanne pointed at the skinny boy. "And this is Raul. Raul's seven." Raul had long hair down in his eyes. He was dirty and needed a haircut. He wore a blue-and-black striped shirt and black jeans.

The Robles children looked poor.

Raul asked, "Do you have a badge?"

Kathryn and David produced their gold shields.

"Wow," Raul muttered.

The other children smiled. Meredith giggled at Raul.

Kathryn told Suzanne, "What we would like to do

is to talk to each one of the Robles children separately. Do you have someplace private we could use for our interviews?"

Suzanne said they could use her and Russ's bedroom. She took them to the room. Russ and David carried extra chairs from the dining room.

Susana, being the oldest, was the first child they interviewed. Kathryn, David, and she sat in a circle in the Reisings' bedroom.

It was a comfortable room, one that had been recently painted, as had the rest of the interior of the house. There was a brass bed, matching lamp tables with lamps on each side of the bed, and two oak dressers. The spread on the bed matched the curtains in the room. They were done in blue and violet orchids. A number of watercolors decorated the walls. The watercolors, also of orchids, looked original. It was a cozy room.

Kathryn asked Susana, "Susana, how old did you say you were?"

"Ten," she said. She had a husky voice. Her hands kept rubbing the sides of her legs as she sat in the chair. The pink fingernail polish on her fingers was wearing thin. It was chipped in places. The sea-green sweater she wore looked like it had stains that washing hadn't been able to get out. There was a reddish stain on the right sleeve, probably from where she had wiped her mouth while eating. Ketchup, Kathryn guessed.

"How do you like school?" David asked.

She shrugged. "It's all right."

He smiled. "What's your favorite subject?"

"When we go to computer class."

"That's good. One of my sons is about your age. He likes computers too."

Kathryn liked how David warmed up to Susana. He seemed good with children. She wondered how well he got along with his sons. She said, "We want to talk to you about Friday, when your sister didn't come home from school."

Susana nodded, but didn't say anything.

"There's no reason to be nervous," Kathryn assured her. "You're not in any kind of trouble or anything. We're just trying to help your sister. Okay?"

"Okay."

David asked, "Do you and your sister get along well together?"

Susana gave a sheepish grin. She said, "We fight a lot. She's sometimes a real pain."

Kathryn smiled. "Do you know if your sister got on the bus Friday morning?" she asked.

Susana shook her head. "No, she didn't."

"She didn't get on the bus?" David asked.

"That's what Mom said."

Kathryn asked, "Did you see if she got on the bus?"

"It was foggy. One time I looked back, and I saw her. The next time I looked back, she wasn't there." She pushed her hands under her stringy hair, raised it, and let it drop.

"When you looked back, she was gone?" Kathryn asked.

Susana nodded. "I looked back, and I didn't see her anymore."

"Did you hear her scream or anything?"

"No."

"You didn't hear any kind of a call or struggle?"

Susana shook her head. "Nope," she said. "Nothing. It was just like it was any other morning."

"She takes a different bus from the one you ride, doesn't she?" David said.

Susana nodded. "It's a bus for handicapped kids who are in special ed," she said. "It used to stop at our house, but when Angela got out of the wheelchair and could start walking on her own, she got to walk to Roger Brown's house. He's paralyzed from the waist down. He's in a wheelchair. They say he's always going to be in a wheelchair."

"How far is that bus stop from the one where you get on the bus?" Kathryn wanted to know.

"A block. But I couldn't see the Browns' house. It was too foggy."

"Are you supposed to help make sure Angela gets on the bus okay?" Kathryn asked.

Silence.

"You are, aren't you?"

"She doesn't like help. When you try to help her, she just screams at you and says she's not a baby." She stood, straightened her sweater, and sat again. "Besides, we don't have to walk her all the way," she said, stretching her sweater down over her knees. "All we have to do is walk with her to our bus stop, and then she walks on her own the rest of the way to her stop."

"But you didn't see her get that far, did you?" Kathryn said. "That's what you just told us, isn't it?"

Silent, Susana stared at the hands in her lap. They were nervous hands. She started to cry. "I told you, I couldn't see her because of the fog," she said. "I didn't lie. I couldn't see her."

Kathryn got up and held Susana. "It's all right, hon," she said, patting the girl's warm back. "We're just trying to help your sister. You understand that, don't you? We're not trying to be mean to you."

"You think you'll find her?" Susana asked in a shaky voice.

In her hands Kathryn could feel the vibration of Susana's words. "You let us worry about that, okay?"

David got some tissue from the master bathroom.

With it Susana wiped her eyes.

Again, Kathryn tried to determine whether there had been any strangers or strange activity in Wainwright Heights on Friday morning.

No, Susana hadn't noticed anything out of the ordinary, nothing except the fog. "You couldn't see anything," she said. "It was bad."

David wanted to know how neighbors and other children at school treated her and her brother and sisters.

She said all the children made fun of Angela—called her retarded.

"What about you? Are they nice to you?" Kathryn wanted to know.

Susana shrugged. She said most of the other children made fun of their entire family because they were Mexican-American. "They call us wetbacks," she said. "I don't care."

David told her that people used to call him the same thing. He touched her hand. He said it was too bad that people had to be mean like that. Then he told her that there was still something confusing to him. "And Agent Stanton might still be a little confused about this," he continued. "If Angela was following you, and then all of a sudden you didn't see her because of the fog—that's what happened, right?"

Susana nodded.

"Wouldn't you have seen her pass your bus stop?"

Susana's voice trembled as she explained that her, Carmela, and Raul's bus came before Angela's bus. "Usually, when we're on the bus, she's still waiting at her stop. Friday, our bus was early. Right when we got to our stop, it was time to get on the bus. So we didn't see Angela go by because she was still behind us."

They asked a few more questions, then Kathryn told Susana she could go back out with the other children.

In between interviews, in the privacy of the Reising bedroom, Kathryn and David agreed that Susana seemed to have been trying to hide something. "Something about the bus being early worried her," Kathryn said. "You noticed how nervous she got when we asked about that?" David said yes, he had noticed that, so they decided to concentrate on establishing the bus schedule.

Kathryn called in Carmela, and, as soon as the girl got seated, mentioned, "You and Susana are almost the same age, aren't you?"

Carmela was quite direct in her response. She said, "She's almost eleven, I'm barely nine."

"Do you two get along all right?" David asked.

"Pretty good."

"You don't fight?" he asked. "I have two sons. They fight all the time."

Carmela admitted that they fought occasionally. "Mostly about her makeup," she said. "I sneak in her room and get into her powder and blush. That makes her real mad."

David mentioned that he had grown up in a family of eight brothers and sisters. He said they had fought all the time.

That set Carmela at ease.

In the course of her version of what happened, Carmela gave basically the same account of what had happened on Friday morning as Susana had given. There was one difference, however. When Kathryn and David persisted about the issue of how the children had lost sight of Angela, Carmela admitted they had run off and left her. They did that every morning, she said. "It's Susana's fault. She likes to tease. We wait until the last moment, then we run out the door, leaving Angela behind. Susana teases all of us like that. She loves to tease."

David said, "So you were late on Friday on purpose?"

Carmela nodded reluctantly. She said, "We didn't mean for anything bad to happen to Angela."

"We know you didn't, sweetheart," Kathryn told her.

David asked if she had noticed any strangers in the neighborhood on that morning, or in recent days.

No, Carmela said, she hadn't.

Raul corroborated his sisters' accounts, only he said he didn't agree with how people treated Angela. He said he knew people made fun of her, but she couldn't help the way she was. "Another car pulled in front of Mom's car," he said. "It wasn't Angela's fault. Even if she wasn't wearing a seat belt, it wasn't her fault. We all almost died, you know." He showed a small white scar on his right arm. "I had to get stitches here"—he pointed to the scar—"and"—he raised his left arm, revealing a larger scar at the elbow, which he pointed to—"here." He pushed his hair out of his eyes. "I had my seat belt on, and I still got hurt. So it's not her fault what happened. I feel sorry for her. She's always been nice to me. She makes me a snack when I get home from school"—he smiled—"it's not very good, but she makes it. And she plays games with me." He said he thought the boogeyman had gotten her.

"The boogeyman?" Kathryn repeated. She wondered why he would suddenly mention such a thing.

Raul nodded. "Yep, the boogeyman."

"Have you seen a boogeyman?" David asked.

No, Raul admitted, but everyone knew he lived in the swamp.

Where was the swamp? Kathryn wanted to know.

In the field across from where they lived, Raul told her. He said it was filled with a lot of trees and mud. "It was Angela's shortcut. Everyone told her the boogeyman lived there, but she said she didn't care. She said she wasn't afraid of any boogeyman."

Kathryn said, "Raul, I guess I'm lost. Are you saying Angela took a different way to get to her bus stop?"

"Oh, yes, she always goes through the swamp."

Why would she go a different way? David wanted to know.

Raul explained that he, Susana, and Carmela ran

off and left her in the mornings. He said it was Susana's fault. He said she made them wait until the last minute—when they would almost be too late to get to their own bus stop—then they would run out the door, leaving Angela behind. He said he thought she went through the swamp because it was the only way she could get to her bus stop on time.

Kathryn held out a notebook and pen. "Raul, can you draw us a picture of the way your sister takes to the bus stop?"

Raul took the notebook and pen. He stared at the blank page for a moment, then made an X on it. "This is our house." From the X, he drew a line up the paper. At the top of the paper, where the line ended, he made a small circle. "This is where we get on the bus." He tore off that sheet and wadded it up. "That's too big," he said. "I won't have room." He made the new drawing smaller. From the circle, which represented where he, Susana, and Carmela got on the bus, he drew a line perpendicular to the first line, creating what looked like an upside down L. At the end of the perpendicular leg, he drew another circle. "This is where Angela gets on the bus." He made a dotted line from slightly above the X straight across to the second circle, creating a triangle. "Angela always cuts across the field to get to her bus. That way she doesn't have to walk all the way to our bus stop and then down the block."

Kathryn took the drawing and studied it. She handed it to David, who put his finger on the dotted line and held the drawing so Raul could see where his finger was placed. "Is somewhere along here where the swamp is?" he asked.

Yes, Raul said, the swamp was in the field.

"And you think Angela cut across the field Friday morning?" Kathryn asked.

"She always does," Raul told her.

"And your mom and dad know about that?" David asked.

Raul became silent.

David told him, "Raul, it's always better to tell the truth. Did your mother and father know Angela took a shortcut to the bus stop?"

He shook his head. "No," he admitted shyly. "We're not allowed in the swamp. It's all muddy, and there's water—like a creek. One boy almost drowned there."

Kathryn and David glanced at each other. A troubling thought occurred to her. Could it be that Angela had been in the swamp all along, right across the street from the house, facedown in the water?

9

By nightfall the wet streets surrounding the swamp were alive with activity. Government sedans, military police cars and jeeps were everywhere. Military tractor trailers roared in and out of Wainwright Heights, delivering giant searchlights from the airport, generators to light them, and a trailer to serve as the FBI's portable command center. The searchlights lit up the field as if it were a baseball stadium. Residents of the neighborhood came out to see what was going on, though they stayed behind the yellow police tape that was being strung along temporary metal fence posts. No one seemed to mind the rain. From under raised umbrellas, the crowd watched the tape being stretched from post to post, completely sealing off the field in the center of Wainwright Heights.

To Kathryn, the swamp wasn't much more than a grove of scraggly trees, bushes, and tall grass. At the trunk of her sedan, under an umbrella held by one of many federal agents crowded around her, Kathryn opened a laminated map. She and five or six other agents wore navy jackets with the gold markings "FBI" on the back and left chest. Another dozen or so agents wore jackets with the large words "Evidence Response Team" printed on their backs.

There were several housing developments around the field Angela had apparently crossed on Friday morning, Kathryn told the agents: Wainwright Heights, Patton Park, and a part of Walker Village.

With the aid of a flashlight, Kathryn pointed out each of the housing developments, then the unlabeled field on the map. She said, "Any of these areas, including the major streets that pass by are potentially significant. And remember this particular location is not far from the reservation limits. Even though the field opens a lot more possibilities than there were before, if this is where Angela disappeared, it helps us to piece together some scenarios." She held the map so everyone could see where she was pointing. With her finger, she traced a line she had drawn in blue grease pencil on the map, then she called attention to the same area by pointing at the field. She said, "This is our way to get in and out of the swamp. No one goes in or out of that particular area"—she pointed at the patch of scraggly trees and bushes—"unless it's by this path." She again traced the route on the map and also pointed it out. "We don't want to contaminate any of the evidence by charging in and out of there like a herd of elephants."

With a red grease pencil and a ruler, she drew a grid on the field represented in her map. She labeled the grid squares with letters of the alphabet. Then she assigned teams of agents to search each grid from the outer perimeter inward, toward the swamp. "David, you, Mark, our photographer, and Kobi Albert of the ERT will go with me. We'll take a reconnaissance trip directly into the swamp. We'll get a preliminary glimpse of what's in there."

Everyone put on green wading boots.

From the car trunk she took a handful of evidence markers—red flags on wire stakes, like the ones electric companies used to mark underground lines through neighborhood yards.

Kathryn, David, Mark, and Kobi set out on the prearranged path into the swamp. Kathryn knew Kobi, a young black woman, by reputation. She was said to

be a stickler for details when it came to collecting
evidence. She missed nothing.

The night was cold, intensified by the dampness. In
the white of the searchlights, the rain looked like
sheets of clear plastic. Kathryn, walking under David's
umbrella, commented that the heavy rains made the
prospects of a productive crime scene gloomy. She was
tired. The past couple of days were beginning to wear
on her. First there was the business with Wendy, then
Randy, then the Robles investigation, including the
disappearance of Major Robles.

David said if they didn't find anything, at least everyone would be able to go home and get a few hours
of sleep. He said it as if the swamp was their last hope
for any immediate leads in the investigation.

It was true, they were running out of possibilities
to follow up on. A good night's sleep might be just
what everyone needed.

He asked her how long had she been with the
Bureau.

It was small talk, but something to keep their minds
off the rain and cold of the soggy field. Fourteen years
she told him, walking.

"Almost one of the good old boys," he mentioned.

She glanced at him. He had one of his subtle smiles
on his face, a smile she was becoming used to. She
asked about Los Angeles.

Los Angeles was filled with too many routine cases,
he told her, which is why he had applied for training
in the antiterrorism program. For a while he had
worked bank robbery, he said. That was the worst
assignment he had ever had. Most of the time all of
the evidence was on bank surveillance tapes. There
was nothing to do but to collect the tape, locate the
robber on the tape, and apprehend him. He shook his
head. "Some robbers would enter the banks, completely undisguised," he said, "commit their crimes,
and leave." It was a simple matter of locating the

robber on the tape and nothing more. Not a challenge at all. As usual he spoke in a quiet, unhurried manner.

She said, "You've been with the Bureau, what, nine years?"

"Yes."

The rain eased.

The closer they got to the swamp, the more marshy the ground became. They entered the grove of trees, careful to note that they were creating a fresh path into the area. Mark, at the front of the detail, began snapping photographs. He led the other agents to the boards that had been thrown across an especially marshy area. There they were: shoe impressions filled with muddy water. A lot of them. Trampled grass. An obvious struggle. Some diluted blood under a leafy plant. Nothing fatal. Not enough blood. A school bag. A flute. Mark took many photographs. He shot systematically, though, so as not to overlook anything through carelessness or accident.

Using her hand radio, Kathryn called the portable command center. She told the agent in charge to contact the military liaison and arrange for a shelter to be erected across the swamp. The liaison, Colonel Spangler, had already studied the field and promised he could raise a canvas awning that would completely cover any crime scene. She told the agent at the command center, "Open our access route to Colonel Spangler, and have him deliver whatever materials his people need. As soon as we get an all clear from our teams in the search grid, we'll let the military in to erect a cover over the crime scene."

It didn't take long. The military team worked quickly and efficiently once it had been granted permission to enter the field. As Colonel Spangler had promised, his team raised a canvas shelter completely across the swamp, like a giant circus tent. Soon the rain could be heard hitting the canvas above where

Kathryn and others searched. Military crews dug small trenches to drain water from the crime scene.

Meanwhile Kathryn and David marked evidence with flags. Each area marked was photographed. Kobi followed, processing the individual evidence. Kathryn and David marked some of the better shoe impressions. They were an adult's impressions. Male, most likely, given the size of the feet and the type of boot. There were several cigarette butts too, a couple floating in water. Someone had been waiting, David said.

Kathryn wondered if it had been Major Robles. Did he smoke? She found an empty matchbook cover lodged in the wiry branches of a bush. The matches were from Arnold's Bar & Grill in Temple, Texas, a nearby town. She marked the bush with a flag.

There was a lot of trampled brush and grass. It looked like Angela had been chased and knocked down. David marked the area for the photographer.

Kathryn's portable phone buzzed. She answered it. It was Grant. He had received word about the swamp. He wanted to know if they had found anything yet.

She told him she was in the middle of her search. "We've got the rain off of us," she said. "The military's raised a tent over the area, and we're about ready to let in a detail of ERT specialists." She asked him if there was any word on the consultant she had requested from the Centers for Disease Control, and the consultant from the military's biological weapons program. She was taking the situation seriously. "What about the Office of Emergency Preparedness?"

He said he had put in the requests and was waiting for responses. He told her he wouldn't hold her up, but he wanted to know the moment she could break for a telephone briefing. She hung up without telling him that already evidence was mounting.

Indeed, the crime scene was rife with evidence. David said it reminded him of some of the surveillance tapes he had seen of Los Angeles bank robbers. That bothered her when he said that because the scene contradicted the apparent planning of the ransom note and everything she knew thus far.

Other agents from ERT arrived.

One reported that on the backside of the matchbook cover, there were fingerprints—protected from the rain. Inside was a thumbprint. All retrievable. Someone else had found some strands of hair, probably Angela's hair.

David tracked the shoe impressions until they disappeared, which gave a clear indication of the direction the kidnapper had gone. The assailant had backtracked to Twenty-fourth Street. Agents marked off an area where it appeared a car had been parked on Twenty-fourth Street. There was an oil stain in the street and some muddy boot impressions near the curb. One set of impressions seemed to match the impressions left in the mud of the swamp, though the impressions were badly deteriorated by the rain. A canvas was raised over that area too.

The crime scene was too disorganized. "It's as if whoever kidnapped Angela, and I'm assuming there was more than one kidnapper, didn't care if they got caught," Kathryn told David when he returned.

David agreed. It didn't make sense for there to be so much careless evidence.

Kobi found a shoe, obviously the shoe of a youth.

Kathryn was impressed. The shoe had been completely submerged in the water and mud. "Kobi, how did you ever see that?"

Kobi didn't give a response, even seemed embarrassed that Kathryn would ask such a question.

Kathryn told her it was good investigative work.

While the ERT team continued its search and continued to process evidence, Kathryn and David headed for the portable command center.

David said, "You think it's the father?"

"His actions certainly make him look like he's involved."

They walked under the same umbrella, the one he carried. Her hand was tucked under his arm. She and he were close enough that she could smell his cologne. Polo. It smelled good. She thought of Randy. That scared her. She didn't know why, but it did. She wondered if he had returned her call.

David told her, "It doesn't make sense for someone to claim to have a biological weapon stolen from a top secret military installation, and not leave a trace of evidence behind there—at least not enough to arouse any immediate suspicion—and then claim responsibility for something as sloppy as this. The two things don't jibe."

It was all too strange. For example, there was the letter that had been postmarked on Thursday, which meant the kidnappers had known they would need to get Angela before the letter reached its destination. It was true, she told him, at least on the surface, there was some evidence of precise planning that contradicted the disorderliness of the crime scene.

He stopped, she with him. "Unless the fog messed up the plan," he commented. Their eyes met. "Fog doesn't seem like something you could plan for. Everyone's told us the fog was so thick on Friday that you couldn't see the nose on the end of your face. Say it wasn't the father—besides, I don't think he smokes. It could be that whoever was waiting for her missed her—didn't see her—and had to chase her through the swamp to catch her. That might have thrown things out of kilter."

But how would the cigarette butts fit into such a scenario? she wanted to know. "The cigarette butts made it look as if someone had been waiting in the swamp for her."

"I think that might work too," he told her. "Say one or more of them was supposed to grab her off of the street right in front of the house, but she slipped past that person. Her diary said someone had been watching her. They would have known her routine. They would have stationed someone in the swamp—just in case she got past the one waiting at the street. Then there would be someone over on Twenty-fourth Street, in case she got past both of them.

"The one in the swamp probably thought all he had to do was wait for some signal, maybe the honk of a car horn or something, and then return to the car. He was probably as surprised as she was when she suddenly showed up in the swamp. That would explain why things were so sloppy."

She squeezed his arm. "Hey, you're pretty good at this," she said.

They continued walking.

Though she didn't say it, she was beginning to think that the sloppy scene, combined with the planned note, meant that there indeed could be a terrorist group of some sort. A terrorist group tended to have a mixed group of members—some more capable than others. There were also the rash of attacks on Mexican-Americans. That might mean a militia of some sort. She was anxious to see what kind of a file Colonel Hendrick, the provost marshal, had put together for her.

At the street, as she and David were ducking under the yellow tape, one of the spectators caught her arm. To her surprise, Kathryn saw Tony Robles when she looked up. He was standing under an umbrella, his face mostly concealed.

He said, "I'm here to turn myself in."

Because of all the people standing around, Kathryn didn't want to call attention to him, or say anything that might be overheard. She took him by the arm. "Come on, let's walk," she told him.

As they walked away from the crowd, Tony asked if they had found Angela.

Kathryn glanced at him, wondering if the question was genuine.

"She's not dead, is she?" Tony stopped.

"We didn't find her," Kathryn told him.

"You found something, though, didn't you?" Tony insisted.

Staring at him, Kathryn struggled with her own conscience. He had lied to her, she knew. Why? Did she, in turn, have any right to withhold information from him? She said, "We have found some items that we believe belong to Angela. There appears to have been a struggle. Angela may have been hurt."

"It's my fault."

She said what was on her mind: "Someone is going to use a biological weapon and doesn't care how sloppy things get. Is that what you're talking about?"

"Yes."

10

Kathryn took her coat off and threw it into the backseat of the sedan while David drove. Tony didn't say anything until they were off Fort Hood. Then he asked, "How much trouble am I in?"

"That depends," she told him. "If you continue to withhold evidence in a criminal investigation, you have a big problem."

He looked out his window.

David drove to the well-lighted campus of Central Texas College, where he parked among other cars. He left the car running, including the windshield wipers, which rose and dropped intermittently.

As soon as they were parked, Tony said, "Today, I found out the truth." He looked pale, especially under the white streetlights that gave him a washed-out look, like someone who was coming down with the flu. The stubble of his beard stood out against his chalky skin. He took off his sunglasses and stared at nothing in particular. "This is bigger than you think. Much bigger."

She said, "You know who has her, don't you?"

Leaning forward, he said, "You don't understand what you're dealing with.

"Try me."

"Let me put it this way: I was digging for information and I was stopped at the last moment."

"You were stopped?" David spoke up. Until that

moment he had been facing forward, listening. He turned to Tony.

"Yes."

"What is all this about?" Kathryn asked.

His sunglasses still off, Tony shook his head. "No. You have to promise protection for me and my family." He leaned back. At that moment the window near him exploded. Glass and water sprayed everywhere.

"Get down!" Kathryn screamed, threw open her door, and brought out her 9mm. Even as she dropped onto the wet pavement at the side of the sedan, David was crawling out over her, his 9mm in hand. "Keep me covered," she told him.

He passed by her. From the back of the sedan, he knelt, poised to raise and fire. "Okay."

Kathryn jerked open the back door of the sedan and dragged Tony out onto the pavement. "Are you all right?" she asked. He was bloody from the glass shrapnel, but hadn't been hit directly by whatever had shattered his window.

"See, you have to protect me!" Tony said. "You have to protect me and my family." His voice was frantic. "They want to kill us."

"Shut up!" she told him, and jerked him by his coat sleeve. She listened. Listened for gunshots, tires squealing, anything. But there were only the sounds of the night. Traffic on the nearby highway passed as if nothing had happened. The wind blew rain.

David eased his head up from the side of the sedan and looked around. He came back down. "I don't see anything," he whispered. Then he blew breath from his mouth. With it came steam from the cold and rain. "Wow, what a rush. Scared the shit out of me." He laughed.

Tony was trembling. Not what she expected, she thought. What kind of a mess had he gotten himself into?

With her portable telephone, Kathryn called in the shooting. She said they needed an ambulance. She stretched out on the wet pavement so she could see under the sedan. She watched for approaching footsteps. If someone comes with an automatic weapon, she thought, we're dead.

"I don't need an ambulance," Tony said. "I'm barely scratched."

"Be quiet."

Now and then, David rose to look over the trunk of the car.

"Did you see what happened?" she whispered to him. It had all happened so quickly she hadn't seen anything, but since the shot had come from David's side, she thought he might have noticed something—perhaps a flash of light.

Peering over the trunk of the car, he said, "Not a thing."

Tony said, "You have to protect my wife and children."

She made another call to the command center and ordered federal marshals to take the Robleses into protective custody. When she put away the phone, she said, "Where the hell is everyone?"

There were no flashing lights, no sirens, nothing.

"Is there a shotgun in the trunk?" she asked David.

"If you think I'm going to open the trunk and look, you're crazy," David told her. "That's all I can say."

She glanced at him.

He had a smirk on his face. "No offense intended."

"None taken, chicken shit."

He laughed.

She laughed too. It wasn't funny, but the tension at that particular moment was so great that it brought about an odd response from both of them. Before she realized what had happened, the two of them were laughing loudly. They were alive. It was a good feeling.

Tony shook his head. "You're both crazy," he said, "downright crazy."

"You see any reinforcements yet?" she asked David, still smiling.

He raised to look over the trunk. "Nope, but if I keep sticking my head up like this, someone's bound to blow it off, then you'll have to do your own looking."

They laughed again.

"I bet it's been several minutes already," she said. It hadn't, but it seemed like it. "Whoever did the shooting is probably sipping a drink on an airplane out of here at this very moment."

David said, "That's why I've never wanted to live in a small town. Do you realize if you had a heart attack or some other emergency in a place like this, you're talking at least ten minutes before anyone shows up. You might as well call a hearse and do it all in one trip."

To Tony, Kathryn said, "When the ambulance arrives, you're going to pretend you've been shot. David, you'll get down too. We'll load you onto the gurney and give the attendants Tony's name. Then Tony, we'll get you out of here. Give David your glasses. David, give Tony your coat." They exchanged the items. While Tony put on David's coat, Kathryn asked him, "Do you mind telling us what's going on?"

Tony told them he was a cryptographer for the National Security Agency.

"We've figured that much out." She said she and David had met Edward Brennan earlier that day.

Tony glanced at her, as if surprised. "They sent him? I wonder why they sent him." He shook his head. "I wouldn't trust him any farther than I could throw him."

While they waited for the ambulance and backup units, Tony told about a military operation that had supposedly happened during the Vietnam era. Brennan, who had been with military intelligence in those days, had supervised the sabotage of American military equipment in order to help exaggerate the war losses. "People like him love war. If there isn't one going on, they start one."

David asked, "Why do you think they sent him? He seemed like he might be someone to be reckoned with in the agency."

"He is, believe me. I have no idea why he's here. To tell you the truth, though, this is the first time I've been in this kind of situation, so maybe it's not that unusual."

"He told us about Exodus-Five," she said. "I understand from Brennan that you know a lot more than what you've been pretending to know."

Tony told them he hadn't said anything because he had been briefed not to talk to anyone without specific permission from his superiors at NSA.

"Who briefed you—when?" David asked.

"My boss at Fort Meade—before I was sent down here."

"I don't think your boss meant us," Kathryn commented. "I don't think anyone would ever brief you like that."

Tony shrugged. "Okay," he said, "don't believe me, but I was specifically told it didn't make any difference who it was, I wasn't to say a thing. I believe even the President of the United States was used as an example. Something to the effect of, 'Even if the President of the United States confronts you, you're not to say a word.'" Tony glanced at her. "Tell me, who has more authority, you or the President?"

"I do," Kathryn said nonchalantly.

David mumbled, "She's telling the truth."

She smiled. "Listen," she said, "all you need to know is we have jurisdiction here, and this is a criminal investigation. And now you know you can talk and better talk because whatever you're involved in

is serious, and these people mean business, and so
do we."

He told them that NSA had a listening post at Fort
Hood. "I've been collecting and deciphering messages
signed MTR. I don't know what the initials stand for.
I think it is some secret group that has it out for
Mexican-Americans."

"What makes you say that?" she asked.

"That's how I've managed to break their code and
follow their messages—by the nature of certain messages that pertained to Mexican-Americans. I guess I
was more sensitive to the messages than other people
in the agency were." Tony looked at David. "I guess
you've heard some of the things that have been going
on down here. It has the Mexican-American community on edge, though no one else seems to care very
much."

David told him, "We're checking into that."

Kathryn said, "Earlier you told us you had gone to
contact these people, but something stopped you.
What was that?"

"I deciphered a message from yesterday ordering a
total communications blackout. I couldn't get to anyone today. Whatever they're going to do, it's all
mapped out, and they're getting ready for the next
move."

From the distance came the sounds of sirens. They
seemed to come from everywhere all at once.

Kathryn stood and flagged down two sheriff's cars
that came flying into the parking lot, one behind the
other. More police cars arrived, as well as an ambulance and several off-duty officials who had responded
to the call for help. She said, "We need blankets. A
lot of them."

State police officers and sheriff's deputies brought
blankets from their cars. She had the officers hold the
blankets open and stretch them out so they would
provide a wall of cover for Tony and David, who lay

on the pavement. The wall blocked out anything that was going on inside its perimeter.

Standing over Tony, Kathryn handed him a bullet-proof vest she had taken from the trunk of their sedan.

He asked, "What's that?"

She told him.

"Why do I need that now?"

"Because someone is serious about killing you—in case you didn't realize what just happened." She nodded in the direction of the window that had been blown out. "And Angela. You think the hit-and-run was coincidental? I think they wanted to kill all of you."

He put on the vest.

A U.S. marshal arrived. Kathryn knew him. Pete Falcone.

She took him aside and told him they needed to get Major Robles to a safe house. "I don't care who asks you, I don't want anyone to know where he is," she told him.

Pete, a marshal in his late forties, was stocky and had a thick head of black hair that had been infiltrated by gray. He said, "That's just like the FBI to call a U.S. marshal when its own agents get in trouble."

She smiled. "Don't get to thinking you're Marshal Matt Dillon of Dodge City, and this is *Gunsmoke*," she told him.

He laughed.

David was loaded onto a gurney, which was rolled to an ambulance, while Tony got into the sedan that Falcone had driven right to the wall of blankets.

Kathryn ordered several other cars to pull close to the blankets, and radio silence. Doors opened and closed. She sent the cars in different directions so that it would be virtually impossible to determine which direction Tony had taken. She remained at the scene in order to give a report to police officers who were trying to piece together what had happened.

So were members of the news media. They were arriving almost as quickly as were additional law enforcement personnel.

One reporter in particular caught her by the arm. "Agent Stanton?" He was a bowlegged young man with long, stringy dark hair. He held out a handheld recorder. Behind him came other reporters. Television camera lights came on, flooding her with whiteness. Microphones and cameras closed in on her. "I'm Roger Worthington of the *Dallas Morning News.* Tell us, Agent Stanton, is there any truth to the rumor that the Mexican girl who was kidnapped from Fort Hood on Friday is the victim of a hate group?"

"No comment," she said, trying to get away from him, but by that time cameras and microphones had walled her in.

"Isn't it true there have been a series of hate crimes in recent days at Fort Hood, hate crimes especially geared toward Mexican-Americans?"

"No comment."

She pushed against the reporters. She wondered where Worthington had gotten his information. With the help of two state troopers, she managed to pass through the reporters. Some distance from them, she looked back. Worthington was standing near the shattered window of her sedan. Speaking into his recorder while a photographer took photographs of the car, he said, "I'm standing near an FBI car that is graphic evidence the hate war has grown ugly down here at Fort Hood, Texas. Tonight, federal agents were fired upon while interviewing a witness. I don't know if the camera will be able to pick it up, but there is blood on the backseat of the car, a definite sign that someone was hurt. A source that asked not to be identified has indicated that a federal witness may have been fatally wounded. . . ."

Someone was talking, Kathryn knew.

The concern about a leak plagued her all the way

back to Fort Hood, where she discovered that Falcone had done his job well. He had set up three different safe houses with law enforcement personnel watching each location for suspicious activity. As it turned out, Tony was in a building in the middle of a field at Fort Hood. It was a VIP quarters for visiting dignitaries. Falcone had established a heavy guard both inside and outside the building.

In a dark apartment on the ground floor of the building, dark despite the small table lamp near the window whose heavy curtains were pinned shut—the colors of the room were evergreen, which made the room even darker—Kathryn found Tony. He was sitting at a circular table near the bed. He looked shaken. There were minor cuts and scratches on his face and arms.

She said, "Before I ask any questions, or hear anything you have to say, I want to give you the facts." He nodded. "I've got you in protective custody, and I'm going to take care of you and your family, but this isn't a game." He didn't say anything, only stared at her with eyes she knew he was having trouble focusing. "This guy Brennan who's here to get you doesn't seem like the kind of person who's going to be too happy when I tell him he can't have you. He's going to raise hell. He's going to raise hell all the way to the top. I already know that."

Tony rubbed his eyes, nodding at the same time. "He will," he said. "I know his reputation. He's an arrogant bastard. He'll raise hell like you've never seen anyone raise hell."

She nodded. "Exactly. And there's something else you need to know. Your daughter Angela has been kidnapped by people who know what they're doing. But if this is a hate crime—I keep hearing that mentioned—you might as well face it right now, whoever has her isn't going to let her go. It doesn't make any difference what you do. They're going to want to hurt

her and set an example with her—an example that
will get people's attention.

"If we're going to get Angela back, it's not going
to be by panicking and giving into terrorist demands.
They want us to give in; they want us to give in a
whole bunch, so they can manipulate us and get as
much attention out of this as they can. I know that
sounds cruel, but it's the truth. We don't bargain or
make deals. Is that understood?" What if it were
Wendy? she wondered. What would she be willing to
attempt in order to get her own daughter back?

Tony leaned forward so that he was close enough
to apparently see her without his sunglasses. "I'm telling you, this isn't small."

She advised him of his legal rights; he signed a
waiver form. "Let's start from scratch. Even if this is
a hate crime, why do you think someone specifically
wanted Angela?"

He shook his head slowly. Start from scratch, she
thought. "I've stumbled upon something, and someone doesn't want me in particular asking questions.
Whoever it is knew I'd be removed from the assignment once the kidnapping took place."

"What do you think you've stumbled upon?"

"I'm not sure, but it's big. Actually, it was from a
transmission sent yesterday—before the communications blackout."

She didn't say anything—waited for him to explain.

"It was a message about you."

She studied him. "My name was mentioned?" Was
Wendy in danger? If MTR was willing to kidnap one
child, would they stop there? "What was the
message?"

"About you finding the diary."

How had the news about the diary gotten around?
she wondered. Everyone knew.

"Whoever got Angela obviously didn't calculate a
diary, and is worried." There was a moment of silence,

during which time he must have sensed what she was thinking because he said, "I'm sure you know that the FBI isn't the only agency capable of eavesdropping and securing such classified information."

She studied him.

"Think of all the times you talk on your radio, on the telephone, or on the computer. Any message you send by one of those means is subject to interception by NSA. We can intercept every electronic transmission in the United States and world. Every single one. I'm not joking."

Why did he keep using NSA as an example? she wondered. Surely NSA wasn't involved.

"It's a fact. I can pick up every transmission you make among your agents. You go about your business as if you have a secure line, but the truth is you don't. There is no such thing."

"Is NSA involved in this?" she asked.

He leaned close to her again. She could see detail in his bloodshot eyes. "I think so. I don't know how, but I think so."

"But how could NSA even get involved in something like this?"

He shrugged. "It's actually nothing new. Think of all the powerful people who have used NSA for dirty work through the years, and for all kinds of purposes. Who can do anything about it? There's no one with enough authority, including the FBI, who can walk into NSA headquarters and turn it inside out. Congress can't do it. The President of the United States can't even do it."

"What are you saying?" The implications of what he was saying were frightening, even to her, who knew the excessive power of the Bureau.

"That things like this happen all the time, and no one ever hears about them." He smiled sadly. "Say I'm an ambitious senator, for example, and I have eyes on the presidency. I have a friend at NSA. My friend gives me dirt, and I'm able to manipulate my way up the ladder by using the dirt. Believe me, it happens all the time. Some say Johnson assassinated Kennedy through NSA."

"And how does the diary fit into this?"

"To MTR, or whoever is conducting this operation, it's big news. No operation would like a loose end like that. I guess one of the reasons someone targeted Angela in the first place is that no one ever expected a girl who had had severe head injuries to keep a diary that might contain incriminating evidence."

"And someone's worried about what all's in the diary?"

"If not, why would the diary become the subject of a transmission? Yes, someone's worried."

She thought of the swamp. Without going into details, she told him how sloppy the crime scene was. How would he explain that if this were a NSA operation? she asked.

"An operation like this will have scapegoats—people to take the fall as things go wrong. When it's all said and done, there will be an entire plausible story for what has happened, one that will satisfy all the inquiring parties, including the FBI. No one will ever know the real truth if what I think is happening is really happening."

She stood. "Tell us what you know," she said. She had heard some of it through Brennan, but she wanted to hear it again.

He repeated what Brennan had told her.

She said, "Okay, one possibility is that someone targeted Angela in order to get rid of you. Aside from that, and her being a potentially nonthreatening target, is there any other reason she might have been targeted?"

Other than that, and the possibility that it was just another in a series of hate crimes, he told her, "The only other thing I can think of is that it might have something to do with her adoption."

She didn't say anything.

"Mary Belle said she told you about that. What she might not have told you is back when we were trying to adopt, we ran into a mess. In fact, it got so bad, there was a time when we almost decided not to go through with it." He went on to tell how his and Mary Belle's best friends at the time were adopting too, and how they insisted on the Robleses getting a blue chip.

"Blue chip?"

"White, healthy, American boy. Mary Belle and I eventually figured out that our friends had a vested interest in the adoption. To be guaranteed a blue chip was expensive, and I think the DiUlios—that was their name—were getting a discount on their own son by arranging for one to be sold to us also. As soon as Mary Belle and I figured out what was going on, we decided to adopt a Mexican child, and to take our chances with whatever child we got." He made a slight whistling sound. "The DiUlios got so mad they wouldn't even talk to us, and we started having trouble with the adoption agency. Then and there Mary Belle and I decided to forget everything."

"But you didn't."

"We almost did." He made a small "c" with the thumb and index finger of his left hand. "We came this close. The agency notified us that it looked like we weren't going to get a child after all, but we suspected the DiUlios were behind that, so that made us mad. We threatened to file a complaint against the agency, and the next thing we knew we had Angela."

"You think something illegal was going on at the adoption agency?"

"We know something was going on."

"And I'm sure the DiUlios canceled their friendship after that?"

He nodded. "If there ever was a friendship. As it

turned out, we never had another thing to do with them—until we moved back to Texas. A few months ago, Mary Belle happened to run into Al over in Temple."

Odd it should be Temple, she thought, and remembered the matchbook that had been found at the crime scene.

"Apparently, he's now practicing medicine down in Austin, and he has a satellite office over in Temple. She had Angela over there to see a specialist—Mary Belle didn't like Angela's doctors here at Hood—and she happened to run into Al. She said he didn't seem surprised to see her. I've wondered in the past couple of days if he wasn't somehow involved in all of this. I did some checking. He's in the Army Reserves, and back when the Gulf War was going on, he was at Fort Detrick, Maryland, to get some specialized training in chemical and biological injuries. Fort Detrick, as I'm sure you now know, is where Exodus-Five is kept."

11

The night was cold and damp like the day, only the darkness made the world close in on Angela. She felt it pressing against her, almost as if it were trying to squeeze the breath out of her.

She had found a rocky place to hide during the day and had been forced to remain there because the soldiers were searching everywhere. They had come almost immediately, so she hadn't been able to get as far away as she had planned. Their own search efforts kept her pinned down.

Oddly enough, she hadn't been hungry since lunch, but now that she was confined to one place, she was hungry. To make matters worse, she was away from the wind and rain, but she could hear them in the trees above her. It sounded like they were whispering about her. She hated that. She hated too that the night was so black. No stars, moon, electricity. No light at all. And she could feel the wetness. Not on her, but all around her, even on the rocks where she sat, knees to her chest, her field jacket pulled around her. With a dog tag between her unburned fingers, she rubbed the letters. The cold wetness, like the night, made her think of death.

She hurt. Her hands, face, and shoeless foot throbbed with pain. When she had been on the move, she hadn't noticed it as much—except for the couple of times she had fallen. Now that she was confined to her hiding spot, though, she noticed immensely. Pain had caught up with her and lingered.

For no apparent reason, she found herself crying. First she cried about the pain, then she cried about the cold and darkness. Then about the men who were hunting for her. Then about her mother and father and family and home. Then because no one loved her. Then because she had caused so many problems for people, made people's lives so difficult.

Why had she ever been born? she wondered. It would have been better if she hadn't.

As abruptly as the crying started, it stopped. Though her face was wet and her nose runny, inside, deep inside, she was drained. The outside cold and wetness had closed in on her, and inside she felt empty. The cold and wetness closed all the way in.

She tried to think of something pleasant. She closed her eyes and concentrated on her house in Maryland. She wished she still lived there, that she and her family had never moved away. If they hadn't moved, she wouldn't have had the accident, and she wouldn't have fallen into the nightmare she was now in. Why had they moved?

It was a warm house, the place in Maryland, especially in the winter when there was so much snow outside. In the morning, when her mother would get her up for school, Angela would take her clothes and stand over the heat register, where the warm air would blow up her undershirt. When she had finished dressing, she would sit on the floor, against the register, wrap her arms around her knees, like she sat now, and fall back asleep.

A flash of light awakened her. She looked around, but the light was gone. All that remained was darkness. That and rain. It had grown heavy. She stared into the blackness, though to no avail. A low rumbling passed through the earth. The flash of light had been the lightning, she decided, the sound, thunder. Don't be scared.

She closed her eyes and tried to return to her house in Maryland when the white light flashed again. Her eyes opened as the light vanished, and she thought she had seen a human skeleton. She pushed back against the rocks. A skeleton? How could it be? She didn't believe in ghosts. She didn't believe in the boogeyman; she didn't believe in ghosts. She could feel her heavy breathing, though, could feel her heart heaving inside her chest. The thunder vibrated in her back.

Not once did her eyes budge from where she thought she had seen the skeleton. She stared for a long time. The lightning flashed, three times in succession. The trees and rocks all moved with each flash. Shadows jumped in the night. Then all was black again. No skeleton. Only her imagination. She lowered her head into her knees and tried to think of her home in Maryland. The thunder rumbled.

Then another sound broke the silence. Like the lightning, the sound was only for an instant. Not the same, though. Unnatural. Static from a radio? She listened hard, turning an ear and tilting her head toward the sound that was already gone. Lightning flashed. A skeleton loomed over her. She screamed. Blackness. She was in its clutches.

"Charlie-delta-one to center," the skeleton said, an arm locked around her neck, a hand over her mouth. The static returned. Her struggle couldn't break the grip. "Charlie-delta-one to center," the skeleton repeated.

"Come in, charlie-delta-one," came an artificial voice through the static. "This is center."

"This is charlie-delta-one," the skeleton said. "I'm on the northeast side of Pine Bluff. I have that article we've been seeking. I repeat, I have that article we've been seeking. It's in good shape, and I'm enroute to center with it."

The skeleton carried her out into the rain and through the darkness. Once or twice the lightning flashed, and she caught a glimpse of the skeleton carrying her, not a skeleton at all, but a soldier wearing some kind of apparatus that fit over his head. It seemed to help him see in the dark.

Soon the soldier was joined by other soldiers, those who carried flashlights that gave off red light. The soldiers seemed to come from nowhere, out of darkness, to greet him. They were slapping hands together and congratulating each other.

Hands took her and began to run in the red light. They ran until they ended up in the familiar setting of the compound she had escaped from earlier that day, only the compound looked empty now, except for the mess hall, which was lighted with fluorescent lights.

Inside the mess hall the camouflaged soldiers carried her. There they strapped her into a wheelchair and bound her mouth with gray tape. All she could think of was her brief freedom, and how good it had been. She was sorry she hadn't kept running. Had she kept on the move, she would have escaped. Why had she stopped? she wondered. Once again, she had failed. Everything she did turned out to be a failure.

That's when she noticed her right hand. It was swollen, red, and shiny. There were black speckles on it. Above her hand, on her wrist, were giant brown blisters filled with fluid. Oddly enough, the hand didn't hurt, though, didn't hurt at all. Where the blisters were hurt, but not the hand. Her right foot hurt, but not her hand.

The colonel appeared. His face looked hard, as hard as a rock. Lieutenant McCabe was with him. Also with him was a new soldier, an older man dressed in fatigues, but without rank on his collar, though he wore a West Point ring. The new soldier had greasy, steel-gray hair and thick glasses that had so many smudges on them she could barely see his moss-green eyes as he studied her. He had a terrible odor about him too, like old garbage. Then appeared a new captain, one who had a skinny face, dark hair that needed to be cut, and a goatee. Captain McCanles was nowhere in sight.

Stopping near her, Colonel Lazarus looked down at her hand and foot. He started to turn away, then he looked again. The hard look in his face was changed by a concerned look in his eyes. He turned to McCabe. "Now look what's happened because of you, Lieutenant McCabe."

McCabe didn't say anything.

"Did you think I was stupid, Lieutenant?" The colonel's voice had raised. "Did you think I believed for a moment that one of our hostage's shoes mysteriously disappeared and nothing went wrong with the plan?"

"It wasn't my fault," McCabe said weakly. "I assumed Captain McCanles did things as he was supposed to do them."

"When, in fact, you knew that he hadn't done them the way he was supposed to do them, isn't that right?" Colonel Lazarus said. His face was red. "I told you to drive by so that Captain McCanles could pull her into the car. Neither one of you even had to get out of the car. Now I learn you decided to make up your own plan. Do you realize the kind of trouble you're in?" He pointed at Angela. "And look what's happened to her."

McCabe looked, but didn't seem to see anything. He seemed to be concerned only about his own trouble. "I didn't make the decisions, sir," McCabe said, trembling. "Captain McCanles decided to change the plan. He's my superior officer. I was obeying his direct orders at the time."

"And what about Major Reising's direct orders!" Colonel Lazarus yelled, hitting a table with his hand.

Major Reising, Angela thought, suddenly surprised. She knew a Major Reising! He worked with her father.

"Captain McCanles told me Major Reising had changed the orders, sir."

Colonel Lazarus stared at McCabe. "Captain McCanles told you the major changed the orders?"

"Yes, sir."

The colonel took a deep breath through his nose. He exhaled the same way. "Then, when I questioned you about the operation the first time, why didn't you say something?"

"Sir, at that moment, I didn't realize that what Captain McCanles had told me was not true. I assumed the major had changed the plan, and that you were asking me if the new plan had been followed as ordered."

"You're lying to me," the colonel said.

"I swear I'm not, sir." McCabe was visibly nervous. He shifted his weight from foot to foot, as if he couldn't stand still.

"Lieutenant McCabe, I can look in your eyes and tell that you're lying."

"I swear to God I'm not, sir."

"Don't swear to God. Don't defile the Lord's name like that."

"I'm not lying, sir."

"Then, tell me this, Lieutenant McCabe, how was it you came to figure out that Captain McCanles hadn't done what he was supposed to do?"

"He told me, sir."

"He told you?" the colonel said in a loud voice that seemed to say he didn't believe McCabe at all.

"Yes, sir, he told me. When we left the mess hall this afternoon, he told me not to discuss the changes you had made in the plan to get the girl. He told me they were top secret changes, and that I wasn't supposed to discuss them even with you."

"Now, why would he tell you that, do you suppose, Lieutenant?"

"He said you would be testing me to see whether I would violate security."

"And you didn't believe him?"

"The more questions I asked him, the more I didn't believe him, sir. So then I said I was going to talk to you, and he got scared. He told me not to talk to you. I kept pushing him for details, and he finally told me he had disobeyed the major's orders, but he asked me not to tell you because he said what he had done wasn't any big deal, and he didn't want to upset you."

"He told you he had violated orders?"

"Yes, sir."

Again the colonel took a deep breath through his nose. He exhaled the same way as before, then said, "So you eventually decided it was your duty to tell me that Captain McCanles had made some changes in the ordered plans?"

"Yes, sir, I eventually thought you would want to know."

"It sounds to me like Captain McCanles is in some big trouble."

"If Major Reising didn't change the plans like Captain McCanles told me he did, then I guess he is in big trouble, sir."

"Not only that, but he concocted an entire story to hide what he had done wrong."

"I guess so, sir."

"That sounds like subversion."

McCabe didn't say anything.

Angela guessed he didn't know what subversion was. She didn't either.

"Lieutenant, I want to thank you for being responsible enough to report all of this to me."

McCabe nodded. "Yes, sir," he said.

"Now, you head for the office and make a full written report. Is that understood?"

"Yes, sir."

To the new captain, the colonel said, "Captain Gillespie, you escort the lieutenant and make sure he writes down everything just as he's explained it here."

Captain Gillespie nodded. "Yes, sir." He and McCabe left the mess hall.

"Captain McCanles!" the colonel said loudly.

McCanles appeared from the kitchen. "Yes, sir." He carried a yellow apple that he was eating.

"I take it you heard all that?"

"Yes, sir, I did," he said, and took a bite of the apple. Chewing as he spoke, he continued, "That's why I came to you right away this afternoon. As soon as I put everything together, I thought you would want to know."

The colonel massaged his chin with a hand. "Okay, let's go over this story another time. How did all this happen, again?"

McCanles took another bite of the apple. "It's like I said, sir, I took the prisoner her meal and left her in the charge of Lieutenant McCabe." He swallowed. "I told him to make sure he got the plate once she had finished eating. It seemed like it was taking a long time for Lieutenant McCabe to return, so I went to check on him." He took another bite of the apple, sucking some of the juice as he did so. "When I got there," he continued, his mouth full, "I found McCabe making sexual advances toward the prisoner. While I listened in, she told him she was scared of me, and he told her he would keep me away from her if she would do what he told her to do. She said she would do anything he wanted if he promised to get rid of me. He asked if she would let him watch her take a shower. She said yes, she would, if he would take care of me. He told her he would make sure I got in big trouble. He said he had a story he would make up, and once he told what he was going to tell, you would make sure I was punished severely." He paused to suck some apple out of his teeth. "I didn't know what he told you was going to be what he made up, but now it all makes sense."

The colonel asked, "And why didn't you come to me immediately?"

"I knew you were busy, sir. I was waiting for things to calm down a bit, not wanting to trouble you with matters I could handle myself."

The colonel nodded. "I see. And how does the fire fit in?"

"I guess that was the other part of his plot," McCanles said. "When they found what looked like the foil remains of a pack of my cigarettes in the burned quarters, I realized what was going on. He set the fire and left my cigarettes there to get me in trouble. Then he came to you later with his story in order to put the finishing touches on his plan."

"How did he get your cigarettes?"

McCanles smiled. "Lieutenant McCabe bums a cigarette from me now and then."

"I see. And how did the prisoner end up escaping? It seems to me that kind of defeated the lieutenant's plan."

Captain McCanles swallowed thickly, as if something were caught in his throat. "All I can figure out is that the fire got out of hand, and when the prisoner saw she had a chance to escape, she bolted."

Angela noticed that the apple McCanles was holding had already started turning brown where he had been eating.

The colonel said, "I guess you know what this means. I guess we all know."

"What's that, sir?"

He took a deep breath before saying, "Lieutenant McCabe can no longer be trusted."

"I never did trust him, sir."

"You're a good judge of character, Captain."

"Thank you, sir." McCanles's pink face reddened.

The colonel nodded. "What we need to do for the immediate moment is to have you keep a low profile for a day or so."

Color drained from McCanles's face. "I'm still in the operation, aren't I, sir?"

"Exodus-Five is a week away. Yes, you're still in the operation, but our immediate task is to take care of the lieutenant. Do you have any suggestions?"

"Yes, sir, I'd like personally to take care of him if you'll give me the chance."

"I don't know. I'm worried about you."

"I guarantee I won't mess up. I'll stake my life on it, sir."

The colonel nodded. "Okay, here's what you do. You go back to the Chrisman place, and I'll send the lieutenant to you. As soon as you finish the job, you return here."

McCanles beamed. "Yes, sir."

"Dismissed." The colonel returned a salute.

McCanles left the mess hall.

"Private Kearnes!" the colonel bellowed.

A skinny soldier with no rank on his uniform appeared, chewing on his red mustache. He had curly red hair that had thinned with age, especially on top, and he looked too old to be a private. Too neat too. His uniform fit him snugly, as if it had been tailor-made. It was starched to a cardboard stiffness.

"Private Kearnes," the colonel said, "get me a pack of Kools from the canteen, and bring Lieutenant McCabe with you when you return."

The private left the mess hall. Within a couple of minutes he was back with McCabe and the cigarettes.

In front of McCabe the colonel opened the pack of cigarettes, removed a cigarette, and handed it to the lieutenant. "Private Kearnes, you smoke. Give me your lighter."

Kearnes produced his lighter.

The colonel took it and handed it to McCabe. "Light your cigarette, Lieutenant, and let's talk for a minute while you smoke."

McCabe said, "Begging the colonel's pardon, but I don't smoke."

"Come on, Lieutenant, we both know you sneak a cigarette now and then."

"Sir, I've never smoked."

"Light it!"

He did so clumsily, but coughed, dropping the cigarette. "I'm sorry, sir, but I don't smoke." He could barely speak. "I'm sorry." He looked sick.

"You've never smoked?"

"No, sir."

"I see." The colonel stood. He towered over McCabe. "Lieutenant, I'm going to give you a chance to prove that what you've been telling me is the truth."

McCabe looked nervous again. His dry face had turned powdery.

"Captain McCanles has disobeyed direct orders, he's lied, and he's engaged in subversion. He's even told us that you're the one who's lying."

"That's not true," McCabe said weakly.

"Then, take care of him."

McCabe shifted from foot to foot. "What, sir?"

"Shoot him in the back. Kill him. It's him or you. Which is it going to be?"

McCabe didn't say.

Colonel Lazarus's voice became firm as he repeated, "Shoot him in the back for all I care, but I want the problem solved."

"Yes, sir." McCabe's voice was not enthusiastic at all.

"He's at the Chrisman place."

"Yes, sir," McCabe said in a voice that was barely audible.

"Dismissed."

Once McCabe was gone, the colonel turned to Kearnes. "Private Kearnes—"

"Yes, sir."

"I'm not too happy about you either."

Kearnes was silent.

"I understand you missed Robles tonight."

Was the colonel talking about her? Angela wondered.

Kearnes didn't say anything.

"In fact, the whole world knows you missed. I thought you were a crack shot."

"There wasn't much time," Kearnes said, chewing on his mustache periodically. "It was an impossible shot."

"Don't let it happen when you take care of Captain McCanles and Lieutenant McCabe."

"Yes, sir."

"Dismissed."

Colonel Lazarus was left only with her and the evil-looking man, the man who had many smudges on his glasses. Lazarus turned to the rankless man. "General Burch," he said, "our hostage needs medical attention."

General Burch shook his head. He was wearing a black undershirt beneath his fatigue shirt. A tuft of curly white hair was sticking out the top of the undershirt, near his Adam's apple. "It's too risky," he said simply. "The cost would be too great."

The colonel pointed at her hand. "Those are second- and third-degree burns," he said. "We need to have a doctor look at them."

Burch stared with his cold, evil eyes. It looked like milk was covering them. "We don't have a doctor."

"But the plan was that the child wouldn't be hurt."

Burch smiled gently. "Think about that statement, Colonel."

"That no one would suffer."

"She won't suffer. Captain Gillespie, I understand,

has some first-aid training. He can bandage her and take care of her. She'll be fine."

"Begging the general's pardon, sir, but those are third-degree burns."

Burch's eyes became like ice. "I said, Captain Gillespie will take care of her." His voice was very firm.

"Yes, sir."

Burch smiled slightly. "Colonel, sometimes you worry me."

The colonel sighed.

"Try to remember the big picture," Burch told him. "Don't go soft on me now."

Colonel Lazarus looked at her hand. He seemed to be troubled, but only for a moment. The look passed.

12

At her motel room Kathryn telephoned Randy. Despite it being two o'clock in the morning, she needed to talk to someone, not necessarily him, but he was the only one she could think of to call at that hour. She wished she could have talked to Wendy, but she knew that would be rude to call at such an hour, especially since Wendy had school the next day. As for Randy, she knew she had already left two messages, but she was certain she would catch him during the middle of the night. To her surprise, after three rings, she got his answering machine. As soon as it gave her the signal for her message, she said, "Randy, pick up. I know you're there. Come on, Randy, I know you got the news. Pick up and let's talk." She waited. He didn't answer. She knew he was listening. "Well, I'm at the motel if you want to call me. You have the number."

She put down the receiver, took off her coat, removed her service weapon by holding the holster while, in one pull, she slipped her belt out of her slacks. The holster containing the 9mm and extra clip of ammunition was left in her hand. She put it on the dresser beside the television. She put her Bureau credentials beside the weapon. Then she reached up under her blouse and unhooked her bra. She removed one arm at a time, freeing the bra at the same time she kept the blouse on. It felt good to have the bra off.

She returned to the phone and dialed Randy's

pager. She keyed in her room number. She hung up and went to the bathroom, where she opened the lid of an ice chest. There were several diet Cokes in what was now mainly water. She reached into the icy water and brought up a can. She popped the top of the can, wiggling the tab until it came off in her hand, and took a long drink of the diet Coke. She dropped the tab in the trash.

The more she thought about Randy, the more perturbed she became. It was rude of him not to return her calls. Had he used her, and now that he hadn't gotten what he wanted, dumped her? She had suspected that all along, but had forced it out of her thoughts. Could it be true?

She looked at herself in the mirror. Her hair was a mess. It had been wet and dry, wet and dry all day.

She heard a tapping at her door. No wonder Randy hadn't returned her call, she thought, smiling at her reflection. He had decided to visit. She hurried to the door, unchained it, and opened it, her arms open at the same time. Her arms dropped.

David stood there wearing a Dallas Cowboys jersey, untucked, jeans, and shower shoes. His dark hair was wet and combed straight back. There was a cigarette stuck behind his left ear. He had obviously just gotten out of the shower. He smelled like soap and Polo. In his hand he held a bottle of what she assumed was either scotch or bourbon.

Embarrassed, she covered herself, realizing she didn't have a bra on under her blouse. "David, what's wrong?"

"I couldn't sleep," he told her. He held up the bottle. "You care to join me in a drink?"

"No, thank you."

"Do you have any ice?"

"David, there's an ice machine down the hall."

"Are you tired?"

"To tell you the truth, I haven't hit the sack yet, but I'm sure I won't have any trouble falling asleep."

"Oh," he said. He looked disappointed. "I thought maybe we could talk for a few minutes."

"Not tonight, please."

"I just wanted to talk," he told her. "Not about work, not about anything in particular. Just talk. Don't you ever just need to talk?"

Yes, she admitted to herself, sometimes she needed to talk. She was sure he hadn't heard the latest about Brennan, hadn't heard that Brennan was on the warpath for her refusal to give him Tony.

She stood away from the door, though she still kept herself covered. "Come in," she told him.

Once he was inside, she pushed the door closed.

He pointed at the sink outside her bathroom. "Can I borrow one of your glasses?" he asked.

"Go ahead. There might be a little ice left in the chest in the bathroom. Help yourself if you can fish any out."

"Can I fix you one?"

"I'm not much of a drinker," she told him. She raised the diet Coke. "This is my poison."

She saw him unwrap one of the plastic glasses and go into the bathroom. She could hear his hand sloshing around in the ice chest.

While he did that, she got a sweatshirt out of her luggage and put it on.

He returned to the counter where the sink was located. As he mixed his drink, his back to her, he looked at her from the mirror. "Believe it or not, I'm not much of a drinker either," he told her. "I like an occasional nightcap, though, especially after a long day, or almost two days in this case." He returned carrying a mixed drink in one hand and his bottle in the other. He showed her the yellow label of the bottle. "You ever heard of it?" he asked, sitting on one of the two queen-size beds in her room.

"Old Taylor?"

He nodded.

No, she told him, she'd never heard of it.

He hung one leg over the other, and sat there with a glass in one hand and the bottle in the other, one of his subtle smiles on his face. "They make it in Kentucky," he told her. "You can't find it most places." He held up the bottle. "My father-in-law turned me on to it while he was still alive. It actually has a pretty good flavor—for bourbon. You want to try?"

She took a drink of her diet Coke. "No, thank you," she repeated.

"I mean just taste it."

She shook her head. "Since I'm not a connoisseur of bourbon, I'm sure I wouldn't like it no matter what kind it was." She sat on the opposite bed, facing him. "Any chance you might be able to patch things up between you and your wife?" she asked. She didn't know why he was in her room at that time of the night, but she wanted to make sure he remembered she knew he was still married.

"Believe me, it's over," he told her, and took a drink.

Beside the telephone was a large rubber band. She picked it up and began to secure her hair at the back of her head. "What happened between you two, anyway?" The rubber band pulled at some of the hairs on the nape of her neck. She adjusted the binding.

He sipped his bourbon. "I like your hair like that," he mentioned.

Still adjusting the ponytail she had made, she said, "Are you avoiding my question?"

"My youngest son, Sean, was hit by a car last year." He took a drink. "Isn't that ironic—I mean, with the Robles girl and her automobile accident? We have these big machines that we create as humans, and then we forget how dangerous they can be. Everytime I think of the Robles girl, I think of Sean."

"Is he all right?"

David smiled. "Nearly perfect," he told her. "But it's been a rough year of surgeries, especially plastic surgery, recovery, and so on, and, as you might have guessed, it's taken its toll on our marriage."

"Maybe you just need to give it more time," she suggested. "Time has a way of healing."

He shook his head. "Believe me, it's over," he told her. "We've both said things now that will never heal." He added, "She's already seeing someone else. Besides, I accept responsibility."

"I don't understand. You mean you blame yourself for what happened to your son?"

"Yes. It was my fault."

She took a drink of her diet Coke. She didn't say anything.

"He was with me at the time. We were in a parking lot—can you imagine someone being critically injured in a parking lot? He stepped in front of a passing car." He closed his eyes, took a big drink of his bourbon, and looked at her with moist eyes.

She thought he looked like he was reliving the experience. "But you said he's fine," she reminded him. "You can't run yourself into the ground, blaming yourself for an accident. It was an accident, wasn't it? And he's fine, right?"

"Of course it was an accident. And he's fine. But I was with him at the time. You never get over blaming yourself when something like that happens. You never want your children to get hurt." He shook his head and went on to say that he wasn't the only one who had blamed himself. "Carol blamed me too. She never said it directly, but I could tell it was there, always right below the surface in our relationship." He shrugged. "Maybe the past two days have taken their toll on me." He forced a smile. "They've been rough," he said.

She told him the time had been rough on her too.

She said she had been thinking about her daughter Wendy. She too forced a smile. "It's funny how you never think about how much your children really mean to you until something like this happens, and you watch someone else go through it. And you realize it can really happen."

He commented that he was glad he wasn't down in the dumps alone.

The smile on her face felt natural. "Just before you showed up, I wanted to call her and tell her I was sorry about anything I'd ever done to upset her."

"You did?" His smile looked natural too, so natural that she saw his teeth for the first time. It was like all the other times he hadn't wanted to loosen up too much.

She nodded, staring at the bottoms of his upper teeth. "I don't know why. I just did. It's like I was thinking, what if something happened to me, and I never got a chance to tell her how I felt."

"Well, it's like you say, it's funny how something like this will do that to a person."

She went on to tell him that she kind of knew what he was talking about when he mentioned feelings of guilt when a son or daughter got hurt. She told how she had had an experience that was nowhere near as traumatic as the one he had suffered with his son, but one which she had never been able to get out of her head. She pointed at the cigarette still behind his ear. "I used to smoke too," she admitted, "and then one day I was involved in an incident that made me stop then and there, an incident I've never forgotten."

It involved Wendy, she said. "When she was three or four—I think she was four—I remember we were riding in a car and I was smoking. Wendy was in a car seat in back. My window was cracked so the smoke would go out. I finished my cigarette, rolled down the window a little, and threw it out. Next thing I know, Wendy was screaming." She shook her head. "My cigarette had blown back in the window, and had landed in her hair." She took a deep breath. "For as long as I live, I'll never forget the look on Wendy's face. She was looking right at me as if I had betrayed her." She finished her diet Coke. "I haven't touched a cigarette since. It's been, well, nearly ten years. And do you know what? To this day, I still feel guilty about what happened."

"Was she burned badly?" he asked.

"No, it singed some of her hair and left a blister. The scar left on me was much worse, I think."

"I bet it did scare the hell out of you."

"Scared the hell out me is putting it mildly."

"And you still think about it after all these years?"

"As if it happened yesterday."

"Great," he said, and finished his drink. "Now I know what I have to look forward to with Sean."

"Things like that are going to happen in life," she told him. "They happen to all of us at some point in time. No one's immune. It then becomes a question of how you react once it happens to you. Do you take on some callous attitude toward life and curse it, or do you fight back and refuse to give in?"

He smiled sadly. "I'm telling you, it's over between Carol and me," he said.

"Okay, so it's over. No one said anything about that. Besides, you'd know that better than I would. But do you just quit living? Don't you still have two sons?"

He raised his empty glass as if making a toast, stood, and said, "Thanks for a few minutes of good conversation. I needed them."

"Any time." She didn't really want him to leave, almost told him about Brennan, but then thought that would spoil a good conversation. She only hoped he wasn't depressed.

"Good night."

"Good night."

She was about to close the door when he turned back and said, "You know what? You're a pretty neat person."

The words embarrassed her. "Thank you," she said. "You are too." Her response sounded stupid, but she didn't know what else to say.

He walked away.

She closed the door. She went to the phone and tried Randy's number again. She didn't want to think about David, didn't want to think that she had enjoyed spending a few minutes alone with him. She got Randy's answering machine, only this time she didn't leave a message.

From her luggage, still unpacked, she brought out an oversize jersey from her alma mater, the University of Texas. She changed into the jersey, turned off the light, put the chain on the door, and pushed the curtain aside to look out the window. Down in the lighted parking lot stood David, smoking a cigarette. He seemed to be watching something, though the parking lot was empty at that hour of the night. She dropped the curtain and climbed into bed. She wondered what he was thinking about.

In bed she tossed and turned, and kept looking at the glowing red numbers on the clock beside her bed. The numbers changed, but she couldn't remember sleeping between the changing numbers. All she knew was that at five a.m., when her portable phone rang, she was so groggy she thought she had been drugged. She could hear the phone buzzing, but couldn't reach it. She had been sleeping with her arm behind her head, and apparently her arm had fallen asleep. In any case, she couldn't coordinate her fingers. When she finally did get the receiver to her ear, she heard the voice of Ken Leubbering, the duty agent at the temporary command center. He said he had received the initial reports about the forensic evidence from the crime scene.

She told him to hold while she got a pen and paper. She turned on the bedside lamp and got her notebook and paper. "Go ahead," she said.

The hair found at the crime scene had been identified as Angela's hair. The blood was hers too. It contained saliva. Apparently, she had been hit in the mouth. The smaller shoe impressions were hers. They matched the shoe that had already been identified by Mary Belle and Tony. The fingerprints were still out, Agent Leubbering told her, and promised to call again as soon as he received a report.

She called Grant in Dallas. He answered right away. She apologized for waking him, but he said he was already awake. Strange, she thought. She reported the findings of the forensic evidence. He told her he had already been briefed about them. Stunned, she asked him who had contacted him during the night. He told her FBI headquarters had briefed him personally. He said, "Kathryn, the director wants me to take over the investigation. I'm packing for the trip right now. I've already talked to Lieutenant General Hale, the base commander down there. He's giving us additional space for an expanded command center. I'll be there in a couple hours."

Having somewhat recovered from the shock of what she was hearing, she said, "I don't understand. What's going on, Grant?" She knew his taking over the investigation was inevitable, but there seemed to be something else going on.

He told her, "This is standard protocol on a high-profile case. You know that. We both knew it was coming." His tone was too cold.

She said, "There's more, Grant. Come on."

"Kathryn—"

She could hear him sigh.

"I'm going to tell you something, but if you ever bring it up in the future, I'll deny ever saying anything."

"I feel like I should be recording this conversation."

"You've ruffled some big feathers at NSA. I don't know what you and Brennan had to say to one another—it may only be a clash of personalities—but the director of NSA's gone to the secretary of defense, who's gone to the President, who's gone to the director. NSA's claiming you're interfering with national security here, and you're endangering the mission of NSA."

"What?"

"Believe me, I know how you feel, and I stood up for what we're doing. I told the director this is a criminal investigation, and we need the freedom to make every inquiry necessary. The director supports us, but you have to realize there's not an agency more powerful than NSA in the world. All NSA has to do is say national security is at stake, and they can basically have whatever they want."

"Which means?"

"Kathryn, please, work with me on this. NSA wants your head on a platter. They've gone to the President of the United States."

She became angry, so angry she didn't know what to say. To hell with NSA. "Go on," she said. "How is it that you propose for me to 'work with you on this'?"

"Keep a low profile for a couple of days. Let tempers cool. Fly back to Dallas. Spend a day or two with your daughter."

"What? You're taking me off the case? That's not standard protocol."

"Kathryn, I can't even begin to emphasize that you don't want the President of the United States asking questions about your job performance. If NSA goes back to him, you might as well kiss your ass goodbye. You'll not only be permanently off the case, but you'll be lucky if you don't end up in a little town out in the middle of Kansas."

She wanted to explode.

"I'll clean this up. I promise. Just give me a couple days."

"So I'm off the investigation?"

"For a couple of days I want you to take some leave." His voice was insistent. "Come to Dallas, visit with your daughter, and keep out of everybody's way. We'll get this thing in hand."

Stunned, she put down the phone. She had never been removed from an investigation. She cried, then her movements were mechanical.

She packed her bags and went down to the front lobby, where there was a stack of Dallas newspapers on the counter. She looked at the headline: FBI SENT STERN WARNING! Below the headline was a large photograph of her sedan, passenger window shattered. She scanned the article by Roger Worthington. It barely mentioned Angela Robles. Instead the article focused on what Worthington found important—a window shot out of an FBI sedan.

13

Angela was done fighting. All she had to do was look at her hand, and she knew she wouldn't fight or try to escape again. She didn't want to hurt anymore. She didn't want to make the soldiers mad.

Her foot looked better. She was relieved to see that it wasn't burned as badly as she thought it had been. A lot of the redness had turned to a pinkish color, though the foot had produced the same kind of watery blisters that were on her arm. Big brown bubbles full of fluid. Both her arm and her foot ached terribly. What scared her the most, though, was not her arm or her foot, but her right hand. It was so swollen and dark red that it looked like it didn't belong to her. It had a shiny, hard surface to it, and a color that was dark brown in a couple of places. What scared her was that the hand didn't hurt. Looking at it, she knew it should have hurt, but it didn't. That scared her. It made her think the hand didn't belong to her anymore.

What also scared her was that she was no longer hungry—couldn't have eaten even if they had forced her to eat—and she no longer had to go to the bathroom. All she wanted was to close her eyes and sleep, or even to die.

Yes, die. She didn't care. She didn't want to go on. She knew she'd never make it back home. When she looked at her hand, she knew there was nothing anyone could do for it. Her life was over.

She closed her eyes and tried to remember her house in Maryland.

Someone touched her shoulder. It was Private Kearnes, the skinny red-haired man who liked to chew on his mustache hairs. Why was he bothering her? she wondered. He was holding what looked like medical supplies.

He told her, "I managed to scare up some Silvadene cream." He knelt in front of her. "To tell you the truth, I don't really know what I'm doing, and I don't know if this is going to help, but the colonel told me to get you comfortable, so that's what I'm trying to do." He started to lay his things out on the floor near a table in the dining hall.

He held up a needle and syringe. "Believe it or not, I was a medic in the Gulf War. I can't remember a whole lot, but I'm the best hope for medical treatment you have right now."

He gave her a shot in her left shoulder. She winced. He was rough with the needle. She thought he probably hadn't given many shots.

He stared at her, as if he had expected the shot would have immediate effect.

Why were they doing this to her? she wondered. Why did they hurt her, then try to fix her? It didn't make sense. Why were they mean one moment and nice the next?

She glanced at the colonel, who was sitting all alone at another table, his head in his hands. A change had come over him. He was not the same person she had met earlier. He was not as relaxed and calm as he had once been. The soldiers who came and went kept their eyes on him, but no one disturbed him.

Not everyone was in the dining hall. Only a handful of soldiers was there. She guessed the others were on night maneuvers.

Suddenly, the colonel stirred. He sent one of the soldiers to make sure the other soldiers were asleep.

He said he didn't trust them. He said time was running out, and he didn't trust anyone.

He got up and walked to where she sat in her wheelchair. He pulled up a chair.

Private Kearnes was getting his medical supplies ready.

Sitting down, the colonel asked her, "How are you doing, young lady?"

He seemed nicer than he had been in the past, but she didn't say anything. She was afraid to.

"Private Kearnes is going to get you all fixed up," he said. "Aren't you, Private Kearnes?"

"I'm going to try, sir," Kearnes said. He unwrapped some gauze. "I'm not a doctor, sir."

She wasn't sure what that was supposed to mean. She wondered if that was supposed to mean she should see a doctor.

"I know, Kearnes, you just do the best you can. That's all I ask."

She noticed that the colonel was staring at her hand. He seemed to be sickened by what he saw. She looked too. It made her sick to her stomach. She looked away.

"Why did you have to try to escape?" the colonel asked her.

It wasn't a mean voice or an angry voice, but a confused voice, as if the colonel genuinely couldn't understand why she had tried to escape.

"See what you did to yourself?" He pointed at her hand.

She looked at it, didn't want to, but found herself staring. Yes, she saw what had happened.

"We don't want anyone to hurt or suffer," the colonel told her, shaking his head. At least she assumed he was talking to her. "Especially a child."

She wasn't quite sure at what particular moment it happened, but at some point a change came over her. For some reason she felt like she had somehow separated from her body and was outside of it. The pain she had experienced earlier had vanished.

She watched as Private Kearnes rubbed white cream on her burned hand. She didn't feel it at all. He was gentle and careful with his movements, perhaps because the colonel was watching him work. For some reason, though, she thought he probably wished the colonel wasn't there; and, if the colonel hadn't been there, she suspected he would have been a lot rougher with her. She didn't care, didn't care about anything except that she wasn't hurting at that particular moment.

When her entire hand was covered with cream, Kearnes carefully wrapped it with gauze. As he did so, he told the colonel, "Sir, I believe you're supposed to leave a burn wound open to air."

The colonel, staring at the wrapped hand, seemed to be in a better mood. He said, "Now, we can't very well have our hostage causing others to ask questions, can we, Kearnes?"

"No, sir."

"Then, we better not let them see what's happened to her, had we?"

"That's a good point, sir," Kearnes replied.

He went to work on wrapping her foot, and was just as slow and careful with it. First he applied a thick layer of white cream, then he wrapped the foot in gauze.

By that time she felt quite indifferent to it all. She decided there was nothing that could get to her, as if somehow she were above it all, experienced no pain, no hunger, no fear, and no concern whatsoever.

The next thing she knew, the colonel was no longer paying attention to her, but had gotten up to address the soldiers who were nearby. Not everyone was there, but there was a handful.

He announced, "I don't like what has happened here any more than any of you do." He wasn't speak-

ing very loudly. "The unfortunate truth is that in war
we see many disturbing sights like this. It's a fact of
life, it's a fact of war. Believe me, I've been in enough
wars to know." He didn't sound sure of himself.

He pointed at Angela, who had been newly bandaged. Even she thought the bandages looked quite
good. They hid the ugliness of what had happened.

"The important thing is to remain compassionate as
well as committed to our objectives."

The more he talked, the more cheerful he became.
"A soldier has to be sensitive to the human condition," he said. "The moment we stop being sensitive
to the human condition is the moment we start becoming killers instead of professional soldiers."

He touched Angela's forehead. He took a deep
breath and let out all the air before he said, "This
young lady has gotten herself into a mess, and rather
than condemn her, which we could have easily done,
we've helped her."

She watched him, even started to believe in what
he was saying. Had the colonel helped her? Did he
really care that much? For the first time she spoke to
him. Her words were so weak she almost didn't hear
them herself. "I'm sorry," she told him.

He smiled gently. "See, everyone," he said. "Did
you hear that? She said she's sorry." He took a deep
breath through his nose and let it out.

She looked at her lap and began to cry.

"See," he said more loudly. "She's sorry."

She cried more loudly. No one moved to help her.

"Okay, that's enough," he told her.

"I'm sorry," she repeated weakly.

"That's enough," he told her. She decided he was
like the others—he probably didn't want to hear what
she had to say.

She stared at her lap, though her vision was blurred
because of her tears. She was tired. She wanted to
close her eyes and sleep now. She wanted to close her

eyes and think about her home in Maryland. She
wished she had never left there, never moved away.
She tried to concentrate on the colonel.

From somewhere he had produced a paper clip and
was stretching it open with his fingers. She felt like
she was the paper clip and he was pulling her life
apart. "It's almost over," he said, as if to reassure her,
"then you won't have to worry anymore."

She tried to stay awake. What did he mean it was
almost over? She looked around. The soldiers all
watched the colonel.

General Burch, the one who looked so evil, had
appeared from nowhere. His gray-white hair stood like
tufts of whipped cream on his head. As he walked
through the mess hall, it was as if he were in a world
of his own.

Colonel Lazarus was happy to see him. "Thaddeus,
we've got our hostage all fixed up, and we're back on
track again."

Thaddeus Burch looked at her through his smudged
glasses. He looked like a timid sort of man, the kind
who was used to acting and speaking when no one
else could see him, behind closed doors, as if he might
be afraid that if he said or did something out in the
open, people would see the person he really was. Angela thought of the assistant principal at her school.
When people were around, he acted like one of the
nicest, most polite men she had ever met, but once
when he had been alone with her, he had slapped her,
slapped her hard. The slap had scared her.

General Burch said, "That's good news because, to
tell you the truth, I haven't been too happy with how
things have been going thus far. That means the people above me haven't been too happy either."

She wondered why the general didn't wear any rank
or name tag. She would have thought he'd be proud
of who he was. Didn't he want people to know he was
a general?

Colonel Lazarus smiled nervously. He said loud enough for the others to hear, "I've made it clear to the men that I'm tired of all these mistakes, and I won't tolerate more of them. Isn't that right, men?"

The soldiers around him didn't say anything.

Burch said, "It's time we move ahead with the operation. None of this should have happened in the first place." He waved an open hand at Angela. "Had it been me down here running things, it wouldn't have happened."

Colonel Lazarus saluted the general. "I assure you, sir, everything's under control."

Burch saluted back. "I hope so, Colonel. I hope so for your sake."

The mess hall door opened and in walked Captain Gillespie, carrying a box. He set his box on a table and approached the colonel, whom he saluted. He said, "Sir, I'm here to give the men their last round of inoculations."

Colonel Lazarus returned the salute. "Very good, Captain. Now, let me ask you, once you give the inoculations, do you think if I put the hostage in your charge, you can keep her under control?"

Gillespie laughed loudly, unnaturally. His goat's beard shook. It was a forced laugh. Too loud for his small body. He said, "She won't give you another worry, sir."

The colonel nodded in approval. "Very well. Tomorrow morning, when Corporal Klock gets up, tell him he's to help you," he said. "He seems like a person who'll follow orders no matter what."

To the soldiers the colonel said, "You heard the captain. Get your shirts off."

The soldiers took off their shirts.

"Line up," the colonel said to the soldiers who were holding their shirts. The soldiers formed a line near the table where Captain Gillespie had left his box.

Removing a silver gun from the box, Gillespie said,

"We've been through this several times now, but I want to remind you that you must remain perfectly still. Just remember that if you happen to make any wrong move, this thing'll blow the back of your arm off." He laughed in a loud, unnatural manner, as if he hoped someone would move, just to see what would happen.

One after another, the soldiers stepped up to Gillespie, who raised his silver gun to their right shoulders, and pulled the gun's trigger. *Poof!* was the gun's sound. One or two of the men flinched, but no one's arm blew off.

In the middle of his work, Gillespie stopped and carried his gun to the colonel, who had taken off his shirt. Poof! Captain Gillespie said, "Now, that wasn't so bad, was it, sir?"

The colonel put on his shirt. "You'll take good care of the girl, won't you, Captain?"

Captain Gillespie laughed loudly. "Of course, I will," he said. "She'll be fine."

The colonel tried to tuck in his shirt. "I'm glad I can count on someone." Frustrated in those attempts, he turned his back so he could unzip his pants.

14

Kathryn caught a flight into Love Field at Dallas, early Monday. She had a window seat and kept her attention fixed on the window, mainly to avoid a conversation with the old man in the seat beside her. She guessed he was in his seventies. Every time she looked in his direction, he began talking. He talked about his wife, about his son, and about the knee he had had replaced. He talked nonstop. She didn't want to talk. She wanted to be left alone.

The sun was shining in Dallas. Clouds cluttered the blue sky above the city of cement and asphalt that seemed to have grown out of the plains by magic. She was glad to be home, looking forward to seeing Wendy. The jet touched down. She collected her baggage.

During the flight, she had been tormented by what had happened. At one moment she had experienced rage; at the next, betrayal. When she really thought about it, though, she realized her entire fourteen years with the Bureau had been the same way. She had given her life to the Bureau, even at the expense of her family. Sure, she knew she wasn't as good a mother as she should have been, knew she never had been cut out to be a mother, but the worst part of it was that she had sacrificed any opportunity to be a better mother to a job that gave back nothing. Women still had no power and authority in the Bureau. It was still a man's world, and that's all there was to it.

With her promotion to the head of the terrorism division at Dallas, a promotion that in itself had surprised her, she had thought all of that would change, but now she realized it hadn't. Anytime a case was important, a man would be called in to take over. That's how it was. Everything was as it had been since the inception of the Bureau. An old boys' network.

She rented a car and drove to Wendy's school. The parking lot in front of the school was almost empty, as school was still in session. Occasionally, Kathryn had picked up Wendy from school. She played the baritone, which was difficult to tote around, so it was not unusual for Wendy to call Kathryn and ask her to pick her up from school so she could bring her instrument home.

Kathryn smiled at the thought. The baritone was huge—barely fit into the trunk of a car—and loud— filled the house with its vibrating brass sounds whenever Wendy practiced on it.

Kathryn's relationship with Wendy had been that way. Wendy seemed to go to extremes to try Kathryn's patience—as if to say, "How far can I push you?" The baritone was one of those extremes, a way of saying that Wendy would pick the biggest instrument she could find and announce she was drawn to that instrument. Needless to say, in this case Kathryn had to concede. Wendy had stuck with it for almost three years. In fact, she could actually play recognizable music.

Kathryn entered the school office and told the secretary that she was there to pick up her daughter. She gave the name and class. The secretary flipped through a card file until she found the card she was looking for, then she spoke into a microphone near her desk. "Mr. Davies?"

A voice came back through a speaker in the office. "Yes."

"Could you tell Wendy Stanton her mother is here to pick her up?"

There was tittering in the background. "Yes," Mr. Davies said.

Kathryn went back to her rented car. She knew Wendy would come out embarrassed and upset. "Why did you have to embarrass me in front of everyone?" she would say. Kathryn looked around at the near-empty parking lot. Was she wrong to take Wendy out of school early she wondered.

Sure enough, Wendy was upset. Kathryn could tell.

"Mom, how could you embarrass me like that?" she asked, getting in the front seat of the car. "Mr. Davies is my favorite teacher, and you embarrassed me in front of the entire class."

"I thought you'd be happy to see me. How about a hug?" She leaned toward Wendy, but Wendy pulled back.

"Mom, I'm thirteen."

Kathryn smiled. She smacked her lips together several times, making kissing sounds.

Wendy smiled and scooted down in her seat. "How embarrassing. What are you doing here?"

Kathryn noticed something she hadn't noticed before. She noticed how straight and white Wendy's teeth were, especially when she smiled. The years of braces had paid off. Wendy was a beautiful girl—young woman. "I wanted to see you."

"Where did you get the car?" Wendy asked.

"Rented it."

Wendy began to dig around in her book bag. "Oh, Mom, I wanted to show you something."

"What?"

"Something I got at church last night."

Kathryn's mom and dad took Wendy to church every chance they got. Kathryn didn't really mind, but sometimes what Wendy learned at church became a source of irritation between the two of them.

Wendy pulled out some blue papers. She said, "Gordon passed these out to us last night. It's for a summer missionary project in Atlanta. A group of us kids are going up to do missionary work for a week."

"Oh, no you're not."

"Yes, I am. Mom, this is missionary work. Grandma already said she thought I'd be able to go. She said she'd talk to you. It's perfectly safe."

"Grandma can talk all she wants, but I'm not sending you off to some strange city by yourself for a week. And Atlanta! Atlanta, Georgia!"

"There are going to be chaperones and everything." She began to read off questions on the application forms and tell Kathryn her answers. For several of the questions, she had written out extensive answers.

At home she was still going on about the trip.

Kathryn mentioned, "I wish you got as excited about your school studies." She sorted through the mail. Bills.

"Why is it that whenever it comes to something I believe, you ridicule it?" Wendy asked, being persistent. She still had the blue application forms in her hands.

Kathryn turned to her. "I don't ridicule what you believe. Please don't think that. I just can't see sending you off to a dangerous city with strangers for a week."

"You do ridicule what I believe. I've finally found a church that I can understand, and you want to try everything possible to keep me away from it."

"Wendy, you go to that church because all your friends go to it. Let's be truthful about it."

"That used to be true. I used to go there because my friends went there, but now I go because I understand what Dr. McCuen is saying. He understands young people. Like last night he was preaching, and he said the difference between boys and girls is that boys think with their minds and girls think with their hearts."

"What!" Kathryn said, shocked by what Wendy was saying.

"See, there you go again, ridiculing everything I believe."

"Wendy, you can't possibly believe that. Girls have minds too."

"But we have bigger hearts."

"I can't believe I'm hearing you say this. My daughter? Girls are just as good as boys. Their minds are just as good, and there's no difference in their hearts."

"That's not what I believe."

What had happened to their relationship? Kathryn wondered. Where had the understanding between them gone? "Sweetheart, I'm not ridiculing you, or anything you believe. But I just want you to make sure you know what you really believe. I don't want you to sell yourself short. You're a very beautiful, very intelligent young lady, and you can be whatever you want to be. You can be anything a boy can be." She thought of her own circumstances and wondered if she really believed what she was saying.

Wendy poured some apple juice in a glass.

Kathryn used the close proximity to her daughter to hug her, but no sooner had she put her arm around her daughter than Wendy pulled away. "Can't I even hug my own daughter anymore?"

"Yes, if you'll let me go to the after-school social on Thursday."

Kathryn thought for a moment. "Maybe." She took advantage of the moment to hug Wendy.

"You mean it?"

"Maybe. It depends on whether you get your schoolwork done and everything."

Wendy screamed with excitement.

"I said, maybe! If"—she emphasized the word—"if you get your schoolwork done. That includes homework and study."

"I promise."

Kathryn looked at her watch. "Good. I've got to run out for a few minutes. I want you to do your homework, then we'll do something special together."

"Okay, Mom."

"Don't be so nice. You'll make me suspicious."

"Can I call Grandma and tell her?"

"Wendy!" Kathryn complained.

"Five minutes," she promised. "Five minutes on the phone, and I'll do all my homework and studying."

"Five minutes. That's it." Kathryn got her coat. "I'll be back."

"Okay, Mom."

The way Wendy was talking sounded patronizing, but Kathryn enjoyed it. "Remember your homework and studies." She went out the door.

On her way to Randy's apartment, she used the portable phone to dial her home number. The line was busy. She kept trying the number until she got to Randy's place. The line stayed busy. She shook her head.

Randy was home, drinking a Coors and watching a football game on cable sports. She could tell he hadn't expected her, though he did invite her in. As she took off her coat, she asked him why he hadn't returned her calls.

He told her he had been on an assignment.

She didn't believe him, but she didn't want to put him on the spot.

He asked her if she wanted anything to drink. His tone was cool.

She asked him if he had any diet Coke.

He went into the kitchen and returned with a diet Coke.

She looked around at the apartment. It was a mess. He needed to wash laundry and dishes. He had always lived like that.

In the living room he pressed the mute button on the television control, though he left the game on.

Apparently, he had been watching television for a while because there were five empty beer cans on the coffee table. The room smelled like cigar smoke.

He guzzled some beer, then belched. He made no effort to control the belch.

She asked him if he had worked that day.

He told her, no, he had taken the day off.

She asked him when he had planned to return her calls.

He said he was planning to call her after the game. He kept glancing at the television set.

Why was he treating her that way? she wondered. She told him she had heard the news about his application to the Bureau.

He told her it didn't make any difference. It was all "water under the bridge," he said.

She could tell he had been drinking a lot. "We both know how badly you wanted in. You want to talk about it?"

"I've already moved beyond that."

She told him it was just as well, and she explained that she had been relieved from the investigation she had gone to Fort Hood for. She said she was considering alternative plans herself—something that would let her settle down more and enjoy life. While she tried to explain what had happened at Fort Hood, she became irritated that he seemed so interested in the television. A couple of times he even watched the game for several seconds. She finally said, "Usually when one is having a conversation, one expects the other party to throw in a word or two."

He told her, "I didn't know we were having a conversation. I thought I was listening to you talk about your work."

The comment stung. "I'm sorry if I'm such an inconvenience to you."

Staring at her, he scratched his beard. "I've been

thinking," he told her. He looked at her. His eyes were glazed.

"Oh?"

He told her, "I'm not getting any younger." He was still fiddling with his beard. He began plucking at the hairs. "The other day I found a gray hair in my beard."

God forbid, she thought and gave him a cold smile.

He got up and went to the sliding glass door. His back was to her. "Now that this thing with the Bureau has passed," he said, "I realize I need to make some changes in my life." He turned to her, pushed back his thick dark hair, and told her, "I need to get back on track with my profession. I've decided I need to put my personal life aside for a while. Maybe I need a transfer to another office. I'm thinking about transferring to the East Coast."

She felt herself plummeting. She wanted to burst into tears. "What are you talking about?"

"I think you know."

She picked up her coat and stood. "I think I better go," she said. Don't cry, she told herself.

"I have a few things at your place. Can I stop by sometime to pick them up?"

She could feel him following her to the door. She turned to him. "You used me," she told him.

He said, "Really, I knew you'd try something like this. I knew it all along. No, if you want to know the truth, I think it's the other way around. I think you used me."

"Used you?"

"Did you hear yourself just a few moments ago?"

She didn't say anything, only stared at him. What was he talking about?

"You've given your entire life to the FBI, and then suddenly you woke up one day and realized life had passed you by. You latched on to me and promised me all kinds of things to try to bribe me into a relationship with you. Well, as far as I'm concerned, you used me."

"This is crazy. I never promised you anything. I thought we had a relationship even before you asked for help getting into the Bureau. I knew I should have said no right then and there—when you first asked for help."

Calmly, he told her, "I see we're locked in a difference of opinion."

She left his apartment without saying another word. Only when she got in her car and was driving away from his apartment did she realize she was crying. What was happening to her world? she wondered. She had lost everything. Even her daughter was in danger of falling out of reach. She tried to call home. The line was busy.

At home she confronted Wendy about being on the phone all the time she had been gone.

Wendy denied it.

"Don't lie to me!" The moment she said it, she regretted it. Don't take it out on her, Kathryn warned herself. Before she exploded, Kathryn went to her bedroom and climbed into a hot shower. With the steamy water beating against her, she tried to calm herself. She was trembling. Maybe she needed a bigger change than she had realized, she told herself. Maybe she needed a new life, a new city.

She got out of the shower, dried off, and wrapped in a towel, went out to the kitchen, where she opened the refrigerator. She was hungry. There was nothing in the refrigerator except three diet Cokes. In the freezer was a package of frozen hot dogs and a package of frozen buns. That was it.

With a knife she pried one of the hot dogs loose, put it on a plate with a paper towel over it, and put the plate in the microwave. While she waited for the hot dog to cook, she popped the top on a diet Coke. She listened to her telephone messages.

There was a message from her housekeeper, Marie. She had accidentally knocked over the gazelle in the living room. "One of the horns broke off," Marie explained. "I glued it back on, and you can barely tell where it broke, but I want to pay for the damage. I'm very sorry. Let me know how much it will cost to replace it." There was a call from the cleaners. Kathryn had a suit coat, two pairs of slacks, and four blouses that needed to be picked up. There was a call from David. He wanted to know what had happened. Was everything all right? he asked. His voice sounded worried. He left his number at the motel.

She didn't feel like talking to him. She let the messages erase, including David's number.

She ate her hot dog without bothering to cook a bun.

Wendy appeared. She asked if everything was all right. "I could tell you had been crying."

Kathryn smiled at her. "That's nice of you to be concerned," she said. "Get ready, and we'll go out and do something together."

They caught an afternoon movie. It was rated "R," so Kathryn made Wendy close her eyes during the sex scenes.

Afterward, they stopped at a pretzel shop and bought giant pretzels and drinks. They walked the mall. Wendy talked nonstop. She talked about music, about clothes, and about boys. She mentioned Kendall and T.J. T.J. was on the football team. While at the games, he liked to pick up the girls and carry them on his shoulders.

Kathryn asked what had happened to Doug.

Wendy acted like she had never heard of a Doug.

Kathryn smiled to herself. At every age relationships passed too quickly.

Wendy pushed back her hair, took Kathryn by the hand, and pulled her into a store, where she took her to a stack of jeans. She drew a pair of Calvin Kleins out of the stack and held them up. "Would you buy these for me, Mom?" she asked.

Kathryn looked at the price. "I'm not paying sixty dollars for a pair of jeans."

"Crystal's mother bought her a pair."

"I'm not Crystal's mother."

Wendy settled for a new CD.

She had always been good that way. She wasn't spoiled, at least Kathryn hoped not.

Later they had dinner at a busy Mexican restaurant. A Mexican woman wearing a colorful blouse and dress stopped at the table. A man carrying a guitar followed. He began to play. She sang.

Wendy slumped in her chair, embarrassed.

It was a good evening together. Kathryn completely forgot about the Robles investigation—until she was paying the check and happened to glance at Wendy, who was gazing into space, alone in a world of her own. For an instant Kathryn thought about the photograph of Angela Robles and her family. In the photo Angela had been staring into space, too.

15

Colonel Lazarus stopped mumbling to himself long enough to pour himself a drink from a near-empty bottle of scotch. "What if it were my granddaughter?" he asked himself, and drank from a dirty glass. "She's seven, for God's sake."

His quarters were simply furnished. There was a bed, a footlocker, and a desk, which is where he was sitting. He never had been accustomed to luxury, had lived out of a duffel bag most of his adult life. In the distant past he had even thought that he was destined for luxury, though those days were gone.

He opened his black leather wallet, which was on the desk in front of him. The wallet was so worn that the photo insert had torn loose. The stack of photographs, each in a plastic holder, lay unattached in the wallet. He started flipping photographs, looking at his grandchildren. There were six of them total—five boys and one girl. One pretty girl with long dark hair. She was his favorite. Terry. Seven.

He took a deep breath, downed the glass of scotch, and opened the bottom drawer of his desk. There sat a small box, its flaps folded in. The sight of the box made him think about his former wife, she had left him many years before, but he still loved her. Always would.

The thought of Vikki was so compelling that he removed the box from the desk, took a flashlight from another drawer, and went out into the night. There was a quarter moon out, enough to give some light to the night, though a haze was upon the earth.

At the back of the building that housed his quarters, he stopped where the drain ran down from the gutter to the ground. It had been raining off and on the past couple of days, and the ground near the drain was soft.

Lazarus had suddenly decided he didn't want anything more to do with Operation Exodus-V. With his bare hands he began to dig in the soft earth, clawing earth like an animal. His nose itched. He scratched it. He could feel the dirt he had left on his nose, so he tried to wipe it away. He dug and dug, then opened the box flaps and removed the lock of Angela's hair, wrapped in plastic. In the moonlight he could see the distinct shape of a curl. He hurriedly dropped the plastic bag in the hole he had dug, but the grave was too shallow.

He went back inside the building and began rummaging through drawers. He found what he was looking for—a spoon. At the same time he noticed he had left dirty prints on papers, notes, and the crude furniture of the office.

He went outside, leaving the door open, and around to the back of the building. There he got on his knees, removed the plastic bag from its shallow grave, and began to dig with the spoon.

"Frank?"

He looked around, didn't see anyone, but knew someone had called.

"Are you out here?"

In his panic Lazarus put the plastic bag back in the box, pushed the flaps down, and carried the box around to the office, where he nearly ran into Thaddeus Burch.

"What's happened to you?" Burch asked.

Colonel Lazarus looked at himself. In a state of confusion he scratched his thick gray hair. "I had some business to take care of," he said. At the same time one of the flaps from the box rose, then another, and another. He realized he hadn't folded them together correctly, and the next thing he knew, he was staring at the lock of Angela's hair.

"What are you doing with that?" Burch asked.

"This?" He held up the box. His confusion grew. "Oh, this." While holding the box, he tried to close its flaps. He couldn't coordinate his hands. "It's not exactly the kind of thing you want to leave sitting around. I had to go out, and so I took it with me." He smiled at himself. "Yes, I took it with me. What are you doing up?"

His eyes on the box, Burch said, "We need to talk."

"Come in. I'll pour you a drink."

They went into the building, where Lazarus sat at his desk. He poured himself another scotch. There was very little scotch left in the bottle. "There's a glass in the bathroom. Rinse it out and bring it here."

"I don't care for a drink."

"Nonsense." Lazarus held up the near-empty bottle. "I have a whole case. Get your glass, General, and join me."

Burch got a glass.

Lazarus poured the rest of the scotch into Burch's rinsed glass. Then he raised his own glass. "To the mission."

Their glasses touched. Burch said, "I hope you mean that."

The officers drank together.

"Of course, I mean it," Lazarus said. "Sit down." He motioned to the bed.

Burch sat down while Lazarus remained at the desk.

"So what has you up at this hour of the night?" Colonel Lazarus removed a soiled handkerchief from his back pocket and began to wipe his hands with it.

"I'm concerned about you."

"My dear general, you have no reason to be concerned about me." He noticed his black-rimmed nails and began to clean them by running the middle nail of his right hand under the nails of his left hand. He saw his fingers were trembling.

"I'm concerned that you might not be able to perform the duties of this operation."

"Drink."

Burch took a drink, watching Lazarus at the same time.

Lazarus was nervous. He said, "Let me remind you that I'm a colonel in the United States Army. I know how to follow orders." He switched hands and began to clean the nails of his right hand with the middle nail of his left hand. "I hardly think it's appropriate for anyone to be questioning my integrity." He looked down at the dirt on his knees and tried to brush it off. His head was reeling from the scotch. He was having trouble concentrating. The flaps of the box had opened again. He tried to pour himself another drink, only to discover the bottle was empty.

Calmly Burch said, "I know you're a colonel in the United States Army—"

Lazarus smiled.

"—but executing the plan is my responsibility. Remember, I'm the one who stuck his neck on the line by volunteering to take charge. If I think there's a problem, I'll make sure I protect the people who have put their trust in me. Right now, I'm not sure you have the stomach to go through with it."

"It's the girl's burns," he muttered. "I'm afraid they're getting infected."

"That's the problem?"

He tried to make some sense of the thoughts spinning inside his head. He gave a shudder when he looked at the box. The damned flaps wouldn't stay down! He began fidgeting with the flaps. "Yes, sir, that's the problem. It makes me sick every time Kearnes changes the dressings."

Burch rose from the bed and closed the flaps of the

box, interconnecting them so they didn't rise again. "We didn't cause those burns," he said calmly. "It's not like we're responsible."

"But, sir, even on the battlefield, we treat prisoners of war better than that."

"Come on, Frank, on the battlefield, we throw prisoners out of helicopters for not talking. We bomb villages and cities that contain children, and we don't even think that a lot of those injured children cling to life for days, even weeks, before dying. We rape, murder, and rob."

"This is the United States of America." Frank noticed his fingernails were still dirty. He began to rummage in his pockets. He found a pair of fingernail clippers. He clipped at his nails. "That makes things different," he said.

"I agree, what's happened to the girl is awful, but what are we going to do? If we dig up a doctor, then we're going to have to kill the doctor because the doctor's going to go back and report what he saw here. We can't have any witnesses."

"They're all going to die anyway. What difference does it make?"

"Exactly, which is why the girl doesn't make any difference."

Fingernail clippings shot here and there as he resumed his clipping. "I don't want her to suffer."

"We can't risk helping her. The FBI's already managed to dig up a few things we hadn't counted on—like the diary."

"Let me ask you a question," Colonel Lazarus said. He stopped trimming his nails. "Why do we have to keep her alive at this point?" He tried to stand in order to brush the clippings off his lap, but he was unsteady and fell back into his chair.

Burch said, "That's entirely up to you. If you want to put her out of her misery, then go ahead."

"I don't want her to suffer."

"Fine. Put her out of her misery. Now, let me ask you one question."

Colonel Lazarus waited.

"Are you up to this, Frank? Are you really up to this?"

Lazarus laughed. "If you're asking if I'm up to this whole damned thing blowing up in our faces," he said, "yes, I am. One thing after another is going wrong, but I'm up to it." He laughed loudly.

"I don't find it funny."

Lazarus smiled. "You're still worried she wrote something about you in the diary, aren't you?"

"She walked right up to the car and looked at me. If she put a description in the diary, her description might eventually be enough to establish that I was here."

Lazarus put away the fingernail clippers. With the dirty handkerchief he blew his nose. He breathed deeply afterward. "The sooner she's dead, the better I'll feel." Again, he stopped talking long enough to pour himself a drink, only to discover a second time that the bottle was empty. He put the bottle down. "As for the suffering, I don't agree with that. I don't care what you say."

A rare smile came onto Burch's face, as if he had suddenly found something they agreed upon. "Then kill her. No one's going to care. The FBI's going to be looking for that anyway. I mean, we've dug around in the gutters, jails, and prisons to bring the right scapegoats together, to make it look like a militia has formed and committed an act of domestic terrorism. We've stirred up the local community for the past couple of months, terrorizing Mexican-Americans. What difference is the dead body of our hostage going to make? Everyone's going to conclude that it's all a part of the terrorists' plan anyway. Kill her."

Lazarus stirred sluggishly and tried to get out of his chair, but he still couldn't get up. He wanted to tell

Burch to leave so he could fall into bed, but Burch
seemed in no hurry to leave. Colonel Lazarus put his
hands behind his head and raised his face toward the
ceiling, but that made the room spin more, so he
dropped his chin.

"We both know that sometimes to have progress,
we must have sacrifice," Burch said. "She'll be part
of the sacrifice."

Lazarus wondered what they had been talking about
to begin with.

"All you have to remember is that this operation
will ultimately save countless lives." He stopped
speaking, and stared at Lazarus. "Are you all right?"
He paused and waited with an inquiring expression.

Lazarus waved a hand to indicate he was fine.

"Like I said, I'm concerned about you."

"Well, tonight the only thing I'm going to do is get
some sleep. Now, if you'll please finish what you're
saying and leave, I'll get a good night's sleep." He
needed to be alone.

Burch stood. "Just don't forget that I have the authority to relieve you from this operation."

"I remember."

"Please do. This is the United States Army. We
can't afford weakness and fear." Burch smiled and
grew more calm. "Listen, Frank, we both know this
operation is going to be a small price to pay in order
to save millions of lives. When a hundred fifty thousand people die from one terrorist attack, the whole
country is going to run to the government and demand
protection. They'll demand we protect ourselves from
the weapons of the future—germs. We'll be saving
cities like Los Angeles and Manhattan—millions of
people—because the American people will finally
allow us to do what they've been so squeamish about
up until now. In a few days the entire world will be
enraged, and the American people will beat down our
door to pour money and authority back into a strong

national defense. Then they'll make you a general, which is what you should have been a long time ago."

Lazarus smiled. He felt better. "I need some sleep."

Burch nodded. "Are you all right?"

"Yes. Please turn off the light on your way out."

Burch did so, leaving Lazarus in darkness.

It took a few moments for his eyes to adjust to the cold white light from the moon, which barely illuminated the room. He barely had enough balance and energy to fall forward into his bed. His face was positioned at such an angle that he could see the box on the desk. What if someone were to search his quarters and find the hair? he wondered. He would be ruined. He wished there was a blind on the window. He thought about draping a blanket over it, but was too drunk to get up. He tried to undress, to get out of his dirty clothes. He couldn't even roll over. All he could do was fumble with the buttons of his shirt by running his hands between his chest and the bed. He couldn't get the buttons unfastened, so he jerked at the cloth, trying to tear off the shirt.

Helpless, he drifted into a strange sleep, where he found himself standing in the middle of a field of tulips, fiery red and pink and orange ones. The night sky was mottled with clouds, through which a full moon shone.

He wasn't sure what he was doing in the field. It seemed he was trying to find his way home. The path he chose was rough. He looked down to discover he was on an old railroad track. The flowers of the field had grown up around the rails and ties.

Suddenly, a bright yellow light hit him, flooded him. The ground shook, and he could hear a huge engine. A locomotive headed straight toward him, barreling down on him from the field of flowers. He tried to get off the track, but one of his feet got caught on something. He looked down. The petals of a tulip had sprouted a child's fingers, which held his pant legs. The huge horn of the train blared.

Next thing he knew, he was awake, groveling on the floor near the door of his room. The floor was vibrating. He could hear an engine.

Over him, his hand on the light switch, stood Burch. "What's wrong, Frank?" he asked.

Lazarus was too terrified to speak. Then he said the only words that came to mind. "I had to go to the bathroom, and couldn't find the door."

Burch said, "The truck is here." He smiled. "Exodus-Five is here."

Frank could hear the truck rumbling. Its horn blared.

"They need us to unload."

Lazarus got to his feet. He was wearing only his skivvies. He couldn't remember undressing. Had someone undressed him? Why couldn't he remember? His head reeled from the effects of the scotch.

In his skivvies he followed Burch out into the early morning that was only beginning to get light. On the bed of a diesel truck whose engine rumbled were many stainless-steel canisters that stood upright. They looked like hospital oxygen tanks. There were red "Flammable" signs on the sides and back of the truck. A civilian holding a clipboard said, "I have a delivery for a tank of oxygen at this address." He glanced at the clipboard. "Are you Colonel Lazarus? He's supposed to sign for it."

Colonel Lazarus signed the sheet on the clipboard.

The civilian unloaded a canister that had a green tag attached to it. Though he struggled with the canister, nobody helped him. He put up the truck's tailgate, got in the truck, and drove away.

Afterward, Colonel Lazarus wished he hadn't signed for the tank. Why had he done it? They would trace the Exodus-V to him. Before he could say anything, Burch held out the box.

Colonel Lazarus didn't want to touch the box.

Burch repeated what he had said the night before: "Are you sure you're up to this, Frank?"

In a feeble gesture Lazarus pointed over his shoulder with his thumb. "Take it inside, and someone'll get it ready to send." He didn't want any part of it.

Burch smiled calmly. "Good enough."

16

Kathryn woke up determined not to be shoved aside, so determined that she barely waited until Wendy had left for school before going in search of Angela Robles's adoption records. The records were in Dallas, she knew, and finding them would give her something to do. She also knew that Grant had told her to take a couple of days off, but she didn't care. Something drove her forward, despite the risk to her own career. What? She didn't know, only knew that had it been Wendy instead of Angela, Kathryn would have wanted someone like herself digging around.

She started at the International Child Placing Services, Inc., only to discover Angela's records didn't exist in the agency's files. Blair Gilman, the social worker who ran the agency, explained that ICPS records only went back to 1986. She said, "You must be thinking of the records for an agency called Intercountry Adoption Services. They used to be at this address, but they went out of business." She chewed gum while she spoke. "We had no affiliation with them. I'm not sure what happened to their records, though I can only imagine."

Was there something wrong with the previous agency? Kathryn wanted to know, noting the sarcasm in Blair's voice.

"They were in deep doo-doo with the state's Human Resources division when they closed." Blair chewed. "There's never been much regulation in this business, and when there's been regulation, there's never been much enforcement, but the Intercountry agency was the exception." The gum popped in her mouth. She smiled. "The state was hot on their trail at the end." Her eyebrows raised. "Is there some kind of new investigation going on?"

Why did she ask that?

Blair shrugged. "It wasn't but a few months ago someone else was looking for the Intercountry agency. Some woman. It's just odd that two people would be looking for the same agency after all these years."

"What did the woman want? Did she say?"

"Only that she was searching for records about an adopted child. I told her all records would be sealed by the court anyway, but she was persistent with her questions."

"Do you remember what she looked like?" Kathryn asked, taking an interest.

"It was a telephone call," Blair said.

"Do you remember a name, an accent, anything?"

Chewing her gum, Blair flipped pages of her desk calendar. She stopped at July 24, where there was a name written in ink. "Angela Robles," she mumbled, surprised. "The same records you're looking for. I didn't write down the name of the woman who called, but I did happen to scribble out the name on the records she was after."

"Are you sure about the name?" Kathryn asked, her heart racing. Why would someone be looking for Angela's records?

Blair turned the calendar so Kathryn could see it. Without a doubt Angela's name was on the calendar. It was on a page that included a lot of doodlings. "It's a nervous habit of mine," she said, smiling at the doodlings.

"Is there anything at all you can tell me about the caller?" Kathryn asked. "Think hard."

Blair popped her gum again. "To tell you the truth,

I don't remember the details of the conversation at
all. I didn't even remember the name of the person
she was searching for until right now when I looked.
All I know is it was a woman asking questions about
some adoption records, and she mentioned Intercountry Adoption Services. I told her the same thing I've
told you. I told her that as far as I knew, Intercountry
had gone out of business, and I doubted their records
even existed any longer. I told her she'd probably have
to go to the courts to get them."

"And has anyone else called?"

"No, that's why I asked if there was an investigation
or something. It's odd that the past several months is
the first time anyone's ever called—except right after
the agency closed back in the late eighties. There was
about a year or so that people contacted us trying to
find out what had happened to the old agency. But
it's been at least six or seven years since anyone's
made any inquiry whatsoever."

The information Blair Gilman had provided, what
little there was, supported Kathryn's theory that someone really had targeted Angela well in advance of the
kidnapping. It didn't make sense, but someone definitely had been searching for information about her.
Why? Who would have even known that Angela was
adopted? It couldn't have been more than a handful
of people, including the biological parents.

Outside, using her portable phone, Kathryn began
making inquiries about the Intercountry agency. Sure
enough, in 1986, the Texas Department of Human Resources had conducted an investigation into the operation of the Intercountry Adoption Services agency, or
IAS, as it was listed on record. The Austin office re-
ferred her call to a social worker in Fort Worth,
Duane Taylor, who had handled the case when it had
been active. Instead of calling him, Kathryn stopped
by his office.

Despite the effort that it took, Taylor, a husky red-haired man in his late thirties, slowly got up from his desk, and using two aluminum canes, walked on unsteady legs around his desk and shook her hand. He had a firm shake. His muscles bulged in the long-sleeved shirt he wore. On unsteady legs, using the canes, he returned to his seat, and literally collapsed into it. Multiple sclerosis, she thought. She had seen it before. An ugly disease.

Yes, he remembered the IAS investigation, he said. It had been his first investigation with the department, he explained, though he had never understood why he had ended up with such a sophisticated case. He said it started when a family complained to the Department of Human Resources. He smiled frequently, not as if he found anything humorous in the subject matter, but as if he enjoyed life and wanted to convey to others how much he enjoyed it. The family had hired a private investigator, he went on to say, who tried to persuade them that their baby might not have died shortly after its birth. "At first I thought it was a matter of the private investigator trying to drain the family of some money," Duane said, shaking his head. "It happens all the time with private investigators and lawyers." He told how the investigator had convinced the family that their well baby had been substituted for a deceased child, and the well baby had been placed in a black-market adoption ring. "It was two or three years after the fact," he explained, "which made it impossible to establish anything for sure. The most I could determine was little more than an old rumor that had circulated at the Dallas Medical Center labor and delivery unit."

Kathryn held up her hand. "May I ask a question, Mr. Taylor?"

"Duane, please."

"Duane, all of this is happening around 1986, right?"

He nodded.

"And if these people were complaining about something that had happened two to three years before that, it would make the child in question—if he or she was still alive—between twelve and thirteen years of age, right?"

"Yes."

She tried to contain her excitement. There were too many coincidences. The child would be close to the same age as Angela. "Was the family you're talking about by any chance Hispanic?" she asked.

"Oh, no. The farthest thing from it."

It didn't necessarily mean anything, she told herself. Think it through.

"The thing I remember best," he added, "was that the people who ended up with the child in question had insisted that it be what we call a 'blue chip baby.' "

"I've heard of a blue chip baby. Isn't it—"

Before she could say, he told her, "Healthy white male. White males in perfect health are still worth a fortune on the adoption market. People have this myth about what constitutes a superior child, and they're willing to pay big bucks to support the myth." It was the first time he didn't smile. His face had a cold expression on it, as if the myth somehow bothered him. "I guarantee you, the adopting family in this case was willing to do and give anything to keep things quiet about the child it had."

"Why didn't someone do a blood test to determine the biological parents?" she asked.

He shook his head. "The judge wouldn't allow it. He wouldn't unseal the adoption records—it's next to impossible to get that to happen anyway—and there wasn't enough evidence to support that an intermediary had been involved in the adoption process. That's illegal in Texas, you know. In other words, if one of the nurses in the labor and delivery department at the Dallas Medical Center had somehow become involved in the process, that person would have been classified as an intermediary, and that would have been a violation of law. It would be close to establishing a black market for babies." He was smiling again. "Naturally, the family who already had the child in question got wind of what was going on, and began to fight even before we could get our case going."

Again she interrupted him. "I thought the judge wouldn't open the sealed records," she said. "How did the family who had the adopted child even know about your investigation?"

With a hand he wiped some invisible dust off his immaculate desk. He kept everything in his office neat and orderly. Smiling, he said, "Believe it or not, one of the families I interviewed contacted them. It was a mess when it happened. Talk about embarrassing." Again, with much effort, he got to his feet, and canes in hand, he walked slowly to the door, swaying back and forth with each step. She didn't know how he kept from falling, though she could see his arm muscles flex as he walked. His arms obviously gave him balance. At the door he said, "Let me see if my administrative assistant can dig up the case. I assume this is part of an official investigation?"

"Of course."

He left the office.

She didn't know why he didn't simply call his administrative assistant on the telephone, though he seemed like a man with a lot of pride. Perhaps his going for the case personally was his way of showing his independence, a testimony that he wasn't going to let the disease in his body get the best of him.

He returned with a manila folder shoved under his arm. As he shifted his weight to close the door, a horrifying thing happened. He collapsed, his head hitting the edge of his desk. She jumped to help, but it was too late.

She knew he had been hurt in the fall, though he

immediately told her he was all right. His face was dark red, deeper red than his hair. She couldn't tell if it was from pain, embarrassment, or anger. She was going to help pick him up, but he asked her if she could bring her chair near him.

She pushed her chair to him. Using it as a prop, he pulled himself to a sitting position. She tried to ignore him, collecting the papers that had been strewn from the file folder. She saw him crawl with his upper body onto the seat of the chair. His chin in the seat of the chair, he asked her if she could steady the chair. She held the back firmly. He pulled himself into a sitting position in the chair. She collected his canes on the floor and handed them to him. He said thank you. Again, with much effort, he got to his feet. On unsteady legs he used the canes to get back to his chair, where he collapsed. He seemed exhausted. When she pushed the file folder across the desk, he flipped it open. One hand turned pages, the other rubbed his head.

She asked if he was sure he was all right. She knew his head had hit the desk firmly.

He said he was fine. He told her, "I have two daughters, one five and the other three. I'm afraid to hold them for fear of dropping one of them or falling on one. Not being able to hold my own daughters is a lot more painful." He smiled. "Here it is," he said, holding up a typewritten document. "As I was telling you, I was trying to collect enough evidence to establish probable cause to open the sealed adoption papers on the baby in question. If I could have done that, I could have gotten a court order for a blood test. It would have established the baby's identity—at least it would have established whether the parents who claimed to be his biological parents, Laura and Kirk Morley, were indeed who they said they were." He waved the document in his hand. "So I got this statement from a family that had been in orientation with the"—he glanced at the paper—"DiUlios, and—"

"Hold on a minute," she said. "What was that name?"

"The DiUlios." He spelled it.

She could feel her heart in her throat. That was the name the Robleses had mentioned. She wrote down the name.

"The statement confirmed the DiUlios' desperation to have a healthy white male baby. It suggested that money had been paid under the table in order to secure such a child. It was the first time that my investigation was beginning to produce some information that was genuinely troubling."

"Who made the statement against the DiUlios?"

He glanced at his file again. "Robles," he said, and he spelled the name. "Tony and Mary Belle."

Be calm. "What happened once you got a statement from the Robleses?"

He laughed. "They gave me a statement, then they got to feeling guilty about it, so they contacted the DiUlios and told them they had given me a statement. Naturally, the next thing I knew, the DiUlios had about five attorneys breathing down my neck. They went after the judge in the case and caused a real stir. He forbade us to continue our investigation. We had nothing criminal or substantive to go on, so we complied with the order."

Kathryn didn't say anything. She watched to see the expression on his face. It didn't change. He didn't seem to be angry.

"I guess I could see his point," he said, sighing. "It was a no-win situation. I mean, even if it did turn out that the babies had been switched, the DiUlios had had the child for almost three years. Imagine the trauma of taking the child away from the only home he had known." He shrugged. "I guess I can't blame the Robleses either. I talked to them and told them they shouldn't have gone to the DiUlios without checking with me first, but they felt they had something in common with the DiUlios, having gone through the same process and everything. They said they wouldn't want someone trying to take away their child unless they knew about it and had a fair chance to fight."

Though he explained he couldn't make her copies of his investigation without a court order, he did allow her to copy notes from it. She was especially interested in the couple who claimed to be the biological parents of the adopted baby. She copied their names, social security numbers, and last-known address.

Before she left, she told him about her meeting with Blair Gilman of International Child Placing Services. "She seemed to indicate that had IAS not closed on its own," she said, "the state would have shut it down."

Smiling, he told her, "I've never seen such poor record-keeping practices. Yes, we would have closed them down eventually, but it was better the way it turned out. There were missing records, forged documents, all kinds of things. But again the judge in the case was right. Why drag all these families and children through the mud? The best option was to let IAS close on its own and let things blow over."

She gave him Angela Robles's name and birth date, and asked him what kind of records they might have on file about her.

To her relief, he didn't try to get up. He used his telephone to make an inquiry.

They chatted about the November weather while he waited for a call back.

The telephone rang. He talked for a couple of minutes, wrote something on a pad of paper, and then put down the telephone receiver. He said, "Unfortunately, this is one of those cases in which we have incomplete records. We don't have her file here.

You'll probably have to get a court order and see if you can open the sealed one."

The news came as a disappointment, but she was still thrilled about what she had learned. She stood.

"There is one thing that might interest you," he added. He explained that his agency kept a log of any inquiries made about specific adoptees and birth parents. He said someone had made an inquiry about Angela Robles on July 24. "I don't have a name of who it might have been, but we do keep a log of inquiries, and the records person told me about this one. I thought you'd want to know."

So it was true. Someone had searched at length for information about Angela. Albert DiUlio had seen Mary Belle in recent months. Had he been searching?

17

Angela came to filled with the sensation that the world was spinning, and she was having difficulty keeping on it. The voices in the distance became clearer. The spinning settled. She realized the voices were in the same room with her, a poorly lighted room cluttered with metal lockers and bunks without mattresses. The room looked like a storage area. She was in one of the bunks, a lower one, and though she lay on a mattress, the bunk above her had none. Her right arm throbbed with pain. She tried to move the fingers of the hand, but she couldn't seem to find them.

She peered through the wire mesh in the upper bunk, at the ceiling, an eggshell color, which was cracked and peeling. It sagged in one place. Where the ceiling sagged, about ready to collapse, there were dried water stains. Spiderwebs, dead bugs, and dust gave the room a haunted look.

She heard a hollow click. In the corner of the room, near the door, sat Corporal Klock, his chair balanced on its two rear legs, and Private Kearnes. Klock was cleaning his handgun. Kearnes was watching. His teeth were chewing on his mustache hairs.

She tried to raise her head from the pillow so she could look down at her right hand. The hand and arm were bandaged. The pain was the worst pain she had ever experienced. She began to weep.

Kearnes glanced at her. He combed his red mustache, using a black comb. Smiling, he said, "She's quite a sport, isn't she? Imagine getting hurt and still sticking with the operation."

Klock said, "Remember, we're not supposed to discuss anything about the assignment." He pulled an oiled rag through the barrel of his pistol. "I take it that means we're not supposed to discuss the hostage."

"I was just making small talk," Kearnes said, smiling. "I didn't mean anything by it."

"I think it's better if we talked about something else," Klock told him. With a slight move of his thumb, he hit a button that caused the extended barrel of his weapon to fly into place. Using his thumb, he lowered the weapon's hammer, then he inserted an ammo clip. Putting the weapon in his side holster, he said, "You look rather old to be a private."

Kearnes laughed. He said, "I used to be a sergeant, but I got busted."

Klock told him, "I thought something was wrong. Not only does your age tell the truth, but you seem like you have your act together too much to be a private."

Kearnes lit a cigarette. He put away his lighter. He had a smile of satisfaction on his face, almost a smile of arrogance.

Angela wondered how they could be so content when she was hurting so badly.

"What'd you get busted for?" Klock asked.

"A fight."

"Tough break. How long you been in?"

"Seven years."

"You going to stay?"

Kearnes shrugged. "Maybe. It depends if I get my rank back."

"What's your MOS, anyway?"

"What?"

"Your MOS."

"What's an MOS?"

Klock stared at him. "Your job assignment. The one you were trained for. What do you do?"

"Oh, that." He smiled and took a puff of his cigarette. "I'm a clerk-typist. Say, I better get Captain Gillespie. He told us to get him as soon as the hostage woke up." He pointed at Angela.

Kearnes opened the door and stepped into the cold daylight. He pulled the door shut behind him.

Klock fell forward and stood. He straightened the MP band that hung from his left shoulder. He walked to her bunk and looked at her. "Can I get you anything?" he asked.

Though he was big and burly, he looked young. Old enough to shave, but young.

"They say you banged your hand and foot up when you fell. You all right?"

She raised her head the best she could. Her right foot was still bandaged. She had forgotten about it. It didn't hurt as much as her arm did. Her head dropped. She couldn't hold it up. Her arm was throbbing with pain.

"That is something—you going ahead with the assignment even though you got hurt. I know we're not supposed to talk to each other, but I just want you to know how much I admire you."

He went back to his chair, unbuttoned his left breast pocket, and removed some cards. He began to look through them. Now and then he would turn a card over and look at its back. When he did that, she could see the picture in front. "Baseball cards," he told her, holding them up. "I've been collecting them since high school. Would you believe I have over thirty thousand of them now. Some of them are worth pretty good money. I have several that are worth over two hundred dollars apiece."

There were voices outside.

Klock put away his cards and buttoned his shirt pocket.

At the same time the door opened, letting in the cold daylight, Klock jumped to attention. He saluted Captain Gillespie. Private Kearnes followed.

Captain Gillespie, who was carrying a folded towel in his left hand, returned the salute. "At ease," Gillespie said.

Klock visibly relaxed.

"How you doing, Corporal?" Gillespie went to Angela's bed.

"Fine, sir," Klock said, behind him.

On the bed beside Angela, Gillespie unfolded the towel. Inside was a syringe and alcohol swab. He said, "Miss Robles, we're going to give you something for your pain. This will help you to relax." He pulled back her bedcovers. To Kearnes and Klock, he said, "Give me a hand so we can roll her up on her side, and I can give her this in the hip."

Angela was pulled onto her right arm and she gave out a scream.

"Not that hip, the other one!" Gillespie laughed loudly. It was an obnoxious, unnatural laugh.

They lifted her onto the other hip. She thought she was going to pass out from the pain. She could feel the cold air on her exposed butt. Then she could feel Gillespie's cold hands touching her, followed by an icy alcohol swab. Just about the time she could smell the alcohol, she felt the jab of the needle. The needle penetrated deep into her butt.

Before she realized what was happening, she had been covered again and was listening to Gillespie, Klock, and Kearnes talk. They were standing by the door, and every now and then Gillespie let out a loud laugh. He liked to laugh. He liked others to hear him laugh. His hair was long, and he had to keep pushing it back from his eyes. Too long for the military, Angela thought. She had never seen an officer with such long hair. And a goatee? He seemed to enjoy talking to the enlisted men. They looked up to him. He liked that. She could tell. His dark eyes sparkled.

Only then did she realize her arm was no longer hurting.

Gillespie was laughing again. He said, "The little bastards always start kissing up when it's time for a promotion." He pushed his hair back and laughed loudly. "I play it for all it's worth," he told Klock and Kearnes. "They want to kiss up, I let them kiss." He laughed. "You might as well enjoy it." He grew serious. He said, "Private Kearnes told me he was talking about our hostage, and you ordered him not to do that."

Klock glanced at Kearnes, who said, "I thought I might as well tell on myself before you did it for me."

Gillespie laughed loudly. He said, "Smart move, Kearnes, and that was good work, Klock. This mission depends upon our ability to stick together, and I'm glad Private Kearnes went ahead and told me what had happened, because had I heard it elsewhere first, I would have lowered the boom on him. And I'm glad you warned him about discussing the operation. I have my eyes on you, Klock. I can tell you're someone who's going to be going places."

Klock came to attention. He saluted. "Thank you, sir."

Gillespie returned the salute. "Keep an eye on the prisoner, Corporal. I'll send Private Kearnes back occasionally to check on you. We want to keep her comfortable. If she's in pain, let him know, and I'll give her another shot. I have orders to keep her comfortable."

"Yes, sir."

Gillespie and Kearnes left. Klock pushed the door shut. He turned to face her. He asked her, "You feel better?"

She didn't say.

He came to the bunk and knelt beside her. "You

know, I have a younger sister about your age. She's
fifteen. How old are you? Sixteen?"

Why would he say that? she wondered.

"I guess that's how old you have to be to do something like this." He shook his head. "You look
younger, though these days it's hard to tell. Last year
when I was taking classes out at Central Texas College, I dated a girl who was twenty, and if you ran
into her on the street, you'd guess she was fourteen
or fifteen. Just a short petite thing. A knockout in a
bikini." He smiled, then he reddened with
embarrassment.

She watched him without saying anything.

"Actually, I have three sisters, but I get along with
the youngest best." He pulled his chair close to her
bed and sat down. "We were the children my aging
parents didn't want," he said. "My older sisters, Barb
and Karen, were born when my mother was young.
She was only twenty when Barb was born. Twenty-
two when Karen was born. Then she didn't have me
until she was thirty-seven, and she didn't have Marilyn
until she was forty-five." He laughed. "She always tells
the story of going to the doctor for a routine physical,
and the doctor telling her she was pregnant." When
she didn't smile, he studied her. "What about you?
Do you have any brothers or sisters?"

She didn't know why he kept asking her questions.
She knew if she answered him, he would hit her.
That's what they always did when she talked. Was he
trying to test her? Her mouth was dry. She wished she
had something to drink. It had been the same way
when she had been in the hospital after the automobile accident and had awakened. They gave her
painkillers, which always made her mouth dry. Nevertheless, the pain had eased, and a dry mouth was
always better than pain.

He told her, "We can talk, you know. No one said
we can't talk. We just can't talk about the operation."

She mumbled, "Help me."

He smiled. "A little actress to the hilt, huh?"

"Please help me." She could barely hear her own voice. She wondered if he could hear her.

He gave her an odd look, one that told her he was puzzled. "Say, why is it they're giving you all these pain shots if you just banged yourself up?" Then he smiled. "Oh, I get it. The pain shots are simulations. Not real. How about if I elevate that hand some?" He went to one of the metal wall lockers and opened it. Inside were pillows. They had been stuffed, one on top of another. He removed two of them. Feathers flew about in the air. "I'm sorry we don't have any pillowcases here, but at least this'll get your hand elevated a little. I know how it is to skin yourself up. It stings, doesn't it?" Holding her right hand up, he slid the pillow under. "How's that? Like I said, they tell me elevation reduces pain." He noticed that the tape on the bandages had come loose during the process of moving the hand, so he began looking in different lockers.

"I'll find some tape around here somewhere," he said. He found the medical supplies. He began to pull out gauze and tape. "I don't suppose it'll hurt to go ahead and rewrap that thing." He brought out a tube of white cream. Examining the tube, the puzzled look returned to his eyes. "Silvadene," he said. "What the hell is this up here for?" He put the tube back on the shelf, but brought the gauze and tape to the bed.

Using a pocket knife, he cut away the rest of the tape, and began to unravel the gauze bandages.

He dropped the arm at the same time she cried out. In an instant his hand covered her mouth. "Ssshhhhhh."

He and she both stared at the bundle of bandages that had come off in his hand. She began to cry.

He looked like he didn't believe what he saw. He said, "My God, what's happened to you?"

"I got burned." She cried.

"Ssshhhhhh." He hurried to the door and slid the bolt into place. Then he returned to her.

"I got burned," she repeated.

"You need a doctor," he said, looking at her hand. "Why didn't they take you to a doctor?"

She didn't say.

"You have to tell me everything. I'm going to help you. No, don't look." His hand pushed her face away. "Please, don't look." She heard him rattling around in a locker. He returned with the cream and spread it all over her arm and hand. "I've got to get this bandaged back up," he told her. "Someone didn't want me to see this, and I can't let them know I saw." He put the pillow up on her chest so she couldn't see him work, but she could feel him wrapping her arm.

"I knew something was wrong," he told her as he worked. "If that Gillespie's a captain, I'm a general." She raised her head so she could see what he was doing. He moved the pillow to block her view. "And if that Kearnes is in the army, he sure as hell isn't a clerk-typist. A clerk-typist would have known what an MOS is immediately." He asked her, "Who are you?"

"Please help me."

He stopped working. Gently, he moved back her hair so he could see the top of her head. "What happened to your head?" he asked, changing the subject. "Where did you get those scars?"

"An accident," she told him. With her left hand she massaged her forehead. "I was in a car accident."

From his holster, he removed his weapon, pulled out the clip, and looked at the ammunition. He even slid one of the bullets out and held it up. "It looks real," he told her, "but we can't take any chances." He returned the bullet to its clip, replaced the clip, and put away the weapon. "Somehow I've got to get to my barracks. I've got another gun there. My own backup piece. I collect guns too," he said, patting the pocket where the baseball cards were. "I know the ammunition I have for it is real."

"I want my mom and dad," she told him.

"Don't be afraid." He looked afraid himself. "What's your name?"

She told him.

"Where are you from?"

She told him.

"Who are your parents?" Then he was asking questions faster than she could answer them. She got confused. "I'm going to help. Don't worry." He sounded worried. "I'm going to help." He looked around. She thought he was looking for someone to agree with him. He looked at her. "Do you know your telephone number?" He was asking questions again.

She couldn't think of the answers, he was asking questions so quickly.

18

To Kathryn's surprise, Grant not only approved her trip to Galveston, but when she told him what she had discovered about Angela's adoption history, he sent David to meet her at the Houston airport on Wednesday morning. Of course, had it been up to her, she would have just as soon not had David tagging along to Galveston, but she didn't push the point. Perhaps she didn't want to see David because she was embarrassed to face him, embarrassed to have him ask why she had been taken off the main investigation, and why she was following leads that would normally go to a rookie. Perhaps she was still reeling from her experiences with Randy. She didn't know, but she did know she wasn't anxious to see David.

She gave him a cool reception when he greeted her at the Houston airport. He, in turn, must have been more perceptive than she gave him credit for being because he simply shook her hand and asked her what he was supposed to do. Not what she expected. A lot of questions, yes. She had expected that. Act embarrassed for her, yes. Ask her what to do—as if there was no question that she was still in charge—no.

She interpreted that to mean that Grant hadn't told him what had happened, and she was thankful. It made their reunion more comfortable.

In the car he said, "You did something to your hair, didn't you?" That was all he said. He drove.

She busied herself looking over the file that Grant had sent with David. It was from Fort Hood's provost marshal, Colonel Hendrick.

"I like it," he said when she didn't say anything. "It looks good pulled back like that."

She seldom wore it back and didn't know why she had pulled it back on that particular day.

On the interstate to Galveston, she asked him if he had read the file Grant had sent. She was still looking at it.

No, David said, Grant hadn't shared it with him.

She summarized what she had read: There had been a rash of attacks against Mexican-Americans, especially against their possessions and property. "The earliest one was on September first," she told him, "and the last recorded one was on October eighteenth." She glanced over at David. "Colonel Hendrick sends a note saying he thinks the incidents have been stopped by the beefed-up security on the post—the attacks were happening at least once a week, and there hasn't been any new ones since the eighteenth."

David gave a short breath through his nose. "He must have forgotten about Angela, and the attempted shooting of Tony Robles."

She smiled. "What do you make of it all?" she asked.

"That whoever's behind this will be keeping a low profile for a while."

"I don't buy it," she said.

She met his glance.

"No, the attacks were real, but it's almost like they were staged, staged to make everyone think there was anti-Mexican-American sentiment at Fort Hood."

"You mean, a diversion?"

"You've worked bank robbery, you know how that works. Stage a diversion and rob a bank. Yes, that's exactly what I'm thinking."

One of his characteristic smiles came onto his face.

He said, "You're not thinking there's some kind of a government conspiracy, are you?"

"Why would you say that?"

"Tony Robles said the same thing. You have Grant on the hot seat, you know."

"What?"

"He's caught a lot of hell for keeping the Robleses under lock and key."

She smiled. "They're still in a safe house?"

"I understand he moved them clear out of state and won't tell anyone."

"Brennan hasn't had a chance to talk to Major Robles?"

David checked his rearview. "Grant said he wasn't going to override your orders."

That surprised her at first, then she decided Grant would let her take the fall if that side of the investigation blew up in their faces. "So why do you mention this business about a government conspiracy?" Tony Robles had spoken of it, but it seemed farfetched to her.

"Because too many things are happening. Too many leaks. And someone at the NSA wants Tony in the worst way. It's like something's up, and someone's trying to cover some butts." He glanced at her. "What do you think?"

Her only response was "That's what we're heading to Galveston to find out."

His smile melted into a general smugness. "Fair enough," he said, then asked, "Did you get my message? I called your home in Dallas." He glanced at her.

"I got it," she told him. She tried to be pleasant. "That was nice of you to call."

He glanced in his side mirror, then over his left shoulder as he changed lanes. Then he made another check of his rearview. "Let's not make a big deal out of this, but someone's following us."

She glanced in the side mirror. Sure enough, there was a red van following. She reached for the radio microphone.

Glancing at her, he said, "Grant told me to tell you to be careful about electronic communications. He thinks we have a leak."

She let go of the microphone. Her head turned toward him, she kept her eyes on her side mirror. "Change lanes," she told him. "Get to the left lane."

David did what she told him.

"Take it up to about seventy-five. Not enough to seem like we're trying to speed, but enough to pass some of these cars."

The red van behind them changed lanes also and seemed to be pacing itself with their car.

"Grant said until further notice everyone's to assume our communication lines are insecure."

She watched the van, thinking about what Tony had said about electronic surveillance. Had the Bureau's security systems been compromised? she wondered. "Take the next exit, and take it at the last moment. Cut right across and take it."

Next thing she knew, he jerked the wheel, and they were on the exit ramp. The red van shot by.

David laughed.

"Damn it, David, you got off too quickly. I couldn't get a license."

He had one of his subtle smiles on his face, a smile of complacency. "I lost them. Doesn't that count for something?"

He took an indirect route to the tourist district of Galveston, where rose-colored and white oleanders lined the streets. There were many cafés and restaurants.

"There," she said. She pointed at the restaurant called Laura's.

David parked the car, and she and he passed through an open veranda to the stylish restaurant whose plant-filled bar occupied most of the lower floor. The bar was still busy with lunch guests. At the bar Kathryn told a large Mexican woman they were looking for Laura Morley.

"She's busy now," the bartender said abruptly. "Come back after closing, or tomorrow before we open. She doesn't like solicitors during business hours."

Kathryn showed her credentials. She said, "Tell her we're with the FBI, and we don't like to be put off."

It wasn't long before a skinny dark-haired woman came downstairs and stopped at the opposite end of the bar. The bartender had moved to that end, and they exchanged a few words, during the course of which Kathryn could see the bartender motioning her head toward her and David. Though the lights in the bar were subdued, Kathryn could tell that the woman with the short dark hair wore a lot of makeup and looked anorexic beneath her beige silk pants and cream-colored blouse. She approached. "I understand you're looking for me," she said when she got to them.

"Are you Laura Morley?" Kathryn asked.

"Yes, why?"

Kathryn opened her credentials so Laura could see them. "We're with the FBI, and we need to ask you some questions. Is there someplace we can talk?"

"About what?" she asked, visibly confused. "I can't think of any reason you would want to see me. Has someone who has worked for me applied for a government job? Maybe you're doing a background check."

"We want to talk about a complaint you and your husband filed with the Texas Department of Human Services about ten years ago."

"I'm divorced."

"We know. This is about an adoption complaint. Is there someplace we can talk?"

Laura took them to her home, a condominium overlooking the ocean. She opened the sliding glass door to the porch, letting in the sounds of the ocean.

"Can I offer you a drink or a cup of coffee?" she asked.

Kathryn said no; David said he'd like coffee.

The kitchen was divided from the open dining and living room by a bar, so Kathryn could see Laura while she made coffee. The condo was furnished in earth-tone furniture and wicker. It was comfortable and well kept. Apparently, Laura's restaurant did well.

Laura returned. She said, "I suppose my ex told you about the money, and that's why you're here."

"Why don't you tell us about the money," David told her.

"Please, sit down," Laura told them. Kathryn and David sat on the sofa while Laura sat on a nearby loveseat. "I don't think you could call it a payoff, but that's what it seems like now. If you're here about the complaint, then certainly you know about the money Dr. DiUlio gave us."

Neither Kathryn nor David acknowledged anything.

Laura shook her head. "It's terrible, but with the good doctor I really saw how money and power can corrupt humans. In fact, we fell into his trap. We accepted his payoff. I guess in a way that made us no better than he was."

Kathryn asked, "What kind of a payoff are you talking about?"

"He called it a settlement to reimburse us for the fees we had paid to private investigators and attorneys. He said he had nothing to hide, but he told us he didn't think it was fair that we would cause harm to his legally adopted child with a lot of false publicity." She seemed to be having trouble sitting still. She went to the kitchen and brought back a cup of coffee for David, who thanked her. "For a long time, I had nightmares that I had sold my son," she continued, sitting again. "You don't know how something like that can haunt you." She lifted the shoulders of her loose-fitting blouse. "I've lost so much weight. I still am haunted, even after all these years—you never forget something like that. I sold out."

Kathryn let her take the conversation the way she wanted it to go.

"I've always felt that our accepting that payment was what led to my ex-husband's and my divorce. We blamed each other. So we split the blood money and went our separate ways." She shook her head. "I've never been happy."

David told her, "I didn't catch how much you said we were talking about."

She told him. "Thirty thousand dollars."

No one said anything right away, but Kathryn was struck by the amount. Thirty thousand dollars was a lot of money. "You must have been pushing some rather threatening buttons in order to get such a response from the DiUlios."

"Oh, there was evidence of irregularities," Laura said, "and we all knew it." She shrugged. "But we also knew the case would never go anywhere. People with power can silence things like that."

"Why do you say that?" Kathryn asked.

"The system is corrupt," Laura answered without hesitation. "The whole system. The people who had responsibility for the investigation dragged their feet and wouldn't do anything. We knew what was happening."

"I talked to a Duane Taylor at the Department of Human Resources in Texas," Kathryn said, "and he seemed to care."

Laura smiled. "Oh, he cared all right," she said, "but he was just a kid. You could tell he didn't know what he was doing, and he was scared to death about his job. He was new at it. I'm sure that's why they gave him the case. After three years, no one took such a complaint very seriously at first. But then when they saw who it involved, everything changed. They gave it to someone they knew was expendable."

"Who's 'they'?" David asked.

"For one, Mr. Taylor's boss, Patsy Thrash. As soon as she got wind of what was going on, and that we were serious, she was determined not to let the investigation go anywhere. She was getting pressure from somewhere." She shrugged. "Or maybe she was only exercising her arbitrary authority. Who knows. But I suspect she dragged her feet because doctors are treated like gods in our society, and Patsy wasn't about to take on the powerful medical establishment. Not for us. She'd break a few laws herself first.

"Every time Kirk and I took Mr. Taylor evidence, Patsy dragged her feet, and she always dragged them in favor of the DiUlios. She wrote off every bit of evidence. Mr. Taylor would keep coming back all apologetic and say that his boss had said the evidence was too isolated. It only involved one child. His boss didn't care." Laura looked directly at Kathryn. "Isn't it strange how if it's just one person, no one really gives a damn?"

David mentioned, "Maybe there really wasn't enough evidence to go on. You said yourself that three years had passed before you had filed a complaint."

Her back straight, Laura sat forward in her chair. She said, "There were definite violations of the law." Her tone was adamant. "For example, we think one of the nurses who worked in labor and delivery had set everything up. If that was the case, she was an intermediary, which is illegal in Texas. The DiUlios probably paid her like they paid us. The DiUlios knew which baby they wanted, and they were determined to have their way—no matter what."

Kathryn didn't ask for the nurse's name. She knew. Instead she asked, "Why wouldn't the DiUlios simply go through a one-to-one adoption process, then—I mean, between the DiUlios and the person giving up the child?"

Laura scooted back in her seat. She said, "There are some obvious reasons for not doing that. For one, the DiUlios insisted on a white male in perfect health. Everyone knew that. There's always a risk in an individual adoption. With an agency the DiUlios could hold out for the child they wanted. They could always turn down an adoption at the last moment.

"Two, the agency gave the adoption process protection. It concealed the parties who were manipulating everything behind the scenes.

"Three, it gave the agency itself protection. For the state regulators, even if a whole bunch of individuals broke every law in the book, the regulators could conclude there was no sense attacking an entire process or an entire agency because of the errors of a few individuals within the agency. Patsy had all kinds of ways of getting out of doing her job. She was as insensitive and incompetent as they come. She literally didn't give a damn about accountability or standards."

Without explanation Laura got up and went to the kitchen, where she got the coffeepot and brought it back to David. She refilled his cup.

"Thank you."

Kathryn said, "What other irregularities were there?"

Laura took the coffeepot to the kitchen and returned. She sat down. "The nurse, the intermediary, helped switch babies. We're sure she did that."

David commented, "It seems a mother would know her own baby. If a baby was switched, wouldn't the mother know right away?"

Laura smiled. She asked, "Do you have children?"

He nodded.

"It's always different for the men. For the woman it's so painful you don't remember much of anything." She continued to smile. "I don't remember most of what happened the night our son was born." Kathryn couldn't remember that much about when Wendy was born. "I remember screaming at my husband, but later when he told me I had pooped in the bed, I didn't remember that." She reddened. "They could have given me anyone's child, and I wouldn't have known it wasn't mine."

"What other irregularities?" Kathryn asked.

"There's an off-limits area of the hospital where the nurses clean the babies, and so on," Laura said. "I know Dr. DiUlio was seen in that area the night the child had died. There were irregularities with paperwork, with exchanges of money, with everything."

David sipped his coffee.

Kathryn asked, "Did you by any chance know a family by the name of Robles—or have you heard that name?"

Laura looked like she was trying to think. She stared off in space and almost appeared to be squinting. "No," she said, "I can't say that I've heard that name. Why?"

Kathryn told her that the Robleses had adopted a child from the same agency about the time the DiUlios had adopted, and the couples supposedly had known each other.

That refreshed Laura's memory. "Yes, I think I know whom you're talking about," she said. "They knew something, and the DiUlios were worried. But for some ungodly reason, this other family—"

"The Robleses—"

"Yes, they contacted the DiUlios and let them know they were being investigated." She nodded. "Yes, I remember them. It didn't make sense. It ruined the investigation."

Kathryn asked, "How is it that suddenly several years after you gave birth to a child some private detective agency came to you with a story about the switching of babies?" It was one of the questions that bothered her the most. Who had stirred up the Morleys?

"I need a drink," Laura said, standing. "Would either of you like to join me?"

No, they told her.

She went to the kitchen, put several ice cubes in a glass, filled the glass with something from a crystal decanter—Kathryn supposed it to be bourbon or scotch—and came back, jiggling the glass with her right hand. She took a big drink. "I was seeing a psychiatrist at the time," she said. She took another drink. "I had never gotten over the death of my son," she went on. "It's like I had carried him for nine months and couldn't get over it. When I got pregnant, I was so careful about everything. I stopped smoking. I stopped drinking. I watched my diet, eating fruits and vegetables that I normally wouldn't eat so my baby would be healthy. I went through morning sickness, mood swings, weight gain, you name it. Then to have him die right after birth, I couldn't accept it. Kirk was so supportive. He didn't believe in psychiatrists, but he supported me. The psychiatrist told me to hire a private investigator and have him investigate things." She finished her drink. "I'm sure the psychiatrist thought the investigator would poke around and give me the hard facts about my son—that he had died of natural causes—but it didn't turn out that way."

David put his empty cup on the table in front of him. He asked, "If you think the DiUlios got your healthy child, what do you suppose happened to the child you got?"

Laura said, "They murdered him."

"Why?"

"There was something wrong with him—not enough for him to die on his own, but enough that he was less than perfect, and the DiUlios didn't want a son who was less than perfect. But they couldn't risk letting the abnormal child live for fear that we might eventually discover he wasn't our natural son—you know, what with medical tests, blood tests, and so on." She shook her head. "I would have taken an abnormal son, even if he wasn't mine, and I would have treated him as my own, no questions asked." Holding the glass in one hand, she stirred the ice with her finger. "They stole my baby and killed the other one," she said. "I know they did." Tears began to run down her face, escaping her attempts to wipe them away with her hand. "Excuse me," she said. She brought the drink to her mouth, only to discover the glass was empty. Her face was wet, her mascara streaked, but she didn't care. She put the glass on a wicker table.

Kathryn said, "One more question—the private detective. Who was it?"

"Lee Watts. He died a year or so ago. I used to keep in touch—sent him a Christmas card, and so on. Then a year or so ago, I got a card from his wife saying that he had passed away."

Kathryn thanked her for her time.

Outside she told David, "I feel sorry for her."

He nodded. "Something like that can really tear your life apart." He produced a cigarette. "Do we have time for a smoke?"

Stopping in the shade of a palm tree, she said, "Hurry."

"Three minutes." He lit the cigarette. "What's the plan?" He moved so the smoke didn't get between them. "Do we see this Dr. DiUlio?"

She shook her head. "Not yet."

He puffed his cigarette, then held it behind his back. "Do you see what I see?"

Yes, she did. There was a white station wagon parked a block away, two men sitting in the front seat.

"Where now?"

"We talk to the nurse."

"You want to figure out who's following us?"

"Not yet." All in good time, she told herself. "Let's get some reinforcements."

19

To find the nurse of record at the time the Morley baby had died twelve years earlier, Kathryn called an old friend, Captain Steve Akers of the Texas Rangers. He worked out of Austin, and she had been close to him and his wife over the years. Steve made some checks with the state license bureau. Tracy Knowles's nursing license was still active, only her name had changed. Her married name was Tuort, and she was living in College Station. Kathryn asked Steve if he would help conduct the interview. She emphasized the matter was urgent. She told him she was flying to College Station from Houston. He said he would be at the local post of the Texas Department of Public Safety.

She then arranged for a National Guard helicopter to fly her and David to College Station. They met Steve at the DPS post, where he took them to a private office so they could talk.

He asked, "What's going down?" as soon as they were in the office. He was a stocky, easygoing man with sandy hair and tanned skin, in his early forties, and managed to keep a pleasant expression on his face most of the time. Dressed in a navy sweater and tan slacks, he looked like he might be off duty. He wasn't wearing a weapon.

She told him about the Robles investigation, and how she was following a series of leads. She also told him that someone had been following them.

"That should be easy enough to take care of if it

happens here," Steve told her. "In a small community like this, we can put an end to something like that right away. Say, how's Randy?"

Mildly embarrassed, she told him she and Randy were no longer seeing each other.

"Sorry, I didn't know."

Kathryn noticed David was watching her, and that made her feel uncomfortable. She asked Steve if he had wrecked any cars lately. Several years before, she told David, she had been riding with Steve when he had decided to head in the opposite direction on a narrow road. Instead of negotiating a turn on the road, he had made a U-turn, completely leaving the road. The state car had bounced across a rugged field. Back on the road, Steve discovered the car wouldn't accelerate to over fifteen miles per hour. It turned out the transmission pan had been dented to the point that the car wouldn't shift out of low gear. It had been a thirty-mile drive to the nearest town.

Steve laughed at the recounting of the story. No, he said, he hadn't wrecked any more cars.

David gave her one of his smiles. She looked back at Steve. "Can we count on your help?" she asked, and sat down at the desk in the small office.

He sat down too, as did David. "What's this important lead?" Steve asked.

She explained about the Morley baby, including details about the history of the Robleses' adoption. She asked what kind of probable cause he would need to get a court order to exhume a body.

He asked what she expected to find if she dug up the body.

Evidence of poisoning, she told him, the kind of poison a physician would know about and have access to. "Since there is no statute of limitations on murder, we figure our Dr. DiUlio might be using his role in a terrorist plot to wrap up some loose ends in his own past, wrap them up in such a way as to protect his adopted son forever—so that things won't ever come back to haunt him. If we can get to the evidence before he can seal the path forever, then we may be able to expose what he's done, and put all this together. There's some kind of a plot, and we're looking for a chink in the armor."

Steve said it would be a tough sell to a judge. The judge would want to know why there was more reason to exhume the infant now than there had been ten years ago when the state investigated the case and hadn't gathered sufficient cause to order an exhumation. "And how does all this tie into the case of the girl who was kidnapped from Fort Hood?"

David said, "We can't figure out why this particular girl was targeted. So far it doesn't make sense why the kidnappers chose her instead of someone else. We're looking for a motive."

Kathryn put her hands in her coat pockets, leaned back, and stretched out her feet. "We're also trying to get something to hold over DiUlio's head so we can get him to talk. We figure he knows something, and if we can drag out the skeleton in his closet, it might be enough to break him."

Steve told her, "It'd be virtually impossible to prove murder after all these years—even if we did exhume the baby's body and discover it had been poisoned."

"It's not about getting a conviction," she told him. "It's about getting something to hold over his head, something that will threaten the stability of his own family enough that he'll be willing to turn government witness." From her pocket, she removed the photograph of the Robles family. The photograph was worn and wrinkled. "That's her"—she pointed out Angela."

Steve smiled. "She's pretty."

She put away the photograph.

Steve stood, put his hands in his front pockets, and rattled some coins in his right pocket.

"Steve, I'm going to level with you, we don't have a hell of a lot to go on right now. This adoption process is the first lead that hints there might be something in Angela's past that could help explain what's going on in her present. We've got to put this thing together and see where it leads. I have to know."

Steve seemed to be counting the change in his pocket. "I see the logic in what you're doing," he said. "In most murder cases, it turns out the victim knew the assailant. You're thinking the same thing with Angela."

Kathryn nodded. "I know someone's been searching for her adoption records. If that someone didn't know her, whoever it was wanted to find out as much as he or she could about her." Then she added the part about Exodus-V. She told him as much as she knew about the biological weapon.

Steve quit playing with the change in his pocket. "Are you for real?"

David said, "The weapon is."

Kathryn nodded. "And we know if whoever has Angela has the weapon and uses it, it'll be the biggest act of terrorism that ever hit the United States."

Steve told them he knew about anthrax from his military days. "I remember as a raw recruit, standing out in a field and holding an imitation atropine syringe, and the drill sergeant scaring the shit out of us about this biological weapon that would kill us within minutes if we didn't get ourselves injected."

She said, "With Exodus-Five, even if there was a magic syringe, you wouldn't have to worry about it. For all practical purposes, Exodus-Five kills instantly. It's been genetically engineered that way."

Steve tried to smile. "Come on, you don't think something like that is really on the loose out there, do you?"

Kathryn and David sat silently.

The pleasant look on Steve's face had vanished.

Finally Kathryn spoke: "I can tell you that someone has gone through a lot of trouble if this is all a hoax."

"And this has something to do with a baby's death twelve or so years ago?"

David said, "It's where we've been led." He said it was thus far the only clue linking the possible theft of Exodus-V from the army and the disappearance of Angela. "Does anyone mind if I smoke?" He lit a cigarette almost as soon as he had asked the question. "If we can figure out why Angela in particular was selected as a hostage, then we might be able to figure out who kidnapped her; and if we figure out who kidnapped her, we might be able to locate the stolen Exodus-Five—if there really is any that's been stolen." He looked at Kathryn.

She looked at Steve. "Right now we're looking for anything that might shed some light on what's happening."

"Then, let's just go put the squeeze on this DiUlio guy."

"The last time someone tried something like that, he unleashed an army of lawyers," Kathryn told him. "This isn't the kind of person you squeeze without having some muscle in your grip. And right now I don't have time for a hassle."

Steve sat down again. He removed a pen from his shirt pocket and rattled it between his teeth. He clipped the pen back in his pocket. "Well, I can tell you that it's going to take more than the parents to consent to an exhumation, so it sounds like you're putting all your hope in this nurse you asked me to find."

She shrugged.

"It's a long shot."

"There aren't a lot of options."

He stood. "Let's go."

They located the Tuort house right as Tracy Tuort was getting out of her car. She still had blue maternity scrubs on. From the backseat of her car, she pulled a sleeping baby from a car seat.

"Mrs. Tuort," Steve said, approaching her. He showed his credentials. "I'm Steve Akers with the Texas Rangers, and these are agents with the FBI." Kathryn and David showed their credentials. "We need to ask you some questions."

In her thirties, she was tall and had long black hair which had been tied back. Her dark brown eyes were large. Her cheeks, rosy. "What's this about?" she asked.

"May we come in so we don't have everyone in the neighborhood wondering what's going on?"

She let them in the new house that had cathedral ceilings. The furnishings were new, a lot of white and navy colors, and the off-white carpet was plush. She said, "Let me put my baby in her crib, and I'll be right with you. Please make yourselves comfortable." She left the room.

Moments later she returned. She sat on the edge of a navy chair. "Now, what can I do for you?"

Steve, sitting in a matching navy chair, commented, "You have a nice home here."

"Thank you."

"Is that your first child?" Steve asked, nodding in the direction of the hall.

"Yes." Her voice was impatient: "I hate to be rude, but what's this about?"

"I have a couple of children," Steve persisted. "They're a lot of fun, but they grow up quickly."

She gave an awkward smile.

"Mrs. Tuort, we want to talk to you about something that happened a long time ago. Is your husband going to be home soon?"

She shook her head. "Not for another hour or so. He teaches at the university. Is this about him? Do I need a lawyer? What happened a long time ago? I didn't know him a long time ago." She was soft-spoken, but her voice was becoming increasingly impatient.

Kathryn said, "Tracy—do you mind if I call you Tracy?"

"That's fine."

"I'm sure you've heard about the girl who disappeared up at Fort Hood."

"I've heard. I haven't followed the story closely, but I've heard."

"We've been looking at her background, and come to find out, she's an adopted child."

Tracy turned ghostly pale, all but her cheeks, which remained artificially rosy.

"Are you all right, Tracy?" Steve asked.

She nodded, but didn't say a word.

David said, "You know what we're here about, don't you?"

Tracy didn't say.

"As it turns out," Kathryn continued, "the Fort Hood people who adopted the kidnapped child had a run-in with some people who had adopted another child, and the run-in had to do with whether these other people may have engaged in foul play in order to get the child they wanted. Does any of this ring a bell, Tracy?"

Tracy wiped some of the shininess from her forehead. She looked sick.

"It does ring a bell, doesn't it?" Steve said.

Kathryn could feel excitement beginning to stir within her. Tracy knew something.

David said, "Tracy, this girl who's been kidnapped is in a lot of danger. Imagine how you would feel if your daughter was in danger like that."

From a shelf under a side table, Tracy brought up a bottle of lotion. She said, "My hands are so sore from washing them all day." She squirted some yellow lotion in the palm of one hand and began rubbing the hands together. They did look chapped.

Kathryn said, "You helped Dr. DiUlio switch babies, didn't you? He wanted a particular baby, and you helped him get it."

"No!" she suddenly said. "Absolutely not. I had no part of it." She wiped away a tear. She took a deep breath. "Excuse me, but I'm just a little scared."

Steve went into the kitchen, which was a part of the open living room and dining area. From the sofa where she and David sat, Kathryn could see Steve get a paper towel from a holder on the kitchen counter. He brought the paper towel back and handed it to Tracy.

"It was my first job out of nursing school." She blotted her eyes with the towel. "You wouldn't believe how bothered I've been about all this over the years. I promise I didn't have anything to do with it."

David asked, "Did Dr. DiUlio switch babies?"

"I don't know. I can't prove anything."

Kathryn prodded, "We're not asking you to prove anything. Do you think Dr. DiUlio might have switched babies on at least one occasion in the unit where you worked?"

"Yes."

David asked, "Did Dr. DiUlio ever pay you any money to keep quiet?"

No. Tracy was adamant.

Kathryn thought of the Morleys. Good question. At least in that case DiUlio had learned that his money could protect him and buy silence. She asked, "Why don't you tell us what happened, Tracy? Or tell us what you think happened. This is a very serious matter. Please, don't hold anything back."

She and Dr. DiUlio had been having an affair, Tracy confessed.

No one said anything.

She had met DiUlio while she was a student in nursing school, she told them, and they had talked whenever they saw each other in the hospital corridors.

Right about the time she had graduated from nursing school, he had asked her if she wanted to stay on at the hospital to work. She had been so thrilled to get a job that she had immediately said yes. One thing led to another, she said, and she and he ended up having an affair. She rubbed her hands together. "Come to find out, he was sleeping with half the nurses in the hospital. He's that kind of a person."

She squirted some more lotion on her hands and began to rub it in. "I was on the night shift in labor and delivery, and he used to stop by and visit me," she told them, rubbing. "I knew about his adoption plans. He always came by to look at the babies. He said he loved to look at them and dream of his own son. I knew the kind of baby he wanted. Everyone knew, only I knew every little detail." She explained how DiUlio had made her feel sorry for him because his wife had had several miscarriages. "He told me all he wanted was a healthy child, but I knew better.

"He started showing up more and more at my workstation. Then one night I was alone with him at the station—I think the other two nurses on duty had gone down to the cafeteria in order to give us some time alone together—and a call light went off. It had been a particularly busy couple of days in labor and delivery, and we had a lot of babies in the unit, including the one that was supposed to become the new DiUlio child." She snapped the lid down on the lotion bottle.

"Anyway, I went to check on the mother whose call light was on. I was gone for maybe ten or fifteen minutes—it turned out to be false labor—and when I got back, there was something wrong, I could tell. I just wasn't sure what it was. You know how it is when you get a feeling?" She looked at each of them individually, but when no one responded, she continued: "Al—that's what I called him—was in with the babies, and he seemed to be trying to get my attention. He kept distracting me. That's when I noticed one of the babies in distress." She began to wipe away tears. "I would have sworn it wasn't the Morley baby, but the next thing I know, that was the name I was hearing." She couldn't keep the tears away. "Everything was happening so fast. We called a code, and all the babies got pushed aside so we could work on the baby who was in distress, and then as quickly as it all began, it was over. The doctor who was running the code called it off." She blew her nose in the paper towel.

David asked, "Was it the Morley baby who died?"

"That's what they said. I even had to look to satisfy my own disbelief because I was sure it wasn't the Morley baby, but when I looked, the baby was wearing the Morley bracelet."

"I would hope there was more than a bracelet involved in the identification," Steve commented.

Tracy nodded. "The records, everything had been changed. Or I was wrong about everything. I mean, sometimes you have to look at it that way. If the whole world is saying one thing, and you're thinking another, don't you sometimes have to think you might be wrong?" She looked at them for an acknowledgment.

Steve said, "If what you're saying is true, and Dr. DiUlio switched babies, that seems like it would be a pretty sophisticated switch. You think he had help?"

"Not necessarily. Today it'd be more difficult to do, but back then?" Tracy shrugged. "I mean, Dr. DiUlio had been living with us. He knew the routine inside out, everything we did. Sometimes he even helped us work—if we got busy. He asked questions about everything. And he knew there was always one or two babies with some kind of problem—whether it be jaundice or something else."

Kathryn asked, "Did you ever confront Dr. DiUlio, or tell anyone about your suspicions?"

"In private, I told him I thought he had switched

the babies. That's when our affair ended. He told me if I ever made such an accusation again, he would make sure I never worked as a nurse or anything else in any hospital. He didn't say another word to me—ever."

Steve repeated Kathryn's question: "Did you ever mention your suspicions to anyone else?"

"Not formally. I was too scared." She began to tear little pieces off her damp paper towel. Each piece she pulled off the paper towel, she rolled into a tiny ball, using her fingers. Kathryn thought of Wendy. She liked to do that when she had a soft drink in a bottle. She would peel off the label and tear it into tiny pieces.

"Am I in trouble?" Tracy asked. She couldn't keep still. "I have a wonderful husband and baby. Please, I'm not in trouble, am I? My husband doesn't have to know about this, does he? I promise I didn't do anything wrong."

Kathryn got up and took Tracy by the hand. "No one's saying you did anything wrong," Kathryn said. "We're only trying to figure all of this out."

Steve said, "If we were to exhume the body of that infant, what do you suppose a medical examiner would find?"

Tracy studied the tiny pieces of paper in the palm of her hand. "Probably, that Dr. DiUlio had murdered the baby," she said.

Kathryn sat back down.

"But you didn't help him, or see him do it, so why is it you believe he murdered the baby?" David asked.

Tracy told them, "After it was all over, and before I confronted Al, I found something in the trash." Her fingers were playing with a tiny ball of tissue. "It doesn't even seem that this could be happening after all these years, but I swear I'm telling the truth."

Kathryn slid forward on the sofa. "What did you find in the trash?"

"A syringe and a vial of potassium."

Steve uttered in disbelief, "Potassium?"

Tracy nodded. "It would have caused cardiac arrest if Al had given the baby an injection of potassium."

"They didn't do an autopsy?"

Tracy shrugged. "Maybe Al had that fixed too. I don't know."

"You never told anyone about what you had found?" David asked.

She said she had told a couple of people. She explained that she had gone home after the infant's death, and had called her roommate from nursing school. Her roommate worked at a hospital in Springfield, Missouri.

What had her friend told her to do? Kathryn wanted to know.

"Not to say anything—just in case the syringe and potassium had nothing to do with the death—but to hold onto what I found."

Kathryn, Steve, and David all glanced at each other at the same time. Kathryn was the first to speak. She said, "You saved the vial and syringe?"

Tracy nodded.

Unable to control her response, Kathryn smiled. "You saved the vial and syringe? For all this time?"

Steve must have thought the same thing because he asked, "And you still have it?" as if he couldn't believe it was even a possibility.

Tracy nodded. "My husband says I save everything." She laughed at herself. "You know how you're supposed to save checks three years, or something like that in case you get audited by the IRS? I have checks from twenty years ago." She got up and went down the hall. They could hear her digging around in boxes. She returned with a sandwich baggie. Inside was a syringe, a vial of clear fluid, and two latex gloves. She said, "Believe me, I've never touched them. I even used gloves to get them out of the trash."

Steve said, "And you think Dr. DiUlio not only switched babies, but he also murdered one?"

"He never admitted that that's what happened, but I've been around enough newborns to know the one that died was going to live. It had some physical problems, but it was going to live."

Kathryn took a deep breath. "Live, but be less than perfect?"

Tracy didn't look at her, didn't look at anyone. "Yes. A beautiful baby, but not a blue chip, or whatever they call it." Undoubtedly, she had heard of the terminology many times from DiUlio.

Steve began to mark the syringe and vial as evidence.

Kathryn said, "I don't want you to think we don't believe you, but would you be willing to take a polygraph examination about all of this?" She wanted to make sure she had covered all her bases. "It's part of our routine in an important matter like this."

Yes, Tracy said, she would take a polygraph.

They left her standing at the door.

Glancing back, Kathryn thought she looked like someone who had had a huge burden lifted from her.

In the car Steve and David were slapping hands together and laughing. They were jubilant.

David said, "Can you imagine that—she kept a damned syringe and bottle of drugs for thirteen years!" He laughed loudly.

Steve laughed too. He said, "Yeah, wait until Sandy hears this. I thought she was a pack rat, but she has nothing on Tracy." He glanced over. "What's wrong?" he suddenly asked.

David, in the back seat, looked at her.

She looked at them. "Don't anyone look, but we have visitors." She had seen the brown sedan when she had come out of the Tuort home. The car was parked almost a block away, but its occupants, two men, were unmistakably watching the Tuort residence.

Neither Steve nor David looked directly at the car, but she knew they saw the one she was making reference to.

Steve started driving. From his left boot he removed a 9mm. He set it on the seat beside him. He told Kathryn, "Throw a round in the chamber, please."

She did and put the 9mm on the seat beside him.

"David," Steve said, "there's a button on top of the seat across from you. Push the button and pull down the seat."

David did.

"Reach back there and get the shotgun."

David brought out a shotgun.

They went over an incline and approached a stop sign. On the right was a car wash. Steve said, "David, as quickly as you can, jump out of the car and take cover in the car wash. I'll wait at the stop sign. When the other car gets behind us, Kathryn and I'll jump out of the car and run to the right side. David, you come in from the back. If they do anything at all, you start blasting with that riot gun."

David didn't even reply. As the car slowed, he jumped out at a full run. He disappeared in the car wash that seemed to be abandoned at that hour of the day.

Steve drove on to the sign, where he stopped and waited.

The car following came over the incline. It slowed for the sign.

Steve asked, "You ready?"

She was watching the car in the rearview. "Anytime you are."

"I'm sure they didn't expect us to be waiting. See, they have to pull right up to us. When I say go, jump out with your piece on the one who's sitting on your side. I'll take the driver. If anything happens, blow the shit out of them and ask questions later."

They caught the occupants of the other sedan off

guard. Weapons drawn, Kathryn and Steve ran up to each side of the other car. David, shotgun aimed in the back window, ran up behind the car.

The occupants raised their hands.

One of them was screaming, "Don't shoot! We're the FBI!"

Kathryn didn't slow until she had the two occupants spread over the hood of their car, their hands stretched forth. Under David's shotgun, she and Steve took the weapons from the two men. Only then did she find their credentials and gold shields. Stunned, she stepped back. What was happening? she demanded to know.

Grant Smythers had sent them, one of the agents called out, his arms still spread across the hood of the sedan. He said, "Can I get up?"

David lowered the shotgun.

Steve stepped back. He tucked his 9mm in the waist of his pants.

Kathryn was too shocked to move.

20

Angela opened her eyes to Corporal Klock. Big and burly, he looked mean, but he didn't act that way with her. He had moved a locker and rubbed away some of the dirt on a window, apparently so he could see the comings and goings of people in the compound.

He turned to her. "Hey, when did you wake up? You should have said something." He yawned.

She mentioned that he looked tired.

He told her he hadn't slept the night before—that the lack of sleep was catching up with him. He said he had lost track of time, wasn't even sure what day it was. He said he thought it was Wednesday, or Thursday, maybe Friday.

Her arm was hurting again, she told him. She could feel it throbbing under the covers, but she told him not to pull back the covers to look because she was cold. There was no heat in the room. She said, "Very cold."

He brought another blanket from one of the metal lockers. He opened the blanket and spread it over her. "I'm sure someone'll be stopping by in a few minutes," he said. "I'll tell whoever it is that you need something for pain." He returned to the window and looked through where he had cleaned. "There's a lot of activity out there. Something's going on." He glanced at her. "Did you sleep all right?"

She shook her head.

"Because you were hurting?"

"I had a bad dream. That's what woke me up."

"A bad dream about what?"

"A giant. He was coming after me."

"A giant?"

She nodded. "I hid from him."

He studied her.

"I hid in a field. Behind a tree."

"What did the giant look like?"

"I don't know."

"You didn't see him?"

She shook her head. "I was too scared to look."

He smiled and glanced out the window. "Then, how did you know it was a giant?"

"I heard him."

He looked at her. "He was talking to you?"

'No. The trees didn't have leaves. They were on the ground. The giant was kicking them up. I heard them. That's how I knew. I knew the giant was kicking the leaves up. He had big feet."

Klock smiled again. "Maybe he was just out for a walk."

She turned her face away.

"I'm sorry," he told her.

Without looking at him, she said, "People always treat me that way—like I'm dumb or something."

"You're right. That wasn't nice. You're a very smart young lady. I'm sorry."

"They don't want me to be a young lady. They want me to be a child. So I act like a child. I act like they want me to be."

Next thing she knew his large cold hand pushed back her messy hair. "Please act like a smart young lady around me." He added: "Your head's warm."

She said, "I don't feel good."

He was kneeling at her bed. There was a troubled look in his eyes. She remembered the same kind of look in her father's eyes when she woke up after the accident. He had a troubled look—like something was wrong he couldn't fix. She wanted to ask Klock what it was that worried him, but she was afraid to. All she could say was, "He was after me."

"Who?"

"The giant."

He rubbed the side of her face. "I believe you. What do you think he wanted?"

She shrugged. "I guess he just wanted to find me."

He still had that worried look in his eyes.

"What are you thinking about?"

"Nothing."

"See, you're treating me like a child again—like I'm stupid or something."

"I was thinking you have an infection."

She stared at him. "I'm still cold."

"I don't think it's a good idea to cover you up too much," he told her. "We need to let some of that heat out."

"Will I die?"

"The infection is in your hand."

For the first time she found the words to say what she felt inside: "I don't want to live." Good. It was out.

"Why do you say that?"

She couldn't feel the fingers of her right hand. Her entire arm hurt, though, all but the hand. "I don't think they can fix my hand. I don't want to live without a hand. That's the hand I write with and everything. How am I going to live without it?"

His cold hand touched her face. "They can fix that hand. Believe me, today doctors can fix just about anything."

She shook her head. "I remember when I was in the accident. The doctor told me if I didn't start taking better care of myself, some day something was going to happen that they couldn't fix. I wasn't wearing a seat belt when I was in the accident."

"How old are you?"

"Almost thirteen. You know that. I told you."

"Have you looked in the mirror lately?"

She smiled through her tears. She was sure she was a mess.

"Well, I tell you what. You're almost thirteen, very beautiful, and you have your entire life ahead of you." He blushed. Even as big and burly as he was, he didn't look like the kind of person who could say such things. "Believe me, they can fix your hand. Don't worry." He unbuttoned his shirt pocket, removed his baseball cards, and began looking through them. As he looked, he said, "Besides, I'm going to get you out of here. I'm working on a plan."

A .45 automatic touched Klock's head. "Don't move," Private Kearnes told him. She hadn't seen him appear. Hadn't heard him. "You move, and I'll blow your head off." Kearnes inched forward. "You didn't know I had a key to the other door, did you?"

"No," Angela pleaded.

"Stay on your knees," Kearnes warned Klock.

Klock settled to the floor again.

"Put your hands behind your neck."

Klock did.

"You know the procedure. Lock your fingers together. That's better."

Kearnes knelt and removed Klock's .45 automatic from his holster. After moving back, he ejected the clip from the pistol.

Klock said, "Do whatever you want with me, but get the girl some help. She has bad burns. You know she does, for God's sake."

Kearnes smiled. "Don't you know you're all going to die soon anyway? You and everyone else. So many dead bodies, no one will ever figure out who did what." He produced a set of handcuffs and handcuffed one of Klock's hands behind his neck. "Put your other hand in the small of your back." Klock did as he was told. "Now, put this one down." Kearnes pulled down the handcuffed hand to the small of Klock's back. There he handcuffed both hands together. "Turn around slowly and sit on the bed." Kearnes moved back. He kept his weapon trained on Klock.

Angela moved her feet for Klock.

Kearnes seemed much smaller than Klock. Angela wondered why Klock hadn't done something. She thought he could have easily overpowered Kearnes.

"What do you mean, we're all going to die?" Klock asked.

Kearnes smiled. "There's a lot you don't know and understand, Corporal."

Captain Gillespie appeared. He seemed surprised to see Klock sitting on Angela's bed, and Kearnes pointing a pistol at him.

"What's going on, Private?" Gillespie asked.

Kearnes said, "I caught Corporal Klock engaged in improper conversation with the prisoner."

"What kind of improper conversation?"

"They were talking about escaping, sir."

Some of the color drained from Gillespie's face. "What did they specifically say?"

Kearnes said, "Your model soldier has figured things out, that's what he said."

Captain Gillespie nodded. He said, "It doesn't matter. They're going to die anyway."

"That's what I told them."

Gillespie said, "I'll send Private Stevens over. You and he bring the prisoners to the briefing so the colonel can decide what he wants to do with them." He left the barracks.

Klock told Kearnes, "You're not going to get away with this."

Kearnes smiled. He said, "You're a little late for that."

Within moments several armed guards arrived. They carried M-16s. One soldier was pushing a wheelchair.

The soldiers were none too gentle about hoisting Angela from the bed and dropping her into the wheelchair. She cried out. One of the soldiers slapped the side of her head. "Shut up, bitch," he told her.

Despite being in handcuffs, Klock threw a kick at the soldier who had slapped Angela. The toe of Klock's boot made contact with the base of the soldier's chin, lifting him into the air. Another soldier was trying to get his M-16 fixed on Klock, but Klock didn't give him time or room. Klock lunged full force into the soldier who was raising the M-16. Klock's shoulder made contact with the soldier's chest. Angela screamed as all the soldiers jumped on Klock, tackling him. More soldiers came running. Still Klock didn't give in. She could see him kicking and fighting under the mountain of soldiers who had buried him.

"Get his feet!" someone yelled.

Soldiers grabbed the kicking boots. Blood and teeth flew.

Next thing Angela knew, the soldiers were beating Klock. They delivered blows to his face, head, and chest. She knew the soldiers were killing him. The floor was bloody. Even when Klock was limp, the soldiers continued to beat him, as if something had snapped inside them and they couldn't stop.

The colonel appeared. He ordered them away. They backed away from the body of Klock, whose chest and head were soaked with blood. Angela was sure he was dead. They had killed him. She looked at the soldiers who stood panting like animals.

The colonel said, "Everyone to the mess hall like I ordered." He was an ashen gray. The stubble in his face stood out.

Two soldiers raised Klock by his arms and dragged him. Angela was transported by wheelchair. She kept her eyes fixed on Klock, watching for some sign of life. There was none. His boots scraped and bounced across the concrete sidewalk as the soldiers dragged him. Now more than ever, she didn't want to live, didn't want to experience what was going to happen next. Or whatever was going to happen next, she wanted it to happen, and she wanted to get it over with, and she hoped there was nothing more to follow.

In the mess hall the air smelled like fresh-baked bread and fish. It was a strange combination. In a corner of the room, under heavy guard, were twenty or so soldiers, including Sergeant Copeland, the huge black training sergeant. He too was bloody, as if he had been beaten. Klock was dumped with the soldiers under guard. Angela was wheeled to the front of the mess hall, near the podium. On a table near the podium was what looked like a miniature city. Angela stared at it. She recognized what she was looking at as Ford Hood. She recognized the bank where her mother and father went all the time, and she recognized her school. There was the airfield too, where all the helicopters were.

The colonel went to the podium. His face was deeply creased, filled with worry.

Private Kearnes yelled, "Attention!"

Everyone came to attention, including the guards of the beaten soldiers, though there was a change in the air. Angela couldn't tell what it was, though she thought there might be less enthusiasm in the room. Maybe it had been replaced by fear.

The colonel said, "We've had another round of problems." His voice was still loud—it carried through the hall—though it sounded less sure of itself. "A few more days is all I ask, and it seems like one thing after another is going wrong now." A few of the soldiers were having trouble keeping still. "I'm disappointed in all of you, that's all I can say." He became silent. It was a long silence, so long that Angela thought it really was all he could say.

He stepped off the podium, walked past the table with the model of Fort Hood on it, and stood near

the soldiers as he talked. "We are in the final hours."
He looked frail. "If it were only about you and me,
and we didn't mind jeopardizing our own lives, ca-
reers, futures, and so on, that would be one thing. But
it's not just about you and me. Now we're involved in
an operation that is about this great country of ours."
His eyes scanned the men. "I'll be damned if I'm
going to let any of you ruin the operation." His face
had turned red with anger. He almost seemed to be
trembling, at least until he took a deep breath. "Do
you understand?"

No one said anything.

Angela thought he glanced at her bandaged hand,
but she couldn't tell.

"All I need is a little sacrifice on your part," Colonel Lazarus said. "Don't you know what sacrifice is
all about?" He spoke like a man who had sacrificed
much.

He began to walk among the men. "Let me tell
you what sacrifice is about, and it'll be a roundabout
explanation, but I think you'll understand." As he
walked, he was twisting his West Point ring. Angela
thought of her father.

"You remember during the Gulf War, there were
all these questions about chemical weapons and nerve
gas and so on?" He looked at the soldiers, but no one
seemed to acknowledge what he was talking about.
"A lot of us knew the United States had gotten caught
off guard in that war. Iraq had us scared. We knew
that the big war of the future was no longer about
nuclear weapons and sophisticated weaponry, but
about germs and terrorism. Cheap weapons that poor
countries could develop and unleash."

Colonel Lazarus pulled up a chair and sat on the
edge of it. He leaned forward, continuing to twist his
West Point ring. He smiled. "To tell you the truth, we
got caught with our pants down, and then we tried to
cover it up." He waved his open hands, as if trying to

flag down some invisible vehicle that was coming toward him. "We knew we were blowing up chemical weapons. We knew there was going to be a Gulf War Syndrome even before anyone started reporting the symptoms."

He stood up. His hands covered his mouth. "Did General Colin Powell know?" he asked, speaking into his hands. He shook his head and uncovered his mouth. "No. Did General H. Norman Schwarzkopf know?" Again, he shook his head. "No." He scratched his left temple. She could see the tiny blue veins in his face. Older people always got them, Angela thought.

Colonel Lazarus was walking among the men again. "No," he said loudly, "you can't tell the generals in charge, and to tell you the truth, it's kind of an unspoken rule that they don't want to know either. You see, they're the ones who always end up getting asked the questions. They're the ones who go before Congress to testify. And when they raise their right hands in front of those cameras and swear to tell the truth, they have to be able to say they knew nothing."

The colonel raised his hands toward the ceiling, almost touched it in fact, arched his back, and yawned. "Yet we knew." He dropped his hands. "All of us planning the Gulf War battles and studying the intelligence knew about the chemical weapons. We knew we were sending our troops into harm's way. It was in our plans. We needed enough exposure to make sure the American public demanded that we get back into the business of chemical and biological weapons again."

He laughed loudly and twisted his West Point ring very quickly. "It backfired on us," he said, stopping. "The damned Congress got so swamped in millions of dollars' worth of taxpayer hearings"—he shook his head—"they always do that. Congress spends literally billions of dollars each year holding hearings on anything and everything—no wonder nothing ever gets done." He stopped speaking. "Where was I?" A few of the soldiers smiled. He smiled back at them. "Oh, yes. It backfired. Congress got all their hearings going, and everyone forgot about the hoped-for objective. We, the military leaders, had set it all up so we could get back in the business of chemical and biological weapons. Congress got us sidetracked with all this business about the Gulf War Syndrome."

His expression became very grave. "We've gone back to the drawing board, and this time, we're going to put it in their face, so to speak. Believe me, this time Congress and the American people will get the message and they won't get sidetracked."

He returned to the podium, where he looked to be reading something, though Angela couldn't see any cards or papers that he read from. "In a matter of a couple of days, a hundred thousand or so people will die in an operation that will get our military back on track—that is, to be the greatest, most prepared military in the world.

"We're going to set off an aerosol bomb of a deadly biological germ, and there are going to be many casualties." He shrugged. "An ultimate sacrifice." He was twisting and turning his ring again. "They taught us at the academy that unless you're willing to sacrifice your own blood, you have no business saying you're prepared to go to war. So the sacrifice of our own blood in this mission—the hundred or so thousand of our people who will die—will give us what we need to save millions, even billions of lives." He stared at the soldiers. "What would happen, for example, if enemy terrorists beat us to the punch and unleashed a deadly biological weapon in the Los Angeles area?"

No one answered him.

The colonel's eyebrows raised. "We're talking about the potential of killing one out of every fifteen Americans in a single blow, an act that would devastate our great nation as we know it. To take away almost seven percent of the population with a single blow is like"—he pointed at Angela—"a body whose hand is suddenly severely burned." He stopped, contemplated the floor, then shook his head slowly. "What we're talking about is an operation that is essentially a humanitarian operation, believe it or not. A surgically precise operation that will cause some local damage, but will benefit the body as a whole."

"You're sick!" Klock, on his feet and so bloody as to be almost unrecognizable, coughed. He spat some blood.

Private Kearnes raised the butt of his M-16 and was about to strike Klock with it when the colonel interceded. He said, "No! Don't hit him." Colonel Lazarus stared at Klock, stared steadily and severely.

"All of you who haven't been inoculated will be discovered as a group of terrorists who have infiltrated the military." Klock was having trouble keeping his balance.

Colonel Lazarus smiled slightly. He said, "I assure you, your presence here is quite authentic. We've set it up to be that way. Everything's been done by the book. Not long from now, of course, you'll be dead. You and everyone else. But this compound will look like any other training exercise at Fort Hood. Look at it this way, in a sense all of the legitimate soldiers will be the unsung heroes of this operation. No one will ever know you were involved, but you will have given us the cover to work right in the center of a military installation. When it's all said and done, we'll clean up all traces of ourselves here, we'll dump the girl off post, and it'll look like someone from the outside drove a launcher on post and launched a rocket into the atmosphere above the post—sort of like the Scud missile attacks during the Gulf War.

"As for me, I'll be conveniently away at the time. Of course, I will be back to mourn the loss of my unit." He smiled sadly. "The entire nation will mourn during what will go down as the most important Veterans Day in history."

Klock must have gotten weak because he sat down.

Colonel Lazarus continued, his voice growing loud: "And, by this time next week, every man, woman, and child in the United States will be begging for the military to protect them! Congress will pass huge budgets and heap tremendous new authority on to our nation's defense system."

"You'll be a murderer," Klock said from the floor, where he had collapsed.

"Be quiet, soldier!" Colonel Lazarus said. "You don't talk to a colonel in the United States Army that way!"

"Murderer!"

Kearnes hit Klock with the butt of an M-16.

"No!" Angela screamed.

The colonel seemed amazed, everything had happened so quickly. His eyes opened wide, he was looking around at the other soldiers.

Sergeant Copeland spoke up: "See, he's gone mad!"

"I feel dizzy," Colonel Lazarus suddenly said, and he massaged the sides of his neck.

Someone brought him a chair.

He sat down. There he remained in the middle of the dining hall, his face pale, a confused look on it.

The door opened. Cool air blew into the room. It was the man Angela thought looked like the devil, General Burch.

Sergeant Copeland said, "Look at him, he's stark raving mad! We need to do something!"

General Burch went to Colonel Lazarus and said, "Colonel Lazarus, are you all right?"

The colonel looked up at Burch. "I forgot what I was talking about," he said, and blushed with embarrassment. He smiled shyly. "Do you ever do that?"

Burch smiled. "Yes, I forget sometimes," he said. "All of us do."

Lazarus shook his head. "That's never happened to me," he said. "Used to be, I never forgot anything."

"Don't worry about it."

Lazarus smiled sadly. "How are those children in Houston?"

"We'll soon know, won't we."

Colonel Lazarus drew a deep, heavy sigh. "More casualties of war," he mumbled.

"Unfortunately."

21

<hr>

Grant Smythers pulled Kathryn aside as soon as she arrived at the Fort Hood command center. They walked down the hall to a quiet place, and he leaned his left shoulder against the wall, his arms folded across his chest. As usual, his right hand had its index finger wrapped around the stub of a cigar, which, at the present time, wasn't lit. He was from the old school: the dark suit, dark tie tight at the neck, and starched white shirt. His black wingtips shined. It didn't matter when she saw him; he always dressed that way, probably slept that way, she thought.

His head tilted, and his right eye squinting as if he were examining her under a microscope, he said, "I apologize about the confusion down at College Station." He had piercing brown eyes that had a tinge of plum in them, eyes that never betrayed what he was thinking. The rest of his demeanor didn't give away much either, except confidence. His lips were pressed tightly together beneath his salt-and-pepper mustache. He had gray hair, white in the temples, closely trimmed and brushed back. On top of his head, the gray showed that he had once had dark hair. She remembered those days.

Watching him with equally steady eyes, she said, "Grant, let's cut to the chase. What's going on? You've been jerking me around for several days now. And we could have very easily had a shoot-out with our own people over a lack of communication."

Without pulling his left shoulder off the wall, he lit the cigar stub and puffed it to life. He was the one of the few people who had the audacity to smoke in her presence. "We have a leak. I know David told you that, at least I told him to tell you. What he didn't tell you is how serious it is." His eyes never left her face, not even when he had lit the cigar. "We have to take every precaution now."

"Starting with me?"

"The Bureau's never had a problem like this," he told her. "This could destroy our credibility. Someone knows our every move. Within the hour you'll know exactly what I'm talking about, and you'll know why I thought it best to provide you with some added protection."

She thought about Wendy. Was she in danger? Don't jump to conclusions. Surely, he would have already assigned Wendy protection had he thought she was in danger.

He asked what she had learned in Galveston and College Station.

All she wanted to talk about was the leak, but she told him about the Morley and Tuort interviews.

"I saw you brought Steve Akers back with you."

She said she wanted to get him on a joint task force. "Can you help make the assignment—that is, assuming I'm still on this investigation?"

He nodded. "You're on the case."

She told him about the syringe and vial of potassium. "We're waiting for test results. Tell me about the leak."

He puffed on the cigar, creating dark smoke. "Any leak is bad, but this is worse than bad. It's a breach of all our electronic security."

She remembered what Major Robles had said about NSA. "We both know who's doing it."

"I've now figured that much out. They're the only ones that could do something this sophisticated and get away with it. The question is, who is involved and why?"

"I'll tell you this much. It's more than NSA being afraid one of our people is going to turn up something that will embarrass them. You could put some pressure on. That would take care of a lot of our problems. At least it'd put NSA on the defensive."

He chewed on the cigar stub. "They're already on the defensive. Now we need to let things play out for a while." He stared hard at her. "Effective immediately, I want you in charge of all field operations in this investigation."

"This game playing of yours really pisses me off," she said. "You've put me way behind in my work."

"I had to make sure NSA cooled off about you. And now I need you to put your ass back on the line."

Great.

He wrapped his index finger around the cigar stub and took it out of his mouth.

"Let me guess, you want to put my ass right out in front so people can take shots at it?"

Staring at her with his right eye squinting again, he said, "For some reason you seem to be the one person who's caused them to squirm."

"And you probably already have a dirty job lined up for me, don't you?"

"Yes, a rather unpleasant one."

Her first thought was that Angela's body had been found.

He pushed himself off the wall. "Let's take a ride over to the hospital," he told her, and took her by the arm.

"Is she dead?" That had to be it.

"We'll talk in the car."

In the sedan, on the way to Darnall Army Hospital, Grant told her, David, and Steve there was now a suspect in the investigation. "The prints you found out at the 'swamp' crime scene matched up," he told them. "He's Michael McCanles from Austin, Texas." He held out a mug shot.

Kathryn poked Steve in the chest. "I should have known he hails from Austin."

Steve smiled. He was sandwiched between her and David in the backseat. In front was Grant and Jeff Parker, a young black agent who was prematurely balding. He looked like he was overweight, but he was essentially the SAC's personal bodyguard, so Kathryn knew he must be good. Jeff, a stubble on his face, kept his eyes on the road. He had never had much to say.

"He's a student at the University of Texas." Grant lit his cigar as they passed around the mug shot. Kathryn cracked her window. "He has an interesting background. His brother's currently on death row down at the state penitentiary in Huntsville." Grant turned in his seat so he could see her. "Kathryn, you remember that bank robbery about four years ago down in Houston, the one where a police officer and one of the robbers were shot to death?"

She vaguely remembered the case. Steve said he remembered. He had gone to the funeral, he told them.

"Michael was allegedly involved in that robbery. The Houston police say he was the getaway driver, though they put him on trial twice without much success. The first time, he got a hung jury. The second time he won on appeal—was down at Huntsville and everything, but the appeals court let him go on some technicality.

"It seems the strongest evidence in the case was a police officer's testimony. He said that as he was arriving at the scene, another car was speeding off, and he saw the back of the suspect, plus one other thing."

"What's that?" she asked.

"He testified he got a glimpse of the suspect's face in the getaway car's rearview mirror."

David said, "Remember that, Jeff, the next time you try to get away with something."

Jeff was watching them from the rearview. She couldn't tell if he was smiling because she was sitting right behind him, but she thought he was. "What was the other evidence?" she asked. "I know they didn't put him on trial with that being the only evidence."

Grant turned back to face the windshield. "They wanted him in the worst way. Anytime a police officer is killed in the line of duty, systems are willing to go to great extremes to have justice. Unfortunately, the evidence wasn't much more than a face in a rearview mirror," he said. "It was basically all circumstantial. McCanles couldn't account for where he was at the time of the robbery. He was seen in the area. You know the scenario."

"So he was the one in the swamp, huh?"

Steve spoke up: "It always happens that way. Someone like that gets off on one thing and turns around and gets involved in something else. That's why you need to catch them good the first time and get them off the streets."

Grant said, "I've ordered him to be picked up as a material witness. He's got a number of connections to extremist groups. In fact, I assume you saw that portfolio on local hate crimes."

She said she had. She also said she was skeptical about the nature of the attacks.

Grant agreed. He said it was a bit too coincidental. "Whoever set up this Robles kidnapping wanted it to look like it was another in a series of similar attacks."

Grant flipped his cigar out the window. He continued: "I'm thinking about releasing McCanles's mug shot to the media. The U.S. attorney is giving us a lot of leeway on this. He's afraid this thing is going to blow up in our faces at any moment, and he wants us to take every measure to get McCanles."

"We don't know where he is?" Kathryn said. "I

thought you said he was a student at the University of Texas."

"He hasn't been to class in several weeks. No one's seen him in at least that long."

Steve said, "Who knows, if you catch him, you'll probably be doing him a favor. He can probably get back in his classes and still pass them by the end of the semester—if he's only missed several weeks."

They laughed, all but David, who asked, "They let them do that there? I thought the University of Texas was a good school."

"Come on, David, all schools are getting that way these days," Steve commented. "I read one story about a faculty and administration fighting because the administration wanted a teacher to pass a student who had only been in class nine times out of fourteen weeks. The administration didn't want any complaints from the student or her family."

Grant looked back at Kathryn. "As soon as you get a chance, I want you to fly down to Huntsville and see if you can get McCanles's brother to talk. We sent a couple of agents over, and the brother seemed willing to talk, but he demanded to talk with someone who had clout. You go down and see what you can work out."

The hospital was in sight. It was a large, several-story building that was surrounded by open fields.

In the back of the hospital, near the emergency room, were several mobile isolation units, yellow trailers, from the Centers for Disease Control. It was the first time Kathryn had seen evidence that the threat of biological terrorism was being taken seriously.

To get inside the central CDC trailer, Kathryn and the others had to pass through two sets of doors. Inside, Grant told one of the agents from ERT to bring out the package. The agent produced a small box. He placed the box on a table. Using a gloved hand to pull up the wrapping that had been cut away, Kathryn looked at the address. There was her name in large black letters: "KATHRYN STANTON, FBI AGENT, DALLAS." There was no other address and no postage. The sight of the box sent a chill through her. She glanced at Grant, who was watching her. He was waiting for her reaction. She knew he was. No wonder he didn't trust anyone, especially her.

Steve said, "Someone has it in for you."

She glanced at him. Was someone leading her into a trap? she wondered.

In a matter-of-fact tone, Grant said, "Postal officials in Fort Worth spotted the package right away and notified postal inspectors, who thought it was a bomb. They contacted Alcohol, Tobacco, and Firearms. Your friend Randy was there. ATF called me, and I contacted the CDC. They dispatched a team to advise us." He raised his hands. "As you can see, they're already getting things set up here and they're real cooperative about helping us—like up at Fort Worth."

He went on to explain how he had been worried that if the package had contained an explosive device with Exodus-V, it might have released enough aerosol to cause a major disaster in Fort Worth. "The CDC team contained the package, then the ATF x-rayed it. There was no bomb. I had them fly it here."

The ERT specialist opened the flaps of the box. Kathryn leaned over the box. Inside was a plastic bag with a twist top on it. Even without lifting the bag from the box, she saw what was in the bag. The specialist lifted the bag that contained a lock of hair. He said, "We've done some preliminary tests. I'm almost positive the hair belongs to the Robles girl."

Grant told the ERT specialist, "Show her the letter."

The specialist handed her a letter in a marked evidence package.

Grant told her, "I knew you were on your way here,

so I told them to hold all this until you got a chance
to see it."

Before she read the letter, she told the specialist,
"I want all this evidence processed, and I want reports
immediately. You personally fly everything to headquarters and walk things from lab to lab. Call me the
moment you learn anything."

The specialist nodded. He began to pack the box.

Kathryn read the letter, Steve and David standing
on each side of her:

Agent Stanton,
   Angela is alive, but thanks to you, she is no better
off. I'm afraid to say she's accidentally received some
burns, not serious ones, but she needs medical attention. The longer you let this drag out, the more serious
her condition becomes.
   By the time you receive this package, we will be
preparing a strong message through a sample use of
Exodus-V. The next time we make a demand, you
won't ignore us. We want the three Lance missiles
and launchers taken to the central hangar at the Fort
Hood airfield.
   MTR.

With the letter was a photograph of Angela. She
was obviously alive, but she looked dazed. Her right
hand and foot were exposed. Without a doubt there
were burn wounds. The hand looked especially
serious.

The ERT specialist commented, "A physician at the
hospital here looked at the photograph and said the
hand seems to have third-degree burns. He says that's
not good."

David sighed. "Oh, God," he said, and turned away.

Grant touched her shoulder. No one talked until
they got outside.

It was cold and windy outside, but the sunshine felt

good. For a few moments the only sound was the wind in a wind sock at a helipad. David lit a cigarette. Grant lit a new cigar. She wished she had a diet Coke. She wished she could talk to Wendy.

Grant said, "Now you know what I meant when I said we have a major problem. Someone knows our every move and is playing a game of cat and mouse with us."

She looked at him. What she didn't like was that for some reason she was at the center of the game. Steve and David were watching her, she could tell, but they didn't say anything. Why had the package been mailed to her? She thought of Randy. Grant said he had been there when the package had been inspected at Fort Worth. Had Randy had something to do with the package?

Grant puffed his cigar, watching her out of his squinting right eye. "Whoever it is knows you've hit a nerve. They want to put the heat on."

Kathryn asked, "On me?"

He nodded. "Which is why I think we should assign some protection for your daughter."

It was the first time he had mentioned it. It made her want to cry. It made her want to get on a plane, fly home immediately, and take Wendy as far away as possible.

He took her by the shoulders. "This is standard procedure," he told her. "Nothing to worry about. I promise you, we haven't heard anything that might lead us to believe that Wendy's in any danger, but with you being an apparent target, it's just best to be on the safe side."

For the first time Kathryn realized what she was involved in was real—very real. She could feel a tightness in her chest, one that seemed to want to cut off her breath. She nodded. "Okay, but I want to talk to her first."

Grant nodded. "One other thing—"

She looked into his eyes.

"You don't have to do this if you don't want to, but everyone agrees it would be most appropriate if it came from you. Would you break the news to Tony and Mary Belle? They should know about the burns. They should know what's going on."

Kathryn asked, "Where are they?"

"Alexandria, Virginia."

"D.C.!"

Grant raised his hands. "You said you wanted them under tight lock and key."

She asked David, "You want to tag along?"

"Sure."

She told Grant. "Have someone make the travel arrangements while I call Wendy. Get the arrangements for Alexandria, then get me to Huntsville. I want to find this McCanles person.

"I also want you to move three Lance missiles and launchers into place out at the airfield. Make them those simulator missiles, or whatever you want, but we need to at least make it look like we're following MTR's demands."

Grant said he would take care of everything.

Steve said he would get to pushing for the lab results on the syringe and vial.

She walked away from where the others stood and dialed her mother's number. She spoke briefly to her mother, then asked to speak to Wendy.

Right away Wendy announced that she had a new tutor in social studies. "I talked to Mrs. Hoepner and asked her what she thought about me having a tutor, and she said it depended on who it was. I told her Paulina Waldman, and she said Paulina was fine because she was making straight As."

"That's good, sweetheart," Kathryn said. "I'm glad to see you're working so hard at your schoolwork. Is tonight the social?"

"Yes."

"You excited?"

"No, Mom," Wendy said sarcastically. "I hate to go, but Grandma is pushing me out the door."

Kathryn laughed.

Wendy asked if Kathryn knew Joe Harris. Kathryn said she didn't think she knew him.

"He's in my grade, but on a different team from the one I'm on. Anyway, he has a brother who's sixteen, and he was in a car accident. They don't expect him to live very long. They say he broke all but three bones in his body, and one of his legs is hanging by a thread. He has internal bleeding, and they took him to surgery, but they couldn't get it stopped. They don't think he'll live another day. Isn't that sad?"

"It sure is. It's terrible." The world was depressing sometimes, Kathryn thought.

"What if something like that happened to me?"

"It'd be awful."

"I think it was awful they made Joe go to school today. They didn't want him worrying, so they sent him to school, but he spent the whole day at guidance anyway."

"That is sad."

"I know."

"Wendy, I wanted to tell you something so you won't get worried."

"What?"

"For a few days there's going to be some people kind of keeping an eye on you."

"Who?"

"Some people that work with me."

"Why?"

This had never happened before. She didn't know what to say. "Since I'm working on a really important case, they want to make sure you're okay—you know, like no newspaper reporters or anything are bothering you." She didn't know why she said that, but it sounded good at the moment.

"Oh. Okay." She didn't ask any questions at all, didn't even seem to be concerned.

Kathryn was scared. She wanted to be with Wendy, wanted to be the one protecting her. She hated that she couldn't be there.

22

A federal marshal met Kathryn and David at Washington National Airport, and gave them a tour of the nation's capital, as a way of indirectly taking them to the Robleses' safe house. It was a clear night. The snow-laden city was well lighted. They passed the Washington Monument. The marshal pointed out the back of the White House. The U.S. Capitol came into sight, but before they got to it, the marshal turned onto I-395. They passed signs for Arlington National Cemetery. Looking out her window, Kathryn saw the Pentagon. There was something about the city that had always appealed to her, something about its being the center of the nation's power. A number of times she had driven in from Virginia, following the interstate that passed through the mountains. At one moment there was the pristine beauty of nature; the next moment there was the heavy traffic of the city.

She smiled. It was just like Grant to hide Tony Robles right under the noses of NSA.

The marshal took the Duke Street exit in Alexandria. As they sped along Duke Street, he asked, "Are either of you hungry? There's a great Chinese restaurant near where the Robleses are holed up."

David told Kathryn: "If you don't mind waiting, I know a nice little place called Calvert Grille. It's here in Alexandria." He asked the marshal, "Have you heard of it?"

The marshal hadn't.

David said, "We can stop there later. I guarantee you'll get a great meal."

Kathryn wasn't thinking of a meal. She wasn't concentrating on the conversation at all. She had been worried all day about Wendy, and now she was worried about facing the Robleses.

David must have sensed her thoughts were elsewhere because from the backseat of the sedan, he tapped her shoulder and said, "Your daughter's going to be fine."

She tried to smile.

The marshal turned off Duke Street. He drove up into a housing development. He said, "This is a part of D.C.'s subsidized housing. Build expensive town houses and get the more affluent to invest so that the less affluent can also have quality housing." The town houses were nice.

The marshal pulled into a driveway. The garage door opened. The marshal drove the sedan into the garage, whose door lowered behind the car.

Inside the house was filled with noise. Children were screaming, and running from level to level of the three-story town house.

The house itself was richly furnished, like something out of a magazine. There were many green plants. Healthy ones. One plant had its streamers of leaves running from the balcony of the second floor to the first floor.

Raul greeted Kathryn. He jumped into her arms, though she felt she barely knew him. He wanted to see her badge again. While Kathryn held the skinny boy in her arms, David showed him his gold shield.

"How do you like our new house?" Raul asked, pushing his long hair out of his eyes.

Susana reminded Raul that the house was not their permanent home. "We're only staying here for a few days."

Carmela came running down the stairs. "Mom said we might be living here forever."

"No, she didn't," Susana said. "She told us we would be staying for a while—that's all. This isn't our house."

The children got into an argument.

Mary Belle came down the stairs.

Kathryn thought she looked pale.

Mary Belle said, "You kids go up and play on the computer." Her voice was not pleasant. It had the tone of someone drained of energy.

Before Carmela left, she told Kathryn, "Oh, you should see the neat computer they gave us."

Susana said, "It's not ours."

Raul answered, "Yes, it is, isn't it, Mom?"

Mary Belle, in a harsher tone, said, "All of you, get upstairs this minute!" Her personality had changed since the last time Kathryn had seen her. She seemed less good-natured, less tolerant.

The children withdrew, arguing about who was going to have the first turn on the computer.

Mary Belle was wearing navy sweats, and her hair was tied up in a bun. She tried to fix a loose strand with her fingers. "Hi, Kathryn," she said, forcing a smile.

The two women hugged.

David squeezed Mary Belle's arm.

Tony came down the stairs. He tried to tuck his knit shirt into his jeans. He was wearing a pair of glasses that had masking tape wrapped around the place where the left stem attached to the frames. He shook hands with Kathryn and David.

Mary Belle said, "They should have told us you were coming. No one tells us anything."

David mentioned, "It's for security reasons."

"Let's go upstairs."

They went upstairs.

The living arrangements were comfortable, even elegant. There was a fireplace, complete with gas logs burning. The formal dining room was combined with the living room. In the dining room was a glass-topped table, surrounded by four wrought-iron chairs, each with a white cushion in it. In the living room, centered around the fireplace, were several chairs and a sofa on an ornate Persian rug, which lay upon hardwood floors.

Mary Belle said sadly, "This is the most beautiful place I've ever been in. Too bad it has to be under these circumstances." No sooner had she gotten seated in a leopard-skin chair than the children were fighting upstairs. She excused herself and went up to the third level.

Kathryn could hear Mary Belle. It was the first time Kathryn had heard her raise her voice. "I want you three to listen to me, and I want you to listen to me well . . ."

Kathryn thought she could see Tony blushing.

Shaking his head, he said, "She's had a rough time of it."

Mary Belle's voice rose again, "If I hear one more word out of you, this computer goes off, and you'll all go to bed, is that clear?"

No one said anything.

"Is that clear!" Her voice was harsh.

Several voices mumbled, "Yes, Mom," and Mary Belle's light footsteps could be heard on the stairs. She reappeared in the living room, her cheeks red. It made her pale face even chalkier. "I'm sorry," she said.

"I hope you have everything you need," Kathryn said, looking around.

Mary Belle tried to smile, but tears came into her eyes. "Of course, we have everything we need, everything but our daughter!" She raised her hands. "Our life has to fall apart before our government finally gives us something comfortable to live in." She glanced at Tony.

He said, "We're on edge."

Kathryn didn't want to say anything, but she knew she had to.

At the same time Mary Belle seemed to sense something was wrong. She said, "What is it? It's something about Angela, isn't it? That's why you're here. You've brought us bad news about Angela."

"Yes, it's about Angela." She didn't try to lie.

Tony got out of his chair and went to sit with Mary Belle. He took one of her hands and squeezed it.

Kathryn shook her head. "Somehow Angela's suffered some burns on her right hand and foot. The kidnappers sent us a photograph. She's alive, but she has some burns."

Mary Belle began to cry, one of the rare times Kathryn had witnessed her cry openly. Kathryn's stomach hurt.

David emphasized, "This doesn't mean we've given up hope, or that we're going to be any less aggressive about bringing these people to justice."

"That's right," Kathryn added.

Tony pulled a handkerchief from his back pocket and handed the cloth to Mary Belle, who wiped her eyes. "We would like to see the photograph."

Kathryn looked at Mary Belle, who nodded. Kathryn held out her hand to David, who handed her the photograph in the evidence package. She, in turn, passed the photograph to Tony.

The parents had a strange reaction, one that Kathryn hadn't anticipated.

They both smiled at seeing the photograph of their daughter and carried on a conversation:

"Oh, she doesn't look so bad," Mary Belle said.

Tony gave out a little laugh. "Yeah, she looks like she's doing fine." He looked up at Kathryn and David.

"You should have seen her after the accident. You remember that, hon?" he asked Mary Belle.

Mary Belle smiled. "She was a mess, all right. Our baby's a fighter, isn't she?"

"Yeah, she's a fighter. She'll fight her way right out of this." He sighed and adjusted his glasses.

Kathryn didn't know what had been more distracting, the sunglasses he had been wearing the first few times she had seen him, or the glasses with the big wad of tape holding them together.

Tony said, "This isn't as bad as I had expected."

For the first time Kathryn saw beauty in the two parents. She saw a certain spirit in them, a will not to let anything get them down. Maybe the reaction they had had was not strange, Kathryn thought. Maybe they had expected to see their daughter dead, sexually abused, and mutilated.

Mary Belle cried in her joy. "She doesn't look bad at all," she repeated.

Tony patted his arm, then announced, "Mary Belle and I have talked. We're ready to go back."

Mary Belle nodded, wiping away her tears. She said, "This isn't us. We know that. The place for us to be is back trying to find Angela. She needs us. She's depending upon us. I can't stand sitting here doing nothing while everyone else looks for my daughter."

David mentioned, "It might not be safe."

Mary Belle looked at him and told him, "I was never so scared in my entire life than to discover that my daughter had been kidnapped." Her voice was hoarse. She asked him, "Have you ever experienced fear like that?"

David took the time to tell about his son. It was the first time Kathryn had heard the entire story. She was proud of him for having the courage to share the story at that particular moment.

Mary Belle gently nodded her head, arched her back, sitting very straight as Tony massaged her back, and said, "Then, you know that at some time you have to stop hiding in fear and stand up to whatever's making you afraid."

No one said anything.

She said, "We're going back and be there for Angela. We're going to help find her, and we're going to take care of her."

Good for her, Kathryn thought.

The children began to fight upstairs.

Mary Belle got up. "Those children will be the death of me yet," she said and left.

Kathryn looked at Tony.

He said, "yes, they'll fire me for going back to participate in the search."

"Or you could cooperate and we could bring those responsible to justice," she told him.

Tony shook his head. "You're wasting your time."

Kathryn motioned to David. They went downstairs, where they found two marshals in a sitting room. One marshal was watching a basketball game on television. The other was reading a magazine.

David asked, "Can one of you give us a ride?"

The marshal who had picked them up at the airport put his shoes on.

In the car on the way to the Calvert Grille, Kathryn told the marshal, "Make the arrangements to get the Robleses back to Fort Hood, and around-the-clock protection."

Without looking over while he drove, the marshal said, "I wish you people'd make up your minds."

At Calvert's, Kathryn and David were greeted by a pleasant man who had thick yellow hair and a yellow beard. He said he was the owner and welcomed them to his restaurant.

From their table near the front entrance, Kathryn looked at her surroundings. It was, as David had described it, quaint, complete with a bar, television, and simple, but tasteful decor.

Kathryn had the cilantro chicken and a diet Coke. The chicken over pasta was delicious. She was hungry. She ate everything. David had the salmon and a glass of white wine.

Over coffee she asked, "Do your sons really fight that much?" She was thinking about the Robles children.

He smiled smugly. "All the time."

"Like the Robles children were fighting tonight?"

Taking a drink of his coffee, he nodded. "Sometimes you literally have to peel them off one another." He smiled. "And I end up yelling at them—just like Mary Belle was yelling tonight." He sucked on his teeth. "You yell until you're literally hoarse. Don't you ever yell at your daughter?"

She shook her head. "Never."

He laughed. "Sure."

It was good to hear him laugh.

She suddenly realized they were looking at each other. Her eyes were staring at his.

23

Although Angela thought Corporal Klock might be dead, he eventually stirred again. Curled in a ball on the floor of the small hut that had been her prison and was now his, he gave an almost imperceptible sign of revival. His eyelids twitched. Then a foot moved.

Angela herself had been sleeping on the floor near him. Not asleep was Sergeant Copeland, and two of the officers, Lieutenants Rivero and Duffy. Other soldiers, under heavy guard, had been taken elsewhere.

Her right arm throbbed with pain, and she was stiff from the cold. She wanted to ask Private Kearnes if he could bring her something for the pain, but she couldn't bring herself to say the words. He sat on a chair at the door, his M-16 in his hands. To control the pain, she tried to keep as still as possible under the blanket Kearnes had thrown over her.

What was that sickening smell? she wondered. She looked around, but saw nothing she thought could smell so horrible. Even in the cold, she wished someone would open the door and let the smell out. It was everywhere.

Klock moaned. His eyes opened, but he couldn't seem to keep them open. The eyeballs rolled this way and that, then up into his head, showing their whites, and then the eyelids fluttered and shut again.

From somewhere beyond her prison, somewhere in the night, came music. Someone was playing a radio. Now and then there would be a burst of voices, like

an argument, then laughter. The noise went on and
on. It sounded like a celebration.

When she couldn't tolerate the pain any longer, she
began to cry. Her tears, warm at first, turned cold as
they ran down her face. She was freezing anyway, so
the icy tears running down her neck made her tremble.

Sergeant Copeland nodded to her and said to
Kearnes, "Private Kearnes, or whoever you are, why
don't you give her something for the pain? You can
see she's hurting. And she's cold too. Give her another
blanket, for God's sake."

He smiled wanly. He said, "Don't give me your
'God' crap. I don't believe in your God."

"Come on, then, you may be cruel, but I don't think
you're savage like the others. Call for someone to
bring her something for pain."

From his starched pocket Kearnes produced a
capped syringe. "I was waiting for her to ask." He
stood. "I know she can talk when she wants to." He
placed the syringe on the chair, removed his 9mm
from its holster, and drew a round into the chamber
as he held the M-16 under his left arm. Then he removed the clip from the M-16, cleared its chamber,
and leaned the M-16 beside the chair. He told the
sergeant to move away from Angela.

As he was nearing to give her a shot, Kearnes must
have seen what she had seen because he said, "Don't
even think about it, Klock."

Klock, whose eyes were open, said, "What?"

Kearnes smiled wanly again. "About making a
move on me. You'd be dead before you got off the
floor."

Pointing his 9mm at Klock, Kearnes yanked back
her covers. She was shocked to see how swollen her
wrapped arm was. The bandages at the end of her
hand, where her fingers were, were soiled with a
greenish color. The stench in the room became
stronger than ever.

"Don't look at it," Klock told her. "Kearnes, she has a bad infection. She needs help."

Kearnes gave her an injection in her right thigh, dropped the blanket over her, and returned to his chair. He reloaded his M-16 and put away his 9mm. "She stinks like a pig," he said. "That's all that's wrong with her."

Klock asked if he could use the restroom.

Kearnes told him to go in his pants, and laughed.

Klock said, "If I do, piss'll run all the way to your feet, and this place will stink worse than it already does. Come on, the bathroom's right through that door." He nodded in the direction of the door. "It's not like I'm going to go anywhere. Take these things off my hands. You can even watch me go."

"I'll be damned if I take the cuffs off."

"Then, you're going to have to unzip my pants and help me."

"You're crazy too."

"At least let me bring my feet through so I can get my hands in front. I promise I'll put them back behind me as soon as I return."

"Go ahead, but make it fast."

When Klock tried to get his feet up through his extended hands, he got his arms to encircle his butt, but he was having trouble bending forward far enough to pull his feet through. He looked too weak. Kearnes, lighting a cigarette, laughed at him. In a strained voice, Klock said, "Come on, Kearnes, give me a hand."

Kearnes, lit cigarette in his mouth, clapped. "There, there's your hand." He laughed loudly.

It took Klock several minutes to complete the process. Meanwhile Kearnes was entertained. He laughed frequently.

Winded, Klock said, "You bastard."

"Like I said, I'm not the one who had to take a piss. And like I said, you should be glad I'm letting you go at all."

Through much effort, Klock pushed himself to his knees, then he was able to get to his feet.

Kearnes said, "Can you whistle?"

"Yes."

"Let me hear you."

Klock whistled.

"You go to the bathroom, but don't close the door all the way, and the moment you stop whistling, I'll come in there blasting with this thing." He patted the reloaded M-16.

Klock said, "Don't worry. I'm not going to try anything."

"Go, and get back here."

Klock nodded. At the bathroom door he began to whistle. When he went inside, he didn't close the door all the way. She could hear him going to the bathroom. He went for a long time, whistling.

When he got back, he tried for several minutes to get his hands behind his back, but he wasn't successful. "Come on, Kearnes, help me," he finally said.

Kearnes said it didn't matter—he could keep his hands in front of him. "You're not going anywhere, anyway." Kearnes leaned back in his chair and stretched out his feet in front of him. He flipped his cigarette toward Sergeant Copeland, who stomped it out.

Next thing Angela knew, Klock was pointing something at Kearnes. Whatever it was looked like a muffler from a car hooked onto the end of a handgun.

Kearnes smiled when he saw it. It was a sick smile, as if he wasn't quite sure what to think. "Where did you get that?"

Klock said, "Believe me, it's real. Just set aside the M-16."

Even as Kearnes tried to aim the M-16, there was a "poof" sound in which a smattering of dark red mixed with chunks of gray hit the wall behind Kearnes. A black spot appeared in his forehead. Angela wasn't quite sure what she saw in Kearnes's eyes. She thought it might be disbelief, or maybe only emptiness. Kearnes slouched in his chair. His hands twitched at his side. The M-16 rattled to the floor. The hands seemed to tremble for a long time, even when Klock hurried to Kearnes and began to search his pockets.

Klock had apparently been looking for a key because when he found it, he immediately used it to unlock the handcuffs on his own wrists. Free of the cuffs, he closed them and put them into his back pocket. He tossed the key to Sergeant Copeland, who unlocked his own hands. As Copeland was about to hand the key to Lieutenants Duffy and Rivero, Klock said, "No, not them. I don't want them running around loose."

Both officers looked shocked, as if they couldn't understand how anyone could not trust their integrity. "They'll kill us," Rivero said through his nose.

Sergeant Copeland didn't make a move. He apparently wasn't going to argue with a man who had a gun, though he mentioned, "He's probably right. When they find Kearnes dead, they're not going to take any more chances—whatever they're up to."

Klock seemed to consider the logic of what Copeland had said. "Okay, rip up a bed sheet and gag them both."

While Klock searched Kearnes's pockets, Copeland used his teeth to start tears in a sheet. He tore off strips of cloth. "Open," he told Rivero.

"You'll be court-martialed for this—" Rivero said, but Copeland grabbed his jaw and shoved a wad of cloth into his mouth. He ran cloth several times around Rivero's head, creating a gag that kept the wadded cloth in place. Then Copeland tied the gag.

Duffy was more cooperative. He seemed like the type who was afraid of everyone and everything, and would do anything anyone told him to do. Without resistance or comment, he submitted to being gagged.

Klock had found another syringe of painkiller. He handed Copeland Kearnes's M-16. Copeland nodded at Klock's own weapon. "What's that contraption?" he asked.

Klock told him it was a homemade silencer. "I bought it from a friend for twenty-five dollars. Watch the back door." As Copeland was walking away, Klock held up the magazine from the M-16 and said, "Here, you might need this."

Copeland mentioned, "I knew it wasn't loaded, but I thought I'd let you play your game." He put the magazine in the weapon, drew a round in the chamber, and went to guard the back door.

Klock knelt next to Angela. "Are you feeling better?" he asked.

She tried to look past him, at Kearnes. "Don't look at him," he warned her. "I didn't want you to have to see that, but there was no other way. They were going to kill us. You have an infection. We need to get you help. I had to do something fast." His face got close to hers, so they could look into each other's eyes. "You think you're strong enough to travel?"

She didn't say. She didn't feel good. Felt weak. The sickening sweet smell in the air made her stomach churn.

"We have to get away from here. Can you help us?"

She still didn't say.

"Please."

"I'll try."

He smiled and helped her up. To Rivero and Duffy, Klock held up his weapon and said, "If you try anything stupid, I'll kill you, and no one will hear a thing." He turned to Copeland and ordered, "Sergeant Copeland, you lead the way. We want to head southeast, but we want to stay far away from the roads because Lazarus will have his men watching them."

Klock wrapped Angela's foot in more gauze to protect it from the cold. Then he put a blanket around her shoulders and, holding an arm around her, walked her outside, where there was a full moon lighting the darkness. Music from a radio still came from one of the barracks. The men were still laughing and talking loudly. The sounds filled the night.

After checking to make sure the way was clear, Klock told Copeland to lead the others to a grove of nearby trees.

Their silvery figures ran across an open space and disappeared in the grove of trees.

Klock whispered, "I'm going to put you up on my shoulders and run with you. I'll try not to be too rough." Without waiting to hear if that was all right with her, he heaved her across his shoulders and ran. She tried not to cry, but let out a couple of small sounds because of the excruciating pain she experienced each time her arm bounced.

Klock and Angela met the others in a patch of silver that had dropped through the trees. Klock was breathing heavily. She thought he was injured more seriously than he had pretended to be. Before, she decided, he was putting on a show for Kearnes, trying to make him think he was too injured to be of any threat. But now it was apparent that the beating he had taken really was serious. He coughed and spat out something that was dark when it hit the pale rocks that looked chalky in the moonlight.

Some clouds moved across the moon, creating blackness for a minute or so.

When it was light again, Copeland asked in a low voice, "Can I make a suggestion?"

Klock coughed and spat out some more of what Angela took to be blood. "What?" he said, clearing his throat.

"We have a long journey to make if we're going to get this girl to safety and get help."

"Okay. So what's your suggestion?"

"If we get out here and the moon goes behind a cloud, I don't especially want to be walking around in the dark with these two characters." He motioned to Rivero and Duffy.

Klock said, "You've got a good point. And what do you propose we do with them?"

"We're not far from firing range Alpha. If we backtrack there and leave Rivero and Duffy tied together so they can't move, it's not likely Lazarus and his men will ever think of searching their own front yard. We can travel faster and safer without them, and we can send back help."

Rivero began to make mumbling sounds through his gag.

Copeland told him if he did that out on the range, he would certainly be discovered by Lazarus. "And you know as well as I do, they'll kill you when they find you."

Rivero fell silent.

Klock gestured for Copeland to lead the way back to the compound. "Okay, we'll do it."

They used the trees as cover in order to backtrack to Alpha, the firing range near the compound. Alpha was not abandoned, however, as they had expected, but there was a group of soldiers working in the bed of a large truck that looked like some kind of a mobile missile launcher. The soldiers were working with a large, stainless-steel cylinder. Lights from flashlights glittered when they hit the giant canister that had a thick base attached to it. Standing on the ground behind the truck was Colonel Lazarus. "Hurry up, I want to get this thing steady for travel, and I want to get it positioned for firing."

One of the soldiers in the truck soon said, "It's ready, sir. It'll travel."

"Okay, drive the truck up to Bravo," the colonel said, "and I'll meet you there."

The truck roared to life, blowing thick smoke into the silver night. The truck drove away slowly, bouncing and shaking.

Lazarus watched it go, his eyes on the men in the bed, who were holding the canister steady. Then the colonel headed back to the compound.

Klock tapped Copeland's shoulder and whispered, "That's some kind of a rocket. Do you think it's the weapon the colonel was talking about?"

Copeland nodded.

"You think it's real?"

"It looked real to me."

"Me too."

While they were talking about what to do, Angela closed her eyes and thought of her former house in Maryland.

24

Outside the Texas state penitentiary's administrative wing, a three-story brick warehouse, David asked if there was enough time for him to smoke a cigarette before going inside. Kathryn looked up at the white clock beneath the pitch of the roof of the building: 8:04.

"It'll take three minutes," he told her.

She put her hands in her coat pockets. His cigarette breaks were always three minutes.

Huntsville, aside from Sam Houston State University and the state prison, was not much of a town at all. It was little more than a way station an hour north of Houston. Strange the prison held some of the most ruthless criminals of modern times, she thought, including a wing of prisoners who were awaiting execution by lethal injection. It didn't seem to be that important a place, yet already eight prisoners had been executed that year at "the Walls," as the prison was called.

David was about to light his cigarette when he said, "How about if I run inside and get you a diet Coke?"

"No, thanks."

"I'm sure they have a machine."

She shook her head. "I'm all right."

"You mind if I grab one for myself?"

She was losing patience with him. Before she could say anything, though, he had gone inside the building.

She felt stupid standing by herself on the front steps of the prison.

David returned with two diet Cokes. He handed her one. "I didn't want to leave you out here watching me smoke."

Though she didn't want to admit it, she had been wanting something to drink. She usually had a diet Coke first thing in the morning, and she hadn't had one yet that morning, things had been so hectic. She had called Wendy, which had been nice, but that had put her behind schedule. Wendy had ended up talking about this and that. Each time Kathryn had been about to say good-bye, Wendy had said something like, "There was something else I was going to tell you—oh, Grandma took me to get my bangs trimmed, but the lady was behind, so we ended up waiting forty-five minutes, then Grandma got mad, and we left . . ."

Opening her can, she said, "Thank you," then mentioned, "I didn't know you drank diet Coke."

"I've decided to make some changes in my life," he told her. "I'm going to stop smoking, lose weight, and get back in shape."

She took a long drink of her diet Coke. "Sounds like I won't even be able to recognize you when you're all through."

A characteristic smile came onto his face as he lit his cigarette. He looked into the hole on the top of his can and said, "I talked to my sons this morning. Sean, the one who got hit by a car, is taking piano lessons."

"That's good. I tried to get Wendy to take them, but she ended up playing the baritone instead."

The smile on his face grew larger. Staring at the ground while he smoked, he said, "I think piano is just what Sean needs—he's so hyper. Maybe this'll settle him down some." He looked at her. "Did you talk to Wendy this morning?"

She told him, yes, she had, and it had been a good

conversation. "Maybe now that she's been staying with my mom and dad, she's started liking me again and hating them." She shrugged. "Anyway, I like it."

A group of trustees filed out of the prison. They were dressed in white. They began washing windows, sweeping, and emptying garbage.

David took a final drink of his diet Coke, a last puff of his cigarette, which he ground out, and said, "Okay, I'm ready."

She drank as much of her diet Coke as she could. She and he went inside the prison, where they checked their weapons at the armory.

At the warden's office they showed their credentials, and Kathryn told the administrative assistant they needed to interview Doug McCanles. The assistant made the necessary arrangements.

Kathryn and David were led deep into the prison. Security was tight, from armed guards in observation towers to guards patrolling the halls. She and David passed through one iron gate after another before they arrived at a room where the interview was to take place. It was a room encased in reinforced glass—a room that the guards could watch from all angles. As she and David waited in the room, six guards passed, dragging a manacled prisoner.

Thirty-year-old Doug McCanles arrived, taking small steps because his legs, hands, and body were chained. A short, fat man with abundant strawberry-blond hair and a pockmarked face, he was wearing a faded green uniform and black boots. He was nothing like she had anticipated. She had expected a hardened criminal, someone who would strike terror in her. Instead he looked gentle, almost pleasant. "Please, sit down," she told him.

The guard who had delivered McCanles withdrew, pulling shut the door.

McCanles sat. He asked her if he could smoke. His voice was polite. His razor-blue eyes watched her.

They were intense eyes, ones that made her feel like they were somehow touching her.

"Go ahead," she told him.

He brought out a package of Kool menthol cigarettes and an orange Bic lighter. With a shake of his wrist, he caused a cigarette to jump. His lips caught it. His other hand lit it. The act was obviously performed to impress others, though he was having a bit of difficulty coordinating his moves because of the chains. He pulled smoke deep into his lungs, held it for a moment and, lower lip extended, blew the smoke upward, around the cigarette, which was still in his mouth. He looked at her through the smoke.

She told him they were seeking information about his brother.

He said he might have information, then asked if she would be willing to go to the governor in his behalf.

She almost laughed, the statement came so abruptly. "I doubt it, but let's hear what you have anyway, and we'll see." She spoke as casually as he had.

His face hardened. Bending forward, he took the cigarette from his lips. "If that's your attitude, I guess we have nothing to talk about," he said. He nodded at his chains and smiled back at her. "Look, I have nothing to lose. As far as I'm concerned, if they're going to put me six feet under, I'll take what I know to the grave with me."

She couldn't figure out whether to take him seriously. She told him, "I didn't say I wouldn't try to do something to help you. I said I doubted it because I doubt you really have anything to tell us. But if I were to do something, first I'd need some damned good information to let me know my efforts were worthwhile. Do you know something that would make me go to the governor?"

He smacked his lips, sucked on his teeth, then bent forward to put the cigarette back in his mouth. He pulled smoke from it. Smoke came out of his nostrils at almost the same time. "Why don't you decide that? Ask me some questions, and see if I'm worth anything to you," he said, the cigarette held between his teeth.

David spoke up: "Your brother's always maintained he had nothing to do with the robbery you've been convicted for."

McCanles smiled and said, "Come on, he was there and we all know it."

It came as a surprise to her that he would say such a thing. Kathryn had carefully read the reports and reviewed the evidence. It didn't make sense that Michael McCanles, who at the time had been working on an undergraduate degree at the University of Texas, would take part in a bank robbery. His academic record indicated that he had everything going for him.

"When that police officer testified he saw Michael in the rearview mirror, he knew exactly who he saw, didn't he?" David said.

McCanles nodded. "He was there. Believe me, he was there. And it wasn't the only thing he was involved in."

Kathryn said, "We're trying to find Michael. Do you know where he is?" Without additional evidence linking Michael to the bank robbery, no one would get a conviction against him. That would pit brother against brother. Besides, getting Angela was her main concern.

Doug leaned sideways, let the cigarette drop to the floor, and ground it out with his foot. "I think that's the kind of information you get after you talk to the governor," he said.

She leaned back, stretching her feet out so they were crossed at the ankles, and shoved her hands into her coat pockets. "Okay, you pretend to know what we might be most interested in," she said. "How about if you tell us something that you think would be enough to send us running to the governor right now. You're going to have to give me something up front."

"I'm assuming you want to know about matter," he told her.

"Matter?" David said, leaning forward as if he hadn't heard correctly.

"MTR."

"Go on," she told him, not moving from her position. She didn't want to jump to conclusions, though she could feel excitement rising in her. It was the first time anyone had pretended to know what the initials stood for.

"The letters stand for Microbe Terrorism Response."

How would he know that? she wondered. How would a man on death row know such a thing? She didn't say anything.

"The army doctors were down here, you know," Doug said. "We have a special unit in the prison, a unit shared by several large pharmaceutical companies. They do drug research here. They experiment on prisoners. MTR was a special experiment that the army conducted. They even told the prisoners the research might be dangerous—you know, like the volunteers might have some kind of a reaction to the drugs." He smiled. "Sure enough, some of them ended up dying. You might have heard, only the prison gave it a different twist for the public. You remember hearing about the prisoners who died by drinking homemade hooch laced with methanol and some other nasty stuff?"

She hadn't heard anything about it.

"That's what the army doctors said. They did the autopsies, and said the prisoners who had died had gotten into some methanol and had tried to make their own alcohol. We all knew it was from the drug experimentation. The army had it all tightly controlled." He stopped talking and stared at her. "You act like you don't believe me. Go to any major prison in the United States, and I guarantee you'll have a pharmaceutical company conducting research. Companies pour their money into prisons because prisoners make great guinea pigs. The companies provide good food and keep the prisoners in a comfortable building with all kinds of luxuries, then the doctors experiment on us. In this case I think the army might have been doing experimentation with some kind of germ. At least that's what I heard. They thought they had a vaccine for it, but it turned out that the vaccine didn't work." He smiled.

Kathryn sat up to the table and folded her hands before her. She asked, "How did you learn all this? After all, you're on death row. How does someone on death row learn such things?"

McCanles smiled. "In case you didn't know," he said, "this is our world. Prisoners run the Walls, just like prisoners run every other prison in the United States."

David asked, "Where's your brother?"

McCanles said, "I'm on death row. You get me off death row, and I'll talk. I'll spend my life in prison. That's fine. But if you plan to kill me, you'll get nothing, not a damned thing. Check out what I told you, and then get back to me if you're still interested."

Kathryn told him, "Oh, we'll check it all out. If what you're telling us isn't one hundred percent accurate, you better let us know now, because we'll check every single detail. And if anything of what you're telling us isn't the truth, we won't be back."

He seemed more nervous. "The only thing the prison isn't going to admit to is that the prisoners who died, died because of the drug tests. The prison's going to insist that the prisoners died from homemade alcohol. That's what the army doctors told them had been the results of the autopsies."

Kathryn and David sent Doug back to his cell and went to the warden's office, where the administrative assistant confirmed what McCanles had said. Drug studies were conducted at the Walls. It was nothing unusual. Pharmaceutical companies had financed the building of a sophisticated wing in the prison, and prisoners routinely participated in drug studies, though the assistant insisted that all studies were strictly voluntary, that prisoners signed release forms, that prisoners were well compensated and cared for, and that the tests were not dangerous.

What abut some prisoners who had died in the drug unit?

"That's all been taken care of," the assistant said. "We have tighter security over there now. Prisoners wouldn't have an opportunity to make their own alcohol. What happened was that one of them found some methanol and mixed it into a concoction that a group of the prisoners drank, and it ended up killing them." He shook his head. "Such materials are never within reach of prisoners now—not even in the drug test unit. They're strictly controlled."

Kathryn asked the assistant if he would be willing to provide a list of the participants, including doctors, of a series of studies known as MTR. Sure enough, Michael McCanles' name was on the list, as was the name of a U.S. Army Reserve physician, Dr. Albert DiUlio.

Kathryn's composure was short-lived. The moment she got outside the prison, she grabbed David by the shoulder of his coat and shook him. "Can you believe this!" she said. "We're on to something here!"

He laughed as he let her shake him.

An uncontrollably large smile on her face, she said, "What a stroke of luck. This is even better than that syringe and vial of potassium."

At the car she got Grant on her portable phone. She didn't explain details, but said she had a lead and was heading for Austin to see the governor. She briefed Grant while David drove to the Department of Public Safety post, where they left their sedan and caught a ride to the hospital. A National Guard helicopter was warmed up and waiting on the Life Flight pad at the hospital.

During the flight, Kathryn made calls to the governor's office. The governor was not available, but his secretary assured Kathryn that one of the governor's representatives would be happy to visit with the agents. Once those arrangements had been made, Kathryn tried to calm herself for the rest of the flight, which didn't take long.

In fact, within the hour she and David were inside the state capitol building. They went directly to the governor's office, where the receptionist Kathryn had talked to greeted them. The receptionist made a couple of calls. She sent Kathryn and David up to the fourth floor.

There, Karen Kershenstein, an assistant to the governor, listened patiently to Kathryn's story. David sat without saying anything. Kershenstein said she had been following the kidnapping story on the news, and took notes. Kathryn explained that Doug McCanles might know something that could lead investigators to his brother and quite possibly to Angela. At the same time Kershenstein seemed interested in the case, though, Kathryn was taking stock of her office. It was a small, windowless cubicle in the capitol rotunda. Not a very important aide, Kathryn thought.

At last Kershenstein leaned back in her chair, and said, "I don't want you to take offense at what I have to say, but I don't want to mislead you either." She leaned forward and, elbows on the desk, rested her chin on top of her folded hands. The desktop was unnaturally bare. "It's not like the governor can pick up the telephone and commute a judicial sentence. You have to understand that the governor is an elected official, which means he can do things for the people of Texas easier than he can do them for representatives of the federal government."

"The daughter of a Texas resident has been kidnapped," David spoke up.

"I understand that," Kershenstein told him, "but let's look at the bigger picture. She's the daughter of a military man, and military personnel come and go all the time. If one comes to Hood, how long does he or she spend in the state—two, three years at most? A lot of people view military personnel as temporary residents. On the other hand, we have the friends and family of a slain police officer down at Houston. If the governor were to commute this McCanles' sentence, we could end up having the entire Houston police force in an uproar."

Kathryn had met enough bureaucrats in her time to know one when she was face-to-face with one. She said, "Are you going to help us or not?" She was prepared to seek an audience with Kershenstein's supervisor. Kathryn needed the information Doug McCanles had.

The young woman's face turned pale. She said, "I'm going to try to help." She straightened and dropped her hands to her side. "I have a suggestion that I think is good advice, a suggestion that anyone else you went to would agree with. I suggest you go to Houston to see the police chief. If you can get his support, it'll be easier to get the governor's support."

Damn it, Kathryn thought, a waste of precious time. Yet she knew if she tried to see another member of the governor's staff, it was likely the new staff member would side with Kershenstein, who had already made a decision. It was how bureaucracies worked. They were slow to get started and next to impossible to steer once they took off in a certain direction. Kathryn and David left Kershenstein at the desk where she seemed to do nothing but sit.

Once in the marble rotunda, David asked, "Why

didn't they tell us all this before we got here?" When she didn't answer, he said, "So are we going to Houston?"

She shrugged. She wasn't thrilled about visiting the Houston police chief. She had met him on a couple of occasions and knew his reputation. Nicknamed "Duke" because he bore a vague resemblance to John Wayne, Billy Hughes was vintage law and order. He didn't strike her as being the kind of person who would support the commutation of a sentence under any circumstances. He would say in this case that the criminals were trying to take the government hostage, and he wouldn't want to yield to their demands. She was almost certain that's the position he would take. At the same time she knew without his support, or at least without his voluntary silence in her endeavors, she would never win the support of the governor.

At the airport she and David caught a Cessna to Houston, where they immediately got an audience with Chief Hughes. She knew she had caught him at a bad time, though—he was returning from overseeing a hostage crisis in which a husband had been threatening to kill his wife. Kathryn didn't waste time in telling him why she had come.

Chief Hughes, who had not bothered to sit down yet, leaned over his desk, and smiling through a brownish-gray mustache, said in a thick voice, "Now, what reason could I possibly have for going along with such a foolish request?"

Though he was an imposing man, she didn't see the John Wayne features others claimed to see. She told him Doug McCanles was willing to help the Bureau locate Michael McCanles, who was linked to the kidnapping up at Fort Hood.

The smile faded from his face. He got serious and dropped into his desk chair. "Does Doug McCanles know something? He wouldn't talk before."

"I guess he's desperate now."

"You know his brother Michael was involved in the shooting down here, don't you?"

She nodded. "That's what Doug told us."

He sighed and said, "I don't know. This puts me in a bad spot. A sort of bird in the hand for one in the bush. If you could get Michael McCanles on something, nothing would make me happier, but—"

She told him, "What difference does it make about the bird in the hand? If McCanles is executed or spends the rest of his life behind bars, he's still off the streets forever."

"He gunned down one of my officers, someone I knew personally and cared about."

She apologized for sounding insensitive, then she said, "The only thing I'd point out is that even if Doug McCanles is put to death, it isn't going to bring back the slain officer. If Doug McCanles lives, he's going to give us his brother."

Chief Hughes stood and reached out with a large hand. She took it. He had a strong grip. "Talk to the president of the police association," he said. "If he'll go along with you, so will I."

It was an encouraging step.

Kathryn and David went to see John Hill, a sergeant in the Harris County Sheriff's Department. A skinny man who looked to be in his fifties and had the face of a mouse, he was not as cooperative. On the wall of his office were a number of diplomas and awards. There was even a law degree. He slipped into his lawyer mode and waxed legalese right away.

He said he was not sure the law would even allow the governor to commute a prisoner's sentence in such a manner.

In the city beyond his office window, sirens rose.

Trying to keep her cool at the same time she was sure she was losing her temper, she suggested that he let the governor and his staff make such a determination. "Right now we're trying to help a child whose life is in danger," she said, "and get a dangerous person off the streets."

The sirens seemed to be everywhere.

Sergeant Hill said, "I know the child you're talking about. You're talking about that little Mexican girl." His tone was one of dismissal. "We can't throw out our entire legal system every time one of those little kids gets in trouble. That'd drain us dry." He leaned back in his chair to look out the window.

David told him, "I don't want to turn this into any type of adversarial meeting, but I'm Mexican-American, and I take exception to the way you made reference to the victim."

To Kathryn's complete surprise, instead of apologizing for his insensitivity, Sergeant Hill acted like he was quite used to such confrontations. He simply said the matter was a federal problem and not a state problem. He opened his top drawer, from which he removed a wet-wipe. He tore it open and began wiping his hands with the moist cloth.

They left him cleaning his hands.

In the halls there was chaos.

25

<hr>

Twelve Houston girls were dead, killed instantly by a highly toxic disease or illness.

The news sent shock waves throughout the country.

An entire section of Houston had been quarantined—cutting off the school where the deaths had taken place, a predominantly black and Hispanic high school, Jefferson Davis High. The National Guard had been called in, and parents and teachers were horrified. The city was in a state of shock. Federal agents, state and local health officials, and officials from the CDC had donned protective suits and masks to begin a thorough search of the school for possible clues to the mysterious deaths. Other officials had swarmed to local hospitals, where there were another eight girls from the same ninth-grade class, all of whom seemed to be suffering from the same mysterious illness, though a weaker version. Members of the news media were arriving from all over the world. They wanted answers and were willing to listen to anyone who would talk.

At a CDC trailer, Kathryn, David, and Bureau forensic specialists introduced themselves to Dr. Jennifer Egan and her team from the CDC. The short, dark-haired woman who had lime-green eyes, the left of which was slightly askew, had flown to Houston immediately upon hearing about the outbreak of strange cases. The trailer and other equipment had been flown in by a military C-131 transport plane. The President of the United States had authorized everything.

As everyone donned protective gowns and gloves, Dr. Egan looked at Kathryn and told her, "We'll be lucky if we can save the other eight." They were in critical condition, Egan explained, and receiving massive doses of antibiotics. Remarkably enough, another six girls had only mild symptoms.

Kathryn asked for details of what had happened.

Dr. Egan said that the twelve girls who had died hadn't even known what had hit them. "The germ they encountered was so toxic that it killed them instantly. Apparently, they were showering after gym class, and an aerosol form of your Exodus-Five was released."

So it was true, Kathryn thought, horrified. Someone had the germ.

There was a somber atmosphere in the trailer as everyone dressed silently, then put on respirators.

It was a short walk to the school, where they passed through the gymnasium to the girls' locker room. Kathryn was sickened by what she encountered in the open shower stall. Young bodies, naked, were lying this way and that in puddles of water—where the germ had dropped them. Worst of all were the ghostly eyes, eyes that still reflected the living world around them. All the eyes were open, filled with terror. The mouths were open too, as though gasping for air.

Kathryn kept seeing Wendy again and again.

To make matters worse, as Kathryn and the others came out of the school, stunned, she learned that one of the eight girls in critical condition had died. The body was being taken to the morgue at Children's Hospital, where an autopsy was being set up for immediate medical information.

A police escort got Kathryn, David, and Dr. Egan to Children's Hospital, which was in a state of chaos. They were led to the morgue, where they re-suited.

From there they were led into a large windowless room. It was all in stainless steel, like a laboratory.

Kathryn saw the young Hispanic girl, naked, upon a stainless-steel table. She looked like she was sleeping, like she might get up at any moment and discover her nakedness.

The medical examiner, in a protective suit, called attention to a row of fluorescent view boxes, upon which hung chest X rays of the girl. An investigator from the CDC, also in a protective suit, began explaining a peculiarity about the X rays. With a Bic pen the CDC investigator pointed at the area between the lungs depicted in the first X ray. He said, "You'll notice here a classic picture of inhalation anthrax—widening of the mediastinum, this space between the lungs, and you can also see evidence of pleural effusion. Dr. Perry has been kind enough to provide us with a normal chest X ray." He put up another X ray and pointed to the bottom of the lung. "See how the bottom of the normal lung is rounded out? These are called the costaphrenic angles. In pleural effusion, fluid fills the bottom of the lungs, as in this case"— he used his Bic pen to point out the lungs of the victim—"where you see the rounded edges, or costaphrenic angles, are blunt." He removed the normal X ray.

The medical examiner, Dr. Perry, led the group of visitors to the table where the victim lay, Myla Estes. Eyes closed but bulging, she was dirty. Even her long black hair, tangled, looked greasy—matted with blood and fluids. Her mouth was slightly open, showing bloodstained incisors. Puncture wounds, stained with orange Betadine, marked where needles and instruments had been attached to her by medical personnel who had worked intensely to keep her alive.

Kathryn tapped the shoulder of a Bureau photographer. He began to snap photographs of the body.

Dr. Perry called out a name: "Dr. Shea, you want to tell us what you know?"

Dr. Lisa Shea seemed as if she were somehow permanently in a state of shock. At least that's how she looked inside the hood that covered her head. Through the window of the hood, her brown eyes looked like they were remembering something they wanted to forget, something that had terrified them. "I saw her as soon as she arrived by ambulance," she said. "Already I could hear rhonchi in her lungs. After that I don't know what happened. She was fine. I thought she was getting better. I administered massive doses of antibiotics, and she was responding well.

"It all took place so quickly. Her lips turned cyanotic, she had trouble breathing, and she developed a choking cough. As you can tell from her hair, she was sweating." She shook her head. "I've never seen such sweating. Profuse diaphoresis." Kathryn could hear a sigh. "She knew she was dying, that was the worst part. She kept telling us she couldn't breathe and that her chest hurt. She kept asking if she was going to die, and I kept telling her no."

A loud fan came to life in the room. Water gushed down troughs on each side of the stainless-steel table where Myla lay. The medical examiner spoke into a gooseneck microphone that hung from the ceiling. "The deceased is Myla Estes, a fourteen-year-old Hispanic female. She is a well-nourished. . . ."Dr. Perry dictated his report as he worked. He made the classic Y incision in Myla's chest, leaving white lines where he had cut. Yellow fat inflated as the scalpel crossed her belly. The smell of bowel filled the room. Not even the fan or the masks were able to attenuate the stench of inchoate bowel.

Dr. Egan asked Dr. Shea, "Lisa, when the patient came in, were you suited up?"

No, Dr. Shea replied. No one had been suited up.

"This was before any of us realized what was happening."

Dr. Egan said, "I'm sure we're going to discover what we've already been told. Exodus-Five is perfectly harmless shortly after it is released into the environment."

As she watched the doctor work, Kathryn realized she had never gotten used to autopsies. It always seemed excessively cruel to cut a body to pieces, regardless of the circumstances.

Dr. Perry worked with efficiency, as if he had done the same cuts thousands of times before and had grown used to them. He pulled on Myla's small breasts, trimming them away from the ribs. From the Y cut, he pulled back all of her flesh and draped it over her arms, as one would throw a soaked coat over a chair to dry. He cut out her ribs in one large section, uncovering a pool of dark red, almost black fluid. Obviously, she had bled internally. Dr. Perry pointed out the blackened areas of Myla's lungs. "Note the necrosis," he said. "Along with the massive hemorrhaging, it gives you an idea how potent the toxin is. . . ."

Outside, photographers and people with television cameras were everywhere. The reporters knew names and weren't afraid to use them. "Dr. Egan," one reporter called out, "isn't it unusual for the Centers for Disease Control to take such an immediate and aggressive interest in a case like this? What's going on?" It was Roger Worthington from the *Dallas Morning News.*

"No comment," Egan said, screened by uniformed police who provided a path for her and the others. Dr. Egan was either used to the questions of the press, or she had been briefed about what she could and could not say.

Worthington called out: "What's going on here? The public has a right to know!" That brought angry shouts from other reporters.

Kathryn pushed forward to one of the waiting sedans.

"Agent Stanton, was one of the victims the girl who was kidnapped up at Fort Hood? Is this an act of terrorism?" Worthington's persistent questions brought a barrage of other questions from other reporters.

Kathryn, getting in the sedan, was sure Worthington was getting information from somewhere, and it angered her. She detested reporters like Worthington, reporters who used the media to create their own little worlds of power, authority, and abuse.

An uneasy silence lingered in the sedan until it was out of the angry mob. Then Dr. Egan said, "It's absolutely incredible to believe our own government created this bug." It was all she said.

David commented that when he was in the Gulf War, he had been through much of the same thing. "Our own government denied that any chemical or biological agents had been used," he said, "and they knew damned good and well there had been agents used."

Kathryn asked him if he had heard the questions about Angela and terrorism.

He said, yes, he had heard them. "I saw who asked them too. That one who did the story when our car was shot up."

Kathryn wondered what the victims of the anthrax infection had experienced during those brief moments. What was it like to be dying and to realize there wasn't a thing anyone could do to help you? she wondered. She asked Dr. Egan about controlling a large act of terrorism involving Exodus-V. "Is there anything we can do in a sort of prophylactic sense?"

Dr. Egan shook her head. She said, "There's no way we can give the entire city prophylactic antibiotics or chemotherapeutic agents. That would be more of a risk than it's worth. Besides, the last thing we want is a resistant strain of bacteria, which is a risk you take whenever you use antibiotics indiscriminately." She looked out her window. "And you know there is no vaccine, don't you?"

Kathryn couldn't tell if Dr. Egan was looking out the window or studying her reflection in the glass.

"But even if we had one," Egan continued, "and we vaccinated the entire city, whoever has Exodus-Five could take the agent to San Antonio, or up to Dallas, or maybe up to Denver." Dr. Egan glanced at Kathryn. "Your best bet is to catch whoever's doing this." She opened a folder from a shoulder case she was carrying. She began flipping pages in the folder, commenting, "The sad thing is that many of us have known for a long time something like this was going to happen—a biological attack."

It didn't take the sedan long to get back to the school.

Houston's FBI office had moved in one of its portable command centers. Kathryn and Dr. Egan went to the center. Inside, agents were hard at work, bustling between communications equipment, lab equipment, fax machines, and computers. A loud humming and buzzing of machines filled the air.

Dr. Egan's chief assistant, a large man with a red face and red hair, Dr. Chris Glynn, appeared. He reported that investigators thought they had isolated the source of the bacteria in the girls' locker room. According to Glynn, a small number of bacteria spores had been collected from an aerosol air freshener in the shower area, a timed freshener that periodically released scent into the air.

Kathryn asked, "How long do these spores stay active? Do we know?"

Dr. Glynn said, "That's the odd thing. This strain of the *Bacillus anthracis* is aerobic like other bacteria in the genus. In other words, it has to have access to air to survive. The generic organism forms highly resistant spores that can survive at least several decades, as long as there's air in the environment. But the way this Exodus-Five has been engineered, it's almost like a malignant form of the original *Bacillus anthracis*. Apparently, without a human or animal host, the Exodus-Five strain will undergo exponential growth in open air for, let's say, the first few minutes, then it's dead." His face became more red. "You must understand that I'm only now coming to terms with all of this, so I'll need to run some studies before I have exact information, but based upon what the army's provided me, I think I'm fairly accurate." He shook his head. "It's one of the most toxic germs I've ever seen."

Dr. Egan sighed. "At least one thing's good," she said. "It means once we disinfect the school area, it'll be safe."

David said he was having difficulty seeing any good at that particular moment.

Dr. Glynn mentioned, "Then, let me put it this way. Exodus-Five is one of the worst germs I've seen, but at least we don't have to worry about abandoning this city for the next fifty years."

Earl Lennette, a skinny black man, arrived. He was the Bureau's special-agent-in-charge of the Houston region, and an old friend of Kathryn's. They embraced. He said he had been out deep-sea fishing and had just returned.

An agent handed Kathryn a telephone. Grant was on the other line. Before she talked to him, she told Earl, "We need to know who manufactures the air fresheners for this school district, who distributes them, and who had access to the school itself—especially the people with keys."

Earl began snapping his raised fingers. "I need some help here," he said, and several agents approached him.

"Yes, Grant," she said, speaking into the phone.

He asked her what was going on. She gave him a

briefing, being as careful as possible not to give too many details over the telephone.

"What can I do?"

She told him, "I want Dr. Albert DiUlio."

"Done. What else?"

"Call the governor. I want Doug McCanles's sentence commuted."

Grant said he would make the call.

She told the others, "I'm heading for Huntsville. Keep me posted."

With that, she and David caught a National Guard flight to Huntsville, where a faxed letter from the governor waited. She knew, of course, that the fax contained no fixed promises, but it did request that the warden allow her as much freedom as she needed to interview Doug McCanles, with the stipulation that if McCanles provided information that led to the arrest and conviction of his brother, his sentence would be commuted from death to life imprisonment without parole. The assistant said the warden had personally talked with the governor and all the arrangements were made.

She and David were escorted to the glassed room where McCanles sat. This time his hands were free, so his movements were more casual. After he had carefully read the fax, McCanles put it on the table in front of him and lit a cigarette. He seemed to gloat over the letter. He said, "This is the biggest moment in my life."

Kathryn reminded him, "Maybe. But don't jump to conclusions." She glanced at David. "Tell us about Michael."

"You knew he was here, right?"

Kathryn nodded.

"He was here and got out on appeal."

"Was he in on the drug tests?" David asked.

Doug lit a cigarette. "Yes, but he was released before they really got going."

That coincided with the information the assistant had given them.

Kathryn could tell David wanted a cigarette. She was tense, and she knew David was too. The stakes had grown tremendously. It was only a matter of time before Exodus-V would be used again. Someone had it. "Where is Michael?" she asked.

"Last time I heard, he was up in Temple," Doug said, taking a puff of his cigarette.

She remembered the matchbook from Temple, the one that had been found in the swamp.

Doug smiled. "Everyone thinks Michael is the good one of the two of us. They think he's the one who went to college and has been trying to better himself. They felt sorry for him when the police kept trying to bring him to trial, felt sorry for him when he got convicted. They said it was only the police trying to frame him and take him off the streets. Of course, Michael did nothing to dispel the rumor, especially when the conviction was overturned." He flicked his ashes on the floor. "Even now when I get letters from our family, they say he's the smart one in the family, and the only reason why he's run off from school is because the police keep harassing him. It's true, he is the smart one. He's the one who plans all the crimes."

What did he mean "crimes"? David wanted to know.

Doug went on to describe a string of burglaries and robberies the brothers had committed together. She and David took elaborate notes, and recorded the interview. Doug left no detail out. He even told them about small crimes, such as how they had stolen a generator from a construction site and had sold the piece of equipment to a private owner. He knew the names of the construction site and the person who had bought the stolen generator.

How had Michael ended up in Temple? David

asked after nearly an hour of details about specific crimes.

"It's where Mamaw lives," Doug replied.

"Your grandmother?" Kathryn asked. She didn't recall any relatives of the McCanleses living in Temple.

"She's not actually our grandmother," Doug told her, "but she's always been like one." He gave an account of how they had grown up with their grandfather, who, divorced, had become engaged to a woman named Maxine Chrisman, now in her seventies. "They were engaged for about seven or eight years when we were boys, and then my grandfather abruptly broke off the engagement and married another woman. Mamaw, that's what we called her, had grown close to Michael and me during those years, so whenever the engagement was called off, Granddad let her keep seeing us. She'd send us birthday presents, Christmas presents, and so on, all the way up until the time we graduated from high school. A lot of times she'd take us places. She'd even have us overnight sometimes on the weekends. It's like Granddad and her were still good friends, and Maxine and Granddad's new wife, Gladys, became good friends too, which worked out just fine because Gladys never had had any children of her own and didn't care that much for children or grandchildren."

According to Doug, Maxine Chrisman had a farm right outside Temple. It was a farm she had inherited from her father's side of the family. He wasn't sure of the details, but he had been to the farm. In fact, he claimed he and his brother had often hidden stolen items and weapons in the barn, which was some distance from the house.

What kind of weapons? David asked.

All kinds, Doug told him, especially military weapons. In fact, according to Doug, when they were in the county jail in Houston, Michael had hooked up with an ex-soldier from Fort Hood, Johnny McCabe, someone who Doug was sure was in a militia.

Both Kathryn and David wrote down the name of the ex-soldier.

"Michael promised me that when he got out, he was going to break me out before they got me to prison." He shook his head.

As she watched him ground out one cigarette and light another, Kathryn was troubled by any alleged plan to break him out of jail. How could such a plan be coordinated? She had a feeling it wasn't the truth. If that wasn't the truth, what else might he be fabricating? She said, "I thought it was policy that suspects involved in the same crime are kept separated while they're in jail," she observed.

He nodded. "You're right, I never did see my brother, if that's what you're thinking. You're wondering how we could have planned a breakout if we never saw each other?" He breathed smoke through his nostrils. "A trustee sent messages back and forth."

The smoke was beginning to nauseate her. She was getting a headache.

"What was that trustee's name?" he said to himself, staring at the window where a guard was passing. "A big, heavyset guy with a crew cut. Damn, I can't remember. Anyway, you guys would be able to find out his name. He supposedly killed two little boys on federal property—Ralph! That was his name. Ralph something. The feds turned him over to the state because they thought he would get a worse punishment if he got convicted, but the state was having trouble getting enough evidence to send him away. I'm not sure what happened to him." He took a puff of the cigarette, then dropped it on the floor and ground it out.

Kathryn was relieved he hadn't decided to smoke the entire cigarette.

"This guy Ralph was the librarian. He got to go around the jail and hand out books."

Doug explained how early on prosecutors had decided to try him and Michael together, which meant for a few times they were going to court at the same time. One time in a holding cell outside the courtroom, he said, they devised a plan of how they could communicate back at the county jail. According to Doug, one of them would take a novel from the library and leave a message in the novel. "Not a note or anything like that, but starting at the front of the book, we would periodically put a tiny pencil dot under a letter. You would follow the letters to build words. Whenever I'd finish a message, I'd tell the librarian—Ralph—to send the book to my brother, that I thought he'd enjoy reading it." He smiled. "We sent elaborate messages back and forth. It turned out to be a good idea too, because the prosecutors suddenly decided to try us separately, and I never saw my brother again. I did hear about what was going on, though, including about the ex-soldier he met."

"What can you tell us about this ex-soldier, Johnny McCabe?" Kathryn asked.

Doug shrugged. "Last I heard he was working as a janitor at a school down in Houston."

She glanced at David. Their eyes met.

David asked, "This Maxine Chrisman, was she involved in what you guys were doing?"

"No!" he said, shaking his head vigorously. He even turned pale. "She's a sweet old lady who hadn't a clue what was going on. She couldn't even walk from the house to the barn. It sits quite a ways from the house."

"Why haven't we heard her name mentioned before?" Kathryn asked. "It seems like if she was such an important person in your lives, some source would have mentioned her—like a presentencing investigation report or something."

"Like I said, this was until we were out of high

school," Doug said. After that, he continued, they had gone their separate ways. "Up in Columbus, Ohio, Michael and I almost got caught when we robbed a bank, and it put a scare in us. We were leaving the bank, and a police car was coming right at us. I mean, Michael and I looked at each other and said, 'oh, shit,' because we knew we were going to have a big shoot-out right then and there."

He smiled. "Back then we weren't ready for that. We decided we were going to come back to Texas and find someplace to lay low for a while. That's when we dropped in on Mamaw. Naturally, she was surprised to see us. We ran a story on her of how we had been working on a construction site up in Ohio and had worked several weeks before discovering the foreman couldn't pay us. By that time we were stone broke—at least that's what we told her. The truth was we had several thousand dollars in cash. We asked her if she could put us up until we could get on our feet. We ended up staying there for six months or so. We even pulled a couple of those small jobs in Houston while we were still staying with Mamaw. We never told anybody about her because we knew her place was someplace we could always go if we were on the run."

"Does she know you're on death row?" David asked.

He shook his head. "Like I said, Mamaw's kind of oblivious to the world around her."

26

Officer Dan Leveque, a transport officer with the Bell County Sheriff's Department, was a distant cousin of Maxine Chrisman. At four-thirty in the morning, Kathryn called the county sheriff, Bud Porter, and asked if he could arrange for a five-thirty meeting with Leveque at Highway 190 and Chrisman Mill Road.

Leveque was on time. A tall, dark-haired man with a crew cut and mustache, he approached Kathryn with a professional air. He had driven up in a battered white Buick, his own transportation, but he was in uniform. He smelled like Old Spice aftershave. Inviting him inside a Winnebago filled with electronic equipment, she introduced herself, Grant, David, and Steve, and told him the FBI was making a raid on the Chrisman property. "We need to get Maxine Chrisman safely out of the house."

"We understand she's in her seventies," Grant said, "and we don't want her to get hurt or have any medical problems during the raid."

Leveque nodded his head as if he understood. "And you want me to get her out?" he asked.

"Yes."

"I'd be happy to help."

Kathryn handed him a portable telephone. "You're married, right?"

Yes, he was, he said.

"Tell her your wife isn't feeling well, and you need someone to stay with her."

They went outdoors, where she told him to follow her in his car. They drove closer to the Chrisman place.

The rural area had been sealed off by Texas Department of Public Safety officers, and the Chrisman house was surrounded. From her car parked under some nearby trees, she watched the house through binoculars while Leveque telephoned Maxine. Sure enough, the frail-looking lady came out on the front porch, wearing a heavy coat. Leveque drove up to the house in his Buick and helped her to his car. He drove the car to Kathryn's car; and Kathryn, after introducing herself and showing her credentials, helped her into the government sedan. Kathryn could see Maxine trembling, so she turned on the car's heater.

Maxine seemed like a pleasant woman, even at that hour of the morning. She looked at Kathryn through thick glasses, which made her dull brown eyes almost as large as walnuts, and said, "You people are up awful early this morning."

Kathryn told her they needed to search the Chrisman place. She produced a search warrant.

Maxine waved her wrinkled hand. "Oh, you don't need that thing," she said. "You just help yourself. Danny, you mean Sharon isn't sick?"

He smiled. "No, ma'am."

Kathryn said, "To tell you the truth, we're looking for Michael McCanles and a friend of his, Johnny McCabe."

Maxine's face turned chalky. "Oh, no," she said. "Now what have those boys done?"

Ignoring the question, Kathryn asked, "Are they in the house?"

Maxine shook her head. She said they hadn't been around for several days that she knew of, though they never stayed at the house anyway, so she wasn't positive. "They insisted on staying up at the old Page place. It's up yonder." She pointed. "Allen Page used to do the farming for me until he got too old and they put him in a nursing home. He'd had a rough time of it. They had to amputate one of his legs because his diabetes got so bad. He finally passed away."

Kathryn asked Maxine if she knew about any weapons or bombs that might be kept on the property.

She shook her head, saying, "I don't know what those boys are up to. I can always hear them back in the hills shooting. They like their guns, they do."

Officer Leveque kept Maxine company, while Kathryn went out to brief agents about the impending raid. She reminded them there was a deadly biological agent hidden away somewhere, probably in the form of a bomb. "We've received mixed signals about this agent," she told them. "At first we were told there was a vaccine for it, but then we learned that the trial runs for the vaccine had failed. Apparently, there was some testing down at the state prison, and some inoculated prisoners died from exposure to the agent. Only within the last few days has the army admitted that there is no cure for Exodus-Five, and no vaccine. In other words, if you are exposed to Exodus-Five, you will die, just like those girls did in Houston."

The agents said nothing. There was a sober mood in the air.

At precisely six o'clock, when the cold, November gray of Saturday morning barely had filtered into the darkness, the elite Hostage Rescue Team from out of Quantico, Virginia, flew over in helicopters. The SWAT team from Dallas attacked Maxine's house, detonating a series of stun grenades to catch off guard any occupants of the house. Kathryn could hear distant explosions of more stun grenades up at the Page place. The teams were swift. Within a minute after each of the team's agents had entered, the leaders radioed that both houses were empty. Another ten minutes, and they gave an all-clear signal. Kathryn and other agents moved in, wearing biological warfare suits, masks, and gloves.

Inside Maxine's house, heavy smoke from the stun grenades still lingered in the rooms.

As Maxine had said, the main house showed no traces of anyone but her.

The leader of the Hostage Rescue Team called Kathryn on the radio. He said they needed her up at the barn.

She drove up the bumpy dirt road to the Page place. There agents had taken off their protective clothing. She took hers off too.

The moment she stepped inside the barn, which looked like it might collapse at any moment, she saw a powder-blue Ford Taurus parked in the barn, its driver's door and the driver's side passenger door open. The two men lying in the bloody dust of the earth were obviously dead, shot to death. One of the men was lying on his back, his head against the rear wheel of the car and his right hand near his head. In his hand was a .357 magnum. Blood stained the bottoms of his combat boots, but there were no prints where he lay. The knees of his jeans were bloody. Kathryn assumed someone had moved him to that particular position. Given the blood on his knees, most likely he had died on his belly. Since there was no obvious wound, she guessed he had been shot in the back, perhaps in the back of the head.

The other man was facedown in the dust, both his arms wrapped around his head, as if he had died trying to protect it. He held a .45 automatic in his right hand. There was no visible wound, though there was a substantial amount of blood in the dust beneath his arms. She guessed he had been shot in the face. She took a deep breath. She could smell hay. It smelled dry and musty, like if she remained in the barn too long, she would sneeze.

Grant said, "So we finally caught up with our notorious McCanles and McCabe team. Some people will like how this story ended."

The man leaning against the rear wheel of the Ford was definitely McCanles. She recognized his pockmarked face and goatee from the photograph she had seen. The skinny man with the dark hair, she assumed was McCabe, though she couldn't see his face. He was basically a nobody. He hadn't ever held a significant job, and hadn't gone very far in the army. He had been a company clerk, a paper pusher, and had made it only to E-4 before being busted twice for dereliction of duty. He didn't reenlist, but went to Houston, where he'd been in and out of trouble. Apparently, that's where he had met McCanles—in jail. The Ford met the description of the one registered to McCabe. The fingerprints on the air freshener at the school were McCabe's. He had once been a janitor there and undoubtedly had kept copies of the keys to the school when he had left employment there.

She said, "I bet when we run things through ballistics, the bullet in McCanles will match the gun McCabe's holding, and the bullet in McCabe will match the gun McCanles is holding. How much you want to bet?"

"No doubt about it, someone wanted to make it look like they shot each other."

She let out a deep breath.

"Got any theories about what's going on?"

"Look at how the dust is all disturbed near McCabe," she said in a low voice.

Grant nodded.

"You know how it is when you stop felons armed and dangerous on the street?" He listened while he stared at the bodies. "You have them get out of the car, put their hands above their heads, and lie face-down on the pavement." She knew he had to see what she was seeing. Both men had undoubtedly lain facedown in the same position, side by side. McCanles had probably been shot first, she said. Then her guess was that McCabe had raised his head to plea for his life, and someone had shot him in the face. She thought of Randy. It was his favorite part of an arrest—making the suspects lie facedown on the pavement, their hands on top of their heads. She said, "I can't help but think that someone ordered them out of the car and told them to assume the position."

"Like a police officer?" Grant said, looking at her. "Kathryn, we're back at our leak, aren't we? An insider is what you're suggesting."

Kathryn pointed at the dead men. "Look at them," she told him. "They look just like they were in the process of being arrested—like right before they were cuffed and searched. McCanles has obviously been moved from that position."

They went outside in the cold morning sunshine. There were agents everywhere. Some still wore protective masks and suits. "You think maybe it's one of our own people?" he asked. Their faces were within a couple of inches of each other.

"For Christ's sake, Grant, you have to admit there have been some strange things happening. There's the whole business of the package addressed to me, as if someone specifically wanted me to receive it. Someone tipped off a reporter both at Hood and down in Houston. He knew who I was and everything—got all the media stirred up."

"What have we learned about him?"

"A legitimate reporter for the Dallas paper. Claims he got an anonymous tip." She shrugged. "That's not the point. The point is, then we go after McCanles and McCabe, but right before we can get to them, someone murders them. Don't you think it's all a bit too coincidental? Someone who knows our every move and gives us what we want at every step. This is more than electronic surveillance."

He pondered her for a moment, then shook his head and said, "I think we're reading too much into all of this."

She was silent.

"Okay, if there's a leak, it doesn't leave us with many possibilities." He lit a cigar. "There would be only a few people with that much access to all our moves."

"Aside from you and me, I can only think of one or two who would be privy to the most privileged information. It boils down to you and me."

"Well, I know it isn't Jeff. I know that for a fact."

"Then that doesn't leave many possibilities at all, does it?"

An agent came out of the barn. He told her they had found a cache of weapons and explosives hidden under the hay in the loft, enough weapons and explosives for a small army. Nothing that wasn't clearly identifiable, though. No bombs. Grant went back inside the barn.

Kathryn walked up to the Page place. She wondered where David was. She hadn't seen him since the raid had begun. It suddenly occurred to her that he knew her every move, and had known her every move. The thought was frightening. Would he betray her? Could she have been wrong about him?

Inside the dilapidated house, forensic specialists were busy. They had already determined that Angela Robles, Michael McCanles, and Johnny McCabe had all been in the house. Their fingerprints were everywhere.

On the floor of the upstairs bedroom, the one with a new lock in the door, an evidence specialist had found traces of Angela's blood. "Probably an abrasion of some sort," he told Kathryn. "There may have been a struggle in which the girl fell or was knocked down. Doesn't look like anything serious—not enough blood." The agent continued his work, packaging a blanket as evidence.

Hands in her coat pockets, Kathryn looked around at the room, at the wood shavings on the floor near the door, and at the window, which a hand had cleaned. Outside, in the distance, she could hear the HRT helicopters still circling.

David appeared, his olive suit wrinkled. He gave her his characteristic smile. "Doug McCanles was right," he said. "They were here." It was like he had just learned the news—that he hadn't even heard McCanles and McCabe were dead.

"Where have you been?" she asked him.

He said he had been talking to a neighbor who might have important information. "He's one of those auxiliary police types—you know, the ones who ride with the regular department part-time." David asked if she wanted to talk to him.

She was about to go with David when an agent called her to the closet. She saw the food on the floor and the open attic panel. She remembered the panel in the Robleses' house. The agent had already put a portable ladder in the opening so agents could climb up and down. She climbed the ladder. Two agents were collecting evidence from an area that looked like there had been a struggle. Most of the attic had been floored in.

"Looks like she tried to escape and put up a fight," one of the agents said, using his lighted flashlight to point out the bloody floor. There were shoe prints in the dust and blood. Some of the prints were of a bare foot.

"Is it her blood?" Kathryn asked. Her eyes focused on the dead wasps.

"We'll know soon enough," the specialist answered, and began testing a small sample.

Kathryn climbed down out of the attic.

David asked her, "What's up there?"

Hands in pockets and staring straight ahead, she walked past him, saying, "Looks like she may have been trying to escape and they caught her." She found herself not wanting to tell him anything. To Agent Baxter, a young man with long blond hair and a beard, she said, "I want to know how old the food in the closet is, where it came from, and anything else you can determine about it."

She went downstairs, where Kobi Albert called her into what had once probably been a living room. On the wall near the front windows was a telephone number written in ink. Kathryn recorded it in her notebook and also noted there wasn't a phone jack in the room. Another number had been written there, but it had been scratched out. "This looks like a Fort Hood exchange," she said to Kobi, "which means that's a long-distance number. Let me know the minute you trace the number. Then let's find out all the long-distance calls that came into that Fort Hood exchange. One of those calls came from here. Probably a cell phone. Let's get a number for that cell phone and all its records. I want to know what other calls came from the phone that was used here." She patted Kobi on the back. "Good work," she told her, "and get back to me quickly."

Kathryn went outside and stood in the daybreak sunshine. She was feeling better. Someone had made a careless mistake. Kathryn was certain a cell phone had been used.

David followed her.

She asked, "Where's this person you think I should talk to?"

"Down at the main house," he told her.

As they walked to the car for the bumpy ride back down to the Chrisman place, she told him, "I want neighbors all around here to be questioned. Find out if they heard anything, saw anything. People must have known about some unusual activity here. They must have seen people coming and going. I especially want to know if anyone saw others besides McCanles and McCabe."

"You think they got in a fight and shot each other?" he asked, getting in the sedan.

"I don't know" was all she said. So he did know about McCanles and McCabe. When had he discovered? Or had he already known?

The radio traffic on the car radio was continuous. She saw a helicopter fly overhead. It made loud chopping sounds, then as quickly the chopping sounds diminished.

"Is there something wrong, something you're upset with me about?" he asked.

She glanced at him. "Right now I have a lot of things on my mind." Even talking to David evoked a sense of betrayal at that moment. All those times he had said he was going to telephone his sons, was he really giving updates about Bureau activities? If not he, who was the leak?

David drove her to the main house, where Maxine was surveying what had happened to her house. She didn't look as happy as she had earlier that morning, even seemed a little perturbed. "I told you there was no one here," she said to Kathryn.

Leveque, who was still present, told her, "Maxine, you don't know Michael like you used to know him. He's become a dangerous man. The FBI was afraid he might be hiding in the house, and you wouldn't even have known it."

"Lord, I'd know if someone was in my own house," she said. She sat down on the sofa in the living room. "And I've known Michael and his brother since they were little boys. They wouldn't hurt anyone."

Kathryn told her about Doug's being on death row in Huntsville, news that seemed to surprise even Leveque. He sat down to hold Maxine, whose eyes got red rims around them. She trembled. "Well, you never know," she said.

Kathryn knelt in front of her and took the old woman's hands, which were cold, dry, and trembling. She said, "Maxine, we've found a couple of bodies up the hill. One of them, we believe, is Michael."

Maxine allowed Dan to hold her, but she didn't weep. At most her eyes remained red with tears.

"Do you have any idea what might have been going on, or what might have happened?"

She didn't.

While Leveque remained with Maxine, Kathryn went outside for a breath of fresh air. There was David and a skinny man with long dark hair and a goatee.

David said, "Agent Stanton, this is Mr. Gillespie. He and his wife live up the road a ways. He says he's met McCanles. Mr. Gillespie, why don't you tell Agent Stanton what you've already told me?"

"It's like I said, I never thought he was dangerous, or anything like that," Gillespie said. "I know he liked his guns. Our place sits in back of Maxine's place"—he pointed—"and you could always hear shooting back there in the woods and fields." He shook his head. "But they minded their own business, and that's all that counts."

Who were "they"? she asked.

McCanles and "Johnny."

Where had he met them? she asked. She glanced at David, who stood listening.

At a restaurant in Temple, a place called Arnold's.

Kathryn remembered the name from the matchbook she had found in the swamp. Agents had had the restaurant under surveillance, but to no avail. It was a local hangout for a lot of people in Temple, including the mayor.

"I'd seen him—McCanles—in and out of Maxine's place here," he said, "and then one day I saw the two of them having lunch, so I introduced myself. You know, I didn't want anyone taking advantage of Maxine, so I thought I'd check them out. We talked for a while. Like I said, they seemed like nice guys. I know they go back there and shoot all day long, but there's nothing wrong with shooting off a few rounds now and then. At least not around here. We all have guns. We all do shooting."

"Maxine said that McCanles and McCabe came and went all the time. Do you know where they were spending their time?"

He scratched his goatee. "As a matter of fact, I do remember when I met him he was talking about some big shot down at Austin. I think they were traveling back and forth to Austin, maybe on business."

"Do you remember a name, or anything?" she asked.

No, he wasn't sure who it was. "I didn't pay that much attention. You know how it is when people start to talk about how the government is too powerful and getting out of hand—you get kind of scared and want to steer clear of them."

"But you do know they had some kind of contacts down in Austin," emphasized David.

"One is all I ever heard about. Some big shot, like I said."

"Do you remember anything else?" she asked.

"No, that was basically it. One day not long after that, the shooting stopped here, so I figured they were spending all their time down at Austin."

She shook his hand. "Thank you, Mr. Gillespie."

He nodded and headed for Chrisman Mill Road.

To David, Kathryn asked, "Where did you say you met Mr. Gillespie?"

"He was one of the people hanging out in front of the place. You know how it is when something like this happens. You have people come from miles around just to watch."

Steve arrived in a state police car. The first thing he said once he reached her was, "Guess what, the reports showed DiUlio's fingerprints on the syringe and vial, plus there were toxic levels of potassium in the infant we exhumed, which isn't the Morley infant."

"He poisoned a baby?" Kathryn said.

"Someone did," Steve replied. "For what it's worth."

She scratched the back of her neck. "You say that like you have bad news."

"The state's attorney says that unless our nurse actually witnessed Dr. DiUlio administering the drug, there would never be enough evidence to charge him."

There was a long pause before Steve added, "I'm sorry. I tried, but all of this should have been taken care of years ago. Enough responsible people were involved that someone should have gotten to the bottom of all this long before we came along. Where is DiUlio, anyway? Have you got him yet?"

Grant appeared. He said, no, the Bureau didn't have him. He had disappeared, but the rumor was that he would be turning himself in with his attorneys sometime soon.

Kathryn put an arm around Steve and patted his back. "Listen, you know we love you anyway."

He didn't say anything.

She looked in the direction of the Page place. Once again, she was one step behind where she needed to be—always a little too late. Where was Angela? Was she alive? What was going on? How did it all fit together? Kathryn turned.

Back on Chrisman Mill Road, Gillespie was talking with a group of local police. The men laughed. Gillespie's laugh was unnaturally loud. It carried in the morning air.

27

Next thing Angela knew, the heater in the Maryland house went out and she woke up nearly frozen.

Morning was at hand. Rivero and Duffy were gone. She didn't know what had happened to them. She was too cold to worry about them. The cold was intense, so intense that, despite the blanket, the cold went down into Angela's right arm, where it stopped at her hand, which felt very heavy. To make matters worse, rising from inside the blanket was that sickening odor that seemed to cling to her, to follow her everywhere she went. She couldn't escape. And her arm hurt like no pain she had ever experienced. Why had they stopped traveling? she wanted to know.

Putting a finger to his lips, Klock motioned for her to be quiet. She obeyed him. Klock looked at Copeland and nodded in an uphill direction. Copeland climbed the embankment.

Angela looked around at her surroundings. They were vaguely familiar. She looked at Klock, who dangled a strip of cloth in the diluted darkness. The cloth moved with the early morning air. Klock had a troubled look on his face. He seemed weaker even than he had the last time she had seen him. His left eye was black and almost swollen shut. It was so swollen that it pulled on his upper lip. His face had a crust of dried blood here and there.

Copeland returned without his M-16, almost sliding

down the embankment. In a low voice he said, "The guard is heavy. It looks like they're rigging the missile on the launcher now."

Klock said, "The wind's not good either. If they're about to launch a missile, the wind will surely carry the germ right across the fort."

Angela asked, "Where are we? I thought you were taking me home." She knew then they were at the other firing range. She had been there before. It was where Klock had taken her in the wheelchair on her first day in camp.

Klock told her, "We haven't forgotten you, dear, but you are very sick. We can't travel anymore."

Copeland smiled. He said, "You've been out of your head, tossing, turning, and talking in your sleep."

Klock nodded. "I'm weak too. I've gotten weaker by the minute. I think I have a punctured lung."

She did notice that he was having more trouble breathing.

"If we tried to travel, they'd catch us," Klock told her.

"I don't feel good."

"I know. You have a fever from an infection. I think it's gangrene. Have you heard of that?"

No, she hadn't. "In my hand?"

"Yes. That's what that sweet smell is. Gangrene smells sweet."

Before he could stop her, she pulled back the blanket. The dressing was gone, the hand, almost as fat as the top of her leg, was puffed with brownish-redness. The backs of her fingers were a crusty, burned black. One finger leaked a greenish fluid from where the crust had split. The smell from the leakage was overpowering.

Klock forced down the covers.

Copeland told her, "You shouldn't look. It looks worse than it really is."

"It's spread," Klock commented to Copeland, who

gave an almost imperceptible nod, though she saw it. To her, Klock said, "If we move you too much, it'll make it worse. We don't want that." He tried to smile. "Besides, with my punctured lung, I'm not up to much anyway. Our best bet is to stop whatever these people are trying to do, and then we'll use their radio to call for help. Help will get to us a lot faster than we can get to it."

She glanced at Copeland; he was watching the embankment. She thought he didn't want to look at her.

Klock told her, "Angela, we need your help. We need to move up to the top of the embankment so we can keep an eye on what's going on. Do you think if Sergeant Copeland carried you up there, you could be real quiet and not make a sound?"

She nodded.

"It's very important that you keep as quiet as possible. If you make any noise, they'll find us."

"I won't make any."

He patted the top of her head. "Do you know that you're a really special person?"

She tried to smile, but she hurt too much.

Sergeant Copeland stood over her. "You ready for this?"

She nodded.

"You sure?" He pulled a handkerchief from the back pocket of his fatigues. "I promise this is clean." He smiled. It must have been at the face she made. "I want you to open your mouth and put this in there. Bite down hard. And any pain you have, bite even harder. Okay?"

She opened her mouth.

He inserted the handkerchief. "That's a good girl." It had a slight taste of chlorine. It reminded her of swimming pool water.

He leaned into her and lifted her onto his shoulder. The next thing she knew, she was going up the side

of the hill. He had her on his shoulder. She cried out
in pain and tried to spit out the handkerchief, but
couldn't get it out of her mouth. Klock was following,
and he kept the handkerchief in—he followed with his
hand clamped on her mouth. They made good time
up the hill.

In the bushes at the top, Copeland, his hand on her
back, gently leaned forward. She could feel herself
going into other hands. When she looked up, she saw
that it was Klock lowering her to the ground. He held
the handkerchief in her mouth for a few moments as
he whispered, "Please, don't make any sounds." They
were in some bushes.

She still wanted to scream out in pain, she hurt so
badly, but after a couple of minutes, she realized they
weren't going to remove the handkerchief until she
was quiet. She calmed. Klock released her mouth and
removed the handkerchief. He whispered, "I'm proud
of you. You did fine."

While Sergeant Copeland caught his breath, she said
in a low voice, "I think I'm going to die."

"Why do you keep talking like that?" Klock said.

"Because it's true." She had a feeling she was.

"Nonsense."

"Why are you lying to me?"

Klock glanced at Sergeant Copeland.

"You're just like my mom and dad. They've lied to
me all of my life."

Klock smiled. "They're probably just being a
mother and father. Mothers and fathers do that
sometimes."

She was angry.

"What did I say wrong now?" Klock asked, touching her left arm.

"I found out. I made calls, and I found out."

"Found out what?"

"That I'm adopted. My mom and dad never told
me, but I heard them fighting one night. They were

fighting about telling me. Now I'm going to die, and don't even know who my real family is."

There was a long silence.

She continued, "I was at Suzanne and Russ Reising's house, and he helped me make the calls."

"He," Klock said. "Is that Major Russ Reising?"

Yes, she told him.

Klock shook his head. "He's messed up in this too?"

She asked, "Is he bad?"

Klock nodded. "Yes, he's bad." To Sergeant Copeland, he added, "He was one of them that helped set this whole thing up. He's been in it from the beginning."

Using a stick, Copeland scratched at the dirt.

She got a glazed look in her eyes.

Klock told her, "Don't worry, sweetheart, Sergeant Copeland and I will be your family. You can count on it, can't she, Sarge?"

"Sure, she can."

"Then, please don't ever lie to me again because my real family wouldn't lie to me."

She was glad they didn't try to lie to her and insist she was going to live. They kept silent about that. Besides, she could feel death. She could smell it. She remembered when she had been in the hospital and had finally gotten well enough to ride in a wheelchair. She had gone to the cancer ward of the hospital. She could remember a distinct smell in that ward. The smell of death. It was the smell that lingered with her now, almost as if it had come back to haunt her. So many things were coming back to haunt her, like the words of the doctor who had told her that if she didn't start taking better care of herself, someday she would do something no one could fix.

Sergeant Copeland parted the bushes so they could look down the hill at the firing line. He asked, "What do you suggest?"

Looking also, Klock told him, "We're three hundred yards from right here."

He and Copeland stared at each other.

Copeland turned his attention to the sky. He asked, "Do you know what day it is?"

Klock looked up at the sky too. "I can't remember. I've lost track of time."

Angela looked up also. It looked like it was going to be a good day, she thought. An autumn day. Wind. Clouds. Blue sky. Sunshine. Cold. She had always liked the autumn. That and spring, though she perferred the autumn. She asked, "Did I miss Thanksgiving?"

Sergeant Copeland said he was sure she hadn't missed Thanksgiving. He pulled back the bushes more so he could watch the distant firing line again, where the shiny cylinder was being worked on by soldiers. He chuckled softly and patted his big belly. He said he would know if Thanksgiving had passed. To Klock, he said, "I think it's almost Veterans Day. Did you know I was in Vietnam?"

Klock looked at him. "No," he replied. There was a puzzled look on his face. "I didn't think you were that old."

"Yeah, thanks, but I'm almost forty-seven. I'll be forty-seven in September. I went to Nam in seventy-one."

"I thought the war was over by then."

"Almost. I got there just in time to kill one child."

She and Klock both watched him.

Copeland turned his eyes to her. "One about your age, dear." He shook his head. "I didn't even know it until she hit the ground and her hat fell off. She had long, shiny hair." He stared into space. "I'll never forget the look in her eyes." He picked up a stick and drew in the dirt. As he did so, he told about a time as a child when he had hunted. It was when he was thirteen or fourteen, he said. He'd been walking through the wooded hills, and in the distance he'd seen a beautiful bird perched on a branch. He said he had casually pointed his .22 rifle in that direction and pulled the trigger. "I thought the bird flew away. I couldn't see it anymore—until I got there and saw it on the ground. It had shiny black eyes. That's what the Vietnamese girl's eyes were like, like the eyes of that beautiful bird. I dropped to my knees and wept."

Klock didn't say anything.

Copeland rubbed his own left chest, as if his heart hurt, or he was thinking about where he had shot the girl in Vietnam.

Was it in the heart? Angela wondered.

Copeland said, "I think it's almost Veteran's Day. Maybe today is Veterans Day." He made a sound deep inside, as if someone had hit him in the stomach. He breathed out deeply through his nostrils.

She felt sorry for him.

"Have you ever been to the Wall?" he asked Klock.

Klock shook his head.

"Angela, do you know what the Wall is?"

Yes, she said, she had read about it in school.

Copeland scratched at a small white scar on his right palm. It stood out on his black skin. "It's black and engraved with the names of fifty-eight thousand Americans lost in Vietnam." He scratched at the scar. "This'll be the first year in a lot of years that I haven't visited the Wall on Veterans Day."

Angela wished she could help him get there.

He looked at her. "It's all coming back to haunt me." Turning to Klock, he asked, "Do you believe in déjà vu?"

"Na." Klock was moving about. His breaths were labored. He seemed to be having trouble finding a position that was comfortable, one that would allow him to get enough breath.

Copeland used his stick to scratch in the dirt again.

Eventually he said, "There's no way we can take them all on. All the weapons and men they have, they'd cut us down in a minute."

Klock didn't argue.

"Do you know who Tim O'Brien is?" Copeland asked, changing the subject.

"Who?"

"Tim O'Brien, the writer."

"Yeah, I know who he is. I read one of his stories in college. A Vietnam story. It was good, the best war story I've ever read."

"That's right. He was the writer who put Vietnam in literature. I met him once."

"You're kidding."

"I got his autograph."

"Is that right?" Klock didn't sound impressed.

"It was at a talk he gave. After the talk he took questions from the audience, and I asked him what he thought of Vietnam veterans." Copeland smiled. "He said he thought all Vietnam veterans were assholes—pardon the expression." He glanced at her. "So after the talk, I went up to him with one of his books, and I asked him if he would sign it. He asked me how I wanted him to make it out, and I said, 'Just make it out from one asshole to another.'" He chuckled softly.

So did Klock.

Angela smiled.

Copeland got serious. "He seemed like a nice guy. I mean, all Vietnam vets are pretty much messed up in one way or another. When I said that about making it out from one asshole to another, he got embarrassed and said, 'Oh, I couldn't do that.' I saw a side of him I hadn't seen before, a good side. Personally, I wish he would have signed it that way. It would have meant something. So much in life today doesn't mean anything, does it?"

Klock was studying the distant firing line. "You

know, when you mentioned that O'Brien writer, and I thought about college, I also thought about something else. A trip I took in college." He was staring. "One spring some of us took a trip to Florida. We were trying to save money, so we took along some camping equipment, and we stayed in the Everglades. I was a gun nut even back then, and I had a pistol with me."

When her grandmother had died, Angela remembered everyone talking like Corporal Klock and Sergeant Copeland were talking—telling old stories. Were the three of them going to die too? she wondered.

"Anyway, we all got drunk one night in camp," Klock continued, "and I suggested we hunt alligators."

Copeland smiled. He was watching Klock with interest.

"We didn't find any alligators, but we came upon a dump site, and down in the trash was an old air conditioner. You know, one of those window units."

Copeland's head was bobbing.

"We took turns shooting at it, and the next thing I knew, there was this loud burst and steam was shooting into the air." He paused, then added, "Do you know what I'm getting at?"

Copeland shook his head. "I have no idea."

"Compressed air. Freon. Whatever it was. When a bullet hit the air conditioner just right, it ruptured the tank containing the compressed air. Steam shot out." Klock looked down range.

"You're thinking about taking a pot shot at this thing?"

"You've seen me shoot, Sarge. I could hit it from here. Put it on semiautomatic and pop the hell out of it."

Copeland rubbed his bald head. "Son, if you shoot

down there and nothing happens, it'll be like stirring up a hornets' nest."

"And if I don't shoot?" He picked up the M-16.

The sergeant didn't say anything.

Angela thought about the wasps she had stirred up in the attic. It seemed like such a long time ago.

28

As promised, Dr. Albert DiUlio surrendered to authorities at Temple, Texas. With him were two well-known attorneys, both of whom remained with him when federal marshals drove him from Temple to CID headquarters at Fort Hood. It was there that Kathryn met him for the first time.

Right away she saw what Tracy and other women must have seen—Albert DiUlio was an imposing, handsome, quite distinguished-looking man with grayish-black hair, a tanned complexion, and solid build. He wore a grape-colored suit and silver tie with grape dots covering it. His entire demeanor spelled wealth and influence.

When he signed waiver forms, he brought out bifocals so he could examine each document carefully. His dark blue eyes, which almost seemed to take on a bit of the grape from his suit, were as hard and flawless as polished marble. Oddly enough, he didn't seem embarrassed in the least that he had been summoned to answer questions about Angela's kidnapping.

"Yes, I know who she is," he said when Kathryn asked him if he knew her. "Who wouldn't know her? She's been in the news for the past week." He had a deep, rich voice.

Her eyes remained fixed on him, and she allowed a slight smile to come to her face. "I would have thought you knew her a little better than that." David leaned back in his chair. She could see him out of the corner of her eye. Was he sending a signal?

"Not really. I knew the family in the past, but that's literally been years ago. Except—"

"Except what?" David asked.

"I met the daughter a while back when the mother visited my office in Temple." He shook his head. "Mary Belle brought her to me, saying the doctors at Fort Hood didn't know what they were doing. I examined Angela as a favor to the mother."

"Mary Belle brought Angela to you?" Kathryn asked. Mary Belle hadn't told her that, had told her only that she had met DiUlio in passing.

"Yes, she brought Angela to me for a consult visit."

"And what happened during that visit?" Kathryn asked.

The doctor stared at her with his piercing eyes. "Nothing."

"Nothing?" David said, leaning forward.

"There wasn't anything wrong with her."

David leaned back again, the front legs of his chair coming off the floor.

"I don't understand," Kathryn said. "Why did the mother bring Angela to you if there was nothing wrong with her?"

"Believe me, I examined Angela carefully. Physically, she had a few limitations that were probably permanent, but nothing major. It wasn't the physical that concerned me."

"What concerned you?" Kathryn asked.

"To tell you the truth, Mary Belle's psychological status was what concerned me."

Warning signals were going off in Kathryn's head, signals that she didn't want to hear.

David said, "Can you explain what you mean?"

"She was riddled with guilt about what had happened to Angela, so much so that I even suggested that she consult with a psychiatrist for herself. I was concerned about her."

Neither Kathryn nor David said anything.

Kathryn felt sick to her stomach. What had she overlooked? What was it all leading to?

"Of course, Mary Belle wasn't happy to hear that. In fact, she was angry with me."

Kathryn asked, "How so?"

Dr. DiUlio leaned forward. "Mary Belle didn't want to hear that the only problem her daughter had was a mother who was so domineering that the daughter could barely breathe."

For a moment Kathryn was almost drawn to DiUlio. He had a certain power and charm about him. He was very believable.

"I'm serious." DiUlio was staring at her. "Mary Belle was so guilt-ridden about what had happened that she would barely let Angela move on her own. I would say, 'Raise your hand, Angela,' and before Angela could do it, Mary Belle would say, 'Go ahead, Angela, raise your hand for the doctor.' I told Mary Belle she needed to let Angela be more independent—let her walk to the bus stop, etcetera."

Kathryn had heard what she needed to hear. It was all falling together. She abruptly changed the subject, asking him about his role with the Army Reserves.

He acknowledged that he had been in the active Reserves, but he no longer was. He was on inactive status, he said.

Had he been to Fort Detrick?

No. He grinned, showing his white teeth. They were flawless. "To tell you the truth, I've never even heard of it."

That's strange, she thought, why would he lie about something like that? His military records indicated that he had been to Fort Detrick.

Had he served on a drug test program at the state prison in Huntsville?

No, he hadn't.

She was confused. Was he a pathological liar? He didn't seem like it. She produced the prison document with his name on it.

He examined it, using his glasses to see better. He wasn't the least bit flustered. "I've never been to the state prison in my life. As a matter of fact, I've never even been to Huntsville."

The emphatic nature of his response troubled her. It was one of those moments when she felt she was at the crossroads to the extremes. Either she had hit the nail on the head, and DiUlio was lying, lying about a lot of things; or what he was saying was the absolute truth. The latter possibility was what troubled her. "It's odd you say you've never been there, but prison officials have produced documentation showing you were there."

"Then, there's something wrong with their documentation. You need to check it out a little more closely because I've never been to Huntsville." He opened his hands, as if to show what was in them. "Look, I have nothing to hide. Surely, they must have a photo on file or something down there. Fingerprints? I don't know, but it's not me." He looked at one of his attorneys. "Richard, what's this all about?"

He wasn't having the typical reaction of someone who had been caught in a web of deception. Instead he was having the reaction of someone who was being falsely accused, the kind of reaction that made her wonder whether she should keep pushing. She went for the kill: "You sure this isn't like that vial of potassium you used twelve or so years ago?"

He broke. "What is all this?" he asked loudly, coming out of his chair. His attorneys grabbed him. "Ask Mary Belle. She'll tell you I wouldn't hurt my own daughter!"

Everyone was silent.

Kathryn thought she could hear her own heart pumping.

"Angela Robles is my daughter." There were tears in his eyes. "I was the one who made the adoption arrangements. I was the one who made sure they got the right child. I did everything because Mary Belle promised me she'd take care of her."

His attorneys both begged him not to answer any more questions.

He nodded, but to his attorneys he said, "I wouldn't kidnap my own daughter."

Outside in the cold, Kathryn stood, too numb to move. She didn't want to think. She knew she was in a state of denial. She would have given almost anything not to have heard what she had heard about Mary Belle.

Someone touched her back.

She could smell cigarette smoke.

"Are you all right?" David asked.

Without looking at him, she told him, "Do me a favor, and follow up on this business about Huntsville. DiUlio's right. If he had been going in and out of a maximum security prison, there must have been some kind of photo ID on file, and so on. Dig all that up. There must have been prints or something on file. Find out about his army records too. I want to know everything. Compare them with DiUlio's public record. If he wasn't at Fort Detrick, there must be some dated medical charts or something to prove he was here instead of there." She stared at David. "I have a feeling our Dr. DiUlio has been set up."

David withdrew soundlessly, leaving her standing alone.

She looked around, but felt like someone was watching her every move.

Ironically, the autumn day she stood in was pleasant, a little cool, but pleasant. A lot of people were out and about. It would be Thanksgiving soon, Kathryn thought, then Christmas. Where had the time gone? She hadn't even begun to Christmas shop. In fact, she suddenly realized she hadn't even asked Wendy what she wanted for Christmas. She decided that this Christmas she would do something special for Wendy, something real special, perhaps take her on a cruise.

As she drove to the Robleses' house, Kathryn had trouble thinking. Perhaps she was having trouble because she didn't want to follow through with all the thoughts that had been stirred up. It was if the thoughts were forcing her in a certain direction, and she didn't want to go.

She found Tony and Mary Belle at home in Wainwright Heights. The children were outside playing, Mary Belle told her, greeting Kathryn at the door. Holding a box of posters displaying Angela, she was smiling pleasantly. "Please, come in. I was just getting ready to walk around the neighborhood and hang posters."

Kathryn took off a scarf that she had wrapped around her neck. "Where's everyone else?" she asked.

They had taken up residence in Killeen, Mary Belle answered. Everyone was getting together later that day to compare notes. They were all working diligently. Kathryn was welcome to tag along to the meeting, Mary Belle told her. She held up the box of posters. "Tony and I are going to walk the neighborhood putting these up. Someone must have seen something. We're offering a reward."

Kathryn folded the scarf in her hands. She shoved the folded scarf in her coat pocket. "Why didn't you tell me that you had been having an affair with Albert DiUlio?"

The question was a bombshell. Mary Belle looked like she had been devastated by it. Even Tony looked like he had been caught off guard, and he was always so cool. He had appeared just as Kathryn had asked

the question, at a point that made it too late for her
to keep it private.

Mary Belle didn't say anything.

Kathryn didn't stop, couldn't stop. "Why didn't you
tell me that you knew Angela was Albert DiUlio's
daughter?"

Again, the question was such a bombshell that Mary
Belle was too stunned to move or speak.

"Mary Belle?" Tony said, staring at her. "What is
all this?"

Mary Belle, a dazed expression on her face, turned
to Tony. She looked as pretty and delicate as she had
ever looked. She was as soft-spoken as Kathryn had
ever heard her speak. "It was a long time ago" was
all she said.

A long silence filled the air.

Kathryn sighed. "Angela is Albert DiUlio's natural daughter?"

"Yes." The word was soft and gentle, barely
audible.

"We adopted his daughter?" Tony emphasized the
word "his."

She looked at him. In her soft voice she asked,
"Does that make a difference?"

He didn't say.

"Would you love her less if she was his daughter,
and more if she was someone else's?"

"Of course not," Tony said, flustered. Kathryn
couldn't tell from the tone of his voice whether he
really believed what he was saying.

Kathryn said, "Mary Belle, I keep saying this, but
it's extremely important that you level with us. Now
it's more important than ever. Is there anything else
you haven't told me?" For some reason she was tired
of asking the question, was actually disillusioned about
it. Why should it be necessary to ask?

Mary Belle shrugged. "I don't know," she said. She
looked down at the girl on the posters in the box. "I

can't think." She looked close to the point of breaking.

Kathryn didn't push. She found herself outside on the front porch, in the cold. Outside were the sounds of children playing. There were sounds of traffic. The sound of distant helicopters.

Tony stepped out behind her, pulling the door shut as he did so.

She looked at him. "Tony, your wife's having a rough time of it," she said. "You probably should see if you can give her a little extra support right about now. She's got a lot locked up inside of her." She shook her head gently. She liked Mary Belle. "That's not good."

He nodded. He seemed to understand what she was saying.

Kathryn was walking away when Tony called to her. She looked back.

"I mentioned this before, but I don't think you believed me."

She didn't interrupt him.

"It's happening like I said it would happen," he told her.

There were several feet between them, but she had no trouble hearing.

"The planners of all this, whatever's going on, have every little detail worked out—as you've discovered. They have everything put together, and if you give it enough time, you'll dig up a complete story. But in the end what will you have?" He shook his head. "You won't have the real story. You'll have the one they wanted you to find, or they'll do something to distract you, and the next thing you know, you'll have forgotten all about us."

Staring coldly at him, she said, "You've been playing this cloak-and-dagger crap too long. I'll get at the truth."

He smiled sadly. "Have you read the book *Moby Dick?*"

She didn't say.

"In it, all Captain Ahab wants to do is to get the great white whale, as if by harpooning it, he will pierce that fleeting truth that constantly eludes him." He shook his head. "As you know, the quest ends with one survivor, Ishmael, floating on a piece of driftwood in the middle of the ocean."

She turned to walk away.

"Kathryn—"

She didn't look back.

"The driftwood. Maybe you'll be one of the lucky ones who latches onto a piece and is saved." He said it as if he had never been so lucky.

29

Kathryn and other federal agents lay in the bushes half a mile from the compound where Colonel Spangler, the military liaison, had led them.

Using binoculars, Kathryn studied the compound. It looked oddly still. In fact, had it not been for a few military vehicles parked there, she would have thought the area completely abandoned. She handed the binoculars to David, who had tapped her shoulder.

To Colonel Spangler, she asked, "You're sure this is the one? You said there were literally dozens of places like this at Fort Hood."

The collar of his field jacket up around his neck to protect it from the cold, the balding colonel shoved his glasses up the bridge of his nose and said, "This is the unit that has the telephone number you gave me. It's commanded by Colonel Frances Lazarus. I gave you the list of personnel here. This is the place you asked about." He was emphatic.

"And what's supposedly going on here?"

The colonel shrugged. "From what I can gather, it's an exercise to study how a diverse group of soldiers work together when trapped behind enemy lines during a war." Other than that, he didn't know much more than that the exercise had been approved at the level of the Joint Chiefs of Staff. He told her, "You know the kind of exercise—some full bird asks a favor of a general, and the general authorizes the bird to play war games. War games go on all the time—every day at every military installation in the world."

David tapped her shoulder again. He handed her the binoculars and told her to look at the firing range near the compound.

She looked in the direction he was pointing. With his coaching, she saw what he had seen—two soldiers bound together. They seemed to be dead, or at least the dark stain on the earth around them was large enough to suggest death.

From the distance came chopping sounds, which grew. A formation of helicopters roared overhead at low level, rushing across the earth. From where she watched, the whole scene looked surreal. The Hostage Rescue Team and SWAT agents, wearing protective masks and clothing, rapelled from the helicopters, detonating stun grenades as they went down. Agents swept through the compound, running from building to building.

Kathryn could hear the explosions of the grenades, the tiny shouts of agents, and the chopping sounds of the helicopters. She waited.

Then the helicopters left, the compound became quiet, and she received the all-clear signal. She and the others moved in, also wearing protective suits and masks.

Everywhere she looked there were somber faces, not at all what she had hoped to see. She knew by the faces what it meant. The compound was empty. She was too late once again. She walked from place to place in the compound, watching agents collect traces of evidence. It was strange to watch them from inside her mask, strange to hear her own breathing. She shook her head in weary cynicism and looked around. David was nowhere in sight. Where was he this time? Before she could ask, a flurry of traffic came over the radio. Agents had made a shocking discovery at a nearby firing range. They were requesting her presence.

A jeep arrived. She got in. The jeep took her to the firing range about a mile from the compound.

It was a pleasant day. The sun was shining. The sky was clear. The masked agents looked out of place, somehow unnatural, as they walked around in the sunlight at the firing range. So did all the dead bodies that lay in the sunlight. Some, in handcuffs, looked like they had been under guard by the others. Kathryn walked among them. Like the young girls in Houston, these bodies had died with their mouths and eyes open. Dr. Jennifer Egan of the CDC took off her mask. Kathryn took her own off. A light wind blew. She could smell death. Dr. Egan called, "We're wasting our time with this equipment." She put away a portable test kit she carried. "The danger is long gone." Other agents began to take off their masks.

Kathryn approached a mobile missile launcher. On the launcher was a silver canister, seemingly ready to be fired. Agent Kobi Albert pointed out the incendiary device at the top of the canister. She said, "It looks like a rather powerful device. Crude, but effective. I'd say the rocket was designed to be shot above Fort Hood, where the heat from an incendiary explosion would cause the pressurized gas in the container to burst into the atmosphere. The Exodus-Five would shower the facility." Kobi showed her several bullet holes. "Whoever shot at this either knew the contents were under pressure, and did it intentionally, or hit it accidentally by some miracle."

Agent Curtis, the HRT leader, said, "Given the direction of the holes and the angle, that's where we headed when we arrived on scene." He pointed. She followed Curtis onto the range. It was a long walk, but she kept up with him. She did not think about the dead men scattered on the field behind her. She thought about Angela. It created an aching sensation within her, one that passed through her entire body.

"The shots at the canister came from someone who was almost certainly an expert," Curtis replied. "It's at least three hundred yards from where the shots were fired."

At the top of a ridge she stopped in the early morning sun and looked down at the three bodies, one a young girl, huddled in the dirt at the bottom of a steep drop. A team of agents were down there collecting evidence. The bodies, locked together, were in the cool shadows, the morning sunlight having passed them by. Kathryn recognized Angela and knelt, where she covered her face with her hands and sighed.

30

The morning was bright with sunshine, though Kathryn could see her breath when she breathed. A fine drizzle had fallen during the night, but by the time the funeral procession had reached the cemetery, the rain had cleared. The granite markers, blacktop road that wound through the cemetery, and string of cars all had a glassy shine to them. The shine made the world look icy.

Kathryn glanced at Wendy, beside her. The collar of her blouse was sticking up out of her coat. As Kathryn fiddled with it, trying to get it back down in her coat, she noticed how soft and delicate Wendy's face looked. She noticed the pockmark at the end of Wendy's right eyebrow. The mark was from when Wendy was a child and had had chicken pox.

It was strange to think that Wendy was there, at her side, strange that she had wanted to be there at all. They walked out on the spongy ground to be near the raised green awning, under which the Robles' family was gathering. Some of them—Tony, Mary Belle, the children, and what looked like the grandparents—sat in aluminum folding chairs, but most simply huddled together. A lot of people were weeping, though in a respectful, subdued fashion, like one is supposed to weep at a funeral. There were a lot of white handkerchiefs visible. All gathered around a rose-colored coffin that contained Angela's body.

Why was Wendy there? Kathryn didn't know. Perhaps because she herself had been so deeply distraught at the death of Angela. Wendy had seemed genuinely moved by Kathryn's emotion.

Perhaps to show support. Wendy had always had a good heart. Perhaps the heart was harder to see now that she was thirteen, but it was still there, and every once in a while, Kathryn caught a glimpse of it.

Or was it because Wendy was awakening to her own mortality? She had heard about a girl near her own age who had died a tragic death and wanted to show respect to that girl. Young people were funny that way, Kathryn thought. Hard to figure out.

Kathryn tried to put her arm around Wendy's shoulders, to draw her near, but she could feel Wendy pulling away, not in any obvious fashion, but in a subtle manner. Instead of being insistent, Kathryn patted Wendy's back, then shoved her hands in her coat pockets, where it was warm. She stared at the casket. What had happened to the days when Wendy had kissed Kathryn good night? What had happened to the days when they had lain in bed together at night and read? What had happened to those days when they had held hands? Wendy had such warm hands.

The minister, at the head of the casket, began to read loudly: "Then I saw a new heaven and a new earth; for the first heaven and the first earth had passed away . . ."

Kathryn's eyes met those of Tony. It was only for a moment, then his eyes went back to the casket; but in that moment, the eyes seemed to say, I told you so.

The minister continued to read: "Jesus said, 'Let the little children come to me; do not stop them. . . .'"

Thoughts of what would happen next, of what leads she would follow, of whether the threat from MTR was over or just beginning, of whether all the Exodus-V had been found—federal agents had raided Bio-Med, Inc., in Austin, confiscating the equipment that had been used to mass produce the anthrax microbe—

passed through her mind; but there was something else. What about the planners of the Fort Hood operation? Edward Brennan of NSA had resigned, as had Brigadier General Thaddeus Burch of the Joint Chiefs of Staff, not because they were linked in any way to the operation, but because each had had responsibility for monitoring and reporting the activities at Fort Hood. Both had failed to keep the proper authorities informed. What about the others? There were certainly others. People high up. How high? Had there been a conspiracy?

The minister had closed one book and was reading from a second book, ". . . We therefore commit her body to the ground; earth to earth, ashes to ashes, dust to dust. . . ."

Kathryn remembered the timid, pathetic look on Angela's face when agents had found her. She would never forget that look, a look innocent, yet resigned.

The minister was praying. Kathryn closed her eyes. She was conscious of Wendy, beside her. She opened her eyes, as if to make sure she was still there. She was.

The minister had a hand in the air over the casket. He was saying a blessing.

Then the service was over.

From the casket the minister moved to the family, where he shook hands with each family member, beginning with Mary Belle, whom he also hugged.

People began to talk and move about.

Wendy asked David, "What are you doing for Thanksgiving?"

Why had she asked that? Kathryn wondered, glancing at Wendy.

He gave one of his characteristic smiles. "I'm not sure yet."

"You're not going anywhere?"

He shrugged.

Wendy looked at Kathryn. "Mom, can't he come to our house? We have room, don't we?"

Kathryn didn't know what to say, the questions had caught her so off guard. She did the only thing she could think to do. She nodded. "Sure."

Wendy smiled. She told David, "We're having my grandmother and grandfather over, but there will be plenty of room." She headed for the car, apparently satisfied she had done a nice thing.

Kathryn went to see Mary Belle, whom she hugged for a long time. Kathryn shook Tony's hand. She noticed he wasn't wearing his West Point ring. The hand looked as barren as his eyes. She hugged the children.

In the car Kathryn looked back at David. He looked sad. She didn't know what to think. Her portable telephone buzzed. It was Grant.

"I just received some interesting news," he told her. "I thought you'd like hear it."

She looked in the rearview. She could see David at his car. He was looking back at the green awning. Had he been a part of it? "What is it?" she asked.

"We have an odd lead."

"What kind of a lead?"

"You know that Derek Klock, the one whose prints were on the M-16 that neutralized the Exodus-Five missile?"

"Yes, the military policeman assigned to the eighty-ninth MP Brigade."

"That's right. And you were skeptical about how someone would know to take a shot at the tank. We've received some additional news about him, news that has a strange twist. Guess what his former assignment was?"

"Are you sure this line is secure?" she asked.

"Believe me, the Bureau's raised enough hell that we have people thinking they'll go straight to jail if they breach our security again."

"What was Klock's former assignment?"

"A courier for NSA. He carried sensitive messages back and forth from Fort Meade to Washington. That was his job—a courier."

"Which means he had contact with high officials at NSA." She hated the implications. So it did add up. How could the United States government have become involved in such a mess? she wondered.

"Exactly. And it was odd how we came across the information. His records list him as being a former courier for the Armed Forces Courier Service. That made his assignment seem unimportant. But the truth is that for national security reasons, NSA had had his records altered so it wouldn't reflect the particular assignment he had had with them."

"So he might have known what was going on from the beginning?"

"It's a strong possibility he knew something."

She started the car and put it in gear. "What about the calls from the Chrisman place to the military intelligence unit at Hood? Any leads on those?" Who else knew?

No, Grand said, but everyone who worked in the office was being questioned. He changed the subject. "Guess what else?"

At the bottom of the hill, she turned onto the main street, leaving the cemetery. "What?"

"This'll please you. The head honchos were so impressed with how you handled the Fort Hood crisis, they're talking about a SAC position."

"What?"

"You know, special-agent-in-charge. Has a nice ring, doesn't it? You derailed a major disaster."

"What's wrong, Mom?" Wendy asked.

Kathryn brought a finger to her lips, signaling silence.

"Listen, it isn't every day a woman in the Bureau is appointed as a special-agent-in-charge of a region," Grant went on, talking in an upbeat tone, "and there's definitely something in the wind. In fact, I heard a rumor there might be an opening up at Denver."

It had been a goal she had worked her entire career for. Why wasn't she happy? And why wasn't she surprised? "What about the Robles investigation?" she asked.

Grant laughed. The sound sent a chill through her. It was one of the rare times she had heard him laugh. Grant wasn't one to laugh. "This investigation could go on for years—if we ever get to the bottom of it all. But it doesn't look like that's your problem anymore. Now, go home. I'll see you back in Dallas, where I'm sure I'll have good news for you."

She put away the phone. "I'm sure you will," she muttered to herself.

"What's wrong, Mom?" Wendy asked.

"Nothing," she lied, feeling like someone had intentionally left her a piece of driftwood in the middle of an ocean.

EERIE SUSPENSE